SHELBY NICOLE MCFADDEN

Grove Hollow

METAMORPHOSIS

MP

MAPLE PROJECTS

A Maple Projects Publication

A GOTHIC PARANORMAL ROMANCE SERIES

A Maple Projects Publication

This novel is purely a creation of the author's imagination. It is a work of fiction, and any connections to historical events, real individuals, religious beliefs, or actual locations are purely fictional. The names, characters, places, and events depicted in this story are entirely fictitious, and any similarities to actual events, places, or persons, whether living or deceased, are not intended on purpose.

First Edition: October 01, 2023
www.shelbynmcfadden.com

For information, address
Maple Projects, LLC.
PO BOX 361
Lewisburg, Pennsylvania 17837

Cover art and illustrations by Shelby Nicole McFadden
Book design by Maple Projects, LLC.
Editing by Grey Moth Editing

Instagram: @grovehollowseries

ISBN 979-8-9888746-0-7

I dedicate this book to the incredible souls who have graced my life and shaped my journey with their love, kindness, and unwavering support.

CONTENTS

What if the universe cuts our souls in two? Creating a reflection of ourselves with an intense soul connection—our *twin flame;* a union with a deep affinity sent to challenge us, mirror each other's insecurities, and break down the walls of our egos; a force so strong it binds us together—controlling intuitions and directing us through predestined events—*fate;* an unconditional love so powerful that a soul could wait lifetimes to find its twin again.

CHAPTER I

BLYTHE HOUSE

GROVE HOLLOW, NEW YORK
OCTOBER 18, 1985

My eyes wander from the monotonous lines on the highway to the ladybug scaling up the door lock. I roll down the car window and offer the tiny bug a chance to break free—something I long for myself, an opportunity to escape this dreadful situation.

"Goodbye, little bugger," I whisper, and my grandfather's playful voice echoes in my mind—those were the same last words he said to me.

"We'll catch up tomorrow," I had promised him as I raced out the door to run a simple errand, unaware that fate had other plans.

Time's cruel, fickle nature deceives us into believing it is limitless and abundant. We fail to appreciate the time we are given, unaware of how little remains. But the grim reality is that death always looms on the horizon, waiting to claim us. It's unavoidable that the ones we love will someday depart to whatever unknown lies ahead, leaving behind a painful emptiness. With each passing day, the echoes of their presence slowly fade away until the sounds of their footsteps and the distinct tone of their voice become distant and forgotten. The memory of their physical presence in a room with us dissipates, reminding us only of their absence.

They say time heals all wounds, except it doesn't feel that way. It's been seven days, and the raw, aching loss of my grandfather still hovers over me like a dark rain cloud. I'm forced to learn to adapt to it, but how can anyone coexist with the idea you'll never see your loved one again? Rather than confronting my hollow thoughts and emotions, I opt to suppress them, hoping that each day will pass without the thought of losing him tormenting me. Finding solace in my state of denial seems to be the best course of action.

As the lump in my throat burns, I push back the tears to prevent the floodgates from bursting open. A tear escapes, and I let the gentle breeze from the rolled-down window dry it away. As the scent wafts in, it brings memories of Oregon's woodland fragrance—a combination of earthy tones and tree oils. The familiar aroma fails to stir up any feeling of homecoming within me. I doubt I will ever feel that sense of home again.

I steal a glance at Toby in the back of the station wagon, my runt of an English Sheepdog. He is lost in a deep slumber with a faint smile, appreciating the warm sunbeams that seep in through the open trunk window. The exit sign for Albany, New York, approaches on the right.

Ronald, my social worker, takes another noisy sip of Diet Coke—his third can since our departure from Portland International Airport. The sound grates on my nerves, leaving me begging for some peace and quiet.

"How much longer?" I ask.

Ronald turns down the radio which is playing "Girls on Film" by Duran Duran. He grabs the crinkled map on the passenger's seat.

"Well, Jade"—he inhales—"if my map is correct, which I hope it is, we take the next exit. Then it's only a few miles until we reach Grove Hollow."

I let out a sigh of relief. I'm exhausted from the constant moving and planning. It's surreal to have left my grandfather's sea shack only a few days ago. Now I am traveling through New York with a couple of suitcases, my treasured collection of classic literature, and my dog.

Now that my grandfather is gone, Toby is all I have left that connects me to him. My grandfather gifted him to me last year on my seventeenth birthday. He had a peculiar way of approaching surprises. I recall him smoking a cigar and reading the paper at our kitchen's Formica table, just like any normal morning. I didn't notice Toby initially; I assumed he was a skinned animal rug from my grandfather's hunting trip. As I grabbed some toast and bacon, a large fluffy dog pounced on me and swiped my food.

"So, you've never met your grandmother?" Ronald asks.

"My great aunt, actually. My grandfather's twin sister," I say, pulling my long hair back with a red ribbon. "And no, I haven't. I guess she and my grandfather weren't very close. I didn't even know she existed until a few days ago."

"Gotta love family drama, am I right?"

I snort out a fake laugh. Unlike my classmates in Oregon, I didn't have siblings to fight with growing up. It was just my grandfather and me for as long as I can remember. After my parents' accident, just a few weeks before my third birthday, my grandfather became my family—my whole family. He was a very private sort of man, so family drama wasn't something I was familiar with.

Ronald switches the station to a different one. They are playing "Edge of Seventeen" by Stevie Nicks. I see his finger on the search button, and I stop him from changing it.

"I like this song. Can we keep it at this station?"

"You got it," he says. "So, this will be a real adventure for you then. You must be so excited."

I continue my gaze out the window. "Yeah, a little."

The scene before me resembles a classic English town from a Charles Dickens novel. As the vintage lamp posts light up, the cobblestone sidewalks and old storefronts come to life. Even though the sun is setting, the town is bustling with activity. Intrigued by the quaint shops, I poke my head out the window to take a closer look. There's a long banner stretching from one side of the road to the other, decorating Grove Hollow's Main Street. The big red letters spell out the details of the upcoming Homecoming rugby match scheduled for Saturday, October 19th, at 7:00 p.m.

Ronald stops the station wagon at a red light. I watch the group of teenagers cross the intersection, dressed in leather clothes, with dyed hair, and distinctive piercings. They are heading toward an old bookshop.

Three girls in cheerleading outfits exit the cafe, the aroma of coffee and cinnamon filling the air. The blonde girl in the center sips her coffee while her friends struggle to divide a pastry.

"Will you guys hurry up? We are going to be late," the blonde-haired girl yells at them and stomps her feet.

I hear a rustling sound from the trunk. I look back at Toby, only to discover he is missing. A shrill scream pierces the air, jolting me into action. Without fully comprehending the situation, I witness the blonde girl collapsing to the ground while Toby engages in a determined tug-of-war over her pastry. I jump out of the car just as the traffic light switches. Toby skips past me, proudly clutching the pastry in his mouth.

"My uniform is ruined!" the blonde-haired girl cries.

"I am so, so sorry!" I take the American Airlines napkin out of my coat pocket and try to dry her skirt.

"Leave it," she says through her teeth.

The world falls silent around us. I can feel the weight of everyone's eyes on me without glancing up. Car horns blare behind us as Ronald's station wagon causes a traffic jam. One angry driver leans out his window and shouts at Ronald to move while laying on his horn.

"I'm sorry, this is so unlike my dog," I lie. He is like this a lot. "Let me help you up."

The blonde girl slaps my hand away and shoots me a fierce glare. "Get away from me!" she spits, shoving me aside.

"You and your dog are going to pay for this. These uniforms are brand new," adds her curly-haired brunette friend.

"Jade, let's go!" Ronald honks impatiently.

"I'm really sorry," I say. I gingerly set the coffee-stained napkin down at her feet and step back. I sense the hushed whispers and pointed stares of the onlookers on the sidewalk. I keep my eyes trained on the ground as I hurry back to the car. Toby pokes his head out the window, wagging his tail.

"I hope that pastry was worth it, Toby," I mutter as I slam the trunk window shut. Slinking back into the station wagon, I hunch down in my seat. I hope no one catches a glimpse of my embarrassed face through the window.

"Goodness, I hope that girl is okay," Ronald remarks, peering at the scene through the rearview mirror. "Your dog really ought to learn some manners."

I ignore Ronald's comment. I lean over my seat to peer through the back windshield. The two girls are helping their friend to her feet. This was not the kind of start I had in mind for my first day in Grove Hollow.

Glad to escape Main Street, we turn onto Fairview Avenue, an old cobblestone road, running parallel to the Hudson River. The two-lane street is unusually wide. Perhaps it was to accommodate horse-drawn carriages in the past. On either side of the road, brick sidewalks and towering privacy walls line the way. Beyond the borders lie colossal, gilded mansions resembling castles with their extravagant designs. I feel like Nick Carraway from *The Great Gatsby* arriving in West Egg for the first time.

"I wonder who lives in these giant mansions," I say.

"These homeowners must be pretty wealthy and powerful to afford estates like these," Ronald says, slowing down the car to take in the view.

"What's the name of my great aunt's street again?" I ask, my attention still fixated on the mansion to my left.

"Fairview Avenue," Ronald replies. "We should be getting close."

I find it unlikely that anyone in my family would reside in these enormous residences. It is much more likely my aunt lives farther along the street, away from these massive estates.

We pass a mansion made entirely of marble. Its pillars are like those of the Parthenon. Despite its grand size, the mansion feels delicate, peaceful, and inviting. A long, winding driveway loops around an Italian marble fountain, leading you to the colorful gardens surrounding the front facade. An iron sign on the brick wall reads: Riverside Estates, built in 1876. My imagination runs wild, envisioning myself as a party guest arriving in a horse-drawn carriage at a mansion as beautiful as this. Women dressed in elaborate gowns and men in finely tailored suits anticipating the excitement of the evening's events. It must have been an enchanting and romantic time.

As we continue along Fairview Avenue, an unsettling mansion catches my attention. The gothic-style estate looms in a shaded seclusion of interwoven beech trees and overgrown brush set back from the road. Its name, Montgomery Manor, is etched on a tilted plaque that hangs by a single nail on the brick wall. I lean out the window to get a better view of the manor. Silence envelopes us, except for the wind whispering through the tree branches. A chill runs down my spine, raising goosebumps on my skin. The dark stone mansion is twice the size of the other mansions on the avenue and twice as intimidating. While some might find the abandoned-looking estate cold and unwelcoming, my initial impression is that it feels sad and forgotten.

"I don't think anyone lives there," I say, taking in the neglected state of the old house.

"Maybe if you're Count Dracula," Ronald quips nervously, earning an eye roll from me. "W-we should probably get going before it gets too dark."

As we approach a gate overrun with vines and dead branches, we can make out a weather-worn sign peering through the overgrown shrubbery. It reads, "Blythe House, built in 1875." Although the old estate's name suggests a warm reception, it seems the property has encountered challenges preserving its former pristine appearance. The once-beautiful chateauesque architecture is now obscured by an unkempt garden of weeds and withered flowers. It must have been decades since anyone has tended to the landscaping.

"Are you sure this is it?" I ask. "Maybe she gave us the wrong address?"

"1306 Fairview Avenue," Ronald reads from a document he pulls out of his bag. "This is the right address."

Both of us stare in disbelief at the grand mansion before us. We let out a gasp as the gate creaks open. Ronald's car gradually makes its way to the mansion's front entrance, where two moss-covered statues of nude female figures stand guard. An elderly man with a comb-over made up of four strands of white hair and dressed in a black suit, slowly descends the marble stairs. His hunched and stooped posture reminds me of the century-old ancient Galapagos turtles. Ronald jumps out to assist him. I head to the back of the station wagon to retrieve Toby, but the timid dog is too scared to leave the safety of the trunk.

"Toby, come on. You can't stay here," I coax, tugging at his collar. He whimpers but eventually hops out and stays close by my side.

"Excuse me, sir. Is this the residence of Ruth Mayfield?" Ronald inquires politely.

"Of course it is," the man replies, his old-fashioned English accent tinted with agitation.

"Oh, great!" Ronald sidesteps as the man shuffles past him.

The older man's arthritic hands reach for my suitcases.

"May I take your luggage, miss?" the old man asks politely.

"Oh, don't worry about it, sir. I can handle Jade's belongings," Ronald says, stepping in front of the man and nodding toward the door. "Why don't you show us inside?"

The man grumbles under his breath. He leads the way back to the house. I tap my hip, signaling for Toby to follow me.

"Come on, don't be a scaredy cat," I whisper to him. He whimpers once more but follows after.

The trio of iron doors, flanked by red and green stained-glass windows, open to a grand foyer, in the Baroque style, embellished with ornate decor. At the center of the room stands a twelve-foot-tall bronze circus elephant, surrounded by a collection of taxidermied safari animals and lifelike tropical plants. A marble staircase makes a U-shape, connecting the left and right sides of the room to the second floor.

At the top of the stairs stands an elegant older woman in a champagne-tulle robe over a silk dinner gown. A long cigarette holder with a wispy plume of smoke rests between her fingers—a partially-consumed cocktail within the grasp of her other hand. Her heavy Jean Harlow makeup and spider-leg-like eyelashes are a feeble attempt to hold on to her youth. Her weathered skin, wiry white hair, and saggy wrinkles overshadow her once-effortless beauty.

"Jade, darling, welcome to Blythe House!" she says, greeting us in a transatlantic accent with her arms unfolding. She gracefully descends the long staircase, sipping her drink through the gap in her teeth. "Nigel, bring the young lady's belongings to her room, will you? Chop chop!"

Ronald and I exchange glances as the older man struggles to lift my suitcases on the first step.

"Oh, I've got it, madam," Ronald offers, taking one of the suitcases from Nigel.

"Nonsense, Nigel is more than capable," she insists.

Ronald bites his nails as Nigel continues his struggle up the stairs.

"You are the spitting image of your mother," she remarks, flashing a crescent moon-shaped smile. I catch a whiff of Chanel, brandy, and cigarette smoke as she approaches. "Except for your father's green eyes—the famous Whitney green eyes. Just like mine."

"Yes, my grandfather had them, too." I grin.

"Yes… I suppose he did."

As I observe her, it's hard to believe they're twins. My grandfather was a simple man who found contentment in the little things. He needed his recliner, small TV, and fishing boat to be happy. He kept the animals he hunted as trophies, while his eccentric sister used exotic stuffed creatures as decorative pieces. Great Aunt Ruth's taste in fashion and style was more bizarre and decadent compared to my grandfather's humble plaid shirts and worn-out denim.

"Thank you for letting me stay with you, Great Aunt Ruth—"

"Let's drop the 'great' part, my dear. I may be old, but I'm not *that* old." She winks and turns to the social worker beside me. "And who might this dashing young fellow be?"

"My name is Ronald Fitz, Ma'am. I'm Jade's social worker. We spoke on the phone last week, remember?" Ronald asks.

Aunt Ruth hesitates for a moment before responding. I think she doesn't remember their conversation. "Of course I do!" she answers.

Ronald fumbles through his briefcase, nearly spilling stacks of papers onto the floor before producing a manila folder.

"Here's a copy of the paperwork I faxed over. I need both of you to sign a couple of these, and then I'll be on my way."

"Of course, of course." Aunt Ruth waves her hand in agreement.

Aunt Ruth puts the long cigarette holder between her lips and signs the papers in a few swift strokes, exhaling a large cloud of smoke. I sign the last document, trying to avoid the wet spot left by Aunt Ruth's cocktail. As Ronald prepares to depart, he says he will check in on me and make sure I am settling in well.

"I'll be okay, I promise," I say to him before closing the door.

"Well, I bet you're famished, Jade, you skinny, scrawny thing! Didn't my brother ever feed you?"

Aunt Ruth places her long red fingernails on my arm and guides me away from the front door. I whistle for Toby, who is shivering at the entrance. He obediently follows us. We step into the enormous empire-styled dining room. The decor is elaborate and unusual, just like the foyer. An intriguing spectacle unfolds in front of the floor-to-ceiling windows—a collection of taxidermy bears wearing charming clothing, each clutching a musical instrument as if caught in a whimsical performance. Their exhibit is accompanied by the gentle melodies emanating from a vintage record player behind them. It's a strange thing to have in a dining room. Undoubtedly, it would make an excellent icebreaker for any stale dinner conversations.

I count the twenty-five throne chairs on each side of the table, their 50s atomic starburst fabric clashing with the formal gilded interior. On the table, elevated centerpieces stand tall with dried flowers, twisted willow branches, and gnarled vines intertwining. With their bewitching presence, the billowing displays only add to the bizarre atmosphere. Suspended above them hang two large chandeliers, their countless crystals shimmering resplendently. Amidst Aunt Ruth's eccentric taste, these fixtures remain untouched, a testament to a different era and a reminder of their enduring elegance.

"This house is so..." I trail off.

"Enchanting, isn't it?" finishes Aunt Ruth. "This place used to be so dull and lifeless. Since inheriting it, I gave it a bit of a facelift. It was designed by Richard Morris Hunt. It took six years to build Blythe House, you know?"

"Wow, that seems like a long time."

"Yes, indeed. It's the second largest house on the block, next to that dreadful Montgomery house. Pity it's in shambles." She sighs.

Two sets of dishes are already arranged on the table, and I sit next to Aunt Ruth. She takes her place at the head of the table, the cozy fireplace behind her emitting a warm glow. What I'd assumed was a stuffed crow perches on the mantle, and I gasp when it takes off and lands on Aunt Ruth's shoulder, offering her a diamond brooch from its talons.

"Thank you, Jankins," says Aunt Ruth to the bird as it flies away. "My crows love to spoil me with presents."

The door swings open behind me, and Nigel enters the dining room.

"May I take your order, madam?" he inquires.

"I'll have the duck," Aunt Ruth says.

"And for you, miss? Duck or lamb?"

"I don't mind either, thank you," I reply.

Nigel casts a glance at Aunt Ruth, appearing uneasy with my indecisiveness.

"I'll have the duck as well," I hastily decide.

"Unfortunately, we're understaffed at the moment," Aunt Ruth explains as Nigel returns to the kitchen. "Since Reggie passed away, I've had to let most of the maids and landscapers go. Nigel's doing his best to manage the household and kitchen staff."

I nod, even though I can't imagine what it's like to run a massive estate like Blythe House. Nigel places an empty bowl in front of me. He pours warm pea soup into the basin. It has a sweet aroma of thyme and onions, making my mouth water. He then does the same for Aunt Ruth.

"Would you care for a cocktail?" Aunt Ruth asks as she pours a generous amount of vodka into her martini glass.

"Oh, no, thank you."

She shrugs and casually drops three maraschino cherries in her glass, causing a small puddle of vodka and tonic to spill onto the cheetah-print table runner.

"Unlike your grandfather, I never enjoyed spending my summers here. He was always into outdoor sports like hunting and fishing." She shakes her head.

"You and my grandfather used to spend summers here?" I ask, surprised.

"Of course, my dear. The Whitney family has been summering here for generations," she says as she applies more red lipstick. "It's a longstanding tradition, you see. The thrilling sailboat races, exhilarating fox hunts, and esteemed duck shootings became the hallmarks of our summers spent here."

I look down as I swirl my spoon around the green broth. I don't understand why my grandfather never showed me photographs or told me stories about Blythe House, especially if the memories of this place hold such significance.

"My grandfather never mentioned visiting this place."

"Well, I'm not surprised. Clyde despised this family and everything we stood for. He called us swine after pearls." She let out a deep sigh and rolled her eyes. "I still can't believe he sold the Manhattan estate after your great-grandfather passed. Within a month, they tore it down to build that hideous high-rise. Some of us value our family's history and believe it should be preserved, not demolished." She gazes at the cherries floating in her cocktail. "I used to adore visiting that place on 57th street..."

We finish our soup, and Nigel brings out the duck entree. He places a bowl of duck shreddings on the floor, and Toby gobbles it up.

"Your grandfather never once mentioned Blythe House? Ever?" asks Aunt Ruth, although it feels more like prying.

"No, not even once," I reply. "I had no idea a house like this belonged in our family."

"Typical Clyde, always keeping things a secret," she says, lighting a cigarette. She doesn't touch a bite of her food. "Well, I suppose you have a right to know about your heritage. Your great-great-great-grandfather, Octavius Whitney, was one of the wealthiest men in America. He and his twin brother, Augustus, ran a highly successful oil and petroleum business out of Pennsylvania. They built an oil empire, drilling all around the country run by the two brothers—that is, until his brother, Augustus, and wife died in the horrible train crash of the Riverton Express Disaster."

She pauses to take a big gulp of her cocktail. "Back in those days, well-to-do families, including the Whitney family, carefully selected their settlement locations. New York City for its vibrant city life, Newport, Rhode Island, for its picturesque ocean views, and a few select destinations down south—though who could stand the scorching heat? Yet, among the privileged elite, a select few took it further, owning wealthy estates in all these places. The one particular town that stood above the rest was Grove Hollow, New York."

"So, what happened to the other Whitney homes? Are they still around as well?" I ask.

"Well, as you know, Clyde sold off the New York estate. My parents sold the Newport home to a bank at the start of the Great Depression. It's a shame, really. I always wished they kept the Newport mansion and sold this one instead. So, Blythe House is the only one that remains."

I feel a deep loss as I learn the other Whitney homes are no longer standing. It was as if a part of my family's legacy was erased from history—a history I am only now uncovering.

"That's why it's crucial we preserve it," Aunt Ruth says. "It's a true blessing that many of the old houses on this street, belonging to the Astors, Vanderbilts, and Rockefellers, still stand tall and proud."

Overwhelmed by this unexpected revelation, my mind spins with disbelief. "So, you're saying that our family was just as wealthy as the Astors and the Vanderbilts?" I ask.

"My dear," she says, a proud gaze directed at my astonished expression, "our families mingled within the same social circle. The Whitneys weren't just wealthy—we were regarded as one of America's royalty among the elite echelons of high-class society."

I rub my forehead, trying to comprehend the magnitude of this information.

"My grandfather never gave the impression we were so well-off. We never struggled, at least not that I'm aware of. We lived off of what we caught, raised, or grew."

Aunt Ruth rolls her eyes. "That's Clyde."

Betrayal bubbles within me. How could my grandfather keep such important family history a secret? I mean, it's not like we were an ordinary family. Was it shame, guilt, or perhaps some other hidden motive?

"I can't believe my grandfather never mentioned any of this to me." I sigh.

Aunt Ruth cocks her head to the side and inhales her cigarette, blowing the smoke onto her half-picked duck. "He got his inheritance and then pretended none of us ever existed."

After dinner, Aunt Ruth retires to the living room for another drink. Toby and I trail behind Nigel as he leads us up the U-shaped staircase to the second floor. We make our way down a hallway lit by the original Victorian sconces. Ignoring Aunt Ruth's quirky decor, I find myself drawn to the refined oil paintings of Victorian men and women that grace the walls. Their sophisticated postures and intricate clothing transport me to a different era. Lost in my admiration, I nearly collide with Nigel as he stops at the last door at the end of the hall.

"Miss Whitney, this will be your room," he says, gesturing toward the door. "It's a spacious, comfortable room with a lovely view of the river. If you need anything, just press the button next to your bed, and I'll be at your service. If you don't mind, I'll let your dog outside to relieve himself."

I thank Nigel, and he takes Toby down the servant steps. I stand alone in my newly assigned bedroom. I find its magnificence overwhelming. My attention is drawn to the romantic Victorian paintings on the walls. I guess hanging my band posters beside them would be inappropriate. Nothing in this room feels familiar. It will take some time for me to adjust. Nonchalantly, I throw my jacket onto the floral silk bedding of the canopy bed and slip off my dirty Reebok Freestyle sneakers. I stretch out on the covers and watch the shimmering light from the crystal chandelier dance across the angelic scene painted on the ceiling. For the first time in days, I feel like I can relax. The long journey that brought me to this moment is finally over. I briefly close my eyes and enjoy the stillness.

Toby interrupts my relaxation as he jumps onto the bed. Nigel enters behind him and hands me a large black box with a red ribbon.

"These are for you for tomorrow."

"For tomorrow?" I ask, puzzled.

"Yes, miss. For school."

It hadn't crossed my mind that I would attend a new school. Nigel leaves, and I place the box on the vanity. The seal on the box bears a crest of two ravens and the letters 'GHA.' Inside I find a pair of tweed plaid skirts, two white button-down shirts, a black blazer, a black sweater embroidered with the raven crest on the left chest, black Oxford shoes, knee-high socks, and a Grove Hollow Academy guideline booklet.

I sit on the tufted couch by the window and browse through the booklet. The cover displays an image of the grand school, with six long rows of uniformed students standing in front. I turn to the first page to find a photo of an intimidating man in a suit and tie—the Headmaster.

"For over one hundred years, Grove Hollow Academy has challenged its students to be intellectually curious, to inspire the community, demonstrate leadership, and strive for their full potential and greatness for over a century..."

Turning the page, I peruse the dress code, arrival and dismissal times, and the school calendar. I tear out the perforated map with directions to the school. As I near the end, I glance at the sports and extracurricular activities sections. The rugby team receives three full-page spreads, unlike the other sports mentioned. I vaguely recall hearing about rugby, but I'm unsure if it's similar to football. Sports have never held my interest.

I turn the page. I see a photo of a blonde-haired cheerleader linked arm in arm with a boy in a rugby uniform.

Pictured Above: Juniors of 1984, Bradley Phillips and Allison Ashmore.

I realize with a sinking feeling that the cheerleader in the photo is the same girl from the incident earlier. I cling to the hope that she won't recognize me.

I open the French doors leading to a balcony spanning the length of my room. Moonlight skims the rippling surface of the Hudson River below. The river's tranquil and calm presence contrasts with the restless energy of the ocean that was visible from my old bedroom, a sight I already miss so terribly. I'm uncertain whether to cry, smile, or pass out. The past two weeks have been a lot to process, from my grandfather's heart attack, the funeral, packing, goodbyes, moving, and discovering my family's hidden history. Now, I'm starting a new school tomorrow. I feel like I am at the threshold of a new chapter in my life.

I look back and see Toby snoring on my new bed. He looks like he's enjoying the extra space of the king-size mattress as opposed to my old twin one. I close the balcony doors and draw the floor-length curtains for privacy. I need to unwind, and a hot bath sounds like a fantastic idea. I grab toiletries from my suitcase and search for a bathroom in the hallway. All the doors are locked except for the walk-in linen closet. I return to my room and ring the bell on the side of my bed. I wait for Nigel, who takes a few minutes to arrive.

"Yes, miss?" he asks.

"I was wondering where the bathroom is?"

Nigel walks over to the wall. He presses a section of the filigree-patterned wallpaper that conceals a camouflaged door.

"It's in here, miss."

"Oh, thanks," I say, embarrassed. "Does Aunt Ruth also use this bathroom?"

Nigel looks at me blankly for a moment. "No, miss. Each bedroom has its own private bathroom in this house."

"Ah, I see," I reply, feeling slightly foolish. "Thank you for letting me know."

"Of course, miss. Is there anything else you need?"

Shaking my head, I respond, "No, that's all. Thank you."

With Nigel gone and the door locked, I let out a deep sigh and smack my forehead with the palm of my hand. How could I have been so ignorant? This huge house, with its lavish decor and amenities, of course, would have more than one bathroom. I shake my head at my naivety.

I fill the oversized clawfoot tub with steaming hot water, pouring in a generous amount of soap. As I sink into the water and feel the bubbles covering me, I marvel at the luxuriousness of it all. What a far cry from the rustic lifestyle I had grown accustomed to back at my grandfather's sea shack. It all appears surreal, as if plucked from my imagination. A tiny teardrop escapes my eye, carrying a hint of bitterness over my grandfather's hidden vault of family history—an important secret kept from me, and I can't help but feel its weight. But as I play with the faucet with my toes, turning the water on and off, I know this is my reality now. Never in a million years would I have guessed my grandfather came from a family like this. That I, Jade Whitney, had a name of importance.

CHAPTER II

THE VISITOR

In the dead of night, I am jolted awake by Toby's guttural growls. I nudge him with my feet to silence him, only to kick an empty bed. I rub my bleary-eyes open. The room is dark.

I pull the blankets up to my shoulders. A chilling draft is blowing over me from the open balcony doors. I must not have locked them before going to bed. As my sight adjusts, I spot Toby's silhouette. He is rigid as stone, with his ears flat and his tail erect, staring at a corner by the vanity.

Fear grips my chest. "Toby, what's wrong?"

Ignoring me, Toby's growls deepen, as his eyes remain focused on the dark wall. Dread prickles my skin, causing the hair on the nape of my neck to stand at attention.

"There's nothing there, Toby. Relax," I say, trying to convince myself.

With a sudden burst of energy, Toby pounces at the wall. The vanity chair knocks over, and a vase of flowers tumbles, smashing on the floor. I gasp as I catch a glimpse of a shadowy figure dart past the reflection of my full-length mirror. But no one else is in the room.

Toby runs out onto the balcony, barking furiously. I worry he will wake my aunt, so I lead him back inside by the collar and lock the balcony doors. As I draw the curtains shut, a sudden movement startles me. I find a massive lime-green creature perched on the glass pane. Its yellow eye-spot markings give the impression it's observing me. Though I don't usually fear butterflies and moths, the creature's wingspan is comparable to both my hands, causing my heart to race. Its intriguing yet unsettling appearance leaves me feeling uneasy. I watch it closely. It flits away like a fairy, disappearing into the night.

I turn to check on Toby, who's shivering under the covers.

"Big baby, it was just a moth."

I nudge his massive furry body to the bottom of the bed. However, I can't shake the feeling that something isn't right. I pull the covers over my head, just in case.

CHAPTER III

AN ACADEMY GREETING

I wouldn't exactly describe myself as having a signature style. In fact, most of the clothes in my wardrobe are far from fashionable; they lean more toward practicality. My grandfather wasn't one to take me shopping regularly, and when he did, it was only to the local hunting and fishing boutiques. While the girls in my class went on shopping sprees with their mothers, I accompanied my grandfather in the pursuit of clam digging during low tide and uncovering the mysteries of tide pools.

He might not have been the nurturing type like my friends' mothers were, but he had a fondness for offbeat amusements. He found delight in tapping maple trees to make syrup and casting a line on his fishing boat, Fiona, which he named after my late grandmother, whom I never had the chance to meet. Perhaps it was these unique interests that made me feel like a tomboy amidst the other girls in Coos Bay. Nevertheless, I embraced my rustic attire and dirty fingernails, for they were tangible reminders of cherished moments shared with my grandfather. They made me who I am.

If I could choose a particular aesthetic, I would opt for a fusion of Victorian and whimsical motifs, mainly because I have a penchant for antique pieces. Even though my clothes lack feminine flare, I have always found a way to incorporate a timeless ribbon in my hair. On my sixth birthday, my grandfather presented me with my grandmother's sewing kit. It contained a treasure trove of ribbons in every imaginable color, fabric, and lace style. With ribbons for any occasion, I choose a black one to match my hair today. I pull my wavy curls away from my face and secure it with a delicate bow.

I've never owned any dresses or skirts, so I am excited to wear my school's tweed and plaid skirt, which I adore. I layer it with a button-down shirt, topped with the school's black sweater with the collar turned up. With my Oxford shoes and knee-high socks on, I take a step back to admire myself in the full-length mirror. For once, I feel pretty.

I enter the dining room and see Nigel arranging an impressive breakfast spread of fluffy pancakes, fresh fruit, and perfectly soft-boiled eggs on the buffet table. I attempt to serve myself, but he insists on doing the honors. He takes great care in pouring me a hot cup of English Breakfast tea. I welcome the caffeine boost after the exhausting event last night involving Toby. Nigel finishes preparing the garnishes for a Bloody Mary and places the cocktail on a silver tray.

"Will Aunt Ruth be joining me for breakfast?" I ask in between bites of my pancake.

"I'm afraid not. Madam is feeling a bit unwell, but she sends her best wishes for your first day at school," he informs me before departing to serve the cocktail upstairs.

After I've finished eating, I inspect the map included in the school booklet. I plot out the quickest route to campus. The most direct path is up Fairview Avenue and across Main Street. I tuck the map into my blazer pocket and sling my bookbag over my shoulder.

"Take good care of yourself." I pat Toby on the head. "Behave and have fun today, all right? No more mischief!"

I step outside and close the front door. I notice three kids, dressed in the Grove Hollow Academy uniform, peering at me through the bars of Blythe House's gate. They quickly scurry off, whispering amongst themselves. It strikes me as odd, but I shrug it off. I make my way up the cold sidewalk, clinging to my blazer for warmth. I hadn't anticipated that fall mornings here would be just as frigid as they were in Coos

Bay. The breeze blowing off the river makes the already nippy fifty-degree temperature feel like it could snow. Luckily, my Sony Walkman's headphones double as earmuffs, the foam earpieces keeping my ears warm. I pop in The Cure's latest album, *The Head on the Door,* and fast forward the cassette tape to track eight.

I hang close to Fairview Avenue's brick wall border, so students on their Bianchi bicycles can pass me. As I approach Montgomery Manor on my right, I pause at the gate to admire the dilapidated mansion from the street. It's eerily quiet. Only the gentle cooing of a pair of mourning doves atop the roof, the rustling of the leaves in the trees, and the swaying of their branches add to the ominous atmosphere. A thick mist hovering above the grass lends a ghostly aura to the estate.

My eyes draw themselves to the third floor. A young man stares at me from the window. A prickly sensation travels up my arm as I watch him.

"Hey there!"

Startled, I stumble backward. I land on the rough brick sidewalk, skinning the palms of my hands. A fellow Grove Hollow Academy student, with quirky white hair and cat-eye eyeliner, offers me a hand, helping me up from the ground. She pulls a handkerchief from her Hussars military jacket and gently cleans the blood from my hands.

"Sorry about that. Are you all right? I didn't mean to startle you," she says at a million miles an hour. "What's got ya spooked? See a ghost or something?"

I look up at the window where the man is standing, but he is gone.

"I'm not sure I didn't."

"You never can tell with these old homes. They are full of ghosts."

"Really?" I say, glancing back up at the window.

"Oh yeah, everyone knows that. These buildings have been here for over a hundred years." Bending down to pick up my fallen Walkman, she glances at the cassette inside. "You like The Cure, too?" she asks with enthusiasm before handing the device back to me.

"They're one of my favorite bands," I say, securing my Walkman in the front pocket of my bookbag.

"Mine, too," she replies with a wide grin. "I'm Aubrey Jackson. You must be new here."

"Jade Whitney." I shake her hand, and we start walking together. "How did you know?"

"Know what?"

"That I'm new to the school."

"Well, for starters, I've never seen you around. Everyone at the Academy knows everyone."

"Oh." I tuck my hair behind my ear. I was hoping I'd be invisible on my first day at least.

"Where did you move from?" Aubrey asks, kicking a stone out onto the street.

"Coos Bay, Oregon. I just moved in yesterday to my aunt's house. It's the mansion just next to this one. It's called Blythe House."

Aubrey stops walking and grabs my wrist hard enough that I wince. There's a look of shock on her face.

"Blythe House? Seriously?" she asks.

"Yeah, why?"

"Blythe House… as in the witch's house? You don't actually *live* there—do you?"

She wasn't referring to my Aunt Ruth, was she? Then I remember the kids' reactions outside the gate this morning; does everyone in town think Aunt Ruth is the village witch?

"I can assure you my Aunt Ruth isn't a witch. She's just a little—"

"Crazy, no offense," Aubrey blurts out. My cheeks flush with embarrassment. "Someone said they saw her dancing around under the moonlight naked in her yard. Three other ladies were with her. They swore it was a witches' gathering."

"Well…" I begin. I haven't known Aunt Ruth for very long, but I don't want to encourage rumors. Aubrey's right eyebrow raises. "She seems really nice."

She lets out a big exhale, her eyes are enormous. "Well, that's good."

We have already reached Main Street. The busy street is filled with students rushing their way toward the Academy. I take out the map from my pocket to find where to go.

"You don't need that." Aubrey takes the map out of my hand. She crumbles it up and throws it into a trashcan. "I'll show you the shortcut."

She guides me down an alleyway sandwiched between the old

bookshop and a video arcade. Big bubble letters on one side of the wall spell out "ART IS NOT A CRIME" in white paint. The other side of the alley displays a painting of E.T. and a quote from Edgar Allan Poe, *"All that we see or seem is but a dream within a dream."*

I scream as a rat scurries past me and climbs up a drainpipe. "Aubrey, are you sure this takes us to school? I don't want to be late on my first day," I ask nervously.

"Trust me, Artist's Alley is the fastest way—come on!" Aubrey replies with confidence.

We turn a corner around a large dumpster and see Grove Hollow Academy. I crane my neck to admire the gothic cathedral-style school atop a hill overlooking the town. Aubrey grips my shoulder and pulls me toward her as a boy on his bike almost collides with us. He wears a varsity jacket with a rugby jersey underneath. I instinctively hide my head behind my hands.

"Watch it, freaks!" he yells back at us.

"You're such a prick, Jake!" Aubrey flips him the finger. "Honestly, I hate this school. Everyone thinks they're so entitled because they're rich. You can't trust any of them either. They are all assholes." She huffs, and her breath lifts her bangs up in the air.

"Really?"

"Absolutely. You especially have to be careful of the cheerleaders. They have a talent for tearing people and their reputations to shreds."

Immediately, the cheerleader from yesterday's incident comes to mind. "Good to know." I gulp.

"Come on, we better motor or we'll miss this light," says Aubrey, tugging at my arm.

We quickly approach a crosswalk filled with academy students. I spot the three kids from outside my aunt's house looking at me. They mutter to the other students around them with their hands covering their mouths. The light changes and we cross the street. As we step through the grand iron archway and onto the Academy grounds, my discomfort grows. The stares of the other students burn into me. It's as though they've never seen a new face before. Meanwhile, Aubrey continues to explain the different cliques at school, and I struggle to focus on her words about jocks and misfits.

"You'll love them. They're my best friends. Wes will love you, too, I know it," Aubrey says, her voice laced with excitement.

"Who?" I ask, struggling to block out the whispers from the onlookers.

"Wes, my boyfriend. The one I said looks like Adam Ant," she explains as I stare back at her, struggling to recall her reference. "You know, the lead singer of the new wave and post-punk group Adam and the Ants?"

"Oh, yeah, right."

As we step into the school, I can feel the weight of the other students' stares and my nervousness settling heavily on my shoulders. But as my eyes adjust to the dim interior, I am struck by the solemn and contemplative atmosphere that pervades the entire building. The walls are made of polished wood, intricately carved with delicate patterns which put the dull concrete blocks of my old school to shame. Marble statues of the school's previous headmasters leer down at us, their expressions grave and dignified. Intricate mosaics and murals ornament the walls, telling stories of the school's rich and illustrious past. It feels like I'm walking into a grand cathedral, but instead of pews, there are rows of lockers and classrooms. Compared to my old public school's tacky decorations and shoddy banners, this place exudes a sense of regalness and studiousness.

"Would you wanna sit with us at lunch?" Aubrey asks, her smile still bright even with eyes watching us—well, me.

"I'd love to," I reply. I could use a friend on my first day.

"Great! I'll meet you outside the cafeteria."

Aubrey and I say our goodbyes for now, and I make my way to the school's front office. I enter the room but notice no one is behind the front desk. I take a seat in one of the empty chairs and wait. The bell rings, and lockers start slamming shut. The noisy chatter of students fills the air as they hurry to their homerooms. After several minutes, a frazzled older woman emerges from a door behind the counter. She fails to notice me in the chair, even with her thick-framed glasses that magnify her eyes.

"Damn heater!" she says, fiddling with the thermostat knobs.

Walking up to the front counter, I see a gold bell resting next to a pile of Grove Hollow Academy booklets. They are the same ones I received just yesterday. I tap the bell's top, surprising the older woman.

"Oh dear, you scared me!" she exclaims, throwing her hand over her chest in shock. "I didn't know anyone was in here! What can I do for you?"

"Sorry about that. I'm Jade Whitney. I'm new here."

"Oh!" she says and nudges her glasses down the bridge of her nose. "Let me find your schedule." She opens the top drawer of a metal filing cabinet and licks her fingers to sort through a row of folders. "Whitney... Whitney... Whit—oh, here it is."

She hands me the folder with a round coffee stain on the front cover. When I open it up, I find my class schedule and locker number 135 written in bold red ink at the top of the page.

"The 130 lockers are outside the office to the right. The 100 room numbers and lockers are on the bottom floor. The second floor has classrooms and lockers starting in the 200's, and—well, you get the idea. Let's see—you have three minutes between each class..."

I flip the page and discover a school site plan with fire exits. It looks like a labyrinth, but at least I have a general idea of where to go.

"Oh yes, the extracurricular wing is pretty big. Do you think you can make your way around all right? I can call for an escort to have someone help you."

"I should be able to find my way around." I hope.

"Wonderful. Good luck on your first day," she says. "Oh! I forgot to mention. Afternoon classes are canceled Friday. The school will host a pep rally outside for the Homecoming game in their place."

I thank her and turn to exit the office. Following the directions given to me by the office secretary, I take a right turn and head toward my locker. The hallway is quiet and empty, which leads me to believe everyone is still in their homerooms. Static blares through the loudspeaker, and the office secretary's voice fills the hall.

"Good morning, Grove Hollow students. Today's lunch will be—"

I'm searching for the 130 lockers, but all I see are lockers starting from the 150s to the 160s. Doubt starts to fill my mind. I double-check my map to ensure I'm heading in the right direction.

"Damnit," I mutter, realizing the office secretary gave me the wrong directions. Instead of making a right, I should have made a left out of the office.

The bell rings, indicating the dismissal of homeroom, just as I finally find my locker. Classroom doors start to open, and students pour out into the hall. My locker is jammed shut—typical—and I struggle to open it. I tuck the folder under my arm and use both hands to pull on the handle. The locker door swings open, causing me to fall backward onto the person behind me. We both fall to the ground in a heap.

"Ah, my head," the boy says.

I scramble to my feet. "I'm so sorry. My locker was jammed, and I—" My words trail off as I lay eyes on the attractive, blond-haired guy on the floor. "I was trying to lift the latch, but then—"

He massages his head; his fingers disrupt his perfectly coiffed blond waves. He lifts his eyes from the ground to meet mine. His furrowed expression softens into a beaming smile, making my insides dance. His hand surrounds mine as I help him up. The moment lingers, and I savor the sensation of our touch before we let go.

"I'm sorry, did you hit your head hard?" I ask him.

"Don't worry, I've had worse head injuries in a rugby match." He laughs.

"Well, I guess it's good I didn't give anyone a concussion on my first day."

He winks. "Day's not over yet."

My cheeks burn, and I nervously tuck my hair behind my ears. I look down at the floor.

"Crap, my papers."

"Let me help you pick those up," he insists, bending down to retrieve my scattered papers. He hands me my class schedule with a smile. "Looks like we have American History together."

I scan my schedule, noting that it's my last class of the day.

"My name's Brad, by the way."

"I know," I blurt out, realizing too late how creepy that sounds.

His one brow curves. "You do?"

"I mean, I saw your name in the school booklet."

Brad takes a moment to recall what I'm referring to.

"Oh, right." He grins, and it's contagious.

The bell rings, signaling the start of class.

"Well, I guess I'll be seeing you around, new girl." He winks again before heading off to class.

He is in no hurry as he walks away in reverse, clutching his books to his chest. The last thing I see is his charming smile before he turns to join the crowd. I stand at my locker, waiting for my feet to come back and touch the ground. I hope I do see you around, Bradley Phillips.

I shake off the image of Brad's captivating smile and focus on finding the French classroom on the second floor. Despite the curious looks from students, I push past the distraction and locate the room.

I take a seat in the front row, pulling out a notebook and pencil from my bag. A girl beside me rushes to finish her French homework before the teacher arrives. I take a moment to jot down the date in the top right-hand corner of the first page of my notebook.

"MOVE!"

I barely complete writing the date before I drop my pencil on the floor.

"Didn't you hear what I said? *MOVE!*"

The cheerleader, Allison, towers over me. Her arms are folded across her chest, eyes ablaze with intensity.

I shrink back in my seat. "S-s-sorry, I didn't realize..."

The girl beside me stops writing and stares, open-mouthed, as Allison tosses my notebook to the floor. She slams her hands on my desk.

"I don't care if it was open. This is my seat," she growls.

"Arrete! Mademoiselle Ashmore, save the drama for the school play. Go find another seat and quit bossing everyone around," a voice rings out.

A petite, middle-aged woman wearing a bright red pantsuit with a matching wide-brimmed hat on top of her permed hair enters the room. She spills a few drops of coffee onto the carpet as she dismisses Allison with a wave of her hand.

"Pouvez-vous faire de la place, s'il vous plaît? Before my espresso gets cold, please," she orders.

"Yes—I mean, oui, Madame Gaël," Allison grits through her teeth.

I go to grab my notebook and pencil from the floor. Allison kicks my pencil and it rolls away. She takes a seat at the back of the room, still glaring at me.

"You can have one of mine." The girl beside me offers one of her pencils.

"Thank you."

"Jean, veuillez distribuer les livres, s'il vous plaît," Madame Gaël instructs, placing a pile of books on the desk beside mine. Jean lets out a big sigh. "While Jean hands out *Les Fables de la Fontaine,* Mademoiselle Whitney can share some facts about herself with the class." Madame Gaël takes a sip of her coffee and reclines in her seat behind her desk, motioning for me to stand in front of the small room. I had hoped to make it through my first day without classroom introductions. My anxiety kicks in, and my heart rate goes from zero to sixty miles an hour. I feel my palms getting sweaty and wipe them on my skirt. I make my way to the front of the class. The pressure of being in the spotlight is making me feel nauseous. I take a deep breath and prepare myself to look anywhere but directly at Allison.

"Oh! What would you like your French name to be?" Madame Gaël asks.

"Well, Annabelle was my name in my French class at my old high school."

"Très bien! We will call you Annabelle. You may proceed."

I nod my head, trying to remain calm. A couple of people are whispering in the back row. My breathing starts to speed up, and I fear I might faint. I clear my throat and try to compose myself.

"Um, d'accord. Je m'appelle Jade Whitney. J'ai vécu à Coos Bay, Oregon. J'aime lire des livres et écouter de la musique."

"Merveilleux!" Madame Gaël exclaims with a smile. "Can you tell us what kind of music you enjoy listening to, Jade? English is fine."

"Sure. I like listening to alternative bands. The Cure released a new album in August, and I bought the cassette."

Allison makes a cutting gesture and jokes with the boy next to her. Madame Gaël gives her a warning look.

"The best band!" Jean says as he places a book on my desk.

"Quel est ton livre préféré? What is your favorite book?" Madame Gaël asks.

"Rebecca, by Daphne du Maurier—definitely."

"A favorite of mine, too," Madame Gaël responds. "Very good! You may have a seat, Annabelle." Madame Gaël then announces, "Speaking of books, we will begin reading short fables by the famous French poet Jean de La Fontaine this week. For homework, I would like you to read a story each night, translate it from French to English, and write in French your thoughts and feelings about each fable." The students in the classroom collectively groan. "Everyone, take out the weekend's homework on the French Revolution. Annabelle, you can sit and listen since you weren't here. Marguerette, what did you get for answer one? En français, s'il vous plaît."

The girl next to me brushes off the eraser dust on the homework.

"Um, the middle class gained political influence—"

"Répondez aux questions en français, Marguerette!"

CHAPTER IV

WE ARE THE MISFITS

I see Aubrey waiting for me at the entrance of the cafeteria. At my previous school, the lunchroom consisted of painted cinder blocks and fluorescent lights. We sat at metal tables with banquet-style seating and red plastic chairs that generated static and shocked our fingers when touching the metal. The dining hall at this school, however, feels exceptionally high-class. Rather than a cafeteria, the lunchroom more closely resembles a great hall at Harvard University. Flying buttresses uphold the expansive gothic dining hall. Oil paintings of boat races and equestrian show jumping competitions hang on the walls in ornate gold frames. A sizable fireplace rests at the back of the room, where cheerleaders and rugby players monopolize the lounge seating in front of it. If you aren't involved in a sport, it appears your place is at one of the regular dining tables.

The lunch line is long, but thankfully, it moves at a reasonable pace. It's hard to hear my stomach growl over the loud chatter in the cafeteria, but I feel it nonetheless. I stand on my tiptoes to catch a glimpse of the food behind the lunch counter. I spot Brad's blond hair a few people ahead of us, and I shift out of line to get a better view of him. He is talking to his friend. His body is energetic as he speaks, and his hands move animatedly. He lets out a loud, raucous laugh that sounds like a car engine. It makes me giggle.

"Who are you looking at?" Aubrey smirks.

"Who, me? Nobody, I am trying to see what's for lunch," I answer. I pretend to check out the lunch counter.

"Looks like"—Aubrey stands on her tiptoes, too—"Caesar salad, lobster mac and cheese, or chicken cordon bleu, I think?"

I watch Brad grab his food tray and sit by the other rugby players by the fireplace. A crowd of people surrounds him as he continues talking.

"Come on now, what would you like? You're holding up the line," says the grumpy lunch lady in an old-fashioned apron.

I hadn't realized how fast the line moved. "Sorry, the salad, please."

The lunch lady grumbles something under her breath. She dumps the salad onto my tray, causing some lettuce to spill over onto the counter. I thank her, but she's already focused on serving the next person.

I follow Aubrey to the side of the room by the arched windows. There's a round lunch table with three other boys already eating their lunch—one of them I recognize as Jean from my French class. The three boys pause their conversation and stop eating as I sit next to Aubrey.

The guy with a floppy mullet takes a sip of his soda and asks, "Who's the new kid?"

"Guys, I want you to meet my new friend, Jade."

They all politely wave. I awkwardly wave back.

"You'll never believe it. Jade lives at the witch's house," Aubrey says enthusiastically.

Everyone at the table looks at me in amazement. Not exactly the introduction I had hoped for.

"You're such a liar, Aubrey," the floppy-mullet-haired boy insinuates, shaking his head.

"I'm not a liar, Davy." Aubrey rolls her eyes. "Don't mind my cousin, Jade. He can be a bit of an asshole at times." She sticks her tongue out at Davy.

"Yeah, I mean, she's not a witch," I say. "She's my aunt. She seems pretty cool."

"Crazy," says Davy. "You weren't joking, Aubs."

"I'm Julian, by the way. You're in my French class." Julian, well,

Jean from French class, offers his hand. I see his fingernails are painted with black nail polish.

As we shake hands, I say, "I thought you looked familiar." Julian holds my hand with a light grip.

"Anyway, witch aunt or not—Jade's cool. I'm adopting her into our group, so she'll be part of The Misfits now," Aubrey declares while slinging her arm around my shoulder.

"The Misfits? Like the punk rock band?" I ask.

Wes, Aubrey's boyfriend says, "We call ourselves The Misfits—you know, like the outcasts of high school." Aubrey is right. He does resemble Adam Ant, with his faded eyeliner and *just out of bed* hair.

"Welcome to the group, Jade," says Aubrey.

I feel a bit out of place among her edgy friends, although they are all friendly and welcoming. Frankly, making a friend on the first day of school is the best thing I could hope for, and I have already made four—even if they refer to themselves as "The Misfits."

Julian wipes his hands on a napkin before saying, "Moving on, what about Friday night? Are we still good to go? I'll need someone to cover my shift at The Mastermind."

"What's The Mastermind?" I ask.

"The Mastermind is only the coolest video arcade downtown. Remember we passed it to go through Artist's Alley?" Aubrey says as she dips a french fry in ketchup. "Jade, do you have plans for Friday night?"

Everyone turns to her with a worried expression.

"Yo, Aubrey," Davy says, "can we trust her even to keep a secret? I mean, you just met her."

"I can keep a secret," I promise.

"We can trust her," Aubrey reassures everyone. "A few friends of ours are meeting us Friday night. We are all going to that creepy abandoned mansion next to your aunt's house. It will be fun. You should come!"

"Montgomery Manor? Are we allowed in there?" I ask.

Wes pulls out two cigarettes from his satchel and nods to Davy to join him for a smoke. "No, but we do it anyway."

"Oh." I am happy to be invited into their plans, but the last thing I want to do is cause Aunt Ruth any trouble. After all, I only just arrived yesterday. "What if we get caught?"

"We won't. No one goes near that place. I'm surprised they haven't torn it down already." Wes sticks a cigarette between his lips.

"Which is why it's the best place to hang out. Secluded. No adults. No security. Please, you have to come!" Aubrey says.

"It's nothing wild," says Julian. "We just hang out, listen to some tunes, and relax."

"Okay, I'll come." If things get too out of hand, I can always head next door to my place.

"Awesome!" Aubrey exclaims. "We're all meeting up at ten o'clock on Friday night. Dress warmly. It gets chilly inside this time of year."

"And bring a flashlight," Wes adds before going outside with Davy.

"Flashlight, got it."

Aubrey gives my hand a squeeze. "We're going to have a blast."

The rest of lunch, Julian and Aubrey chat about an upcoming show at The Underground, a music hall underneath the old bookshop on Main Street. I allow myself a moment to tune out and escape the day's chaos.

Periodically, I glance over at the fireplace lounge area. Brad has Allison on his lap with his arm around her tiny waist. I can't say I'm surprised to see them together. A cheerleader and athlete dating is a high school cliché. I'm in an envious trance watching her twirl her fingers in his hair. I wonder if a misfit and a jock could ever date outside of typical social norms.

The remainder of the day is uneventful, which suits me just fine. The only time I have to introduce myself was in math class. Thankfully, I don't have to stand up, and it's over quickly. By the time the bell rings for the last period of the day, I'm so tired I can barely muster the energy to climb up to the third floor. But then I remember that my last class is American History, which gives me the strength to keep going.

There are only four classrooms on the third floor—it's less crowded than the floors below. The American History classroom is dark, with the only light coming from the half-closed blinds, giving it a cozy feel. An American flag hangs on the back wall, stretching the entire length of the room. Each walnut bookshelf is stocked with historical literature, with books referencing every decade.

I sit in the back row, hoping I haven't taken anyone's seat. I place my notebook on the desk. I look up when I hear Brad's distinctive laugh outside the classroom. We make eye contact as he enters the room, but I quickly shift my focus to the windows. My breathing picks up as he takes the seat next to mine. He continues talking to his friend in front of him while I distract myself by taking out a pencil from my bag. Brad and his friend discuss the upcoming Homecoming game against St. Mary's on Saturday night.

"Coach has been working your ass off in practices. You're going to kill it this weekend. I know it!"

"Thanks, Jake," Brad says. "Are you going to go?"

I glance over to see Brad and his friend Jake, the same guy who had insulted Aubrey and me this morning on his bike, looking at me. They are awaiting my response.

"Sorry?" I ask.

"Are you going to the match?" repeats Brad sweetly.

"The one this Saturday?"

I know it's the one they are referring to. I'm just a little shell-shocked that Brad is asking me if I'm going.

"Yeah, you know, the Homecoming game?" Jake says. I don't think he recognizes me from this morning.

"Oh, I haven't given it much—"

"Everyone open up your book to chapter four."

I am cut off by a tall man with a Tom Selleck mustache entering the room. With a strong, intimidating presence, he exudes a stern and militant nature. His brawny physique and sharp features suggest that he's not one to be trifled with. His sudden entrance silences the room, and students hurry to pull out their textbooks. Brad shoots me an apologetic glance. I decide to hold off on my response for now.

"Come on, everyone, I haven't got all day. You should have had your books open and ready before I entered the room." The teacher claps his hands impatiently.

I scan the front and sides of the room for a pile of textbooks like in the other classes but come up empty-handed. I raise my hand and wait for the teacher to glance up from his lesson plan.

"Yes?"

"I don't have a textbook," I say to him.

The teacher rolls his eyes and lets out an irritated sigh.

"You all know what happens if you don't bring your textbooks to my class," he says in an agitated voice. "I deduct half a letter grade at the end of the semester."

The teacher's authoritarian demeanor makes it difficult for me to speak up and explain my situation. Instead, I freeze.

"Mr. O'Connor? Sir, she is new here and doesn't have a textbook," Brad explains.

Mr. O'Connor peers up from his desk and gets a good look at me for the first time.

"In that case, I apologize," he says with a prolonged tone. "I don't have any more books available. How about sharing with Mr. Phillips for the time being until I can arrange for another one?"

A rush of excitement fills my chest upon hearing his suggestion. Brad moves his desk closer to mine and places his textbook between us.

"Thank you," I whisper to him.

"You're welcome." His mouth curls into a subtle smile.

"I would like you all to silently read the first section on page 349 while I finish grading the assignment from last week," says Mr. O'Connor.

I lean over to view the textbook, keeping a respectable distance from Brad despite being inches apart. We both begin reading the first page. I force myself to concentrate on the excerpt about Andrew Carnegie and his influence on the steel industry, but my brain fails to retain the information whenever I smell Brad's oak and rosemary cologne.

"Mind if I turn the page? I can wait if you're not done yet," Brad asks kindly.

I pretend to finish the page, even though I've barely made it through the first two paragraphs. "Yeah, go ahead."

He turns the page, and his left hand accidentally brushes against mine. I can feel my heart skip a beat. We both jump at the unexpected contact.

"Sorry," he says.

"It's okay," I reply, trying to hide that his touch has left me feeling a little breathless.

For the next fifteen minutes, we read through the remaining pages of the section together. Brad seems careful not to brush hands again. The longer we sit together, the more at ease I feel. The fluttering in my stomach is less intense, and my breathing slows to a moderate pace.

Just as we're finishing up, Mr. O'Connor distributes the graded assignments from the previous week. I catch a glimpse of the red-circled sixty-four percent on Brad's paper. I quickly glance at the classroom clock, pretending not to have seen it.

"Not your finest work, Mr. Phillips," Mr. O'Connor says.

"What did you get?" Jake whispers to Brad. "I can't believe he gave me an eighty-six. He's such a hard-ass."

Brad shows him the paper with the sixty-four percent at the top.

"Dude, Coach is gonna kill you if you get below a C in this class! He'll have to bench you!"

"I know." He groans.

Brad lowers his voice and leans closer to Jake. I vacantly look out the window, so it appears I'm not overhearing their conversation.

"Allison and I were in a fight last week, and I didn't have time to study."

"Again? Dude, you guys are always fighting. What was it about this time?"

"The rise of steel," Mr. O'Connor clears his throat and starts writing on the chalkboard. Brad stops talking, and Jake turns around in his seat. Mr. O'Connor begins to write the dates 1850 to 1970, his chalk squeaking as it slides across the board. My ears listen to Mr. O'Connor's lecture, but my mind trails off. I wonder what caused the argument between Allison and Brad, even though it's not my business. Out of the corner of my eye, I notice Brad tearing off a piece of paper from the bottom of his notebook. He scribbles on it and then folds it into a small square. He slips the paper under the cover of the book beside my hand. I wait for Mr. O'Connor's back to turn before opening the note.

I NEVER GOT YOUR NAME, NEW GIRL

I bite my lip to stifle my grin so Mr. O'Connor doesn't catch on. Discreetly, I slide the note onto my lap. I write my name before folding it into a tidy origami square. I then slip it back under the book that Brad and I share. As he takes the note, a tingling sensation courses through my body as our fingers touch. I can no longer suppress the uncontrollable smile that spreads across my face. Brad directs his attention back to the board, waiting for Mr. O'Connor to turn around again. The corners of Brad's mouth turn upward as he unfolds the note.

The bell echoes through the classroom, announcing the end of my first day. In a flurry of movement, students rush to gather their things and head out the door. Meanwhile, Brad moves his desk back to its original position, taking care not to scrape the floor in the process.

"Thanks again for letting me borrow your book," I say.

"Don't mention it." He smiles.

"See you tomorrow." I wave to him as I exit the classroom.

"Hey, Jade!" Brad calls out to me in the hallway. "If you're planning on going to the match on Saturday, there's a costume party at my friend's house afterward. You should come."

"Isn't it a bit early for a Halloween party?"

He shakes his head, grinning. "No way. It's going to be a blast."

I stare back at him—at his hopeful expression. "I'm not much of a partier."

"Well, if you change your mind, I'll be there," he responds with a hint of playfulness.

I tilt my head to the side, feeling a blush creeping up on my cheeks. "I'll think about it."

"Great." He winks. "I'll see you later, Jade."

With a final wave, he turns to join Jake, and the two vanish down the stairwell. My cheeks ache from the wide smile plastered on my face. I make my way to my locker, where I find Aubrey waiting for me. Though I suspect she notices my foolish expression, she doesn't comment, thankfully.

"Hey, why don't you hang out with us at Artist's Alley?" Aubrey asks, bright-eyed.

"I should probably head home. My Aunt might get worried about me on the first day," I reply.

"Aw, come on! I'm sure it will be fine. You don't have to stay long."

"Well, maybe for a little while." Concern loiters within me. I worry Aunt Ruth might grow anxious about my whereabouts, much like my grandfather did whenever I ran late. "But then I really need to get going."

"Awesome! Do you like to paint?" she asks.

"Not really. I'm not much of an artist," I admit, half-jokingly.

"That's okay. I'm not great, either. Davy is the artist of the family. You can just hang out with me on the sidelines."

Aubrey wraps her arm around my shoulder as we leave the school grounds and make our way to Main Street. The clouds are heavy and gray, and I button up my blazer to keep warm.

"So, you made it out alive on your first day," Aubrey says, putting her nose ring back in.

"It's a miracle." I let out a sigh of relief. "By the way, thank you for being so kind and introducing me to your friends. Everyone seems really cool."

"Of course! I'm glad you like them. It's always hard being the new kid in this town. Julian only moved here last year, you know? If it weren't for us being friends with him, I don't know what would have happened to the guy."

"What do you mean?"

"Well, when Julian moved here, he didn't know anyone. Just like you. Except it was worse for him because people suspected—well, they suspected he was different," she says, looking downcast. "Anyway, the jocks were bullying him in the gym locker room, calling him all sorts of horrible stuff. One day, a couple of them cornered him in the shower. They beat him up pretty badly. Luckily, Wes and Davy were in the same class and stopped it. They got suspended for a week."

"That's horrible! At least the jocks got what they deserved."

"Oh no, it wasn't the jocks who got suspended." She shakes her head. "Only the three of them: Wes, Davy, and Julian."

My mouth drops. "What?"

"I know, right? Basically, you're golden if you play a sport, particularly rugby, in this school. You're untouchable. You can get away with murder; especially if your family is really wealthy."

"Who all were involved in the incident?" I ask.

"Pretty much everyone on the rugby and baseball team, I think." She flicks her cigarette ash on the pavement and inhales again. Surely Brad wasn't a part of that group. He seems too nice of a guy to hurt someone. "Anyway, now that Julian's a Misfit, no one messes with him anymore. I think people are a little afraid of us, and we like to keep it that way."

I guess I picked the right group to be friends with. Having companions who can offer security in an intimidating environment could be an advantage to someone as shy and timid as me.

We find Wes and Julian in Artist's Alley between the bookshop and the arcade. They are in the process of painting a face on the brick wall. While smoking a joint, Davy is reading Kurt Vonnegut's *Slapstick* novel on the ground.

"Hey, newbie," says Wes with a paintbrush between his teeth.

"So, you are allowed to paint on these walls?" I ask.

"Well, this side that we're painting on belongs to the arcade my parents invested in." Julian adds more paint on his brush. "And the other side is the bookstore that Mr. Willoughby owns."

"Mr. Who?" I ask.

"Mr. Willoughby is the retired Harvard professor who owns the old bookshop," Aubrey explains.

"Mr. W's the freaking man," Davy says without looking up from his book. "He encourages all forms of creative expression."

"He sounds awesome." I cock my head to the side to examine the unidentifiable figure on the wall. "What are you painting?"

"David Bowie, of course!" Julian says. "See the lightning bolt outlined? It's from the cover of the *Aladdin Sane* album."

"Oh, I see it now," I say. Maybe once Bowie's face is painted it will be more obvious.

"Want to paint something?" Aubrey asks, lighting a cigarette for Wes.

"Nah, I don't want to ruin anyone's work," I say, fully aware of my limited artistic abilities. I would be afraid that my lack of skill might adversely affect the overall quality of their work, and I don't want to intrude on their creative space.

"Nonsense! Come on. It doesn't have to be anything amazing," Wes says, handing me a paintbrush. "Just paint what comes to mind."

"Well, all right. Why not?"

I take the brush and dab a bit of white paint on it. I attempt to paint a portrait of Toby, except it looks more like a Muppet than a dog.

"Jade, are you excited to come with us on Friday?" Wes asks. The way he said it sounded more like a challenge than a question.

"Um, yeah, definitely."

"Good," he says firmly.

"Well, I'm excited. It will be like your initiation night." Aubrey laughs while reading over Davy's shoulder.

"Except without any hazing." Julian points his paintbrush at me. I am certain he noticed my wary face.

"But remember, you have to keep it a secret," Wes repeats.

"Of course, it's no problem," I say as we continue to paint on the brick wall. "So, do you guys always meet up at Montgomery Manor?"

"We used to meet up at the graveyard by Aubrey's house. But we got caught trespassing last year, so now we go to the mansion instead," Wes explains.

Aubrey stands up and begins painting a flower. "It's sort of becoming a monthly tradition."

"And now that we know someone who lives next door to the place, there's even less to worry about," says Davy, peering up from his book.

"Why's that?" I ask.

"Well, if anything happens, we can dart over to your house," he explains.

"You mean like if we get caught?"

"Or we run into one of the old ghosts that were murdered in the house… lurking around every corner in every dark room." Aubrey cackles like a witch and bends her fingers to make them resemble talons. *"Mwahaha—"*

"Oh, come on, Aubrey! Really? You're going to freak her out," Julian snaps.

"Murdered? Someone was murdered in that house?" I shudder; remembering the mysterious young man I saw standing in front of the window this morning.

"Not just someone—it was a whole family."

"Yeah, but it was like a hundred years ago, and no one knows who did it," Julian adds.

I gulp a mass of air down my throat. That just made the already eerie mansion more disturbing.

"There's nothing to worry about," Wes says. "It's all just stories to keep bored kids like us off the property."

I feel a couple of raindrops tap on my head. I still have another fifteen minute walk home.

"Let's make moves to the arcade, guys. It's going to start raining," Davy suggests, and they begin packing up.

"Well, I think I should probably get going, too." I drop the paintbrush into the paint can.

"Hey, I hope I didn't scare you," Aubrey says to me in a hushed tone as I gather my backpack and books. "I didn't mean to—"

"Oh, no—I don't really believe in that stuff anyway," I say, but the memory of someone swiftly passing by my mirror last night resurfaces. I try to make sense of it, seeking a rational explanation, but I'm struggling to find one.

"Okay," she says. "It will be a lot of fun Friday, I promise. Plus, I think the dudes think you're pretty cool."

"Thanks again for making today easier for me."

"No problem. Wanna walk to school tomorrow with me? I can meet you outside your gate?"

I give her a wide smile. "I'd love that."

We say our goodbyes, and we part ways on Main Street. The sky darkens, and raindrops bounce off every surface, drenching my blazer. By the time I approach Montgomery Manor on Fairview Avenue, I hear thunder rumbling in the distance. I can't believe people were murdered in this house—*this house.* The house next to mine. I tremble at the thought. I try to avoid tripping over the tree roots poking through the sidewalk as I run by the creaking gate of the mansion. I refuse to look up at the window where I saw the young man standing earlier. The idea alone sends chills down my spine. What if there are such things as ghosts?

CHAPTER V

THE DEATH CARD

"Aunt Ruth?" My call echoes in the foyer.

"In here, dear."

I follow a sweet melody—the sound of a harp playing—and find myself in a cluttered drawing room where Aunt Ruth is surrounded by dusty antiques and a cloud of cigarette smoke. In spite of the chaos, she looks angelic as she plays her massive pedal harp. Suddenly, Toby barks and jumps off a nearby couch. He's wearing a top hat fastened to his head with a black ribbon tied around his collar.

"I hope you don't mind, I have been calling him Reginald all day. He reminds me of my late husband, in a way. Doesn't he look so dashing?" Aunt Ruth laughs maniacally.

"He certainly does." I shake my head. Toby looks absurd.

In some ways, Aunt Ruth's idiosyncratic personality is comforting. It puts me at ease and helps me feel more at home in this unfamiliar setting.

"Thank you for taking care of Toby while I'm at school."

"Oh dear, please, it's no bother at all. Reginald and I are going to be the greatest of friends."

She takes a small bell out of her kimono and rings it three times.

Nigel enters the room, leaning against the doorframe for support as his slouched body struggles to maintain its composure. Beads of sweat glisten on his forehead, which he wipes away with a tired gesture. "Yes, madam?"

"Did you pick up my evening gown from Harrold's?"

"Yes, madam. It is hanging in your closet."

"Very good. Call the limo driver and remind him to be here at six o'clock. I don't want to be late like last time." She snaps her fingers. "I apologize, I won't be able to dine with you tonight. I am attending a dinner party in the city this evening with some old friends. I'd cancel, except we do this every year and it's been in the books since January."

"Of course, it's no problem. I have some homework I should get started on anyway."

"What sort of homework? I hope they didn't give you too much on your first day," she says as she continues to strum.

"Just some French homework. Our teacher gave us a reading assignment."

"Ah, le français est la langue de l'amour," she sings. Her eyes haze over as she gazes out the window. "The French language is one of the most romantic languages, don't you agree? I had a short summer affair in my forties with a French writer. Guilliam was his name. He had the most seductive gray eyes that made you go weak in the knees."

I take a seat on the couch and Toby hops up next to me. "How did you two meet?"

"At the theater in Paris. Yes, it was a wonderful fling we had. Our mutual friend, Laurie—well, you probably know him as Sir Laurence Olivier—introduced us."

My eyes pop open in shock. "You know Laurence Olivier?"

"It's Sir—and yes of course. We met at London's Central School of Speech Training and Dramatic Arts. We still write to one another from time to time. Anyway, Laurie's wife at the time, Vivien Leigh as you know, God rest her soul, and I met him backstage after his performance of *Romeo and Juliet.* Laurie introduced me to his friend, and that was that. Guilliam and I had a two-week-long passionate affair. Traveled all around the coast of France. We stayed in five star hotels and dined at all the restaurants—sparing no expense."

"That sounds so romantic. But why only two weeks? What ever happened to you and him?"

"Well, all good things must come to an end, as they say." She gets up from the harp and floats her way over to the liquor cart to make a whiskey sour. "He had to go back to his wretched wife and that was the end of that," she claims, taking a generous sip of her drink. She twists her tongue between the gap in her teeth. "Enough about me, how did your first day go?"

"It went"—I replay the eventful day in my head—"better than expected."

"Wonderful!" She toasts her glass. "Any dashing young fellows that caught your eye?"

I tug on a strip of my hair and play with the end of it. My eyes are doing the same dreamy thing Aunt Ruth's did when she was thinking of Guilliam.

"I know that look. You can't fool your ol' auntie now."

"Nah, it's nothing."

She looks unconvinced.

"Really, it's nothing." I blush. "I mean, I met a cute boy today. He seems really nice."

Aunt Ruth sips her cocktail waiting for more details.

"That's all," I say.

She makes a disappointed face as she sets her whiskey sour on the coffee table. "Ah, I see… How about friends?"

"Well, I did meet a girl on the way to school this morning. She's really cool and introduced me to her friends. In fact, they invited me to a"—I pause, searching for a different word for "party" that doesn't sound so precarious—"a get-together this Friday night."

"Great! There's nothing worse than an empty social calendar, my mother used to say. Makes for a boring person." She looks at her gold wristwatch and her eyes perk up. "Speaking of social calendars, I should get moving! Sorry to cut our chitchat short, dear," she says, chugging the rest of her drink and slamming it back down on the coffee table. She wraps her fingers around my chin. "It really is wonderful having you here."

Her warm comment makes me grin. "Have a great time tonight,

Aunt Ruth."

"I always do," she exclaims matter-of-factly while exiting the room.

At around 6:30 p.m., I hear Aunt Ruth shouting at Nigel, followed by a car door slamming shut. I glance out my bathroom window and watch the headlights disappear among the trees.

After changing out of my school uniform, I pull on my olive green sweatshirt with an embroidered albacore tuna on the front. I got it as a souvenir from the Coos Bay Fishing Tournament I attended a couple of years ago. I'm amazed it still fits me. I was fifteen at the time and feeling skinny and unformed. Now that I'm almost eighteen, my body has changed. I have more curves, with little wider hips and a growing chest. Although, I'm still pretty scrawny overall.

As I get dressed, I hear what sounds like small pebbles hitting against the windowpanes. The rain pounds relentlessly, and the wind howls outside. There's a knock at my door. When I open it, I see Nigel standing there, drenched and clutching a few logs under his arm.

"Miss, we might lose power in the storm. Do you mind if I light a fire for you?"

"Not at all," I say, letting him in. "Do you normally lose power during thunderstorms?"

"Oftentimes, yes. Lots of old trees on this block."

He stacks the logs neatly inside the fireplace. Using a lighter from his chest pocket, he lights a crumpled ball of newspaper and throws it under the wood. It doesn't take long before the logs are ablaze.

"That should do the trick," he says, slowly getting off his knees from the hearth. "Are you sure I can't have Chef Martin make you anything for dinner?"

"No, thank you." I'm not used to being waited on. I've always been independent and taken care of myself. Although I appreciate the offer, it just feels strange and uncomfortable. "Honestly, it's not a big deal. I'm used to making my own meals. It doesn't make sense to go through the trouble of making a big dinner for just one person."

"If you're sure, miss. I'll be in the study. If you should need anything, ring for me."

I bid him farewell with a nod. I hope the man can finally get some rest now that Aunt Ruth is out of town for the night.

Retrieving my worn-out copy of *Les Fables de la Fontaine,* I climb onto the bed. I lie on my stomach with my head resting on my hands. I open to the first poem, *"The Fly and the Ant"*, which is accompanied by a child-like illustration of an ant and a fly by a tree stump. Toby snores deeply on the tufted couch. It must be nice to be a dog with no homework to do.

Halfway through my translation, I let out a loud yawn. The sound of the rain hitting the side of the house and the fire crackling makes the room feel cozy. My eyes start feeling heavy, and I struggle to keep them open...

I am awoken by the booming of thunder. My notebook paper is soaked in drool. I wipe it off with my sleeve. Toby whimpers and climbs onto the bed with me.

"It's okay, bud. It's just a storm."

Another lightning flash illuminates the room, followed by a loud crash that shakes the house. The flame in the fireplace is nearly extinguished making it hard to see around the room. I grope the wall with my fingers in search of a light switch. When I flick it up, no lights turn on in my room. The power must have gone out after all. A deep growling noise startles me. I quickly realize it's just my stomach, reminding me of my hunger. I prioritize finding something to eat and making moves to the kitchen.

A candelabra has been lit just outside my bedroom door, presumably by Nigel in case of an emergency. I take it with me as I make my way down the dark hallway, the silence broken only by the occasional thunder. My body trembles under the flickering candlelight as I recount what Aubrey said today: *All these old houses have ghosts in them...*

"Ghosts aren't real," I remind myself, glancing over my shoulder down the dark hallway, just in case.

I find the kitchen. Apart from the refrigeration system, the kitchen appears unchanged since the house was initially constructed. The original copper pot rack hangs above a long wooden prep table with numerous pots and pans. It's easy to imagine the countless dinners prepared on that table over the years. A series of wood-burning ovens span the length of the wall. A row of toques hangs above them, paying homage to the chefs who once prepared meals within these walls.

I discover a British pork huntsman pie inside the refrigerator in a ramekin. A note is attached to it bearing my name. Under it is a message advising me that the pie doesn't require heating. Nigel must have left it for me. The aroma of sage and onion wafts toward me as I remove the lid from the ramekin, causing my stomach to growl even louder. I devour the pie and wash the dish in the tub sink. As I rinse the ramekin, I hear laughter from another room. I had assumed that Aunt Ruth wouldn't return tonight.

Following the sound of the voices, I make my way down a narrow hallway that leads to an open-air atrium. The source of the voices comes from a partially open door at the end of the hall.

The walls are fashioned with weathered iron and glass, suggesting this area is a conservatory. Above, a pane in the ceiling is shattered. A sizable metal bucket rests below it, collecting rainwater as it drips through. Three crows sleep atop a lemon tree. While I find these creatures beautiful, I also see them as dark and mysterious. As a lover of classic literature, where works like Emily Brontë's *Wuthering Heights* and William Shakespeare's *Macbeth* associate black birds with omens of death, I feel uneasy walking by them.

"Oh! Jade, please come join us!"

Aunt Ruth rises from her seat and motions me toward a table where three older women sit, wearing flashy evening gowns, fur coats, and expensive-looking jewelry. It's like I've stumbled into a room of young girls playing dress-up and hosting a make-believe tea party.

"This must be your beautiful niece you were telling us about, Ruth," says the petite older woman with the brightest pink lipstick I've ever seen.

The woman with faux butterflies in her beehive hairdo pats the chair next to her. "Have a seat next to me!"

"Jade, I would like for you to meet my closest grade school friends, Eileen, Lolly, and Mable."

I smile at her friends. "I thought you were going into the city for the night?"

"I did. We all went to the theater and had dinner and returned in the limo. It was my turn to host the sleepover."

"Sleepover?" I thought sleepovers were just a thing you do in your adolescent years.

"Yes, it's our yearly sleepover," Aunt Ruth repeats.

"We haven't missed one yet! Since we were six-years-old." Lolly claps her hands and her ruby bracelets jingle, her beehive hairstyle teetering.

Eileen pushes her thick Windsor glasses up the bridge of her nose and starts shuffling a deck of cards. At first glance, I think they are playing a card game. As I look closer at the cards, I see it's not playing cards on the table, but cards made up of strange illustrations. In the center is a white candle surrounded by sparkling gemstones. Eileen closes her eyes and starts humming.

"What game are you playing?" I ask.

"It's not a game, hon, it's *tarot,"* Eileen says, lifting one eyebrow.

"What's tarot?" I whisper.

"They are divination cards," Aunt Ruth says between puffs of her cigarette.

"Like fortune telling cards? Do they work?"

"Oh, yes! When we were young teenagers..." Mable looks over at Eileen who is side-eyeing her and she drops her voice a couple octaves. "When we were young teenagers, we would get together for sleepovers. Just like tonight. Eileen's mother used to read the fortune telling cards for her soirées just for fun, but she was really good at it."

"It didn't take long before many folk got wind of her talent," Aunt Ruth interjects. "It became a tradition at her parties. Her mother would let us stay up late and read our cards for us. I really can't remember an instance when any of it didn't come true!"

"Her poor mother—we must have driven her crazy." Lolly giggles.

It's heartwarming to listen to these elderly friends share their childhood memories, but they stimulate a bittersweet feeling. It reminds me of the special friendships I missed out on during those early years of never having close friends.

"Remember she told us dancing under the moonlight would bring us good fortune? Just so she could get a moment of peace?" Aunt Ruth chuckles. "We believed everything she told us."

"We did that a couple years back." Mable gets up from the table to make a cocktail. "It was when Ruth brought back Absinthe from her Paris trip. Somehow or another we all went skinny dipping. Oh, I haven't felt so free since!" She cackles.

Wow, so Aubrey was right! That kid who saw a bunch of old ladies dancing naked under the moon wasn't lying.

"Time for another drink?" Mable asks and puts a drink in front of me.

I take a sip and shut my lips, so I don't spit it out. "Oh, this isn't lemonade!"

"Of course not! It's a French 75, honey!" Eileen laughs.

"Oh, go ahead darling, drink up—live a little!" Aunt Ruth brushes her hands toward me. "Drinking age is eighteen in some states."

Eileen draws three cards from a pile and places them in a row in front of Lolly. She flips the first card revealing an image of a sun and a baby riding a horse.

"So, how does this card game—I mean tarot—work?" I watch curiously as Eileen flips another card.

Aunt Ruth lifts her hands up in the air, like she's speaking to God himself. "Tarot tells us stories and cycles of our lives. They are our spiritual guides, our celestial allies, illuminating our path through what's yet to come and what has passed."

The idea of angels utilizing the cards to reveal my future seems ludicrous. Yet, four women almost four times my age are gathered before me, convinced of the cards' enchanting power.

"Knowing your future is kind of scary, isn't it?" I contemplate aloud. I find the idea of knowing one's future unsettling. It raises the question of whether having such knowledge violates the fundamental principles of life.

"Oh, no, dear. Think of it as valuable insight," Lolly says.

"Would you like a reading?" Eileen asks.

"She is really good—just like her mother was," Mable says. "She predicted a windfall for me a few years back, and I won a large sum at the Kentucky Derby that year!"

"And then you spent it all on those silly scarves from Hermes." Lolly giggles.

"Not all of it." Mable gives her a sidelong glance. "Plus, I adore my scarves."

I love the childish banter between these old friends. If it's true that a good friendship keeps you alive longer, then these four women could live centuries. I hope to find the kind of friendship these four have one day. Who knows, maybe The Misfits will fill that role.

"Come on, give it a try," Aunt Ruth insists.

I hesitate to answer. Knowing the details of my future might put me in a vulnerable position if the cards are legitimate. What if the tarot cards reveal something I'm not prepared to hear? I bite my nails, unsure if I would be ready to explore the unknown.

"Well," I begin, still hovering between doubt and indecision, "all right, but I don't know what to do."

"No worries, dear. We will guide you through it," Aunt Ruth says.

Eileen shuffles the stack of cards before handing them to me.

"As you shuffle the deck, concentrate on what you would like to ask the cards. When you are ready, cut the deck into thirds."

The room is hushed, except for the raindrops pattering against the glass ceiling. As I try to perform an overhand shuffle, I feel the weight of the cards in my hands. Sitting up straight, I inhale deeply, allowing my breathing to steady my spinning thoughts. With closed eyes, I formulate a question. I want to seek insight into the upcoming year and uncover what I desire most: to build close relationships with people who wholeheartedly accept me for my true self. I long for a sense of belonging, to be understood, and to have my intrinsic value acknowledged beyond superficial judgments.

I open my eyes and divide the deck into three equal piles.

"Perfect. Now stack the three piles into one any way you feel is right."

I do as Eileen says. She grabs the deck and lays out the first card: The High Priestess. The second card from the pile is The Lovers followed by the Two of Wands. Lolly, Mable, and Aunt Ruth exchange looks as Eileen rubs the sides of her temples with her long green fingernails.

"Honey, can you tell me about the two lovers you might have asked about?" Eileen asks.

"Two lovers? You must be mistaken—"

"No, darling. The cards are showing me two people. Two men to be specific. If you don't know who they are, they are coming your way."

I suppress a laugh, feeling like the tarot cards are playing a joke with me. Centering my question around friendship, I had never thought it would lead to the unexplored terrain of romance. Finding love always felt distant and implausible for a shy tomboy like me. I never experienced the ease of developing relationships or being seen as desirable—let alone by *two* guys. I stare at The Lover's card; a naked man and woman look up at an angel in the sky. I play with my hair, wondering how images on three cards could predict something so unimaginable.

"You are going to come to a crossroad and you will need to make a decision." Looking down at the three cards, she puts her index finger over the top of her lip. "The cards also advise you to be careful and deliberate in your choices."

I find that last bit alarming and totally unexpected. The seriousness of the message shifts my perspective as if the cards warn me to take their advice more seriously. I swallow a gulp of air as I process the possibility that this could all come true.

"A lot can happen in a year," Lolly advises in a hushed tone.

"Yeah, I guess we'll have to see," I say, scratching my head.

Lolly and Mable both yawn simultaneously.

"Well, ladies, it will be 4:00 a.m. soon," Aunt Ruth says, looking at her wristwatch. "What do you say we pack up and get some rest? After all, it is a school night." She winks at me.

Eileen begins to pack the tarot cards into a rose decorated metal tin. As if by magnetic force, a single card drops out of the stack and lands face up. A flash of lightning illuminates the glass room with a crash of thunder following. All five of us stare at the card with the skeleton knight riding a white horse. Their eyes crawl up from the card to meet mine.

"The Death card," Eileen whispers. "Be ready for a big change, Jade."

The dark hallway leading to my room doesn't feel so ominous with Aunt Ruth's friends bickering about tomorrow's breakfast outside of their rooms. I wish them all goodnight before going into my bedroom. The fire is completely extinguished and it's cold and dark inside. There's just enough light peering through the curtains that I can see the edge of my bed. I realize that I never finished my French homework, so I'll have to complete it during homeroom tomorrow, instead. I load up my backpack and sit it next to my school uniform.

I gently move Toby to the foot of the bed, watching as he takes a deep breath and falls back asleep. I feel envious of his ability to switch off so easily. My mind is racing, and even though my eyes are closed, I can't seem to calm down. The image of the death card keeps playing over and over in my mind. If the cards were predicting my future, who are the two men they spoke of, and what decision must I be careful about? I'm overthinking so much that it's giving me a headache. I rub my temples to try and relieve the pressure. For my first full day in Grove Hollow, it feels like so much has already happened. Will every day be this eventful? If that's the case, I fear I won't ever sleep again.

CHAPTER VI

THE PHANTOM INTRUDER

Thursday night, I wake up to the sound of my bathroom window opening and closing. I lie motionless, except for my heavy breathing that causes the covers to rise and fall. I am paralyzed with fear and unable to move. The doorknob clicks, and the door slowly creaks open. I hear shuffling footsteps across my bedroom floor at a steady pace.

The vanity drawer slides open, and its contents are rummaged through. With shaking hands, I peer over my covers, but there's no one there. Suddenly, the drawer slams shut, and another one opens. My stomach drops when I see my copy of Daphne du Maurier's *Rebecca* floating in the air and the pages turning before it's tossed onto the floor. Other items from my vanity, such as a hairbrush, lavender body lotion, and my grandmother's ribbon box, are also thrown onto the floor with it. I glance over at Toby, who is still fast asleep on the couch. How could he sleep through this? Am I just imagining things? The invisible entity opens my armoire door, causing the hangers to rustle on the rack.

"W-w-what do y-y-you want?" I dare to call out.

The activity comes to an abrupt halt. I wait nervously under the covers, trembling with fear and unsure what to expect next. I hear the footsteps glide across the room and stop by the foot of my bed. Intense dread washes over me as the weight of a person presses down on the covers. I let out a piercing scream in terror. I throw the covers back over my head. The weight lifts and the sheets are flat again.

"Please go away, please go away," I whisper with tears falling from my eyes.

I remain paralyzed beneath the safety of my blankets, uncertain how much time has passed, but it feels like an eternity. Finally, I hear the fading footsteps retreating through the balcony doors. Summoning my dwindling courage, I cautiously emerge from beneath the bedding. As I search around, I'm shocked to find the room immaculate. It's as if no one had ever broken in.

CHAPTER VII

STAYING AWAKE

"Jade, come on," Aubrey says, shaking my arms.

"Huh?"

"The lunch bell rang, we gotta go to study hall."

I rub my dry, heavy eyes and realize the lunchroom is almost empty.

Aubrey hands me a packet of Twinkies and says, "I noticed you didn't eat anything. You can have these—they'll tide you over."

"Thanks," I mumble, wishing I could have another couple hours of sleep.

"Why are you so tired today? Did your aunt have another party or something?" she asks as we head to the library on the second floor.

I let out a big yawn. "No, I wish. I've been up since 3:30 in the morning."

"Insomnia?"

"No." I exhale. "I think my aunt's house is haunted."

Her eyes grow in size.

"Haunted? Like with a real ghost?" Aubrey asks, and I can hear the excitement in her voice.

"Yeah, I think so, anyway. I don't know." I shake my head. "I swear I saw someone—well I couldn't really see them, but a book was floating in the air, and my stuff was getting thrown around my room. I'm sure I felt it sit on my bed, too. When it left, I looked up from the covers and it was like nothing happened. The room was back to normal. I don't know, maybe the lack of sleep is causing me to hallucinate."

"Could you have sleep paralysis? I heard you can get that if you're over exhausted."

"Maybe." I yawn again.

We stop at the girls' restroom opposite the library, and Aubrey heads to a stall while I station myself at the sink. Tucking back my hair, I splash cold water on my face, already feeling more alert. I gaze at myself in the mirror. I pull down my eyelids to inspect my sleepy eyes, their puffy bags accentuated by the fluorescent lighting.

"I can't wait to go home and take a nap. That's if I can ever sleep again."

"Hey, I have an idea!" she says through the stalls. "Why don't I come over tonight? We can rent some movies, and I'll be there if the ghost shows up again. Maybe then you'll get some sleep."

"Really? You would want to do that?"

"Sure, that's what friends are for," she says. My heart leaps with joy at her referring to me as her friend. "Plus, waiting for a ghost sounds exciting."

The door swings open and it slams against the tiled wall.

"Well, well, well... look who it is. Samantha and Danielle, looks like we have company," Allison sneers.

The girl with the high ponytail flicks her hair to the side. "Loser's bathroom is on the third floor."

The three of them approach me. I'm surprised at how fast adrenaline can awaken an exhausted body. I feel my hands shake as I hold on to the edge of the sink. Allison's eyes narrow and I see a smirk form on the edges of her mouth.

"Get out of my way."

She shoves my body to the side so she can stand in front of the mirror. I fall and knock the metal trash can over on my way down. Used napkins spill out and litter the floor. There's a throbbing sensation at the top of my arm. I grab it tight with my hand. The three of them stand around me laughing.

"Pick these up," the athletic girl with dark curly hair demands.

"What?"

"You heard Danielle, clumsy—pick these up," Allison hisses.

"Are you deaf or just stupid?" Samantha shouts and punts a ball of napkins at my face.

The toilet flushes and Aubrey kicks her bathroom stall open.

"Hey! Don't you all have something better to do?" Aubrey grabs my hand and helps me up from the floor.

"You should feel right at home with all this trash on the floor," Danielle snickers to Aubrey.

"I've always wondered what your mom had to do to the Headmaster just to keep you in here," Allison says. "What is she on, boyfriend number five?" The three of them laugh so loud it echoes off the walls and rings in my ears.

Aubrey's face turns red. Her eyes begin to water, but she stands her ground. "Bite me, Allison."

Allison scoffs and looks down at Aubrey's tight fist. "What are you going to do, punch us?"

Aubrey moves her hand as if she's going to strike but lets her arm drop. "As much as I'd love to hit that stupid, ugly face of yours, I have better things to do. Come on, Jade."

"Pfff—just what I thought. You're all talk," Allison says.

"Go ahead, walk away losers!" Samantha calls from behind.

Aubrey slams the door shut as we exit the bathroom. A group of freshman girls stare at us from across the hall.

"Thanks for standing up for me," I say to Aubrey.

Aubrey doesn't say anything, and just looks down at the floor. I stop just as we enter the library. Aubrey comes to a halt, too, but doesn't look up.

"Are you okay?" I ask.

"Oh, yeah, I'm fine," she replies, but her eyes brim with tears. A blast of heat courses through my body as anger stirs within me, directed at Allison for causing my friend to almost cry.

We pick one of the long, empty tables in the back by the stacks. I sit across from her, facing the door. She still won't make eye contact and her nose is pink as she sniffles.

"I'm sorry about what she said—Allison. That was a horrible thing to say about your mom," I say.

"Don't worry about it." She shrugs and turns on the brass piano lamp on our table.

I decide not to press her about the bathroom incident any further. It's clear Aubrey is affected by the comment about her mother, but whatever that was about is none of my business. I'm hoping she'll come to me if she wants to talk about it. Instead, I pull out my French homework and start reading tonight's fable, *The Frog and the Ox.* Aubrey rests her knees against the edge of the table to recline back in her seat. Instead of studying or working on homework, she doodles on top of her trapper keeper covered in stickers.

"I hate her. Allison is such a bitch. She doesn't know anything."

"I can agree with that—"

"Everyone in this fucked-up school thinks I'm poor because my mom and I live in an old farmhouse on the edge of town, past all those stupid, ritzy mansions. It's my dad who pays for me to come here, you know? It was part of the agreement when he and my mom split."

She tilts her head so I don't see the tears building up as she continues to doodle.

"I'm sorry, Aubrey."

"Everything is handed to her on a silver platter. All because her family comes from a long line of money. The rich folk here are privileged assholes who think they can do anything to anyone."

"Like my grandfather always said, wealth robs the brain of compassion," I say, feeling a pang in my heart as his words resurface in my memory.

"He was right." She brushes her nose with her sleeve. "Sorry, I shouldn't be unloading all of this on you."

"Don't apologize," I say with a weak smile. "You sound a lot like my grandfather."

"How so?"

"He looked down on people who had money, even though society does the opposite."

"That's strange, considering you're, like, wealthy."

I fiddle with the corners of my notebook. "Growing up, he kept that part hidden from me. It wasn't until I arrived here that I learned about my family."

I look up at Aubrey, who is giving me pitying eyes. I decide to change the subject.

"You know, if it weren't for you, Allison would have beat me up… or at least Danielle. She's so big… and scary."

"She really is," Aubrey admits. "We need to get ourselves thicker skin."

"Would that help me from getting more bruises like this?"

I pull up my sleeve to show the bruise forming and her jaw drops.

I hadn't noticed Brad sitting diagonal from us until now. His back must have been turned when we entered the room. He sees the bruise on my arm, and I immediately roll my sleeve down to cover it.

"Damn, that bruise is wicked! Is that from Allison pushing you?" Aubrey asks.

"Yeah, it was."

"Shit, I should have punched her when I had the chance."

I shake my head. "No, it's probably best you didn't."

"Well, she deserves a good punch in the face at least," Aubrey adds, and we both laugh.

By the last period of the day, word gets around about the incident in the bathroom. People say Aubrey foamed at the mouth, her eyes turned red, and worse—she punched Allison. It's incredible how a little gossip can quickly transform into a rumor with little to no evidence. Whispers follow me as I walk up the stairs to the third floor. I do my best to ignore the people gawking.

"What people talk about is their own affair," my grandfather would say.

Static comes through over the loudspeaker: "Aubrey Jackson, please report to the Headmaster's office."

Oh, no.

I'm so worried for Aubrey, that I don't hear the audiovisual boys behind me wheeling in the projector. Mr. O'Connor taps his foot with his arms crossed.

"You boys were supposed to set the projector up *before* class begins," he barks.

"I know, Mr. O'Connor, but Madame Gaël needed it for her AP French class," one of the boys says to him. Mr. O'Connor lets out a loud sigh.

"Miss Whitney, I made a note to have the school order more history books. Unfortunately, they won't be here until next week. You'll have to continue sharing until then."

"Thank you," I say to Mr. O'Connor, but his back is already turned.

Brad walks into the room and overhears the tail-end of my brief conversation with Mr. O'Connor.

"So, you don't have a book yet?" he asks me as he sits.

"Not until next week."

"Good," he says in a delighted tone and pushes his desk next to mine. "Looks like you're going to be my book partner for at least another week."

I hide my smile. Sharing a book with him has been the highlight of my days. As I unpack my backpack, a sudden spasm of pain shoots through my arm, and I clutch the bruise.

Brad frowns. "Listen, I heard what happened in the bathroom. I saw your bruise in the library and I thought maybe it was from Allison. If so, I apologize—"

"There's no need for you to apologize. It's okay, really." I lower my head and rub the top of my arm. His lips twist sideways, betraying a hint of doubt toward my words.

"Now class this isn't let's-mess-around-because-we-are-watching-a-movie time. Nobody is to talk through the documentary," Mr. O'Connor warns as he pulls down the projector screen over the blackboard. A picture of a railroad train with the title, "The Evolution of the Steam Train," shows up on the white screen. "If I catch any of you talking or sleeping, it's an immediate detention, got it?"

I pray my heavy eyes can stay awake in this dark room.

"You are to spend the first few minutes reading chapter seven, sections one and two, before we begin. This will go over the material in the documentary we're about to watch, so be sure to read *thoroughly,*" he instructs.

Brad opens our books to the proper page. We read together silently.

Luckily, his cologne isn't as strong today and it's easier to concentrate on the reading. It doesn't take us long to finish the assigned sections. I decide to write down some notes in case we are tested on the material. Brad lightly taps his fingers on the side of the book. I recognize the rhythm as the 20th Century Fox Fanfare and let out a funny snort through my nose. I try to cover it up with a cough, so Mr. O'Connor doesn't expect any tomfoolery. A chuckle escapes Brad and we both bow our heads to hide our wide grins. Mr. O'Connor must have heard us as he stands up from his desk to look around the room. We straighten our mouths quickly and pretend to read the book. A pencil drops onto the hard floor, making a loud noise in the quiet room. A boy's chair squeaks as he leans over to grab it and muffled laughter follows.

"All right, that's enough time. Everyone lift your heads up from the pages," Mr. O'Connor grumbles. "Let's start with the documentary. Miss Sanderson, can you press play for us?"

In the front row, a girl with feathered bangs reaches out and presses a red button on the projector beside her. The room darkens, and the black-and-white documentary commences.

"The steam generated by the engine creates pressure, causing a piston to move back and forth within a cylinder..." The narrator's voice drones. I can already feel a yawn welling up within me, which I quickly smother with my hands. I fight to keep my eyes from growing heavy in this dark room. The projector's warm light, the narrator's monotonous voice, and the unstimulating documentary content add to the challenge.

Suddenly, Brad nudges my arm, and my eyes jolt open. He slides his notebook over to me.

YOU ALMOST FELL ASLEEP!

I look up at Mr. O'Connor, who is sitting on a stool, scanning the room like a World War II aircraft radar scanner. I write back:

do you think he saw me?

Brad takes the pencil off my desk:

I DON'T THINK SO.

I rub my eyes and write back:

I don't think I can make it through.
I should accept a detention now.

He puts the pencil to his chin, the eraser side up, as he thinks. He then writes:

I COULD MAKE SURE IT DOESN'T HAPPEN AGAIN?

Mr. O'Connor lets out a sneeze and I write quickly:

HOW??

I see Brad's left hand come up over the open textbook. I watch curiously. He grabs my right hand and drags it under the desk and onto his lap. An electrical impulse travels down a special pathway through my chest. My heart is beating so fast it hardly has time to rest between intervals. Is this really happening? I hyper-fixate on the feeling of Brad's fingers intertwined between mine, especially the tip of his thumb on the side of my palm. I bite my lip so hard it could bleed. The last thing I want is Mr. O'Connor suspecting something from my wide grin. He squeezes it twice and then rests.

"One squeeze if I see your head bobs. Two squeezes if your eyes shut," he whispers in my ear and it sends goosebumps from my neck to my spine.

I suspect he didn't intend for me to notice the slight blush on his cheeks, but I do. His focus remains fixed on the film. My mind struggles to absorb the content. I can't concentrate on anything in these unexpected and thrilling conditions. Throughout the entire duration, I wonder if his kind gesture is purely platonic or carries a deeper meaning...

As the documentary progresses, I feel his thumb gently caressing the side of my palm. At first, I thought it was unintentional, but then he did it again, sending tingles up my arm. I brush my thumb against the outside of his index finger, and he responds by giving my hand a gentle squeeze. Despite the sensations stirring inside me, I somehow keep a straight face. I don't want this documentary to end.

But it does.

A kid next to the door turns on the overhead lights. Brad drops his hand and our fingers unlock. His head is turned as he tucks the textbook back into his bag. Jake helps him drag his desk back.

"Ready for practice?" he asks Brad.

"Yeah, man. I hope Coach goes easy on us today," he says, swinging his backpack over his shoulder.

As I pack up my stuff, our eyes meet from across the aisle. The warmth of my cheeks drains as he shows me a look of indifference.

He gives me a head nod. "See ya."

"See ya," I reply, bewildered.

CHAPTER VIII
WAITING FOR GHOSTS

While walking home from school with Aubrey, my mind drifts away, consumed by thoughts of Brad and our intertwined hands during class. Uncertainty takes hold within me, and I question whether it was simply a friendly act or held deeper significance. Aubrey shoots me a curious look, jolting me back to reality.

"You good, Jade?" she asks.

I'm not ready to tell her about the hand-holding. "Yeah, just thinking about the bathroom incident. By the way, I heard you got called to the office. Did everything go okay?"

Aubrey lets out a frustrated groan and tells me they didn't believe her when she denied hitting Allison.

"But Allison didn't have any bruises to prove it," I say, rubbing my own bruised arm.

"Right! Believe me, I had the strong urge to hit her."

"So, what happened in the end?"

"Well, since there was no evidence, they issued me a warning."

My jaw drops. "A warning? For something you didn't do? That's ridiculous. I don't understand how she could get away with something like that."

"Her family donates a lot of money for school funding, so I imagine that's why they sided with her. Such bullshit."

Aubrey unfastens the two scrunchies holding her braids in place. She loosens the strands of her messy white hair, and they cascade in wavy curls. As I nervously nibble on my nails, I express my hope that we won't have any further run-ins with Allison or her friends.

Aubrey scoffs. "I'm not scared of her. They're just bullies. Anyone who messes with my friends will have to face me. Besides, there are worse things than being suspended."

"Really? Like what?"

Aubrey responds, "Like not standing up for yourself. It's better to speak up than to be silent. Never make yourself a victim, Jade."

"I wish I had your courage."

"You can," she says confidently. "Seriously, next time Allison confronts you, stand up for yourself. I think you'll be surprised by the amount of courage you will have."

"I'll try," I reply, tucking my hair behind my ear. The thought alone makes me nervous.

We walk across the street to The Rewind, a newly renovated video rental store designed by Wes's dad's interior design firm. The modern store has colorful neon lights reflecting off the square tiled walls, making it look prismatic. In the center of the store, an art installation of TVs stacked on top of one another like a tower plays various movies of different genres. The store smells like movie popcorn, making me hungry.

"Wow, this place is incredible. Our video rental store back in Coos Bay was so small and dull compared to this place," I say.

"It's neat, huh? Come on, let's find something fun to watch while we stay up and wait for ghosts."

We split up. Aubrey heads toward the horror section while I stay close to the drama and comedy sections. I pick out *Sixteen Candles* and *Young Frankenstein.* Both lighthearted, comical, and easy to watch. Just what I need. I take my empty VHS cases up to the register.

"Will this be all?" asks the boy behind the counter, his thick, round glasses lending a quirky look to his appearance. He places the VHS tapes into their individual cases.

"Not yet. My friend is picking some movies out, too."

Aubrey comes up to the counter with a pile of movie cases. She drops one on the floor, and I crack up.

"How many movies do you have?"

"I figured we might need some options."

"It's a three limit movie rental, Aubrey," the boy says in irritation.

"Oh, whatever, Randy. Just check us out, okay?"

Randy, puts his hands up in defense. "Okay, okay—fine!"

He gives in and scans her five movies through the system: *Ghostbusters, Nightmare on Elm Street, Poltergeist, The Exorcist,* and *The Shining.*

"*The Shining?* Really, Aubrey? I'll never fall asleep again after watching these!"

"Consider this research. We gotta know what kind of ghost we're up against."

Randy stares at us with a confused face. "That will be six dollars and twelve cents. They're due back in a week."

Aubrey searches through her backpack.

"Shit, I must have left my wallet at home."

"I got it," I offer, giving Randy a ten dollar bill.

"Thanks, I'll pay you back," Aubrey says, and I can hear the embarrassment in her voice.

"Pay me back by being on ghost-duty so I can get some sleep."

Randy's one eyebrow raises as he counts the dollar bills.

"What, are you guys ghostbusting or something?"

"Actually, Randy," Aubrey says, snatching the plastic bag from his hand and I grab the change, "we are."

"With what? A proton pack?"

"No, you idiot!" She rolls her eyes as he laughs. "Oh, nevermind. Come on, Jade. Let's get out of here."

"Good luck with Slimer!" shouts Randy. I can hear him laughing at his own joke from outside.

Aubrey offers to carry the bag of VHS tapes as a thank you for paying for the movies.

"No way, it's really not a big deal," I say and grab one of the bags from her.

"I swear I would have paid for them if I had my wallet on me."

"I know you would have. You can spot us next time—but fewer scary movies, okay?" I say, trying to lighten the mood to prevent Aubrey from feeling embarrassed.

She smiles. "Fine."

While walking toward Blythe House with Aubrey, we pass by Montgomery Manor. As we discuss our mutual love for new wave music, my attention is drawn to the window where I had previously seen a young man. An eerie feeling washes over me. It's not solely because of the previous murders but because of a strange connection that seems to exist between me and the house. Noticing I'm distracted, Aubrey halts and looks at the mansion with me.

"It's creepy, isn't it?"

"It feels lonely. Like everyone in this town has forgotten about it," I whisper in response, empathizing with the familiarity of that kind of loneliness. I reach out to touch the gate. I run my hand along its cool, wrought iron bars as if I'm trying to give the melancholic house some kind of comfort.

Rain starts to fall, tapping against our heads. We hasten our pace toward Blythe House, following the brick path. Nigel greets us at the door, and we remove our wet shoes and hang our blazers.

"Damn," Aubrey says with her mouth wide open looking around at the elaborate gilded interior meshed with the bizarre decor. "Holy shit, this place is crazy!"

"I know, it's like a museum." I follow her eyes as she looks up at the chaotic decorations.

"A freaking awesome museum," Aubrey says, in awe.

"Your aunt is in the drawing room," Nigel says, giving Aubrey a disapproving look.

We find Aunt Ruth playing the harp again with a long cigarette between her fingers. One of her crows flies above us and lands on her shoulder. Aubrey claps her hands as though this is a sideshow act at a circus, when in reality this is just an ordinary day at Aunt Ruth's. Toby runs into the room dressed in a bowler hat and a monocle. He jumps on Aubrey and gives her a big lick on the cheek.

"Reginald! House manners!" Aunt Ruth gets up from her harp and holds her hand out to greet Aubrey as Toby gallops from the room.

"Aunt Ruth, this is my friend, Aubrey Jackson," I say.

"Nice to meet you, dear. Any friend of Jade's is a friend of mine. Please, won't you two sit down for some tea?"

We sit on the tufted couch in front of her. The crow is still perched on her shoulder. Nigel pours tea into three teacups. It's too hot to sip, so Aubrey and I put ours aside. Aunt Ruth drains her flask of brandy into her tea. Aubrey looks at me and giggles.

"Your house is amazing," Aubrey remarks. "I've always wondered what the inside of these mansions looked like."

"Thank you, dear. Almost all the decorations are from a set during my acting days," Aunt Ruth says proudly. "See the palm trees? They're fake. They're from the set of *South Pacific.* Oh—and that big sign over there that says, *Mushnik's Flower Shop* that's from—"

"Little Shop of Horrors," Aubrey finishes.

"That's right." Aunt Ruth seems impressed by her theater knowledge.

"We performed that for the school play my Freshman year. It's one of my favorites."

"Mine, too." Aunt Ruth gleams.

"Jade never told me you were an actress."

Aunt Ruth coughs up her spiked tea. "She didn't? Why, I worked alongside some of the greatest: Cary Grant, Clark Gable, and Lauren Bacall." She lets out a small laugh. "I must admit, the attraction of fame and fortune seduced me during those times. Speaking of which, did you know, I even had a short affair with Humphrey Bogart?"

I cut in before Aunt Ruth can continue another one of her daily erotic love affair stories. "Aunt Ruth, would it be all right if Aubrey spends the night?"

"Of course, dear. I will have Nigel prepare one of the guest rooms in the other wings—"

"She can camp out with me in my room."

"Very well," she says and takes a big gulp of her tea. "So tell me, Audrey, what part of the Hollow are you from?"

"It's Aubrey," I correct her.

"My apologies," Aunt Ruth says, waving her hand.

Aubrey clears her throat and fidgets with her hands. "Well, you know, just off Blackhill Road."

"Blackhill Road? That sounds oddly familiar," Aunt Ruth says, bringing her fingers to her chin.

"You probably recognize it. It's the road at the end of Fairview—with the old cemetery."

"Ah, yes! The Blackhill Cemetery," Aunt Ruth recalls. "Almost every Grove Hollow pioneer is buried there—your ancestors included, Jade."

My eyes widen as I learn that my distant relatives have been laid to rest nearby. I feel a newfound and unexpected connection to this town beginning to materialize, knowing my bloodline is deeply rooted in its soil.

"We'll have to go check it out sometime." Aubrey nudges me with a smile.

"Yes, yes. I have a burial plot there myself all ready for me," Aunt Ruth adds, "along with the other Whitney's."

The crow caws and both Aubrey and I jump.

"Brings back memories of a date Errol Flynn once took me on and we stopped at Père Lachaise Cemetery in Paris. Have I ever told you the tale of my romantic entanglement with Errol?"

"Well, Aunt Ruth," I say to her, grabbing Aubrey's hand and pulling her up from the couch, "we have some homework we need to catch up on before we watch the movies we rented."

Aunt Ruth sets her teacup down and shoos us with her hand. "I won't keep you ladies. Enjoy your evening."

Once we make it to the second floor, I turn to Aubrey and whisper, "Thank goodness we left when we did. Sometimes her love affair stories can take up to an hour."

Aubrey giggles. "Your aunt is quite the character!"

"She really is." I open the door to my bedroom.

"I can't believe this is your room," Aubrey says as her fingers sweep the floral wallpaper, her eyes focused on the chandelier. "*And* you have a balcony?" She opens the French doors.

"Yes, and it overlooks the river, too," I reply, settling down on the bed and rubbing the hand Brad had held earlier. "So, which movie should we watch first?" I call out to her.

Aubrey twirls back inside and shuts the doors. I grab the bag of rental movies and dump them on the bed.

"Definitely *The Exorcist,*" she insists.

I shudder. "No way! I'll never be able to sleep after watching that!"

"Okay, fine." She makes a ticking noise with her tongue. *"Nightmare on Elm Street?"*

I groan.

"Wait, I have an idea," Aubrey says, holding up *Nightmare on Elm Street* and *Sixteen Candles* behind her back. "Pick a hand. Whichever movie it is, we'll watch it."

"Sounds fair."

I point to her right side. Her face falls as she holds out *Sixteen Candles.*

"Yes!" I exclaim.

"Fine, but next time it's my turn to choose the movie."

Chuckling, I respond, "Hopefully, by then I'll have dozed off."

Nigel presents us with a large bowl of popcorn and sodas on a silver tray. He kindles a warm fire for us and sets up the VCR, turning it to channel three. The opening theme to *Sixteen Candles* emanates from the TV as he exits the room, leaving us to our viewing pleasure.

"We really ought to be watching *Ghostbusters,* though," Aubrey grumbles.

"I prefer Jake Ryan from *Sixteen Candles,* personally."

"Ew, he's too pretty." Aubrey grimaces.

"How can anyone dislike Jake Ryan?"

"Give me Matt Dillon in *The Outsiders* any day."

"And Rob Lowe!" We both say at the same time and erupt into laughter.

"It's great having a girl in the group," Aubrey muses. "Don't get me wrong, I love all the guys, but nothing beats a girls' night."

"Absolutely," I reply, not entirely sure what a girls' night is.

"Do you miss your friends from home?" she inquires, handing me the popcorn bowl.

Lowering my head, I confess, "I never really fit in with the girls back in Oregon."

"Really?" she asks, looking surprised.

"I was kind of a tomboy," I admit, feeling embarrassed.

Aubrey grins and grabs a handful of popcorn, tossing it into her mouth. "Well, you're cool in my book."

"You guys are pretty great, too." I'm grateful for a friend like Aubrey who makes me feel comfortable being myself.

A loud boom of thunder makes us jump.

"Damn, this storm is crazy," she says, glancing toward the balcony where a tree branch falls into the river below.

Halfway through the movie, a sudden, deafening crash comes from outside, and the television abruptly shuts off. Aubrey hops off the bed to investigate, but the TV stubbornly refuses to turn back on. Just then, there's a knock on the door. Nigel saunters in, logs in hand to add to the fireplace.

"Hopefully the power comes back soon," he mutters in his flustered British accent. "Would you ladies prefer dining in the main room, or shall I bring dinner up here?"

"Upstairs is great, Nigel. Thank you," I say, not wanting to miss a chance of the ghost returning.

"I can't believe you have a butler," Aubrey says to me after Nigel leaves.

"I am still trying to get used to it," I reply.

"Get used to it! Some of us would die for one," she and I laugh. "So, what should we do now that we've lost power? Are you tired?"

"I'm not tired yet." I shrug. "I think the thunder woke me up a bit. How about a game?"

"What games do you have?" Aubrey inquires.

I glance around my room and realize I don't own any board games.

"Maybe we can play a card game? I'll see if Aunt Ruth has any cards. You can stay here if you want."

Another crash of thunder rumbles through the house, and Aubrey shivers.

"I think I'll come with you," she says, huddling close.

"Are you afraid to be alone with the ghost?"

She scoffs. "No way, I ain't afraid of no ghost," she says. I raise an eyebrow in disbelief, and we both giggle.

We start our search for cards in the living room where Aunt Ruth is dozing off on the living room couch with Toby snoozing by her feet. In an attempt to not wake her up, we tip-toe around the room. Toby glances at me, and I signal him to stay quiet. He goes back to sleep, resting his head on Aunt Ruth's feet.

With no luck at finding cards, I whisper to Aubrey, "I wonder if there are any cards in the study?"

"Let's go take a look," Aubrey whispers back.

The study is cluttered with plants, taxidermy, and bric-a-brac, making it hard to find anything. I investigate Aunt Ruth's writing desk while Aubrey wanders over to the drawers in the bookshelves. The bottom drawer of the desk contains only old bills and papers. I open the drawer above it and come across a few black-and-white photos.

One photo catches my attention; two children dressed in early 1900s attire standing outside Blythe House. The estate looks considerably different from how it is now; no vines are climbing up the walls, and the gardens are overflowing with flowers and shrubs. It's a beautiful sight. I notice the birthmark on the boy's cheek as I examine the photo. This must be a picture of my grandfather and Aunt Ruth. They look so joyous and carefree.

As I look at the photo below it, I see a young Aunt Ruth cradling a baby boy in a rocking chair. My grandfather stands behind her, beaming with pride; the baby must be my father. It's heartbreaking to see my grandfather so happy, looking down at his beloved baby boy, not knowing that he would have to bury his only child twenty-five years later. My nose begins to tingle. Tears roll down my face, landing on the only photo I've ever seen of my father.

I remember catching my grandfather in a vulnerable moment when I was seven. It was the only time I saw him cry. I was peering through a sliver of the partially opened door, witnessing him poring over old photo albums. The next day, when I went to look for the albums in his room, they were nowhere to be found. His involvement in World War II created a barrier that made it difficult to broach the subject of his personal past. Therefore, the courage to ask about the photo album and the reason for his tears never found its way to me. I'm wondering if these painful memories are why my grandfather never had photos displayed around the house.

Despite my urge to take the photographs with me, I resist and return them to the drawer. As I close it, I spot an envelope hidden between the desk and the drawer. I recognize my grandfather's handwriting on the address and retrieve the aged paper. I glance at the study door to ensure no one is coming in, and Aubrey is still preoccupied with the bookshelf.

September 06, 1970

Dearest Ruthy,

I received your letter. I understand you wish to buy the deed for The Whitney Mansion in exchange for Blythe House. I know you, dear sister, and I know how much you love the estate in Manhattan. You must understand, I cannot meet your request. Aside from the various details I cannot disclose in this letter, you know the money won't be around for much longer. Collins says it's more likely I'll get a buyer for this estate than for Blythe House. The last thing I want is for her to grow up how we did. Trust me, this is best for Jade.

Anyway, it is done and I won't hear any more of it.

Your brother,
Clyde A. Whitney

P.S. Please dispose of this letter after you've read it.

"Found some cards!" Aubrey shouts.

I quickly slide the letter back into the envelope and tuck it away where I found it.

"Awesome!" I respond, wiping my teary eyes.

"Are you okay?"

"Yeah, just some dust in my eyes," I lie.

"You can definitely find a lot of that in here," she jokes, and I chuckle.

We go back upstairs, through the dark hallway, and into my bedroom. Aubrey teaches me how to play Gin Rummy. Using her impressive skills, she wins all three rounds.

Around six o'clock, the power comes back on. Nigel brings us a platter of steak and fries and a rich chocolate mousse. Aubrey devours her meal and finishes my fries as we chat about her romantic encounter with Wes at The Underground and watch the end of *Sixteen Candles*. I help Aubrey set up a bed on the couch, and to my surprise, she suggests we watch *Young Frankenstein* instead of her choice of horror films. I suspect Aubrey is too afraid to watch anything scary.

"If I fall asleep, wake me up if you hear the ghost, okay?" she requests.

"Of course." I stifle a yawn.

"Thanks for being a good friend, Jade."

"Thanks, you, too." I smile at the thought of Aubrey becoming the closest friend I ever had.

I pull the covers up to my chin, fluff my pillow, and prop myself up for a better view of the movie. Aubrey's audible mouth breathing leads me to think she has already dozed off. Despite my best efforts, I struggle to calm down my racing thoughts about my grandfather's secret letter. He indeed wanted to keep all of this a secret from me, but I fear I'll never find out the "why" part. I fight to stay awake, but it seems like I am not far behind Aubrey in terms of sleepiness.

I wake up and find the flickering static from the television casting an eerie glow throughout the darkened room. Aubrey remains sound asleep on the sofa. A cold breeze blows my hair as I shuffle across the chilly room to silence the TV. As the wind creeps through the balcony doors, they emit a haunting creak, conjuring a ghostly sway in the curtains.

I move to close the doors but stop in my tracks as a shadowy figure catches my eye in the full-length mirror. A young man is sitting on the edge of my bed; his features are obscured by the darkness. Though my heart pounds in my chest, I whisper softly, "Who are you?"

The hairs on my neck prickle as I see him shift his posture through the reflection of the mirror. He rises from the bed and moves toward me with a melancholic grace. I spin around to face him—but he is no longer there. It is only Aubrey and me in the room.

I struggle to take a breath as I witness the balcony doors slowly shutting on their own. Without a second thought, I race toward the doors. I peer out into the darkness of the balcony, but find no one there. Shaken, I retreat back to the safety of my bed, pulling the covers around me as I keep my eyes fixed on the balcony doors.

CHAPTER IX

BIG BUFF BRAD

In the dimness of my room, Aubrey readies herself for school before my mirror. She is humming the melody of "Midnight Rambler" by the Rolling Stones, swaying her hips rhythmically from side to side.

"What time is it?" I ask, rubbing my eyes.

"It's almost half-past six."

"Ugh. I envy your energy," I grumble.

"Do you mind if I borrow one of your ribbons? I promise to give it back."

"Sure, borrow whatever you'd like," I say, still half asleep.

I trudge my way to the bathroom. The room is still humid from Aubrey's shower. I take a quick rinse in the bathtub to avoid wetting my hair. I have no motivation to style it this morning. While I prepare myself, Aubrey rewinds *Young Frankenstein* and watches a portion of it. I keep my eyes shut while I brush my hair, knowing it's not as restful as sleeping, but at least it gives my tired eyes a break.

I pull back my hair with a thick, maroon-lace ribbon. However, I'm not satisfied with how my hair frames my face. No matter how many times I attempt to pull my hair back, the persistent frizz refuses to settle down.

"Here, let me help," Aubrey offers.

From her backpack, she grabs a small can of Aqua Net hairspray. I shut my eyes as she sprays the front of my hair. She expertly uses a comb to tame my unruly mane. When I open my eyes and look in the mirror, I see her skilled handiwork, and the frizz has vanished. I thank her.

"Any ghostly visits last night?" she asks, making my stomach drop as the memory of the chilling encounter floods back.

"Well," I start, ready to confess about the young man sitting on my bed. But the fear growing on Aubrey's face hinders me from spooking her too much. "Nope. I think you were spot on. It was just sleep paralysis."

"Great! Now you can snooze easy without any spooky surprises."

I force a laugh. "Yeah, I hope so."

I glance at my exhausted eyes in the mirror, wondering if it was all just a strange dream... or will the elusive visitor pay me another visit tonight?

"Wait, let me help you hide those eye bags." Aubrey pulls out a compact from her backpack.

"Ugh, so they are noticeable."

"Don't worry, I'll make them go away," she says.

She blots nude powder foundation under my eyes and dabs it with her makeup sponge. I look back in the mirror. The saggy skin has successfully been camouflaged.

"They might come back as the makeup wears, so take this and reapply it every hour or so."

I tuck the compact in the front pocket of my bookbag. "You're like my fairy Godmother this morning."

She looks at her wristwatch. "Hey, we might have time to grab some lattes before school. Let's get you some caffeine."

The storefronts on Main Street proudly display signs in their windows wishing the Academy's rugby team good luck for tomorrow's Homecoming match. Many of the shops have adjusted their hours, closing early in the afternoon to accommodate the game.

We make a pit stop at the cafe before cutting through Artist's Alley. Aubrey, a seasoned coffee drinker, takes it upon herself to order a mocha latte for me. The warm beverage has an immediate effect in taking the edge off my drowsiness.

As we step inside the school, we discard our empty coffee cups in the trashcan near a ladder where two students struggle to hang a Homecoming banner in the breezeway. The hallways are decorated with long strands of black and red crepe paper and balloons hanging from the ceiling and lockers. I'm amazed by the town and school's dedication to their sports teams.

"Ugh, I forgot. Today's a half day," Aubrey moans.

"What's so wrong about that?"

She digs her fingers into the skin of her forehead and drags them down to her chin. "Because we have to sit through the rugby pep rally game."

"It's better than sitting through a class, right?"

"I'd prefer schoolwork over watching rugby."

Wes is waiting for Aubrey at my locker. After exchanging a quick kiss with Aubrey, the pair head off to their homerooms. Meanwhile, I swap out the textbooks in my backpack for the ones I need for my morning classes. Using the mirror inside my locker, I apply some foundation under my eyes. As I look at my reflection, I catch a glimpse of Brad and his rugby teammates walking down the hall with their sports bags. Brad's gaze meets mine through the mirror, but I quickly shut my locker door as they pass.

"Good luck today," I say to him.

He doesn't say anything, but gives me a feeble smile with a headnod. His response surprises me, as it contrasts with his friendly demeanor from yesterday in American History class. I'm left puzzled, unable to understand his sudden change. Was it something I did?

At lunch, Aubrey nudges my arm to look over at a cheerleader. She is bending down to grab her fork off the ground and three guys in rugby jerseys are whistling at her. She shakes her hips so her skirt shows more of her black spankies. She giggles while straightening herself up. One of the bigger rugby guys picks Samantha up and twirls her around in the air, and she squeals in mock protest. Aubrey wins the world record for the most dramatic eye roll.

"God, they need to grow up," Julian huffs as he sits down at the table.

"A pep rally? As if any of them need another reason to blow up their egos," Wes says, taking an angry bite out of his pizza.

"They just love showing off their uniforms, don't they?" Aubrey complains.

"Their uniforms aren't that bad," Davy says as he leans back in his chair to get a view of the cheerleader's short skirts.

"Gross, dude." Aubrey throws a napkin at his face. He falls backward on his chair and we all laugh.

"ARE YOU READY, RAVENS?" calls a short cheerleader in pigtails.

"Oh, no—here it goes," Wes slaps his forehead.

"Here goes what?" I ask.

The group of rugby players and cheerleaders shout a school chant and the rest of the lunch room joins in:

"RAVENS FLY HIGH! RAVENS FLY HIGH!"

Brad enters the lunch room with his confident gait. His red and black striped jersey hugs tight against his chest, defining every ab like a chiseled rock wall, and exposing his strong upper arms. My eyes are drawn to his thigh muscles protruding under the seam of his high black shorts. It's like Michelangelo used Brad as his muse for carving David. Every inch of his body is perfectly sculpted.

"You have some drool running down your mouth," Julian whispers to me.

I wipe my mouth. "Sorry."

"He may be an asshole—but even I can't look away from his bod," he admits.

The lunchroom resounds with the repeated chant of Brad's name. Three cheerleaders, among them Allison, grab the crowd's attention with a synchronized cartwheel routine near the tables. Allison executes a flawless landing, yet her wave of the pom-poms lacks the usual enthusiasm. Through her impeccable makeup, the swollen bags under her eyes and her reddened nose show signs of recent tears. Confusion overtakes me as I scratch my head, wondering why she was crying. Suddenly, the room erupts into applause, and everyone rises to their feet, offering a standing ovation.

"I'm going out for a smoke. I have a headache from all this screaming," Wes says, a cigarette bobbing up and down between his lips.

"I'm coming with," Aubrey says and Davy follows.

A teacher lowers their hands to turn down the volume of the cheering. Julian continues reading his book for English Literature with no interest in watching the pumped up crowd. I, on the other hand, can't look away. The cheerleaders follow Allison, like little ducklings, to the opposite side of the room. They stand in a line and shout more cheers and the students join in.

Brad slumps into a seat in the lounge area by the fireplace. I watch as he runs his hand through his wavy blond hair with an air of frustration. When one of his rugby buddies tries to engage him in conversation, he appears disinterested and lacks his usual charismatic energy. He picks at his food listlessly, his head lowered. I put two and two together; something must have happened between Allison and him.

Following lunch, a collective announcement directs everyone to gather at the outdoor stadium for the highly anticipated Homecoming pep rally. I make my way there with Aubrey and the rest of the group. When we arrive, we spot an unoccupied row at the highest point of the bleachers, where we all sit. While my friends shiver in the cold, I can't help but feel like the odd one out without a fashionable leather jacket. However, despite my coat's lack of trendiness, I take comfort in the familiar warmth provided by my rustic corduroy coat. Its sherpa lining has been my companion during countless trips on my grandfather's fishing boat, always ensuring I stay snug and protected from the elements.

"My butt is freezing sitting on these cold-ass bleachers," Julian says, hunched over, blowing warm air on his hands.

"Just be glad you don't have to wear a skirt," Aubrey whines, cuddling close to Wes.

"This is so stupid, why the hell are they making us come outside for this shit? We should have the option to go home and omit ourselves from this torture," Davy grumbles. He puts his Walkman's headphones over his ears and reclines against the chain linked fence.

"This should help with the cold," Wes says, pulling out a whiskey flask from the inside of his jacket.

"Sweet!" Julian grabs the flask from Wes. He takes a big swig.

Aubrey's next to steal a sip and waves the flask in my face. I admit, I'm a bit chicken about the idea of drinking in front of teachers, but I cover the flask with my hands and throw back a small gulp. It burns on the way down. As soon as the whiskey enters my stomach, I feel a warm blanket cover the inside of my body. Davy finishes the rest and lets out a loud belch.

There's clapping as the Headmaster stands behind a podium with a microphone. I've only seen him in portraits in the hallway, so it's my first time looking at him in person. He gives a speech on how Coach Roy will lead the boys to victory this weekend against their rival team, St. Mary's Catholic School. Everyone cheers—except for my group of friends. There's a boost of adrenaline in the stadium as the cheerleading squad tumbles out onto the field, waving their pom-poms in the air. A marching band coordinates themselves into a G and an H formation and plays the school's alma mater.

Allison leads the cheer squad into an intricate pyramid and the band starts playing "We Are the Champions," by Queen. Wes, Aubrey, and Julian sing along to the song. Two guys a few rows forward turn around and glare at us, which only makes them sing louder. The cheerleaders continue their choreographed performance full of tumbles, backflips, and vigorous stunts. A person in a funny-looking raven costume, that looks more like Sonny the Cuckoo Bird from the Cocoa Puff's cereal, dances alongside them. I find the show entertaining to watch. The Headmaster walks back onto the podium and the raven mascot does the chicken dance behind him. The office secretary takes her cane and shoos the mascot away. The crowd of students cries with laughter.

"All right, all right. Please rise and cheer on the Grove Hollow Academy Rugby Team!"

The cheerleaders and the band form two straight lines down the middle of the field. A pair of girls at either end hold a paper banner with the school's crest. The rugby team charges through the banner ripping it down the center. Unlike football, where the players wear a lot of protection gear on their bodies, rugby players wear very little padding—if any. I can't imagine how cold they must be right now. The crowd cheers, *"RAVENS FLY HIGH,"* in unison. The last one to run out from behind is Brad. His face is serious and determined. He and the rest of the athletes run to the center of the field.

"This is bogus, I am getting out of here," Davy says.

"Same. You guys wanna come, too?" Wes asks.

"I'd love to, but I can't risk another warning or else I'm in detention," Aubrey admits.

"I'm staying here," Julian says to them.

"Jade?" Wes asks.

"I'm going to stay here, too."

"All right then. See you tonight, guys," he says to us.

With all the commotion this week, I almost forgot all of us are meeting at Montgomery Manor.

"Sorry, I forgot the time we are meeting tonight," I ask.

"Don't sweat it, we're meeting at ten o'clock," Aubrey replies.

"Remember, don't forget a flashlight," Julian says. "It gets dark in the mansion."

I move my hands up and down on my arms as my body shivers with goosebumps. I'm unsure if it's from the cold or the thought of entering the creepy mansion at night.

I shift my attention to the field. The rugby team divides into two squads. The Headmaster pulls a coin from his pocket, placing Brad and another player on opposite ends. Skillfully flipping the coin, he catches it in his palm. With triumphant applause, Brad's team appears as the coin toss winners, earning them the advantage of starting the game with possession of the ball.

"I'm starting to regret not leaving with them while I had the chance. Sports are so boring," Aubrey complains.

"They're not too bad to watch," chimes Julian.

"Uh-huh." She gives him a side-eye accompanied by a smirk. "Especially, a bunch of guys with buff bods in tight clothes, right?"

Julian rolls his eyes, but the smile left on his face tells me he agrees. I didn't mind watching either. In fact, I haven't kept my eyes off Brad since he ran out onto the field.

Although I am not well-versed in the game's intricacies, Brad is a skilled and strategic player who moves quickly and expertly among his teammates. He charges down the field with incredible power with the ball in hand. As I watch in anticipation, I bite my nails while gripping the edge of my seat with my other hand. The opposing team's players rush toward him, determined to take the ball away. Despite their efforts, Brad outpaces them and sprints toward the in-goal area. The crowd, including myself, holds their breath as he approaches the goal line. Finally, he crosses the line, scoring a point for his team. Overcome with excitement, I rise to my feet and clap my hands. Aubrey is surprised by my outburst, but Julian also joins in with applause.

"That was really close," he says.

The rest of the game is equally as exciting. Aside from one kid getting knocked-out, Julian describes it was a pretty tame match compared to last year's pep rally. Brad's team won the game. All the players lift him up in the air as they cheer his name. The Headmaster dismisses us and we are free to leave to go home. I look back at the field and notice the rugby team stays as Coach Roy gives them a pep talk.

Julian, Aubrey, and I are the last out of the stadium. The parking lot is full of classmates hovering by their luxury cars.

"So, are you excited for tonight?" Julian asks me.

"If I'm being honest, I almost forgot," I reply and the two of them laugh.

"Hey, Jade—hold up a second!"

I turn around and Brad is running out of the stadium entrance. Aubrey and Julian exchange looks.

"Did… did I just hear Brad call your name?" Julian whispers.

"I'll be right back," I tell them.

As he continues to run toward me, I meet him halfway. Two girls say hi to him, and he half-heartedly waves back. He bends down and clutches his bare, sweaty knees with his hands.

"Hey," Brad pants.

His cheeks are flushed from all the exertion. Beads of sweat pour down from his messy, wet hair, and he flips the front of his hair from his eyes. I didn't think it was possible for him to be any more attractive, but I've been proven wrong.

"Hey, what's up?" I smile in spite of my nerves.

He lets out a cough to catch his breath.

"I wanted to see… if you've given some thought… about… the

costume party… at The Willows… tomorrow?"

"Oh." I bite my lip and scratch the back of my leg with my shoe. "I don't have a car, so I don't think I can make it."

He tilts his head to the side. His eyes squint and the corner of his mouth moves upward. "What if I pick you up?"

I look behind me. Julian and Aubrey, who are acting like curious cats, are whispering to each other. I don't think they would approve if I went to a party with Brad. It's disappointing my friends lump him together with the other jocks, even though he seems genuinely caring and kind. I wish they'd give him a chance.

"I can't tomorrow. I'm busy. Maybe some other time?"

"Sure," he says with disappointment in his eyes. "Maybe some other time." He slumps back toward the stadium.

"Hey, Brad!" I call back to him and he turns to face me. "I'll be cheering you on at the game!"

His posture straightens and his frown transforms into a wide grin. I give him a smile in return and walk back to meet Aubrey and Julian.

"What did Big Buff Brad want?" Aubrey asks.

"He wanted me to go to a costume party with him."

"Brad? Bradley Phillips wants to take you to a costume party?" Julian looks baffled. "Why?"

"I'm not sure." I shrug. I feel like the best way to stay out of trouble is to say as little as I can right now. Aubrey has a peculiar look on her face, like she's devising a plan.

"But he invited you?" she asks.

"Yeah, but like I said, I'm not going to go."

"Why not?"

I hesitate before answering, "I don't know—I'd feel uncomfortable, I guess. I wouldn't know anyone."

"Where's the party at?" Julian asks.

"The Willows."

Aubrey jumps in front of us, and we stop walking. "A party at The Willows?"

"Oh, you've heard of it? What is it? A restaurant?"

"No." Julian chuckles. "It's one of the old mansions on your street."

"Everyone's heard of the radical parties at The Willows!" she shouts.

"They are legendary for being wild and crazy! Even people from the city travel up to go to them—we should go!"

Julian throws his hands in the air dismissively. "Aubrey, are you crazy?"

"Come on, Julian! Imagine how fun it would be to crash it."

"Let me remind you, we *never* get invited to these parties—and for good reason. We hate those kinds of people and they hate us! Plus, we weren't invited—Jade was."

Aubrey throws her arms around my shoulder and Julian's. "Duh! But if Jade gets an invite, then we are invited by association."

"I don't know about this," I mutter.

"Listen, it's a costume party. We'll cover our faces so no one will recognize us," she suggests.

"But what if they do find out it's us? You know they'll kick us out, or worse, beat us up." Julian gulps.

"No one's beating anyone up, okay? Plus, we'll have Davy and Wes with us. Come on, Jules. When will we get another opportunity like this?"

"All right, fine," he agrees. "I have to admit, I've always wanted to dress up and go to a costume party at The Willows."

"We can't go to the party without you, Jade." She lifts both her hands up. "You in?"

I'm torn. Part of me wants to go, but, on the other hand, the cautious side of me is worried. The last thing I want to do is stir up any trouble, especially since Brad was kind enough to invite me.

"Please?" Aubrey begs.

I guess, what's the worst that can happen? Brad did invite me after all, and no one said I couldn't bring a friend or two… or four. I would feel more comfortable knowing someone at the party, anyway.

"Okay, let's do it."

CHAPTER X

MANHUNT

In the crisp late-October air, I hold onto my corduroy jacket while making my way up the sidewalk from Blythe House to Montgomery Manor. The dark street makes it hard to see the mansion in the shadows. A thick, murky fog blankets the ground, swallowing the surroundings in an uncanny stillness. My eyes climb to the window where I once spotted the young man, realizing it could have been him who haunted my room the other night. The thought sends a prickly sensation through my body, prompting me to quicken my pace.

I hear distant chatter coming from the front gate. At first I don't recognize Aubrey without her school uniform. She's wearing fishnet stockings, a white crop top, and a tight leather skirt. Her makeup is more dramatic than usual—thick cat-eye eyeliner, blue glitter eyeshadow over her eyelids, and black lipstick on her face. Her hair is teased to add volume to the top and the sides. As I stand next to her in my rustic farmer-like overalls and plaid shirt, I feel frumpy in comparison.

"Jade, you made it!" she says, lunging forward and giving me a hug. "This is Davy's and my cousin, Greg, and his girlfriend, Sarah. They both go to public."

"Public school she means," Greg corrects her and reaches out to shake my hand. Her cousin and his girlfriend both have the same punky look as Aubrey.

"Nice to meet you both. You all look so cool."

Aubrey pats me on the back. "And you look hella warm!"

"Come on, let's get moving," whispers Wes from the other side of the gate.

With a few jabs of his screwdriver, he's able to pick the lock and the gate opens with a groan. We move some of the brush to get through. The grass and overgrown shrubs are so high they come up to my waist.

"This place is like a jungle," Sarah says, swiping away a tree branch.

"Where's Julian and Davy?" I ask.

"They're coming. They had to stop and get supplies."

"Oh," I say, wondering what she means by supplies.

We squeeze through a broken window into a crumbling ballroom. The room's gilded shine has lost its luster due to the accumulated dirt. I stand in the center and admire the sad fresco mural on the ceiling. It's cracked from years of decay and neglect. Two thirds of the crystals in the chandelier above us have fallen onto the checkered floor like sad teardrops. I wonder when this once-magnificent fixture saw this ballroom last come to life. Aside from the chandelier, the only thing left in this room is the lone grand piano. Even covered in dirt, it's still very grand.

"All right, guys, our usual spot." Wes sets his flashlight on the floor.

"Are the same people coming as last time?" asks Aubrey.

"I think we are waiting on two more people," Greg replies.

Still in awe over the ballroom, all I want to do is explore the rest of the mansion before the party arrives. There's an unexplainable curiosity I have for this place. Maybe it has something to do with the haunting young man I saw in the window. I can't tell if I am more scared or hopeful to see him again. I tap the top of Aunt Ruth's flashlight that I borrowed from the utility closet. It flickers on, then off, and then finally on again.

"Don't go too far! You might get lost!" Aubrey shouts to me.

"I won't! I just want to look around."

The first room I enter is a library or study of some sort. I'm surprised by the number of books still on the shelves, mostly about engineering and the railroad. I smirk thinking how excited Mr. O'Connor would be about them. Scattered across the floor are dampened newspaper clippings. They make a swishing sound under the soles of my boots as I continue to explore.

There's a large oil painting on the wall behind a mahogany desk. Part of the canvas is slashed in half, and it looks like it was done intentionally. I lift the loose linen to reveal a portrait of a man's face. His blue eyes are cold and serious as they stare back at me. My light shines through the two holes on the plaster wall underneath the painting—small enough to be bullet holes. I rub the back of my neck where goosebumps start to climb. No doubt these holes are evidence from the murders here.

An ear-piercing scream slices the air, causing me to jump in alarm and let go of my flashlight. My heart beats fast with adrenaline as I grab the flashlight from the floor, eager to uncover whether my friends have encountered the ghost. However, my hopes dwindle as Sarah yells for Greg to put her down, accompanied by the explosive notes of an out-of-tune piano. A touch of disappointment passes over me. I had secretly hoped for a chance to meet this mysterious person that could be haunting me. With the arrival of new voices, I assume the rest of the party has finally arrived. Pausing to calm my breathing, I prepare to join the others.

I make my way back to the ballroom, following the terrible rendition of Chopsticks. Julian and Davy have arrived and are holding on to the party supplies: a cassette player and two brown bags. I'm unfamiliar with the two other guys accompanying them—they look too old to be high school students.

"I don't believe we've met," says a tall gangly guy with face piercings and a red mohawk. He takes my hand and brings it to his lips. I retract my hand and feel a creepy chill crawl up my skin.

Aubrey giggles. "Jade, this is Eddie, and this is his friend, Ted. They're friends with Wes's older brother. They bought the goods for us," she says, shaking a clear bottle of alcohol.

"Nice to meet you, Eddie," I say, wiping my hands on my overalls.

Julian puts a Depeche Mode cassette tape in the stereo. Everyone seems to know the words to the first track. Wes rummages through the brown bag and pulls out the red cups.

"Don't feel like you have to take one," Aubrey says to me.

"It's okay."

She pours a small portion of alcohol in my cup. "How's this?"

"That looks good, I think," I say, uncertain about the appropriate amount to consume. I'm a little nervous about drinking, given my lack of experience with alcohol and the unfamiliar feeling of being intoxicated. Glancing around, I see everyone else at ease, confidently sipping their beverages. I bring the cup to my lips to blend in, like everyone else. "Why does this smell like nail polish remover?" I gag.

"It's vodka. Here." Aubrey pours a generous amount of soda in my cup.

"Thanks," I say. I pinch my nose and throw it back.

"So, I spoke to Wes and Davy. They said they're down to go to the party tomorrow," Aubrey says.

"Great." I'm still feeling uneasy about my friends crashing a party Brad invited me to.

"No clue what we'll come dressed as, but we'll figure it out."

"Why don't we go as something themed?" Julian suggests, joining the conversation.

"That's a great idea!" Aubrey pours vodka into his cup. "We can brainstorm tonight and come up with a plan."

"What about you, Jade? You in?" Julian asks.

I shake my head, a shyness creeps in at the possibility of coordinating a bold or edgy costume. I prefer to stay within my comfort zone and plan for something safe and easy.

"You guys go ahead and plan something. I might just go as something simple since it's so last minute," I say.

Both Aubrey and Julian shrug. "No problem," they both say to me.

Everyone gathers around the cassette player, and I feel my social anxiety creep in. My shy personality makes it hard to naturally thrive in crowds. Whenever I feel uncomfortable in a social setting, my first instinct is to sit back and observe a room. I would do this often at birthday parties back home in Coos Bay, not that I was invited to many. I prefer to watch people interact rather than fret over whether or not I'm dull. Being a wallflower may make most people feel small and awkward, but I consider it great spectating fun. From what I see, everyone's energies naturally flow with one another. Maybe it's because everyone here fits under the same sub-genre: anarchic. Ironically, that is the last word to describe rule-following, quiet me.

Aubrey, who has the most energy of them all, is organizing a dance to the music with Julian and Sarah, while Wes and Greg watch as they talk to Ted and Davy. They poke fun at Davy for having to make out with a girl named Tonya at the last party while playing spin the bottle. I really hope that's not a game we will be playing tonight.

There is one person here that I'd rather not observe from across the room. I don't know why, but he makes me uncomfortable. Maybe it was his initial hand-kissing introduction that felt invasive, or his occasional glances over in my direction, but he gives me the creeps. One thing's for sure, I'm not interested in getting to know Eddie any more than I need to tonight.

"Hey, everyone, why don't we play a drinking game?" Wes asks the room.

"How about Never Have I Ever?" Sarah suggests.

"How do we play?" I ask the group as we sit down in a circle.

"What? You've never played Never Have I Ever? How old are you, twelve?" Ted teases.

Julian gives Ted the side-eye.

"I haven't been to many parties," I admit, feeling the heat of embarrassment on my cheeks.

"It's easy," Sarah says, sitting next to me. "We put up five fingers. Everyone admits something they hadn't done before. If you or someone playing has done any of the things mentioned, you put a finger down."

I glance down at my hands nervously, recognizing the level of attention that will be directed toward me while participating in this game.

"And you take a shot," Davy adds, pouring more alcohol into my red cup.

"What happens if you have all of your fingers up at the end?" I ask.

"Well, you probably will have at least a couple down," she says, holding her cup out for a refill on the vodka. "But, even so, the person with the most fingers up wins."

"All right, let's begin," Davy declares and sits down next to Ted.

I scoot over for Aubrey to sit next to me. Wes pats his hand on the open spot alongside him.

"Sorry, Jade. The boyfriend wants me next to him," she says.

"Don't worry, babe, I'll sit next to you," Eddie says. He claims the spot to my right. I shift my body as close to Sarah as I can get.

Davy lifts his hands up. "Five fingers up, guys. Eddie—you first."

"Never have I ever made out with a guy."

Aubrey, Sarah, and Julian put a finger down. All five of mine remain upright.

"Okay, okay—cheap one, Eddie. All right, Jade you're next," Davy says.

"Um, never have I ever"—what have I never done before? I think hard—"been to a drive-in."

There's a lot of unimpressed faces staring at me, and it makes me nervous. Did I do something wrong?

"You mean like doing it at a drive-in?" Greg asks.

"Doing what?" I ask.

Sarah whispers to me. *"Doing it* means having sex with someone."

"Oh, yeah, that's what I meant." I pretend. In fact, that's not at all what I had in mind. Only one person puts their finger down and it's Ted. Aubrey and Wes look at each other and giggle, but neither of them put their fingers down. It's Sarah's turn to go next. Her "never have I never" is that she's never gone to third base. I catch Greg giving her a wink. I'm guessing that will change soon. I'm catching on quickly that this game is intended to reveal everyone's intimate details. If that's the case, I'll be the winner of this game in a landslide, having zero experience with a boy.

"You didn't put a finger down," breathes Eddie into my ear.

"Yeah, I know," I reply, scooting myself closer to Sarah. Any closer and I'll be on her lap.

It's Julian's turn. His "never have I ever" is streaking in the river. Most of the group, except Ted, Eddie, and me, put their fingers down.

I feel Eddie's hand creep up my back and grab the side of my waist. I jump to my left and knock Sarah into Greg.

"Sorry," I mutter.

I search for the exit, running through excuses to leave in my mind. I drag his hand off my waist, hoping he gets the hint. I don't want to make a scene in front of the group. I just hope this game ends soon. A couple more people have a go at the game. I look around and notice I'm the only one with all five fingers still up.

Wes lets out a yawn. "Almost everyone has all their fingers down," he says. "Why don't we play a different game?"

"Sounds good to me!" I shout, jumping up on both feet to get away from Eddie.

"You were going to win anyway. You had all of your fingers up," says Greg.

Rather than admitting my lack of experience, I respond with an uneasy laugh.

Ted shouts over the group, "Anyone down to play Manhunt?"

"Yes! I love Manhunt!" Aubrey yells and bounces up and down.

Julian explains the object of the game. It's basically like hide and seek; one team hides while the other team finds them. Sounds easy enough.

"But first, we all take shots?" Greg suggests.

"I'm always down for shots," says Sarah.

With much difficulty, I hurry to finish my first drink before Ted pours more vodka in my cup.

"Jeronimo!" Davy shouts.

Everyone whips their heads back to swallow their drink.

"Come on, Jade—swig it!" Sarah nudges.

My eyes squint shut. I make a sour face as the vodka hits my tongue and slides down to my stomach. My mouth tastes like I chugged rubbing alcohol.

"Yuck!" I shake my head and brush my tongue with my hands.

"Okay, now that's settled, let's split into groups," says Wes. "Aubrey, Julian, Sarah, and Ted—you guys are on my team. The rest of you will be on Davy's team. Oh yeah—and we hide first!"

"Hey! Unfair!" Davy cries.

"I'd get counting if I were you!" Wes sticks his tongue out at him. Hand in hand, he and Aubrey run out of the room.

"You know those two are going to lock themselves in a room," says Davy, shaking his head.

"We'll give you five minutes to hide and that's it!" calls Greg.

Our group waits in the ballroom. Eddie pours himself his fourth drink. I watch from the old piano seat as Greg and Davy debate if Duran Duran is considered an alternative rock or pop band.

"Duran Duran is pop as hell!" Greg exclaims. "They're closer to the B-52's than Echo and the Bunnymen!"

"They are totally alternative—they're English new wave, for crying out loud!" Davy argues. "Their music is even influenced by Roxy Music and David Bowie! The founders of alternative rock!"

I start playing Beethoven's "Moonlight Sonata" on the old piano and the music drowns out their argument. The out-of-tune keys sound haunting, like it belongs in Phantom of the Opera. I bet this old house misses someone playing on the piano.

"Ladies and gentlemen, she plays piano," garbles a clearly drunken Eddie as he staggers over to the piano. He presses his weight against the bentside of the piano, and I shudder. I ignore him and continue playing.

"Where'd you learn to play?" he slurs.

"My grandfather taught me."

He nods his head. "Cool. I like a girl who plays piano."

I don't acknowledge his comment or look up. Instead, I continue to play.

"So, you have a boyfriend?"

"No."

I should have lied, because he inches closer. He bends over, as though he's about to sit on the bench with me. I stand up so quickly, the bench makes a loud screeching sound across the checkered tile floor.

"Do you think it's been five minutes?" I call over to Davy and Greg.

Davy looks at his watch. "Shit, yeah, it's been almost ten minutes. We should split up. Greg and I will take the bottom part of the mansion and you two will take the top."

Before I have a chance to suggest switching Eddie for Greg, Davy and Greg run out of the room. Eddie chugs his drink and lets out a loud belch.

"Come on, let's go," I say with a sigh.

Unlike the U-shaped staircase at Blythe House, there's only one set of stairs that goes straight up to the top floor. I walk behind Eddie to keep an eye on him. It's amazing he hasn't lost his footing with all the alcohol in his system. We finally reach the second floor and are met with a long dark hallway. It spreads to both the left and right of us.

"Why don't you take that side and I'll go this way," I say to Eddie, who has to lean against the wall for support.

"It would be more fun if we went together."

I step backwards. "It would be more *productive* if we didn't."

"Fine," he says, waving both hands in the air. I shake my head as he stumbles down his side of the hallway. Finally, a moment of peace.

The first room I search in is a pink and gold bedroom. The air is musty and damp from the hole in the ceiling. I let out a sneeze and it echoes off the four rose-patterned walls. A massive painting of a beautiful woman wearing a pale-blue Victorian dress lies shattered on the floor. I'm careful not to step on the broken glass as I move my way around the room. The mattress on the bed is missing, with only the canopy frame remaining. I imagine at one point the bed was decorated with expensive feminine linens, pillows, and lace. What a shame. There's a writing desk by the window that catches my eye. Out of curiosity, I look over the contents on the top of it and pick up a letter:

My Dearest Cornelia,

I am delighted to hear your son is returning from his trip soon. We were worried he might miss the whole summer season! My daughter will be happy to hear. Church bells will be ringing before we know it!

We look forward to seeing you both soon.

Sincerely,
Mortega

I place the letter back down on the desk and pick up another:

Willy,

Your father and I are relieved to hear the voyage to Mexico City went well, despite the turbulent waters. We support your research under the observation of Dr. Wallace. However, your father is concerned you are distracted with your archeology hobbies. It is important you take time when you're home to go over the books. We must wait until your return to discuss more on the matter.

Until then, please be safe for your Ma.

With Love,
Ma

There's a loud crash in the hallway, and I drop the letter.

"Aubrey?" I call out slowly into the dark hallway.

I shine my flashlight on the floor. Scattered in little pieces is a Majolica flower vase. Eddie is hanging on to the table where it once sat.

"What are you doing? I thought you were going to search on the other side?" I remind him, irritated.

"I did—I was—" He hiccups. "I just wanted to see you."

I scoff. "Why don't you wait in the ballroom? I'll finish looking up here."

"Why don't we go into one of these rooms together?" he asks, with his tongue half out of his mouth.

"I'd rather not," I reply with the utmost disgust.

He shuffles toward me, the ceramic pieces crunching under his feet.

"Come on, I know you feel it, too."

"Feel what?"

I start backing away. As I do, I bump into a door and raise my hands to protect myself. "Eddie, please go downstairs."

"I just want one kiss," he slurs, and I smell his boozy breath.

He moves closer, and my heart pounds with so much intensity I can hear it. As he lunges for a kiss, I desperately search for a way out. My fingers come across a doorknob. Hoping it's not locked, I turn it, and the door swings open. Without hesitation, I step back into the room and forcefully slam the door shut in Eddie's face. I hear a resounding thud as he tumbles onto the floor.

"What the hell?" he groans in pain.

I grab my flashlight and lock myself inside the room—praying the lock works. Eddie's shadow moves under the door. I step back, holding my breath.

"Let me in!" he yells, and I see the doorknob jiggle. "Fine. Fucking bitch."

His footsteps gradually fade away. It feels like an eternity before I can finally draw a deep breath. As the adrenaline wears off, all the energy drains out of my body. Holding the flashlight steady becomes a challenge. There's a dusty bed in the center of the room. It's a relief, as I desperately need a place to rest. I don't want to risk being trapped by Eddie in this pitch-black mansion, so I plan to stay here until Manhunt is over.

I cast the light from my flickering flashlight across the bedroom. Vines and tree branches have made their way through the plaster, exposing the inside to the outside elements. A myriad of sketches and depictions of both human and animal forms haphazardly adorn the walls, and I move to get a better look. Stepping closer to examine the talented artwork, I unintentionally trample over dozens of Victorian travel guides and classic novels of various genres scattered on the distressed hardwood floor. Amid the chaos, a book about precious gemstones and minerals catches my attention with its gleaming mother-of-pearl embellishments illuminated by my flashlight. I flip through the old book and find the corners of a page about the Koh-i-noor diamond folded. Someone must have read this page over and over again, as the paper is worn and delicate. There's even a paragraph circled in ink:

The Deadly Curse of the Koh-i-Noor Diamond. The word Kohinoor means "mountain of light" and the stone itself is 186 carats. A curse is associated with this diamond, affecting any man wearing it. The lives of male rulers who owned the Koh-i-Noor diamond suffered a life full of violence, murder, mutilation, torture, and treachery. A Hindu description of the diamond warns that "he who owns this diamond will own the world but will also know all its misfortunes. Only God or women can wear it with impunity."

It is silly to believe in the curse of a diamond. How can a mere stone have control over a person's destiny? With a shake of my head, I place the book on the bed and dismiss the notion.

My attention is suddenly drawn to a black and white photograph lying on the floor, where a young man's piercing gaze catches me off-guard. I pick up the photo and read the name and date typed below it: William M. Montgomery II, 1884. His handsome face exudes a sense of mystery, with neatly styled dark hair and a sophisticated look. Tracing my finger along his square jawline, I pause at his expressionless lips and powerful stare. His fiery yet light eyes leave me entranced, unsure whether to feel chilled or swept away. I can't resist the allure of the photo and tuck it into my back pocket—being a lover of vintage items.

Perhaps there are more trinkets I can find in this room to bring back. I hit the side of the flashlight, and it flickers as I stand up to explore the room. I pick up one of the old atlases and something scurries from under it.

"Ah!" I scream.

I jump backwards and my foot falls through a flimsy floorboard. The rat hurries away and hides under the bed. I feel a stabbing pain through my ankle. A broken wood plank cut the side of my overalls and my skin. Steadily, I guide my foot out from the floorboard, careful not to scrape it again. I see something shiny shimmering underneath. I grab the gleaming item and inspect it. It appears to be a green gemstone locket carved into a beetle. Its legs on either side are connected by a circular red stone. It's a stunning piece of jewelry. A metal clasp is situated where the beetle's green elytra wings meet, but my attempt to open it proves useless as it remains locked shut. With my flashlight, I beam the dying light beneath the floorboard, hoping to uncover more hidden treasures. To my surprise, it's empty. I find it odd that this strange item was concealed in such an inconspicuous spot.

"Jade?" Aubrey yells from outside the door.

I tuck the necklace into my pocket.

"Jade!" she shouts again.

"In here!" I yell back. When I open the door, I give her a big embrace. I'm so thankful to see her.

"Is everything okay? We heard a scream."

The group carries on below us on the main floor. I feel nauseous when I hear Eddie's voice.

"What's wrong?"

"Nothing... nothing. It's just..."

Her eyebrows contort into a v-shape.

"I-I saw a rat," I stammer.

She lets out a big sigh of relief. "Ew, gross." She shakes her body in disgust. "Come on, everyone's been found. It's your team's turn to hide."

I want to confide in her about Eddie's attempt at kissing me, but I don't want to stir up drama among the other party guests. I look down at my feet and see the blood tracks under my boots. It's the perfect excuse to make a quick exit.

"Actually, my foot went through a floorboard and I cut my ankle."

"Ouch!" She lifts up the end of my pant leg. There's a three inch cut that looks worse than it feels. "Do you think you need stitches?"

"I don't think it's that bad. I think I might head home and dress it though, so it doesn't get worse." I feel kind of thankful to have an excuse to leave the party—even if it's at the expense of my ankle. The thought of staying here, in close proximity to Eddie, makes me uncomfortable.

"Want me to come with you?" she asks.

"I should be okay."

We walk down the hallway and I have a difficult time walking without limping. She links her arms through mine.

"I'm walking you home."

"Are you sure? I don't want you to miss the party," I say.

"Absolutely. There's no way you're walking home like this—even if you're only next door."

"Thanks, Aubrey." I give her a heartwarming smile.

We return to the ballroom and Julian and Wes help me sit down on the floor.

"This might sting, but it will help clean the cut," Julian says as he opens the almost-empty bottle of vodka.

He pours the alcohol over the wound on my ankle, and a howl escapes my lips. He bites off the end of his plaid cuff and tightly wraps the fabric around my injured ankle, applying gentle pressure. Eddie, standing in the corner of the room with his arms crossed, watches the scene. I notice the gash on his forehead caused by the door slamming in his face. That part makes me feel good, at least.

"I'm going to walk Jade home," Aubrey tells everyone.

"I'll help her get home, too," Julian offers.

"Are you sure?" I ask him.

"Yeah. I'm getting bored," he says, and the three of us walk outside.

I don't say much as we walk to Blythe House. I was hoping neither of them would notice my silence as they chatted about their Manhunt hiding spots, but they do.

"Something's up, I can tell," Aubrey says.

"I didn't want to say anything, but I noticed you're more quiet than usual," Julian agrees. "Which says a lot."

With a sigh, I take a deep breath and admit, "I didn't want to say anything because I didn't want to cause any drama, but Eddie tried to kiss me."

Aubrey's eyes widen in shock. Julian crinkles his brows.

"Ew, gross!" Aubrey exclaims.

"Are you okay?" Julian asks, his tone worried.

"I'm fine," I reassure them. "If anything, I'm more grossed out at the thought of Eddie being my first kiss."

Aubrey shivers and makes a sour face. "I'd be grossed out, too."

All three of us laugh. The thought of Eddie being my first kiss is revolting. I want my first kiss to be with someone special, someone I have a deep connection with. Someone who makes my heart flutter like a hummingbird's wings, beating fast with excitement with just one look into their eyes. I bite my lip, wondering if that could be Brad.

CHAPTER XI

COSTUME PARTY

I stay awake until midnight, anxiously awaiting the ghost's return, but eventually, exhaustion takes over. I drift off to sleep before I can see if they appear again.

The next morning, I yawn as I thoughtlessly brush my hair while taking turns staring at the beetle locket and the black and white photo of William Montgomery on the vanity top. I grab the necklace and attempt to pry open the beetle's wings again. I'm not surprised it doesn't open, but this only adds to my curiosity of what rests inside this unusual locket. I set the necklace down and pick up the photo. I didn't think it possible for his eyes to appear any brighter, but in proper lighting, I've been proven wrong. I find myself wondering if they are gray or blue. I guess I'll never know what color those icy eyes are. I set the photo down and quickly dress myself. I want to make sure I catch Aunt Ruth at brunch, in case she slips out for the day.

I walk into the dining room to find her face buried in a newspaper. She takes a puff of her cigarette and blows the smoke into its pages.

"See here, Nigel? Didn't I always say they were going to take every inch of this town and build a development on it?"

"Another development, madam?" he asks, adding more Belgium

waffles to the serving dishes on the buffet.

"Yes!" she exclaims, her voice filled with frustration. "Those developers behind the construction of the flashy Sherwood Estates neighborhood, with their gaudy mansions, have now acquired additional land to build even *more* tacky homes! Our town is becoming overcrowded!"

"But surely having more people moving here means the town will thrive, won't it?" I impose on the conversation as I sit down at my usual seat.

She shakes her head. "You would think so, until they try and buy our house and build a shopping mall on it!"

Nigel places a dish of waffles, bacon, and eggs in front of me. I don't have much of an appetite, so I nibble on a couple pieces of bacon.

"Aunt Ruth, do you have an old costume I can borrow?"

She pops her head over the newspaper. "Whatever for, dear?"

"Well, there's a Halloween party I'd like to go to tonight—if that's all right with you? But I don't have a costume for it."

She taps her index finger on her chin and her eyes light up. "Why don't you join me today? I had plans to go shopping in the city. Perhaps, we can find you a costume there? No better place!"

I've always wanted to spend a day in New York City and see what the Big Apple is like. "That sounds amazing!" I exclaim, causing Nigel to cover his ears with his hands.

"Perfect! We'll make a day out of it. Nigel, get the car ready for us!"

Our drive to Manhattan takes approximately two hours, and we arrive around two o'clock in the afternoon. Aunt Ruth says there's never a dull day in New York City, and I can see why. The bustling urban oasis is exciting and energetic. Generally, I find city life intimidating and prefer the low-speed countryside. The one exception is that I love that you can be whoever you want to be here. In a small town like Grove Hollow, Aunt Ruth comes across too eccentric and showy. It scares people. However, in Manhattan, she fits right in. For instance, we just passed a man with a voluminous pompadour wearing skin-tight acid-wash jeans and a neon pink mesh tank top under his cropped black leather jacket—or the lady walking out of the Duane Reade drugstore wearing a matching cheetah coat with her Bichon Frise. No one batted an eye at either of them. I can understand why Aunt Ruth's heart is here.

"Are you going to be all right to walk with that ankle?" Aunt Ruth inquires as we make our way toward Fifth Avenue.

"I should be okay. It doesn't hurt as much now. I think it's healing."

"Good, because we have a lot to fit in if you want to be back in town for 7:00 tonight for that Homecoming game," she says. "Any thoughts on what you want for a costume?"

"Maybe something easy, like a witch or a black cat."

She makes a disgruntled tisk with her tongue and shakes her finger side to side. "No. No. No—none of that will do. This is the one time out of the year you can go all out and dress up however you want! Don't settle. Let me take care of it—really, I insist."

Of course the ex-actress would see this costume opportunity as an exciting project. I just hope she doesn't go *too* over the top and turn me into something ridiculous.

"I've also been thinking, we really need to get you out of those frumpy frocks. God only knows where my brother took you to go shopping," she comments as we walk up Fifth Avenue. "We absolutely must update your wardrobe. You're a Whitney, after all. It's time you dressed like one!"

I open my mouth and then close it. It's best not to argue with her. I know she won't take no for an answer. I wish my last name didn't have a prerequisite for being high maintenance. The idea of dressing up and wearing designer clothes might sound exciting to most girls, but the thought of shopping for them frightens me. It's less pressure to admire and dream about them instead. Really, I don't mind my rustic look. It's safe, comfortable, and I think I pull it off all right.

"We must hurry. Come along dear." She waves her hand up in the air for me to follow.

A man dressed in a black suit opens the door for us. The department store we enter is called Bergdorf Goodman and it's the epitome of high-end luxury. The boutique lighting highlights the expensive jewelry and colorful designer clothes on display. So far, I haven't seen one article of clothing half-folded or thrown on a rack like the boutiques back in Oregon. Everything is organized and arranged with purpose. A sophisticated-looking woman approaches us from the floor, wearing dress trousers and a sequin blazer with broad shoulder pads.

"Mrs. Mayfield, how lovely to see you again." The woman kisses Aunt Ruth on both sides of her cheek like the French do.

"Janice, dear, I'd like to introduce my niece, Jade. She and I are shopping for some new clothes. Perhaps you could steer her in the right direction? I would like for her to wear whatever the Upper East Side teenagers are wearing these days," Aunt Ruth commands the woman. "We will be buying a lot of clothes today, so treat her well." She hands Janice a one hundred dollar bill.

Janice bows. "We will take good care of her," she says.

"I'll just be over here looking for some new outfits for the winter season," Aunt Ruth says to me.

Janice's eyes narrow as they scan and assess my bulky knit-sweater, light-wash jeans, and my dirty Reebok Freestyle sneakers. At least I wore my favorite ruffled blouse underneath. It's probably the nicest thing I own.

"Is this your casual attire?" she questions, her disapproval evident as she coughs to conceal it.

"Oh, yeah." I tuck my hair behind my ears and look down at the floor. "I mean sometimes I wear boots."

"Hm..." Janice scratches her chin as she continues to examine me. She asks me to turn around slowly several times like a rotisserie chicken. "Right, okay we have some work to do."

Janice uses her pager to call for some back-up. We go up to the fourth floor where we meet another lady and a man.

"Quinn and Rita, get the young lady's measurements. I'd like to curate a selection for Mrs. Mayfield's niece with some basics as well as some cosmo-looks. Let's start with casual day-wear and then move to evening. Maybe a couple power suits. Thierry Mugler, Azzedine Alaia, and Chanel to start, and then move into Armani."

"What about contemporary patterns?" Rita asks Janice who looks back at me.

"Relaxed and nothing busy, wouldn't you say?" Quinn suggests.

Janice nods. It was like the three of them were speaking a different language in front of me. Janice claps her hands and Rita starts my measurements. Quinn begins sourcing an assortment of outfits from the

Chanel section and moves into Vivienne Westwood, Gianni Versace, and eventually to Giorgio Armani. I feel out of place as I stand in the center of the floor watching the two professional stylists at work.

"Would you care for a drink while you wait?" Janice asks.

"Yes, please."

I'd do anything to preoccupy myself.

"Please, have a seat. I'll send someone up shortly."

Moments later, a man holding a gold tray offers a glass of champagne. The champagne is light and bubbly with a strawberry aroma. I've never known an alcoholic drink to taste so delicious. I sit on the leather settee near the fitting rooms and wait until I'm told what to do. I watch as Quinn hangs on the dressing room rack the first set of clothes: colorful blazers in various patterns and materials, button downs with embellished collars and textures, pants and knee-length skirts in all different designs, and blouses in both whimsical and daring styles.

"Rita, can you pull some shoes and accessories from floors two and five?" Quinn says in his handheld transceiver.

There's static and Rita's voice comes through on the other end. "What size?"

Quinn looks down at my feet, presses a button, and talks through the speaker again. "Size seven."

Wow, he's good.

The first "casual" outfit Quinn assembles is a white-lace blouse with a sapphire cameo brooch connecting the high-top collar, which I love. He pairs it with dark-blue suede slacks and a plaid blazer. Rita sets a pair of red heels on the floor. I slide my feet through and they fit comfortably.

"Let's have you step over to the mirror," he directs.

Carefully, not to hurt myself with an already injured ankle while wearing heels, I walk to the runway mirror to look at my reflection. I am shocked by the person looking back at me. I feel bold, refined, and confident, almost as if the clothes have reawakened a dormant aspect of my personality.

I had reservations about updating my style, but every outfit I've tried on has exceeded all my expectations. It's as though Quinn and Rita could read not only my personality, but they knew how every inch of fabric would hold on to my thin frame before I tried it on. It feels unreal to be wearing anything outside of cotton and denim.

"Goodness, you could be a model on the cover of VOGUE," Aunt Ruth comments, as she sits down on the settee.

"Just wait until you see what I've picked out for her evening wear," Quinn says, proudly.

The first evening dress he selects from the rack is a stunning black and gold beaded gown. Curious, I slip into it. To my surprise, it has a deep plunging neckline and exposed back extending down to my waist. I've never felt so attractive. I step out of the dressing room to showcase the outfit. The dress shimmers under the lights with every step, leaving everyone around me in awe.

"This is the most beautiful dress I've ever worn in my life." I beam.

Quinn clarifies, "This piece belongs to the collection of Maxime Silverstone, an up-and-coming fashion designer making waves in the industry. It draws inspiration from the 1920s Egyptian Revival Robe de Style dresses."

Aunt Ruth's eyes get large, and she grins. "This would be perfect for tonight's costume party! We can transform you into Cleopatra! I still have the wig and all the necessary props from when I portrayed her in a play!"

"You really think this could work?"

"Absolutely! Darling, you're going to turn every head in a room wearing that dress."

Aunt Ruth delights in the mini-fashion show by Rita and Quinn. Afterward, we meet them at the register with the many items, and Aunt Ruth generously pays for them.

"Here, keep this." She hands me a credit card from her wallet. "You never know when it might come in handy during emergencies."

"Thank you, Aunt Ruth," I reply, almost speechless. I've never had a credit card before, so I carefully put it away in my bag.

When we return to the car, I check my watch and notice it's after 5:00 p.m. Concerned about being late for the Homecoming game, I ask Aunt Ruth how long it will take to get back to Grove Hollow.

"If we leave now, we should be able to get you back in time for the Homecoming game at seven," she reassures me. I hope she's right.

Unfortunately, we encounter heavy traffic on the George Washington

Bridge. I can sense Aunt Ruth's irritation at my anxiousness as she smokes her third cigarette. She glances at me as my legs bounce up and down in the front seat. Meanwhile, I keep checking the clock on the dashboard, worried that we won't make it to the Homecoming game on time.

"Relax, dear, you're shaking the whole car," she snaps at me.

"I'm sorry, Aunt Ruth. I'm just nervous about missing the game."

"Well, there's not much we can do now," Aunt Ruth says, honking the horn at the cars in front of us, but it's useless. The line of vehicles has barely moved in twenty minutes.

It takes over an hour, but we finally exit the city. Aunt Ruth's Rolls-Royce Silver Spirit speeds down the interstate, causing my stomach to churn with motion sickness as the car swerves on the back roads.

As we approach Grove Hollow, I notice people on Main Street wearing red and black with painted G's and H's on their cheeks. When a group of cheerleaders and rugby players cross the street, I realize I've missed the Homecoming game. Damn.

"I'm sorry about the game, dear," says Aunt Ruth as we pull up to the house.

Nigel opens the driver's side door for her. Toby comes around my side of the car to greet me.

"It's okay," I say in my most convincing happy voice. I told Brad yesterday I'd cheer him on, and now I missed the game entirely. I feel like such an asshole. At least there's still the party this evening to make up for it.

Aunt Ruth orders Nigel to unload today's purchases and bring them to my room. There must be at least twenty shopping bags and hat boxes stuffed inside the trunk. We make our way to the dining room and wait to be served.

After dinner, I retreat to the library. I hear a clock somewhere in the room chime nine times. To pass the time before I have to start getting ready, I browse the collection of books on the shelves.

"For your nerves," says Aunt Ruth. She enters the room with a cocktail and hands it to me. For once, I take her up on her offer. "What time is your costume soirée?"

"My friends are picking me up at ten o'clock."

She slams the whiskey decanter on her drink cart.

"Goodness! Dear, why didn't you say something? We have less than an hour to prepare you! I'll bring up the makeup and cocktails—Pip-pip!"

I find the black and gold beaded dress from its bag and go to step into it. Aunt Ruth enters my room holding one of her frilly ostrich feather robes. Nigel is behind with his eyes closed as a respect for my privacy. He is balancing in his arms Aunt Ruth's makeup caboodle, a wig, and a glass of brandy. He leaves the room without a peek.

"No, dear, you can't get ready in your dress! Here, put this on while we get you ready," she says with a cigarette between her lips. I slide my arms and half-naked body into her silk feathered evening robe; I appreciate it not being see-through.

"Oh, you don't have to be so modest around me. Nothing I haven't seen before." She half laughs and half coughs. "Sit in your vanity chair while I unpack the makeup. We'll have to tuck your hair into my wig from when I played Cleopatra," she says, tucking my hair under the short, black wig. I look unrecognizable already.

"Your face is pretty, of course, but let's make it more dramatic and accentuate your eyes!"

She uses a black eye pencil to fill in my brows. Next she contours my green eyes to create a cat-eye look, gradually blending out the edges to create a smoky effect. She applies a subtle hint of teal eyeshadow around my eyelids to further enhance my eyes.

"You never want to overdo it with rouge. Too much and you'll look like a clown. Always apply a light coat on either side of your cheeks," she coaches.

I open my mouth just enough, so she can administer the fire-engine red lipstick. Lastly, I climb into my new black dress and step back to take a look at myself in the mirror.

"You could give Elizabeth Taylor a run for her money." Aunt Ruth proudly puffs a cloud of smoke into the air while admiring her work. "You need a necklace for that bare neck. Let me see what they put in your bags at the shop."

"Oh! I have a necklace that will go perfect with this outfit."

I grab the beetle locket from the vanity top. Carefully, I clasp the delicate necklace around my neck.

"What a fabulous and peculiar locket," Aunt Ruth says, wide-eyed. "It's perfect."

I hurry downstairs, careful of my ankle. A black Mercedes-Benz pulls into Blythe House's circular driveway. I peek through the window by the front door and see Aubrey, Wes, Davy, and Julian inside the luxury car. Davy's mouth drops as he gets out of the car. My eyebrow moves upwards and I hold back a laugh.

"Are you okay?" I hobble toward him.

He shakes his head. "Yeah, sorry. You look different." He grabs my arm and helps me to the car.

He holds the door open for me and I sit between him and Julian in the back. Aubrey turns around in the passenger's seat with her mouth hanging open. In fact, everyone's mouth is hanging open.

"Jade, you look like a movie star! You're Cleopatra, right?" Aubrey asks.

"Oh good, I'm glad you can tell. I wasn't sure if it was obvious."

"I'm loving the short hair. Is it real?" Julian asks while running his fingers through the wig.

I titter. "No, it's a wig."

"What do you think about our costumes?" Aubrey asks, fluffing her teased white hair.

The four wear tight studded leather pants, distressed shirts and jackets, and makeup on and under their eyes. Everyone, except Aubrey, is wearing black hairband mullet wigs.

"Um… a heavy metal band?"

"Getting warmer," Wes says behind the wheel.

"Uh…" I blank on an answer. "Is it a specific band?"

"We're Mötley Crüe!" Aubrey impatiently answers.

"Oh, I see it now."

Davy pulls out a bottle of tequila from a paper bag and opens it. He takes a swig.

"Woo!" he says, shaking his head while wiping the alcohol from his chin. Then he offers the bottle to me. "Jade?"

Feeling uncertain, I hesitate to grab the alcohol. I consider the legality of drinking in the car and the necessity for one of us to stay sober to drive us home.

Aubrey notices my apprehension and reassures me, "Don't worry, Wes is our designated driver tonight."

With a sense of relief, I reach for the bottle Davy is offering. I take a swig and plug my nose. I wish we were drinking something tastier, like strawberry champagne, instead. I cringe as the taste of the alcohol mildly burns my throat on the way down.

I pass the bottle along to Julian, who takes his turn. "Next time remind me to bring limes and salt." He winces as he takes a swig.

"Do you think we'll get caught going into this party?" Davy asks.

"That's what the masks are for," Wes says behind the wheel. "Aubrey, babe, mind passing them out? We're pulling up soon."

I didn't realize how close The Willows was. The car ride felt like five minutes and we never left Fairview Avenue. Wes parks the car close to the front gate. The massive Italian Renaissance mansion has several willow trees shading the front. I'm guessing that's where it got its name from. Every window in the three-story house is lit, and shadows dance behind the curtains.

"Should we do one more shot?" voices Aubrey.

"Wouldn't hurt," I reply, matching her nervousness.

I stretched out my hand to take the bottle of tequila from her. Her eyebrows shoot up as I swallow a mouthful.

"Give me some!" Julian says with a sour face. "Okay, one more, just in case."

"I guess this is it. We're really doing this," says Wes.

The four of them tie back their Zorro masks.

"Well, at least no one will recognize us," Davy states.

I'm crossing my fingers he's right. The last thing I would want is to cause a scene if my friends get caught attending the party alongside me.

I cling onto my necklace, weaving the beetle locket in and out of my fingers. I've never been to a party like this, like the crazy parties you see in movies. My fidgeting feels more extreme the closer we approach the door. I hold my breath as we step inside the mansion. The inside is just as ornate and magnificent as the outside. Unlike Blythe House, the renaissance style interior has new postmodern decor and furnishings. The owners spared no expense, either.

I didn't think there would be so many people at the party. Maybe that's a good thing—we'll draw less attention to ourselves. The costumes range from generic Halloween themes like vampires, monsters, and even a guy in a chicken suit, to sexy cowgirls, police officers, and Playboy bunnies. It seems as though no one cares what you are dressed in as long as you're drinking and dancing.

"You guys go ahead. Davy and I will find us something to drink," Wes says.

I follow Aubrey and Julian to the ballroom. The room is surrounded by strobe lights flashing against the gold ceiling and walls, transforming the room into a nightclub. The DJ is dressed in a Frankenstein costume and is blasting, "Hungry Like the Wolf," by Duran Duran. Two drunk girls, dressed in cheetah-print lingerie and cat-ear headbands, swing from the massive chandelier hanging from the ceiling. Both of them are taking turns drinking out of a champagne bottle. A ball of orange crepe streamers gets tossed from across the room. I duck down, and it hits the Michael Myers mask on the naked male statue.

"What a place!" Julian shouts in my ears.

"What? I can't hear you over the madness!" Aubrey shouts in response to him.

"I said what a place!"

A girl dancing next to us knocks me to the floor, and Julian and Aubrey help me up.

"Let's move somewhere else! It's too crowded by the door!" Aubrey yells.

We make our way over to the opposite side of the room where it's less packed.

"Here works!" Aubrey tells us as we find a spot in front of the DJ booth.

The turntable booth is pumping out music at an ear-splitting volume, which explains why there's a vast open space by the booth. Julian takes my hand and twirls me around in a circle, and I feel myself loosen up.

Davy and Wes arrive, each holding cups filled with beer. As someone new to the beer world, I find the taste pleasantly bitter and prefer it over stronger spirits due to its smoother quality and enjoyable carbonation. Meanwhile, Julian's impressive moonwalk across the dance floor captures the crowd's attention, resulting in cheers and applause. In no time, a circle forms around us. Davy and Wes enthusiastically join in, showcasing their dance moves inspired by the Twist Dance from the Blues Brothers. The spectators cheer even louder, totally entertained by the performance. Once they return to the circle, a girl dressed as a vampire swoops in, clasping Davy tightly. I watch in shock as they begin passionately kissing.

"Does he know her?" I yell to Julian. He shrugs his shoulders completely unfazed.

Aubrey tugs at my arm, urging me to join her in the heart of the dance floor. My nerves take flight, but her contagious energy instantly infects me, easing my tension. While attempting to mimic her effortless dance steps, I become aware of my lack of coordination, but I surrender entirely to the music, releasing all of my fears.

The music pulses through the room. I suddenly become aware that Aubrey has returned to the sidelines joining the rest of the group. The spotlight seems to have found me, and I notice I'm dancing alone, center stage in front of the entire crowd. I'm a little embarrassed, but my friends cheer me on. I bask in the attention with all eyes on me.

I come to a stop as the song ends. A sudden sense of awareness drives through me, causing the hairs on my neck to stand on end. It's as if my body, in its entirety, is rousing itself to the presence of something unknown. Compelled by an invisible force, my body turns, and my narrowed eyes center on a guy dressed in an enchanting, old-fashioned Victorian costume. He casually leans against the dim-lit wall at the room's far end, studying me. Time stands still as our eyes meet. I feel an extreme thrill of familiarity, reminiscent of déjà vu as if I am experiencing a past moment all over again. I don't know how to make sense of this strange sensation.

I rejoin Aubrey and tug at her shirt. "Who's that guy over there, Aubrey?"

She stands up on her tiptoes and looks around the room.

"What guy?"

"The guy—over there by the back wall in the old-fashioned costume," I say.

"Who?"

"Him—don't you see the guy?" I attempt to point without being obvious.

"Meh, if there's a guy staring at you it's probably because you look so good tonight! Consider it a compliment!" she yells over the music. Wes grabs her hand and pulls her away from me to dance.

Maybe she's right. I should be flattered by the attention. Yet, the intensity of his gaze electrifies me, and its energy courses through my heart, charging my chest with power. I feel a connection between us, and I'm mysteriously drawn to him, like a moth to a flame. I suspect he's aware of my staring because he tilts his head in speculation. I shift away from the other dancers to get a better glimpse of him. I watch him take a deep breath and shake his head dismissively before departing to the other end of the room.

"I'll be back," I tell my friends, but they're too engrossed in the music and dancing to notice.

I look for the guy in the Victorian costume in the foyer. The crowd in the hallway is packed, but through a small opening of people, I see him heading up the stairs. Before I can put my foot on the first step, a hand grabs mine from behind.

"Come with me."

CHAPTER XII

THE LOST SOUL

The person pulls me so quickly into a dark-lit room that I stumble into their chest when we abruptly stop. They gently guide me away with both hands. I look up, and my heart races when I realize it's Brad.

"Are you okay?" he asks, laughing softly.

"Yeah, I think so," I reply. Looking around, I notice we're not alone; a group of party-goers sits by a fire, playing a card game.

"Sorry about that, I didn't want anyone to see—" He stops himself. "I mean, I wanted to catch you before I lost you."

"Lost me?" I raise one eyebrow.

"Yeah, I was making my way into the ballroom and saw you were heading for the stairs."

This unexpected meeting with Brad causes the guy dressed in a Victorian outfit to slip my mind entirely. At a relaxed speed, Brad's hands let go of my arms. I step back, giving us more space in between.

"To tell you the truth, I almost didn't recognize you at all."

"Really?" I go to tuck my hair behind my ear, but forget it's covered by a wig.

"Yeah, you look different. Your hair is shorter."

"It's a wig." I blush.

He laughs. "I figured. Let me guess"—he puts a finger to his chin—"you're some kind of Egyptian queen?"

"Cleopatra, actually."

I tilt my head to the side to get a good look at his costume. His half-wet hair is slicked back, and he is wearing a black tailored suit. My eyes are drawn to his half-opened, button-down shirt that exposes a hint of his chest. I'm finding it difficult to hold back a grin.

"I'm stumped. Who are you supposed to be?"

"I'm James Bond. Can't you tell?" He takes out a fake plastic gun from his back pocket. His lips purse, and he blows the top of the barrel.

I giggle. "Ah, I see it now."

He leans against a bookcase that's covered in fake spiderwebs, and I do the same.

"So, I thought you didn't have a ride?" he asks.

"I found one."

"Oh, from who?"

"Oh, no one special." I tuck my fingers behind my back.

"Was it a guy?" he asks with a strange, curious tone.

"No, no… it was my… aunt who dropped me off," I fib, not wanting to blow my friends' cover.

"Oh yeah, I heard something about that. You live with the… um…" He searches for a word.

"The crazy witch?" I flash a knowing grin at him because he looks so ashamed. "She might be a little crazy, but she's pretty cool. Definitely not a witch."

A guy with a tray of drinks walks by us and Brad grabs one for me.

"That's a relief." He laughs into his cup. "So, you must live on Fairview Avenue, too?"

"Yeah. The house has been in my family for years, I guess. I never knew."

"You know, a lot of families with old money own these homes on this road. I live just a couple streets over in Sherwood Estates. It's the neighborhood with the large homes that were built a couple years ago."

I remember at brunch today, Aunt Ruth commented about Sherwood Estates, describing the houses as tasteless and gaudy. I fake ignorance, shaking my head instead. "I'm sorry, I'm not too familiar with the area."

"Oh, that's right. You've only been here like—what, a couple of weeks?"

"Just a week," I correct him. "It feels like it's been a year, to be honest."

"Yeah, I bet." He lifts the corner of his mouth and nods.

Victory echoes from the card table. A player boasts about winning again, prompting Brad and me to turn our heads in their direction. Brad looks back at me, and I can tell he's searching for something to say. It feels different talking to him outside of school for some reason. I wonder if he also feels the awkwardness between us. I sip my drink, expecting him to break the silence, but he remains quiet and sips his drink, too.

"How was the game? Did you win?" I finally ask.

"Oh," he says, his face falling. "You didn't go?"

"I wanted to." Damnit, I feel like an asshole. "But my aunt and I got stuck in traffic in the city."

"The city? You mean New York City?" He looks surprised. "What were you doing there?"

"My aunt wanted to take me shopping. She said I needed a more sophisticated wardrobe." I use my two fingers to make quotation marks in the air.

"Really? I'm sure you look great in everything." I catch the quick sheepish smile before he hides it behind his cup.

I feel myself blushing more. "Thanks."

When his cup lowers, his grin looks twisted like he's hiding something.

"What?"

"Nothing." He pauses. "It's just that you look really hot tonight."

"You must have had too much to drink," I tease, knowing someone as handsome as Brad couldn't find someone as undesirable as me attractive.

"No, I mean it. You always look pretty," he says.

I'm left speechless as his words confirm the unimaginable. I see his gaze soften, filled with an amorous quality. My hands quiver as I steady my drink.

"I think you always look pretty, too—I mean hot, not pretty."

Brad laughs. "Really? You think I'm hot?"

I give him a blank stare. "Doesn't everyone?"

His mouth droops down a couple degrees. He lowers his head and folds his arms.

"Maybe... but I want to know if *you* think I am."

It's like someone lit a match and set my face on fire. My cheeks are burning up and I wonder how red I look.

"Yeah." I gather up all my strength and courage to look him in the eyes. "I—I do."

I've never had a guy look at me the way he's looking at me right now. Not like this. Not in this dreamy way where it's weakening my knees. I struggle to catch my breath.

"I'm glad you decided to come out tonight," he says in a hushed voice as he moves closer.

"Me, too."

A spectrum of emotions shoots through my body as he leans in with his lips—only inches from mine. I've always wondered what my first kiss would be like. I imagine it would feel like seeing a new color for the first time, something you can't quite comprehend or put into words. And now I'm about to find out. The background noises of the card players fade away into silence. A moment elapses where nothing happens. Something feels off. I open my eyes and find Brad wearing a conscience-stricken look of regret and the players at their table looking at us.

"I should go check on my friends and make sure they're not getting super wasted."

"Oh." With a heavy sigh, I slump, my heart sinking in my chest. The weight of guilt settles on me, knowing I want Brad's kiss more than anything despite his committed relationship. Yet, he surprises me with an unexpected peck on my lips. In an instant, moral restraints crumble, boundaries blur, and I embrace the liberation as my spirits soar freely.

I stand in awe, rubbing my lips as he leaves. I feel like I am in a dream, floating through a mist of clouds as I walk out of the room. Except the cloud is made of marijuana smoke. It makes me cough uncontrollably.

"Want to partake?" A guy with red glazed eyes offers me his joint and almost falls on me.

"No, thanks."

As I walk backward away from them, my hurt ankle gives out and I fall into the person behind me.

"What is your problem? You almost made me spill my spritzer, asshole!"

I could recognize that voice blindfolded. I feel sick to my stomach as Allison, Samantha, and Danielle all turn to face me in their matching angel-winged costumes.

"Oh, God. It's you," Danielle hisses in her raspy voice.

"Funny, I don't remember anyone letting losers into the party," Allison says in a testy voice. "Unless you were invited, which I highly doubt, you're not allowed here."

"Prepare to get kicked out, bitch," Samantha states, rubbing her hands together.

Aubrey's words about standing up for myself echo in my mind. I say in the most bold tone I can muster, "I *was* invited."

Allison lets out a laugh that sounds similar to a cackle. She moves closer to my face and her eyes narrow. "Who the hell invited *you?*"

I stand up straight and look her right in the eye.

"Brad did."

Both Danielle and Samantha's faces go white and their jaws drop. I know I shouldn't have said it, but it felt *so* good.

"Liar."

"Feel free to ask him yourself, Allison." I am feeling empowered for standing up for myself.

"Should I call security?" Samantha asks.

"No, I think we can handle this ourselves."

Allison's fingers crinkle the sides of her plastic cup as she tilts it. Before I have a chance to process what is happening, her red spritzer is trickling down the front of my dress. She shakes the empty cup to make sure every last drop has poured on me. Tears form in the corners of my eyes as the cold drink slides down between my breasts to my stomach. The bottom of the dress feels heavy as the fringe soaks up the liquid.

"Looks like we're even now. Karma's a bitch, ain't it?" she says with a wide smirk.

"Aw, is the little baby gonna cry now?" Samantha pretends to pout.

I feel a large ball in my throat as I desperately hold back the flood gates. I want to slap her face and call her all sorts of horrible things, but the only thing I can manage to do is run away. I hear the three of them laughing all the way to the bathroom. The line is long, and I'm not confident I can hold back the tears while I wait. Paying no attention to the couple making out on the steps, I try for a bathroom upstairs. Every door is locked except the one at the very end of the hall.

I peek my head inside the pitch black room. "Hello?"

I close myself inside. My head collides with the door, and I slump to the floor, hugging my knees against the rush of emotions. The pressure behind my eyes lessens, and tears course down my cheeks, smudging Aunt Ruth's perfect eye makeup. All I can think about is going back home, not to Blythe House, but back *home.* I continue to weep into my knees, wiping away as much of the mascara as possible with the back of my hand. I fume over how the night unfolded. If I hadn't taken Aubrey's advice to stand up for myself, which had the opposite effect, I wouldn't be crying up here. In exasperation, I hurl the wig across the room, and my hair cascades down my back. I'm trapped in a vicious cycle of unpleasant encounters with Allison. It's as though fate is playing a cruel joke on me.

A shiver runs down my arms as I notice the slightly open balcony door. Maybe getting some fresh air could help me reduce my stress levels and provide a physical reset.

The terrace is serene and quiet, much like the balcony outside my bedroom, albeit smaller and without furniture. As I hold the beetle locket between my fingers, I allow myself to cry. Watching the river's gentle ripples helps soothe me, and my breathing steadies. I notice a layer of stratus clouds approaching the waxing crescent moon. It won't be long before the bright crescent shape is concealed.

I hear the sound of feet sweep along the stone balcony floor. I turn my head and see there's someone leaning against the railing a few feet away from me. It's so dark in that corner I hadn't noticed him. I let out a gasp and jump to the side.

"Sorry, I didn't realize anyone was out here," I manage to say, hastily brushing away my tears. Although I can't make out the person's facial features, the outline of his silhouette reveals that he's watching me. Sniffling, I use my hands to hide my tear-stained cheeks, feeling embarrassed for intruding on his solitude with my emotional outburst. The person remains motionless, offering no words in response.

"Are you a student at the Academy?" I ask, silently hoping he isn't, as the idea of someone from my school witnessing my tears would elevate my embarrassment.

He adjusts his stance, leaning against the railing with his elbows.

"I used to be," he answers with a low, husky tone tinged with confusion and surprise. "But that was a long time ago..."

His refined foreign accent catches my ear as I listen to him speak. It sounds like it might be from some part of England. It occurs to me he likely isn't from Grove Hollow. Either way, this realization brings a sense of relief, as it eliminates the possibility of him being familiar with the town.

"Are you from the city?" I ask with a sniffle.

He laughs softly and says, "No."

"Oh." I nervously drum my fingers on the railing.

As a moment passes, he asks, "Are you a student at the Academy?"

"Yeah, I just moved here a week ago."

"Really?" he asks with interest. "How come you moved here?"

"It's a long story," I reply. The last thing I want to think about right now while my emotions are on a roller coaster is the *why* part. "What brings you to the party then if you're not from the city or the Academy?"

He pauses.

"It's a long story," he echoes.

I sigh, accompanied by a faint chuckle. It seems neither of us feels like sharing much information.

"What made you come out here to cry?" he asks instead.

Now I pause to answer.

"Pardon me. That was impolite of me to pry. You'll have to excuse my conversational skills. They are somewhat out of practice."

"It's fine." I sniffle, rubbing away the last bit of mascara on my face. "Someone poured their drink on me."

"Whatever for?"

"If I started from the beginning, we'd be here all night."

"I've got time," he says in a way that gives me chills.

As I open my mouth to begin my story, the blanket of clouds rolls away. The faint shine of the moon reveals the guy is wearing a Victorian-style costume. My heart leaps at the sight of him, and my mood lifts with the excitement.

"Wait a second, I recognize you from the ballroom. You were watching me from the back wall," I say as I see a faint grin spread across his face.

"I didn't think you could see me," he replies.

Rubbing the back of my neck, I try to extinguish any signs of flattery. "I happened to notice," I say. "What's your name?"

He heaves a deep breath and raises his shoulders. "I am no one," he admits with traces of emptiness. "I am but a lonely soul, barely existing."

Raising an eyebrow at his gloomy response, I cannot help but interject with playful banter to lift the somber mood. "Well, Mr. No One, I'm certain you're someone."

He leans his head to the side. "Why don't you reveal your name first?"

"All right, easy enough. It's Jade," I reply with a lighthearted grin. "See? It's not too complicated at all. Now it's your turn."

The young man hesitates.

"You have a name, don't you?" I tease again, but my tone is more uncertain as I wonder why he's so guarded about telling me who he is. "If you don't tell me, I'll just have to go back inside." When his reply is silent, I turn back around to go inside the bedroom.

"Wait!" his shouting startles me and I rotate myself to face him.

"Yes?"

"Where did you get that necklace?"

"This?" I say, grabbing the beetle locket in my hand. "I found it."

"How? Where did you come across it?" he asks, his tone shifting toward a seriousness that makes me nervous.

"I found the locket in an abandoned mansion."

"An abandoned mansion?" he repeats. "Which one?"

"Montgomery Manor."

"That's not possible," he mutters.

"That's where I found it. Under a floorboard in a bedroom."

He drops his head and clutches the side of his hair, like he's attempting to grasp the meaning of my words. When he looks back at me, he likely notices my confused, wide eyes as I try to understand his unexpected behavior.

"My apologies," he says, straightening up, "but could you please consider giving me the locket? It belongs to me, and I've been looking for it for years."

I pause, contemplating what I should do. I feel uneasy after talking to this person, possibly due to his unwillingness to reveal his name and his excessive interest in the locket. I'm considering asking him how he came to know about the necklace, given that I discovered it hidden under a dusty old floorboard in an abandoned house. But there's something more about him that confuses me.

"Please?" he pleads with urgency.

I feel the weight of the locket in my fingers. If it holds such significance for him, I suppose I could just hand it over and be on my way.

"Sure." I unclasp the necklace and offer it to him.

He slowly walks toward me, almost gliding. Emerging from the shadows and into the light from the bedroom window, the silhouette of his profile is etched out. My eyes grow large as I look into his eyes, a clear-blue shade that rivals any diamond's brilliance. I feel the blood drain from my face as I realize I'm staring at the young man in the black and white photo, the one I found on the bedroom floor at Montgomery Manor.

I let out a low shriek, covering my mouth with trembling hands. I shake my head, attempting to comprehend what my eyes are witnessing.

"N-n-no, it can't be..." I step back in fear. Clutching the locket tightly in my hand, I turn to leave, but he blocks my path again. I let out a cry of alarm.

"I'm sorry, but I cannot allow you to leave until you hand me the necklace," he says firmly.

Shaking in terror, I beg, "Please, don't hurt me."

His tone and posture soften as he replies, "I promise I won't hurt you."

Curiosity overtakes my fear. I need to know if he is who I think he is. "What's your name?" I whisper.

He hesitates before responding. "If I tell you, will you give me the locket?"

I nod. He steps closer, causing me to back away until I hit the balcony railing. I tremble uncontrollably as he looks at me with his piercing eyes.

"My name is Will," he says. He pauses before disclosing the rest of his name. I can feel my heart pounding as he's about to confirm what I already know. "William Montgomery."

My gut feels like a ton of bricks has been hurled into it. It can't be true. The man standing before me is William Montgomery, the one who was murdered with his entire family years ago. None of this makes sense. The adrenaline streaming through my body makes me feel dizzy. I place my hand on my forehead, steadying myself against the balcony railing.

"Perhaps you should sit down," he suggests.

Slowly, I lower myself to the ground. He kneels beside me.

"None of this is real," I murmur. "How can this be happening? You're supposed to be dead. It's been years since you and your family were killed."

"About a century, to be precise," he responds with a nonchalant shrug.

As I unclench my fist and examine the beetle locket, my mind is flooded with questions. I found the necklace in *his* house.

"Why is this necklace so important to you?" I ask.

A heavy sigh escapes him. I observe his jaw tightening as he looks up at the sky above.

"It's the only thing I can recall before everything faded into darkness," he responds in a gentle, subdued tone.

"Darkness?" I repeat, wrinkling my brow.

Our eyes meet. His are full of grief, remorse, and frustration. It dawns on me.

"Death." I gasp, covering my mouth as I shiver at the very thought. "So, you really are... *dead?"*

"Yes." He has a distant look in his eyes. "This green beetle, I remember it so vividly. I can still feel it resting in the palm of my hand. When I opened the locket, everything around me vanished. I thought, maybe if I could find it, I could escape this... this purgatory."

"I don't understand. If you're dead, how is it possible that I'm talking to you right now?"

"I'm not dead enough to *not* exist or alive enough *to* exist."

"A *ghost."*

"That's one way of wording it," he says, staring at the cold balcony floor.

"Is this normal? You... talking to people?"

He runs his fingers through his dark hair and drags them down over his face. "No, it's not. Up until now no one's been able to see me—apart from you tonight."

I tuck my hair behind my ear. "Why is that?"

He looks at me with a sad expression, shrugging his shoulders. "I'm unsure," he says. I feel sorry for him.

I look down at the locket in my palm. The moon's glow reflects off the beetle, and it shimmers between my fingers.

"Here," I say, picking up the chain and dangling the necklace in the air. "The beetle's wings are locked, by the way. I've tried prying the wings open, but it must be sealed shut."

As I hand over the necklace, he extends his hand to take it from me. We both gasp as it passes through his palm like his hand is made of mist. The locket falls to the floor with a clink. We both stare at it in disbelief. He tries to grab it, but it slips through his fingers each time.

"I cannot believe it!" he cries, trembling and in shock. "I've searched tirelessly for years, and when I finally discover the beetle locket, I find myself incapable of carrying it! My hopes of crossing over are gone." Frustration washes over his face, and he covers his head with his hands.

"Maybe I can help you?"

He lifts his head up. His eyes have now changed with pain and bitterness. "How?"

"Well, I don't know exactly," I say and his arms fall to his side. "But, we'll figure it out—"

"Jade? Are you in here?" I hear Aubrey's voice call from inside the bedroom.

"I'm out here!" I yell back to her.

"What are you doing out there? We've been looking for you everywhere!" she yells. "Let's motor! They found out about us, and we are getting kicked out!"

"Can you meet me tomorrow afternoon at one o'clock at Blythe House?" I whisper to him as I hurry to clasp the locket around my neck.

"Blythe House?" His face perplexed as we stand up together. "You're a Whitney?"

"Yes, that's my last name," I say.

"I knew I've seen you before." His mouth curves into a gentle smile, and his expression solidifies with confirmation. I arch an eyebrow. "I can meet you there tomorrow," he says.

"Jade!" Aubrey's voice gets louder as she approaches the balcony.

"Coming!" I turn to him quickly one last time. "My bedroom is last window on the left side of the back of the house—"

"I know which room it is," he admits.

Before I can ask him how he knows, Aubrey calls my name again.

"Goodbye, Jade," he says.

"See you tomorrow, William—"

"Will."

I turn around. "What?"

"Just Will."

A small smile tugs at the corner of my mouth. "Goodbye, Will," I whisper, a farewell meant only for him to hear.

Aubrey grabs my hand and guides me back into the bedroom, moving with such urgency that I fear my ankle might falter. We hurry down the stairs, my fingers tightly gripping the banister while leftover dizziness persists. Did I just have a conversation with a ghost? The surreal encounter leaves me questioning the boundaries of reality.

"We gotta hurry before someone starts a fight!" Aubrey pants.

"How did anyone find out?"

"The girl Davy was making out with was one of the rugby player's sisters. He recognized Davy even with the mask on!" Aubrey says, jumping over the last three steps. "We were wondering where you went. You never came back to the dance party. Were you up there the whole time—and why is your makeup a mess?"

I cough through the cigarette smog. "I—"

"Jade!" I hear Brad's voice from behind and Aubrey and I turn around. "Are you leaving?"

"Our friends are getting kicked out," I say.

Aubrey squeezes my hand and tugs at it.

Brad seems to have noticed that my makeup is a mess, as his face drops with concern. "Let me drive you home."

"No thanks, bro—she's coming with me," hisses Aubrey. I notice her swift defensive reaction, making me wonder why she's so eager to claim my company.

"I think she can decide for herself," he says flatly.

I let go of her hand. "It's okay, Aubrey."

Her eyebrows come down and together. "If that's what you want to do." She looks Brad dead in the face and says, "If I so much as hear you did anything to hurt her, I will cut you into a million pieces—okay, bro?"

Brad's squints. "You have nothing to worry about—bro."

"I'll be fine, Aubrey." I give her a sincere smile.

She pats my shoulders. "Call me tomorrow?"

"Sure thing."

Aubrey races out of the house to search for the guys outside. I feel this immense guilt for not choosing to go home with her. After all, she is my friend, and I showed up at the party with her. But the guilt gets pushed aside, and the butterflies set in as Brad takes off his blazer and wraps it over my shoulders. I follow him outside to his red Ferrari. He opens the front door of the passenger side for me and shuts it once I'm seated. My nose is hit by the scent of his cologne mixed with the leather. I pinch my arm to make sure this isn't a dream. When he opens the driver's door and enters, my body goes numb from the jitters.

"Are you sure you don't want to stay?" I ask.

"Nah," he says with a side-smile and turns the car on. "When you've been to one party at The Willows, you've been to them all."

He puts his hand on my headrest and rotates his head to look through the back windshield. I wish there was a trick to staying calm. I feel my hands shaking from the excitement of spending time alone with Brad—even if it is only a couple-minute drive away. I grasp my fingers around the beetle locket, taking one last look at the mansion through the side mirror before we pull out of the driveway. The experience of tonight is like a surrealist painting brought to life, where real life and the imagination blend together in a disorienting and hallucinatory manner. It feels impossible to make sense of it all. My mind is still trying to unravel the inexplicable events of the night.

"I'm glad you came out tonight," Brad interrupts my trailing thoughts. He glances over at me with a sweet smile.

"Me, too."

My breathing accelerates as he reaches over and holds my hand. He gently strokes the side of my index finger with his thumb, just like he did in class Thursday. I watch his eyes squint as a car with bright headlights passes us. The intensity of his concentration on the road only amplifies his attractiveness, casting an air of confidence and rugged masculinity that steals my breath away.

"So, how'd you get mixed up with those outcasts, anyway?"

"Who? Aubrey and the guys?"

"Yeah," he says, lifting his hand from mine to put his car in a new gear.

"They're nice, really."

His head bobs up and down, but I can tell he doesn't agree.

"What?" I ask.

"Nothing, it's just—well, I can't picture you hanging out with people like them. They're weirdos and you're not."

I raise a brow.

"Well, maybe I am a weirdo, too, and you just don't know it yet."

He laughs. "Oh, really?"

"Mmm-hm." I give him a playful smirk.

"I guess that means we need to hang out more, so I can find out for myself just how weird you are, huh?"

I force a smile to show my approval, but I can't help but feel bothered by him calling my friends "weird." They're some of the nicest friends I could ask for—maybe he doesn't know them well enough.

He squeezes my hand, and I hold onto it tighter. I see the gate to Blythe House a few yards ahead of us. I wish this car ride could go on forever; I don't want it to end. He presses the button, and the rusty gates open. There are no lights on in the house except for the foyer. He releases my hand and pulls into the circular driveway. He rests the side of his head against the headrest, and I do the same. His eyes lock with mine.

"I like you, Jade. I want to get to know you," he says, playing with my hand.

"I'd like that." I beam.

He pulls my hand close and leans into me. This is the moment I have been dreaming about since I first saw him at my locker. I close my eyes. A wave of heat rushes through my body as his warm lips encompass mine. They are softer than I'd imagine for someone so strong. It takes me a few seconds to learn what to do with my lips. I follow his smooth rhythm, and the kissing feels more natural. He grabs the back of my head to keep it steady. The tip of his nose breathes warm air onto my cheeks. My heart feels like there's an explosion of a million fireworks. His pace slows down, and he pulls me away. I bite my lip. I never wanted it to end.

"Let me walk you to your door," he says sweetly.

"Sure."

He opens the car door for me. When I stand up, I am a couple inches from his face. My head dips down in surrender to the overpowering flush that takes over my cheeks. He retakes my hand, giving it a little squeeze, and we walk side-by-side to the front door. Before I go inside, he gives me one last kiss goodnight. It's tender and light.

"See you at school." He winks.

CHAPTER XIII
AN EMPTY WORLD

The curtains are parted slightly. A beam of sunlight penetrates the room like a sharp blade, and my eyes burn as they adapt to the striking brightness. I lay still, lost in thought, as I look up at the canopy for what seems like an eternity. Last night's events seemed as magical and farfetched as a fairy tale. The kiss from Brad was definitely real; I replay that in my mind with every detail savored. But the bizarre encounter with a ghost seemed unreal. Ruby slippers with magical powers, enchanted spinning wheels, and beetle lockets belonging to ghosts only exist in story books. It doesn't make any logical sense. I had to convince myself that it was the result of drinking too much alcohol. None of it could actually have happened, right?

With a sluggish pace, I drag my feet to the bathroom. The cascading hot water of the shower washes away the throbbing headache that had been plaguing me. Lacking the energy to dry my hair, I let it air dry, knowing full well that it would turn out frizzier than usual. I fasten the front part of my hair back with a white ribbon. The clothes Aunt Ruth bought for me yesterday are hanging in my armoire. I feel my headache return as I sort through the garments, wondering where to begin. Why can't I be like most girls who don't feel overwhelmed by choosing an outfit? Although tempted to wear my pajamas all day, I consider the thought that Aunt Ruth might spring an impromptu trip on me. I settle on a pair of black trousers, a plaid sweater vest, and a white button-down blouse with a ruffled Peter Pan collar. Despite feeling mildly hungover, I can take comfort in my cute look.

Amidst all the things I love about Blythe House so far, the breakfast spread crafted by Nigel and his diligent kitchen staff takes the cake. Today more than ever. He apologizes for the cold food, as he was expecting me to be up earlier. He goes into the kitchen to warm it up. I lay my head on my arms until he returned with the eggs, home fries, and bacon. It smells heavenly.

"Here you go, miss. This should help you recover, too," Nigel says, placing a cup of black coffee and two Tylenol in front of me. I trust he has plenty of experience nursing Aunt Ruth's hangovers.

"Is Aunt Ruth around today?" I ask.

He shakes his head. "I'm sorry, miss. I thought she might have told you. She is organizing a new play at the Palace Theater in Albany. They have their first meeting today as the opening show will be in January."

"Oh. I didn't know that," I manage to say through a mouthful of bacon.

"Will you, uh, be wanting lunch, too, miss?" Nigel asks as I'm licking my plate.

The clock above the fireplace reads quarter-till noon. I hadn't realized how late I slept.

"No, thanks, Nigel. I'll skip lunch—maybe even dinner," I answer, feeling full and queasy. "I might go back upstairs and lie down for a bit."

Nigel chuckles. "I'll have a pitcher of water brought up for you."

I sort through the movies Aubrey and I rented. I decide to rewatch *Sixteen Candles.* The movie's storyline of the attractive, popular guy falling for an ordinary girl resonates with my own situation with Brad. It sets my mind spinning with thoughts of him. Even though I intend to rewatch the film, I doubt I'll be able to focus on it, as our kiss has consumed my thoughts since I woke up.

I open the doors of the balcony to let in the fresh air. The cold wind on my face makes me feel better. I curl up in a ball under the blankets and sip on the water Nigel left for me. I wonder if Brad is thinking about the kiss, too? What if he's not? Or even worse, what if he regrets it?

Midway through my movie, Toby's incessant barking outside disrupts my focus. I turn up the volume on the television as his bark grows more fierce. I want to get up and investigate, but the other part of me knows it's likely the geese from the river stirring up trouble again.

I'm startled by the shadow of a man moving over the TV and onto the wall. I let out a shriek and accidentally knock over my cup of water onto the bed sheets.

"Relax. It's just me."

Standing in the balcony doorway is Will. I blink several times and rub my eyes. He's still there.

"I'm a bit early," he says, walking into the room.

"I—I thought you were a dream. This is a dream. I am dreaming, right?"

He shakes his head and sits on the couch next to the bed. "No. Not a dream, I'm afraid," he says with a grin.

"How'd you get on the balcony? Did you fly?"

He presses his lips together to hold in a laugh. "I'm not like the ghosts you see in films. I climbed up the lattice."

"Is this something you do often?" As the idea forms in my mind, I consider the possibility that it was him who came into my room and sat on my bed a few nights ago.

"It's become a nightly ritual of mine," he replies nonchalantly.

I clutch the covers closer to my chest, realizing he had invaded my privacy. My embarrassment gives way to irritation, and I yell, "It was you! You had no right to come into my room like that."

His deep laugh ricochets off the walls. "I apologize. I didn't think anyone was in here. This room has been empty for years."

"How do you know that?"

"I've been searching these old homes for decades for that damn locket. Almost every night. Speaking of which, I believe that's why I'm here."

"Oh, right." I grab the locket on the vanity and rummage through my bookbag for something to take notes on.

"What are you doing?" he asks.

"I'm grabbing a pen and a notebook."

"Whatever for?"

With the locket clutched in one hand and the pen in the other, I position myself against the headboard. "We need to start at the beginning. You'll tell me everything you can remember. I'll channel my inner Sherlock Holmes and record it all."

He raises an eyebrow, catching on to my reference. "So, I'm the reliable and supportive Dr. Watson in this scenario?"

I can't help but let out a laugh. "You got it."

He smiles, tilting his head in amusement. "All right, Sherlock, let's start from the beginning."

"Great." I click the tip of my pen. "Tell me all you remember, okay?"

He reclines on the couch, assuming a patient's posture on the verge of divulging their life story to a therapist. He seems to have a problem relaxing, as his muscles remain tight with tension. As he narrates his tale, his gaze remains fixed on the ceiling.

"I remember waking up alone at the manor in my bedroom. All was the same; my room was unaltered, and the house was in an identical state as I recalled. But I sensed something wasn't right. I had difficulty recounting facts, events, or specific details. My entire life felt like a jumbled heap of indistinct photographs. At first, I thought I might have indulged in too many spirits the night before. But when I looked around, the house was empty, and our servants were preparing the furniture with dust covers. I soon realized no one could hear, feel, or see me—"

"Did you know then you had died?" A cold chills crawls up my back as the words slip from my mouth. I can't imagine coming to the realization that you're no longer alive. What sort of emotions, thoughts, and fears would come into your mind?

"I wasn't consciously aware of it, but I sensed it on some level," he responds quietly. "Over time, after a couple of decades, you start comprehending it."

"Do you remember how you… how you were—"

"Murdered?" he interrupts my stammering, and the corner of my mouth slides sideways. "The last thing I remember before everything went black was opening the beetle locket. I don't even remember what was inside. There was a loud bang, and then everything around me vanished. It wasn't until I came across a newspaper article about my family's murder that I pieced together what had happened."

"Did you ever find out who killed you?"

"No, I'm afraid no one ever did."

I jot down everything with my right hand, while my left fingers graze the top of the beetle. I make a new heading on the page for notes relating to the locket.

"Where did you get the locket from?"

He scratches the bottom of his chin and squints. "I wish I could remember. I don't know for sure, but I have my suspicions. I found an old journal of mine a long time ago. It was tucked away in a drawer in my dresser. Inside are illustrations and notes on my travels to South America. Perhaps I found it there."

I jot down notes, underlining critical points on the page. "Why were you in South America?" My eyes remain steady on the paper, but I feel his eyes watching me. I look up and see the warm orange light of the afternoon sun casting a gentle glow on Will's face. He continues to study me. I look away, focusing on anything but his eyes.

"What?" I ask finally, and drop the pen on the paper.

He jumps up with a sudden burst of energy, taking me by surprise. My mouth drops open in astonishment, and my eyes widen with confusion. Swiftly, he grabs the notebook from my hands and throws it to the floor, making a delightful tinkling sound as it lands.

"Enough sleuthing for today. Let's have some fun," he says.

"What about—"

"It's been a century since I've had a conversation with anyone. I don't want to spend it reliving my death."

"Fair enough," I say, standing up with him. "What should we do?"

"I have an idea," he says, exiting toward the balcony. "Meet me out front by the gate."

He refuses to spoil the surprise when I ask him where he's taking me for the second time. I follow him to the front of the Montgomery Manor gate. It's a busy Sunday afternoon, and the road is bustling with cars. Will hops over the wall covered in vines, and I worry about getting caught.

"People are going to see that I'm trespassing, Will."

"Don't worry. You don't have to enter through the gate. Meet me over by those bushes."

He gestures toward a cluster of unkempt shrubs that jut out from the wall and onto the sidewalk. I position myself in front of them, waiting for further instruction. As I glance back, I notice the curious looks of passing drivers. I must seem silly standing still in front of the withered brush.

At last, I hear the sound of rustling leaves. Will's hands start clearing away the tangled foliage, revealing a gap in the wall created by fallen bricks.

"Follow me."

Once the coast is clear, I maneuver through the narrow opening in the wall, closely tailing him. We embark on a dirt pathway that meanders alongside the tranquil river. While it should be unsettling to follow a dead stranger down an isolated and shadowy trail, I strangely feel comfortable and trust him.

A portion of the river diverges, transforming into a thin stream. Crossing a bridge to the opposite bank, he stops near an ancient stone wall. I assume we've reached a dead end until Will reveals a concealed door beneath a tangle of ivy, which he pushes open. As I step through the entrance, I'm greeted by a delightful, overgrown Victorian garden. The untamed nature of the flora serves as a gentle reminder that beauty can thrive amid imperfection and that there's a unique charm to wild and unrestrained things. Surrounding its border are unusual colored flowers and exotic plants. The border is a living, breathing work of art. A stunning display of nature's beauty and wonder. We walk along a stone path that feathers out into a rockery displaying various ferns, alpine, and rock plants. A charming marble gazebo overlooking a quaint pond sits on a small hill. It paints the quaintest setting I've ever seen.

"It's beautiful here."

"Thank you. I visit this place often," he begins. "My father commissioned this garden as a present for my mother's birthday. Whenever I went on my travels, I would bring back flowers and greenery for her to plant and remind her of me while I was away. At least, that's what I've found in my journal. I've tried my best to tend to the garden, but I must confess, I'm not much of a gardener. I would rather indulge in the simple pleasures of reading, sketching, and watching the daytime creatures doze off as the nocturnal animals take over."

"I admire that. I guess time slows down when you have all the time in the world."

Will laughs under his breath. "Yeah, I suppose it does."

We walk up to the gazebo and sit on a marble bench. Apart from the birds chirping in the trees and the frogs croaking amid the lily pads, it's quiet and serene.

Leaning forward, Will places his elbows on his knees, causing his dark hair to sweep before his face and obscure part of his eyes. He fidgets with the gold ring on his pinky finger, twirling it clockwise and then counterclockwise. There is a rose at the center of the ring that bears embossed words around it.

"What does your ring say?" I ask.

"It says *Memento Mori,* it means 'remember that you will die' in Latin," he responds with a soft, reflective laugh that suggests a hint of irony regarding his circumstances. "I think, in some ways, it pays as a reminder to cherish things that truly matter and to avoid becoming consumed by wealth and status."

I smile weakly, as the words remind me of my grandfather and his similar views. "That's a really humbling way of looking at things. And also very interesting to have on a ring."

His lips curl into a gentle smile. "It's my family's signet ring."

"What's a signet?"

He laughs at my poor pronunciation. "You seal envelopes with hot wax and stamp the ring on top to make the seal."

"It's a shame that sort of practice isn't common anymore." Maybe the Whitney family has a signet ring, too.

"A lot has changed over the years," he says with some resentment in his tone.

There is a shared silence between us, as we admire the two swans floating in the pond. They both use their necks to search for food underwater. Their feathers make a loud rustling sound as they shake their wings.

"Did you know swans mate for life?" he asks.

"I didn't know that," I say, staring at them. "I wonder how long they've been together."

"Since April of 1961. They've been here ever since."

"Wow, that's six years before I was born."

The swans are lucky to have found a mate for the last twenty-four years. If Will has been coming here since before I was born, I wonder just how old he really is.

"How old are you, Will?"

He takes in a deep breath and exhales. He turns to look at me and his hair falls away from his face. In natural light, I discover just how bright his irises are. They convey a depth of wisdom, intelligence, and confidence.

"How old do you think I am?"

I inspect every inch of his face. He looks too old to be my age but not old enough to be over twenty-five.

"Twenty?"

He grins and shakes his head, the top of his hair tosses to the side. "Close—one hundred and twenty-one."

I laugh. "How is that close?"

"I was twenty-one when I died. I had just celebrated my birthday in July before everything paused. Since then, I haven't aged in the physical sense."

"So, you've been dead for a hundred years."

"This year marks my centennial." He lowers his head.

"My birthday's coming up soon—next week," I say, tucking my hair behind my ears. "The big eighteen."

"Ah, you're transitioning into an adult."

"Yeah, I guess so," I say, somberly.

"Why do you say it like that? Like it's a bad thing."

I shrug. "I guess it's because it's the first birthday I'll be spending without my grandfather." A piece of my heart breaks thinking of him.

He says, with genuine concern, without shifting his gaze, "I'm sorry to hear that."

"Every year, the two of us would bake my cake together. Well, he'd bake it, and I'd decorate it." I let out a subtle laugh as I remember the comments my grandfather would make about my terrible decorating skills. "I guess it will just be me this time."

"I'll help you make a cake." He perks up.

"Really? Can a ghost bake?"

"I am still human."

My eyebrow flares upwards.

"Well, perhaps I'm not entirely human," he confesses with sadness in his voice. "The touch of human flesh eludes me—no hand-holding, no embracing, no physical connection at all."

I frown, struck by the thought of a life empty of human touch and the inherent loneliness it entails.

"However, I can hold and interact with any inanimate object, so it is possible to help you bake. It could be a fun experience, and you wouldn't have to do it alone."

"All right." I beam. "But you're going to have to help me eat it."

His chuckle trails off. "I will leave that task to you. I don't eat food."

My eyes widened. "You don't eat? As in ever?"

"I don't have to. I'm dead."

I shake my head. "But food tastes so good!"

He shrugs. "I have lost the ability to taste food. All of it is flavorless to me."

The concept of existing without the need for sustenance or the desire to consume food is difficult to fathom. It's hard to wrap my head around Will being real. He looks and acts like a living person, yet his body is no more real than one's own reflection; you can see it but you can't touch it. Is this what happens when you die?

"Do you think everyone ends up like you? Like a ghost, I mean," I ask with my grandfather in mind.

He pinches his lips together and shakes his head. "No, I don't believe so. At least, I've never met anyone else like me."

"Oh," I say with some relief. My grandfather's passing still feels fresh, and the thought of his whereabouts brings a twinge of pain to my chest. "Sometimes, I worry I'll never see my grandfather or parents again. Like this life is all there is, and when you pass away, you vanish completely. Eventually, your whole existence is forgotten."

"You will see them again," he says matter-of-factly.

"How do you know?" I say, pushing back the tears. "How do you know if there's anything on the other side?"

He lets out a sigh. "Just because something is not visible to the naked eye does not mean it does not exist. Sometimes you have to believe in its reality," he says as his hand passes through mine, as transparent as the wind, to make his point. "I think that's why I'm so determined to find out my connection with this necklace. There has to be more than this on the other side. I think that locket is my key."

"But, wouldn't it be better to stay on this earth and live forever rather than pass over into the unknown?"

"Loneliness is the worst, most bitter pain one can experience. This is just an empty world for me."

I can relate to his words, as I am no stranger to the deep void that loneliness has on a person. While I may not fully comprehend Will's exact circumstances, the thought of wandering the world alone, feeling abandoned and helpless, is unimaginable. And he's done so for a hundred years. I have a deep sadness for him, and I am eager to offer any help I can to alleviate his pain.

"We're going to figure this out, you know," I say to him.

He leans back on the bench. "What makes you so sure?"

"Because I'm not going to stop until we do."

I could have sworn I saw his eyes glimmer like crystals. It makes my stomach tumble, but in a good way.

We move down to the edge of the pond. I sit on the bank while Will skips stones across the water. We talk until the sun nearly disappears. At one point, Will describes what it was like watching the town transition from the Victorian-era to modern day. I find it fascinating he experienced all the various decades of this century. I enjoy listening to him talk; his deep voice makes him a natural storyteller.

"The town used to be a hub for the mob?" I ask, surprised.

"It was so close to New York City, secluded enough not to draw attention, and there's lots of money here. I believe there is still a speakeasy under the bookshop where they used to store old brandy barrels. Nowadays, I rarely leave the manor except for when I visit the bookstore after hours. I borrow books for my personal reading and occasionally listen to the music emanating from down below. It seems the place has transformed into a sort of social hall."

"It's called The Underground. It's a nightclub. My friends go there sometimes for concerts." I watch as he nods his head and throws another rock into the pond. "So, do you just steal books and skip rocks all day?" I ask teasingly.

He gives me a puzzled look before bursting into laughter. "What's wrong with that? Besides, a book can take you anywhere."

"There's nothing wrong with it. I would love nothing more than to have infinite amounts of time to read books, trust me. But, I mean, you have the ability to travel unnoticed. Wouldn't you rather go explore the world than escape in a book?"

Will pauses to look down at the smooth rock in his hand. "It's an irony that I find myself unable to escape. According to my journals, my heart longed to travel the world when I was alive, dreaming of exploring far-off places. But now that I'm dead, I find myself not wanting to leave Grove Hollow, even with the freedom to travel anywhere if I so desire." A faint chuckle escapes him, and he has a far-away look in his eyes. "I once ventured as far as New York City—just once—only to find myself returning before long. Someday I hope to visit my mother's family estate in Asheville, North Carolina," he murmurs softly, his voice heavy with longing. "But I fear that day is still far off."

"Why do you say that?"

He waits for a moment, his expression troubled. "There's something unexplainable that keeps me tethered to this manor..." He trails off. "It's as though some invisible force holds me back, preventing me from wanting to move beyond the town's borders." His downcast eyes give away the possibility there is more to his situation than he is willing to share. Considering we only just met, I choose not to delve deeper into the matter, as it seems personal.

Casting his last stone into the calm pond, he takes a seat next to me on the soft grass. "But enough about me," he says, his voice lifting. "Tell me, why have I never seen you before at Blythe House?"

"Well, it wasn't until my grandfather passed that I found out the place even existed," I say, sticking my hands in my coat pocket. "I had no idea my family was so wealthy and prominent until I moved here."

His eyes widen in astonishment. "You mean to say you had no knowledge of belonging to one of the wealthiest families in America? How is that possible?"

I shrug my shoulders. "I guess my grandfather wanted to keep all of this a secret for a reason," I say.

"Interesting," he remarks. "Where were you residing before you arrived in Grove Hollow?"

I tell him about Coos Bay, Oregon, recounting the story of my parents' accident and my grandfather's passing. I reminisce about my childhood memories, a time when friendships were scarce, and I found companionship with my grandfather, allowing me to relate, to some extent, to his loneliness. During my storytelling, he is watching me intently. I end my tale at my arrival at Blythe House. He reclines his arms behind his head on the grass and stretches his legs out. I can tell by his pensive look he's visualizing my entire life story. Whether he finds it interesting or not, I'm not sure.

"Are you considering staying here for some time?" he asks.

"I believe I will. I can't think of any other place to go. My aunt is the only family I have left."

He nods, seemingly satisfied with my answer.

"Why do you ask?"

"Selfishly, I must admit, you're the first person I've talked to within a century. I'd hate to cut it short," he confesses, and we share a laugh. "However, I should escort you home before it gets too dark."

Lost in our conversation, I hadn't realized that the garden had become barely visible as the darkness fell around us with the sun almost entirely set. Making our way toward Blythe House, our literary discussion persisted, fueled by our mutual passion for great books.

"Do you mind if I have a look at your library?" he asks when we enter the house.

"Not at all," I whisper to him, in case anyone else is around.

I lead him to the small library connected to the study, where he runs his fingers along the gilded walls and examines the Victorian paintings.

"It's so interesting," he begins to say, his voice carrying a distant tone of reminiscence, "how much has changed, and yet a few things remain the same."

"Did you visit Blythe House a lot when you were alive?" I ask.

He takes a moment to answer. "I believe I used to come here. There's a feeling of familiarity to this place." He trails his hand over the books on the bookshelf. "I suspect my parents were acquaintances with your late family members. After all, we were neighbors."

It's strange to think that at some point, Will may have known my distant relatives or even caught a glimpse of my grandfather as a young boy. Though we are strangers, our history links us together.

I watch as he takes a black book off the bookshelf and flips through the pages.

"What did you find?" I ask.

"Moby Dick. I definitely remember reading this book as a child. Probably because I loved it so much." He looks down at the cover with a joyful expression. "Do you think your Aunt would notice if I borrowed it?"

"There's so much stuff here. I don't think she'll notice if anything is missing."

Toby runs into the library and kisses me on the cheek. He turns in the direction of Will. He drops his ears and growls.

"Can he see you?"

"He probably senses me. I get that a lot from animals, especially cats," he says, unconcerned.

"Good evening, miss. I thought I heard you talking to someone."

I spin around in surprise to find Nigel watching me curiously.

"Nope, just me talking to myself," I squeak, trying to act like it's nothing out of the ordinary.

"I see. Well, I came in to ask if you changed your mind about dinner. I will need to give the kitchen staff enough notice."

"No, thank you. I'm still feeling full from breakfast."

Aunt Ruth's liquor cart slides across the floor from the other side of the room. Nigel glances over in shock. I dart my head at Will. He stands completely still with a guilty look on his face.

"Maybe just send something small to my room. Thanks, Nigel!" I rush my reply.

"As you wish. I will bring it up to you shortly."

I feel like I was holding my breath the whole time. I wait for Nigel to disappear across the hall to the dining room before talking to Will again.

"That was close!" I exhale.

"Why does your Aunt have so much clutter? You can hardly walk without bumping into something."

"We should probably stick to my bedroom if we are to meet. Come on, let's go upstairs."

I glance around the corner to ensure no one is around before motioning for Will to follow me. When we get inside my bedroom, he takes a seat on the edge of my bed, staring at the green beetle locket resting atop my pillow. I grab it and join him.

"I wonder how old this is," I ask, looking at the locket with him.

"Who knows if we'll ever find out."

"What do you think will happen once we figure out how this beetle will help you?"

"I don't know. I've wondered that so many times. For all I know, there might be nothing I can do and I'll remain trapped in this vacant shell for all eternity," he says.

I shift myself to face him. "What do *you* hope, then?"

"I *hope* it makes me human again. To be flesh and whole, where I can talk with people. I want to finish the life I started." His face falls and he looks down at the floor. "Seeing as I was murdered, my odds are not good. So, if that is the case, I would like to go where all the other souls go in the end."

"It seems so… final."

"All goes onward and outward, nothing collapses. And to die is different from what any one supposed, and luckier."

"Walt Whitman," I remark, recognizing the poet's famous, poignant words about the supposed fortune in death.

"That's right." He nods, with a subtle upturn of the lips, and lowers his head. "It's the natural progression of life—how it's meant to be."

Considering the uncertainty of what lies beyond us after we die, I struggle to embrace Will's optimistic perspective. The thought of our attempts to solve this mystery leading to a permanent outcome leaves me disheartened. He raises his head, and our eyes connect briefly. I get the feeling he can sense my sadness about the possible consequences as he lets out a deep sigh. Trying to hide my disappointment, I force a smile.

"May I request a favor?"

"Of course," I reply softly.

"Will you always wear the locket to keep it safe?"

Leaning in slightly, I nod gently.

"Do you promise?"

"I promise."

He places his hands over mine, and they glide through them like a frigid mist. I clench my hand into a fist. It's like a silent understanding passes between us in the moment's stillness, forging an unspoken bond. Suddenly, I feel this intangible connection with Will. Our paths cross, guided by an otherworldly force, as we unravel the deep significance concealed within the mysterious locket we hold.

With a final glance exchanged, he gets up from the bed and heads toward the balcony. "I should leave, so you can eat and get some rest."

The words to ask him to stay are on the tip of my tongue—I've been loving the comfort I feel in his company, but my responsibilities force me to think ahead and prepare for a new school week.

"Can I see you tomorrow?" he asks.

Without thinking twice I say, "Of course."

"Great," he says with a lingering smile. "Goodnight, Jade."

"Goodnight, Will."

CHAPTER XIV

THE WOLF AND THE LAMB

My mind is in a whirlwind of conflicting thoughts and feelings as I prepare for school. On the one hand, I have this newfound mission to assist a ghost, and on the other, there's the anticipation of seeing Brad again after our Saturday night kiss. It's all so new to me. No guy has ever shown interest in me before. I always assumed it was because I dressed more like a fisherman than a girl. But now, here I am, grappling with the meaning of a kiss. Is he genuinely interested, or was it just a kiss and nothing deeper? Really, Brad and I hardly know each other. Ironically, I feel closer to Will, whom I met only a day and a half ago, than I do with Brad. If I don't sort out my thoughts soon, I'll have a tough time focusing on anything else today.

I had laid my uniform on the vanity chair last night, ironed and ready to wear. Today, I decided on a more feminine look by ditching the sweater in favor of a blazer and button-down. I notice Aunt Ruth's makeup bag on my vanity. Determined to enhance my plain features, I make the bold choice to dive into the world of cosmetics, regardless of my limited experience. I start with a light coat of blush on my pale cheeks. Then a few strokes of mascara to my lashes, making my green eyes appear bigger and brighter. I consider using eyeshadow, but I'm overwhelmed by the numerous shades available and decide against it. Instead, I comb my tangled hair, which settles into loose waves, albeit still frizzy. I tie it back with a thick red ribbon made into a big bow. School policy forbids jewelry, but I sneak the beetle locket around my neck and button my blouse high enough to conceal it. I don't feel as pretty as I did on Saturday night, but I'm not far from it.

Aubrey is waiting for me outside the gate on her bike, and we start down the sidewalk together. She pedals slowly. She is quiet and not her usual bubbly self. I realize I forgot to call her yesterday because of Will's visit. I feel guilty for being so absentminded.

"I'm really sorry I forgot to call you yesterday."

"It's cool," she replies. "How was the rest of your Saturday night?"

"It was good."

"Cool," she says again without any enthusiasm. "Everything go okay with you and pretty boy?"

I scrunch up my face, feeling uncomfortable. "Yeah, everything went fine. Brad dropped me off, and I went to bed." I try to make it sound like it was no big deal, even though it was the most magical night of my life.

"Oh," is all she says.

I tuck my hair behind my ear and look down at my feet. I'm not too fond of the tension between us. My grandfather always said, *"Don't let bad silences linger."* It's best to clear the air as I start my second week. So, I guess now is a good enough time to approach the topic of Saturday night.

"Look, Aubrey," I begin and she stops pedaling, "I'm sorry if I made the wrong decision to have Brad take me home after the party. I should have left with all of you."

Her shoulders move up and down as she huffs. "It's not that I'm upset you didn't come home with us. I mean, you're allowed to like whomever you want. It's just"—she lets out another big sigh—"it's Bradley Phillips. He is like the king of the douchebags, you know? Remember I told you what they did to Julian?"

"I remember," I say, unable to make eye contact with her. "But, he's not like those other guys. He's nice."

"He was there when it happened, Jade."

"What? He beat up Julian?" There's no way that's possible. I just can't see him doing something like that.

"Not exactly, but he was there. Which means he is just as guilty."

I grab a strand of my hair and tug on the end of it.

"Look, I'm not saying you can't like him. Just be careful, okay? I don't trust any of those jocks, especially Brad."

"Are Wes, Davy, and Julian going to be mad when they find out?"

"Don't worry about them. If the dudes somehow find out, leave that part to me." She gives me a weak smile.

"So, you're not mad?" I wince.

She hops back on her bike and starts peddling again.

"No, I'm not mad. Just promise you won't become one of those asshole-wannabes and forget about us when you two start dating exclusively and become popular."

"That part you don't have to worry about."

As we walk past Montgomery Manor, I search the windows for Will, but he's nowhere to be found. It's hard to remember that he's not just a figment of my imagination. I decided not to tell Aubrey about Will, fearing it would make me the target of relentless teasing and mockery if it ever got out. The last thing I want is to be labeled as another village witch, like my Aunt Ruth.

Students crowd the school courtyard as usual. We squeeze into the breezeway. Aubrey asks if I'll come with her to her locker near the gym. I don't need anything from mine, so I agree to go with her. My heart rate speeds up as I see Brad standing next to his rugby friends by the trophy case.

"I just want to say hi real quick," I say to her.

"Okay." She frowns. "I'll wait here for you."

Walking toward him, I can feel her eyes on me from behind. With both nerves and excitement competing against each other, I cling my books tight to my chest to hold myself steady. Brad notices me approaching, and I can sense his body tensing.

"Hey!" I wave at him.

His friends turn to look at me with confused expressions. He puts his hand on my shoulder and guides me a few feet away from his rugby teammates.

"Hey, what's up?" he whispers.

"I just wanted to come over and say hello."

"Oh, hey." He seems nervous as he peers over his shoulder at his friends.

"I had a really good time Saturday night. I couldn't stop thinking about you all weekend."

"Oh yeah?" He scratches his head and shifts his weight as if he's about to walk away.

His discomfort takes me by surprise. I feel embarrassed. I shouldn't have come over here.

"Listen, I have to get to homeroom. I'll see you later, okay?" he says, patting my arm. He walks away with his friends following him.

I stand there, stunned. It's like nothing happened between us on Saturday night. As I walk back to Aubrey, I hear one of his friends ask, "what was that about?" It feels like someone plunged a dagger into my heart when I hear Brad reply that I was looking to interview him for the school newspaper. What a huge mistake. I can't believe I thought there could be something between Brad and me. I'm such a fool.

"Everything okay?" Aubrey asks from behind.

I'm trying my best not to cry from mortification. "Yeah, I'm fine."

"Come on, forget about that asshole. Let's meet up with the dudes," she says, swinging her arm around my shoulder to comfort me.

I can't stop thinking about my conversation with Brad this morning. Every time I replay it in my head, I feel more and more foolish. How could I think it would be anything more than just a kiss? I'm the first in my French class, so I try to distract myself by rereading the La Fontaine poem we studied last night. More people come in, and we all wait for Madame Gaël, who is running late. Allison walks in and coughs the word "slut" in my direction. Two other girls in the back row laugh along with her. I try to ignore her taunts and keep reading the fable. I can hear her whispering to the other girls.

"Mike and Ian saw them that night in the study. They said they saw her throw herself on him," one girl says with a snicker.

"What a bold move for someone who showed up out of nowhere," Allison says to the other girls, loud enough for me to hear.

"Maybe she got kicked out at her last school for attacking other people's boyfriends," the one girl says, and they laugh together.

"I can't believe she had the nerve to go after Brad like that," Allison starts again. "I'm not surprised he had to push her away. How desperate can one person be?"

The other girl shakes her head. "I don't know how she thought she stood a chance against you, Allison. Everyone knows he's been in love with you since freshman year."

"Exactly. She didn't stand a chance," Allison says confidently.

My fingers shake as I grip my book tightly. I try to focus on the words on the page, but their whispers become louder. I can feel more eyes on me as the other students listen in on their conversation. My stomach is in knots as I swallow the ball in my throat. I can feel a tear escape and roll down my cheek. I want to run out of the room, go home, and hide under my covers.

"How insecure do you have to be to spread lies about others?" Julian sneers at Allison, coming to my defense.

Before Allison has a chance to reply, Madame Gaël enters the room. She orders everyone to turn to the fable assigned last night to us, *Le Loup et l'Agneau—The Wolf and the Lamb,* to discuss as a class. I get out my sheet of paper with my notes, grateful for the interruption.

"The Wolf and The Lamb is one of my favorite fables," Madame Gaël says as she sits on the edge of her desk. "Jean, why don't you tell us your English translation from the French fable and then we will open the discussion."

Julian clears his throat and begins to recount the fable. "A lamb comes to a stream to drink some water. A little upstream, a wolf also drinks from the same water source. The wolf turns to the lamb and says, *"How dare you muddy the water I'm drinking."* The lamb, being gentle and polite, responds, *"I'm sorry, sir, but you are mistaken. You are drinking upstream, so I am not muddying the water for you."* But the wolf is not satisfied with this explanation and becomes angry. He accuses the lamb of insulting him at the same stream a year ago. The lamb points out that he is barely a year old and couldn't have done such a thing. The wolf then accuses the lamb's father of insulting him, but the lamb apologizes on his father's behalf. Despite the lamb's attempts to appease the wolf, the wolf becomes even angrier and decides to kill and eat the lamb as a lesson."

"Very good translation from French to English, Jean." Madame Gaël looks around the room. "Who would like to go first to talk about their take on the fable? How about you, Céline?"

Allison sits forward in her chair. "My take on the fable was that the wolf was upset that the lamb tainted the water with mud. The mud ruined the drinking water for everyone who could be drinking further down the stream. The lamb acts like they're weak and helpless, even though it knows what they are doing, using it as leverage to plead innocence. To top it all off, the lamb doesn't even apologize for ruining something that doesn't belong to her!"

"Fascinating and a rather untraditional perspective, Céline. So, you do believe the wolf was justified for killing the lamb?" Madame Gaël asks, intrigued.

"Obviously," Allison says with a roll of her eyes. "The lamb should know better than to take something that doesn't belong to her—and the same goes for girls who try to steal other people's boyfriends. They should expect to face the consequences of their actions."

Julian looks in my direction. He notices I'm clutching on to my pencil so tight it's ready to snap.

I interrupt Allison, clearing my throat. "The wolf didn't care that the lamb apologized to him," I say, my voice shaking. "His plan all along was to kill the lamb. His excuses were a way to justify his desire to kill an innocent creature. The wolf lied and tried to make the lamb seem less innocent to benefit himself."

"In your opinion, Annabelle, what is the takeaway from the story?"

"I think Annabelle should change her name to *Jezebel,*" a girl whispers to Allison, and they both laugh.

"The tyrant can always find an excuse for his tyranny. Just like a bully will always find an excuse to bully," I say as her eyes narrow on me.

Julian claps his hands.

"Great discussion!" Madame Gaël joins Julian in his clapping. "This is why La Fontaine's fables are so intriguing. His work has a moral lesson, as you know. Depending on how some of us interpret the poems and apply them to our life experiences, the lessons can sometimes have completely different meanings. Excellente, Jean, Annabelle, and Céline!"

Even though I didn't confront Allison for her hurtful gossip, I am relieved that I stood up for myself—at least this time I didn't get a drink poured on me.

By lunchtime, word of the quick kiss at the party between Brad and me has spread through the entire school. I suspect one of the card players from the party must have told everyone. The rumors circulating aren't in my favor—they portray me as the aggressor, forcing myself onto him like some desperate, untamed animal. Even though Brad was the one who initiated the kiss. Amidst the commotion caused by these false narratives, I find comfort in absentmindedly toying with the beetle locket, almost forgetting I've also formed a friendship with a ghost.

With my back deliberately turned away from Brad's area, I sit silently at our table, barely picking at my forkfuls of ravioli di Zucca. The gossip has completely spoiled my appetite. Aubrey shoots me an uncomfortable glance as if she had just tasted a mouthful of worms. I can tell she's harboring something to say.

"What is it?" I finally ask.

"I didn't want to tell you this, but apparently Collin Fetterman told everyone in my English Literature class your aunt made you a love potion to help you win over Brad. He even went as far to say he saw you put it in his drink the night of the party."

I bury my head in my hands. Everything is getting so distorted.

"No doubt Allison is the source of all these rumors," Davy sneers.

Aubrey puts her hand on my arm. "If you want, I'll beat her up for you. You just tell me when and I'll do it."

"I just don't understand how everything became so twisted." Taking a moment to collect myself, I continue, "Brad kissed *me,* but it was only a quick peck on the lips!" Fortunately, nobody has discovered that Brad and I shared a *real* kiss in front of my house that night. The thought of that rumor spreading far and wide fills me with anxiety.

"Jade, Brad may seem like this super nice guy, but he is no different than all the other jocks here. They're nothing but liars and cheats," Wes states.

Julian glances over my shoulder, his eyes fixed on Brad's table. "He should man up and tell everyone the truth about kissing you," he says. I resist the urge to turn around and look at Brad's table myself.

"Ugh. I don't feel like talking about this anymore." I slam my forehead against the table and everyone's trays bounce up.

"Well, I have something that will excite everyone," Wes says, pulling out a piece of paper from his satchel. It's a concert poster he made in art class for a band called Moxie Youth. The poster is made of cut paper on a neon pink sheet; I admire the DADA design work that went into it.

"It looks so sweet!" Julian says. "I'm totally amped."

"Who are Moxie Youth?" I ask, happy to talk about anything else.

"It's our band!" Aubrey hoots. "I thought I told you? We started it over the summer. Next Thursday is our first gig at The Underground."

"Next Thursday? That's my birthday!" I exclaim excitedly.

"And it's Halloween—say you'll come?" Aubrey begs.

"I'll be there. You can hang with me," Julian says.

"I'd love to come to your first gig—but do we have to dress up in costume again?" I don't think I have it in me to wear another costume.

"Some people will—just come looking street," Aubrey says.

I'm unsure what "street" means, but I interpret it as casual clothes.

"What kind of music do you play?" I ask.

"We are like a new wave post-punk alternative rock band," Davy explains.

My jaw drops. "That's a mouthful!"

Davy laughs. "Aubrey plays bass, I'm on drums, and Wes is on vocals and lead guitar—"

"And I'm the band's groupie." Julian winks.

"We mostly do cover songs right now, but we have a couple original songs that we are working on," Aubrey says.

"Great, I can't wait."

"How's about a smoke break anyone?" Davy grabs his pack of cigarettes.

"I could use some fresh air," I admit.

Loving nothing more than to escape the presence of Brad, Allison, and the swirling gossip, I abandon my half-eaten lunch and join Aubrey and the guys outside in the atrium. They engage in an animated discussion about their desire to attend the sold-out Orchestral Manoeuvres in the Dark and Thompson Twins concert at Madison Square Garden in December—two bands I love. Their company feels effortless, as if I'm an integral part of the group. I feel deep gratitude for friends like Aubrey, Julian, Davy, and Wes, particularly when I find myself at the center of hurtful rumors.

A substitute teacher rolls a TV cart into our American History classroom, and students in the front clap and cheer. Not only is Mr. O'Connor not teaching today, but we also get to watch a movie.

"Mr. Ryan, how's it goin' man?" A guy in the front row holds up his hand and Mr. Ryan gives him a high-five.

"Yes, Mr. Ryan's subbing!" another kid cheers as he walks into the classroom.

Mr. Ryan appears to be a popular substitute at the school. It's easy to see why, with his laid-back demeanor. He's a plump man with a walrus mustache, round glasses, and a bow tie with suspenders. I feel relieved that Mr. O'Connor is out today, but my comfort is short-lived when Brad sits beside me. I can feel him looking at me, but I pretend not to notice.

"All right, all right, everyone." Mr. Ryan starts reading instructions from a sheet of paper provided by Mr. O'Connor while the class carries on, "Mr. O'Connor has here… *we are to watch this five-part documentary on Industrial America. You will have test questions on the video for your final, so pay attention,* he writes."

He gives a packet of papers to a girl in the front row to hand out. It looks like we are to fill in the blanks while we follow along with the movie. Everyone groans.

"Oh, to be a teenager again," Mr. Ryan says with a laugh and claps his hands together.

"When will Mr. O'Connor be back?" The girl passing out papers asks.

"He'll be out for a week at a teacher's conference." Everyone cheers and claps their hands with excitement.

Mr. Ryan struggles to connect the VHS player to the TV, and a student in the front volunteers to help him. I look over the fill-in-the-blank worksheet, which has a lot of empty spaces for us to fill in. As someone who suffers from anxiety, I always find it difficult to follow along with a movie and fill in the answers. The material is rarely interesting, so paying attention to it requires a lot of effort, to begin with. Then adding a worksheet to the mix makes it even more challenging. I'm always too distracted by my worries of missing an answer, so I never retain any critical information from the video, which is *always* on some sort of quiz or test.

"Jade," Brad whispers surreptitiously.

I don't look over. I see him write something on paper from the corner of my eye. Brad gets up to sharpen his pencil at the pencil sharpener. I glance at him and then quickly look away, not interested in what he's doing. He slides a note onto my desk when he returns to his seat.

ASK TO GO TO THE BATHROOM. WAIT FOR ME THERE.

I crumple the piece of paper. I have no intention of skipping class to meet with Brad after the way he treated me in front of his friends—as if I were a nobody. I walk up to the front of the room with the ball of paper in my hand and toss it in the bin. Brad slumps in his seat with his hands over his forehead. But then my heart overrides my brain—I hope I don't regret what I'm about to do. Just as the documentary starts, I ask Mr. Ryan if I can go to the restroom.

"No problem-o!" Mr. Ryan chirps.

I glance at Brad one last time before leaving the classroom. Whatever this is, it better be worth my time.

I wait outside the bathroom for the American History room door to open, tapping my foot impatiently. After five minutes with no sign of Brad, I'm about to give up and go back when he finally emerges from the classroom. If my eyes were longbows, they'd be shooting a thousand arrows at his chest.

"Sorry for the wait."

I tap my foot harder against the floor so he hears it. "This better be worth it."

"Follow me." He grabs my hand and pulls me in the opposite direction of the classroom.

I pull my hand away. "What about class?"

"Mr. Ryan won't notice we're gone."

"I meant the worksheet. We need to turn it in. Not to mention the material will be on the final!"

"Forget all that. Come on."

He starts walking down the hall without me. I hesitate, looking back at the American History room, but I give in and follow him.

There's an old wooden door at the end of the hall that I've never noticed before. A heavy padlock hangs on the Georgian door handle. Brad pulls down the lock's body, and the shackle lifts. The door opens to a narrow staircase leading up to a fourth floor that I hadn't seen on the school's map. It's a small space with only two stained glass windows lighting the dark hallway. The last door at the far end opens to a dusty shower room that looks like it hasn't been used in years.

"Where are we?"

"It's the old shower room from when this place was a boarding school," he says. "None of the teachers know the lock doesn't work, so students come up here to skip class or to fool around."

I peer up at the spider weaving its intricate web between the pointed arch above us. Not exactly the most romantic place I'd pick to do it with someone. He sits down on a wooden bench between a row of lockers. I sit beside him, leaving a twelve-inch gap between us.

"Why did you bring me here?" I try my best to mask my unease, but my belly tingles.

He grabs my hand and squeezes it gently. If I look up at him, I fear I'll lose all my ability to stand my ground. I can't forget that I've had a miserable day all because of him. I was taunted and gossiped over. Most of all, he acted as though nothing happened between us Saturday night. There's no reason this boy deserves any of my attention right now. Yet, here we are, holding hands, and I'm not wanting any of this to end.

"I needed to talk to you without any distractions."

My heart sinks. I know he really means he wants to talk to me without anyone else around. My eyebrows pull together, and I slide my hand away from his.

"You made me feel like a fool, Brad. What happened Saturday night—those kisses may not have meant anything to you, but they meant something to me."

"It *did* mean something to me, Jade," he says, grabbing my hand again. "I wouldn't have kissed you if it didn't mean anything to me."

"Then why did you act that way toward me this morning? Are you embarrassed by me?"

"No," he insists. "It's not that."

"Then why?" I snap.

"It's hard to explain."

"Try then."

He positions himself away from me. "It's Allison. She and I are technically together, even though we're not really."

I lift a brow. "That doesn't make sense."

"We've been fighting off and on. It started over the summer when I found out she had met someone in Venice. Since that trip, things haven't been the same between us. I thought maybe I could get over it and pretend it never happened. I'm putting on a convincing show, at least. Then you bumped into me that one morning."

"Am I just some sort of rebound then? To get back at her?"

"What? No!" He shifts himself back to face me. "I haven't been able to stop thinking about you since that day."

I don't want to admit that I've felt the same way about him since we met in the hallway by my locker.

"What about Allison? Where is she in all of this?"

He scratches one side of his neck. "It's complicated."

"How so?"

"Well, my dad works for her father. He's one of the richest bankers in America. He wants to make my dad a partner in his business next year. So, you can see why I'm treading on thin ice if anything happens between her and me."

"That doesn't seem fair. Your parents are adults, I'm sure they want you to be happy."

He makes a soft snort with his nose. "Allison and I have been together for four years. Our parents are expecting us to get married after college."

"Married!" I shout in disbelief. "You're only seniors in high school!"

He shrugs. "They're old fashioned. It doesn't help that she comes from one of the richest families in the country. My parents are pushing for it."

I can't imagine having that sort of pressure from his parents. In some ways, I feel bad for him.

"Can we keep this all a secret? Just until I figure it out?"

"I don't know how this will work out, Brad. Your parents are expecting *marriage* with Allison and your dad is tied to hers. Not to mention, it doesn't feel right going behind everyone's back." Even Allison's.

"I'll think of something. Just give me some time."

I bite the edge of my lip, unsure of what to do. In the back of my mind, I hear Wes's voice saying, *"They're all liars and cheats."* But he seems genuine. I feel compelled to take the risk and trust him.

"I meant what I said. I want to get to know you." His voice lowers. "We can meet in secret."

"So, am I to become your paramour when you and Allison marry?"

He lets out an uneasy laugh. "It won't be forever. We just have to be careful around everyone else. If word gets out about you and me, Allison will tell her parents, and my dad's position at the company could be in jeopardy. I promise it won't be for much longer," he says, bringing his hand up to my cheek.

Under his gentle touch, I feel the wall I have built between us start to crumble. His hands glide to the back of my head, where the clasp of my beetle necklace lies. He draws nearer, and my heart races. A mixture of nerves, anticipation, and uncertainty fills me. His kiss begins tenderly, a delicate caress. Yet, it quickly transforms into a passionate embrace, and I willingly surrender to its power. I savor the sweetness of his breath, overcome by pure bliss. I forget all about the gossip and chatter as the world around us melts away.

CHAPTER XV

SHERLOCK AND WATSON

I stare out my balcony window in a daydream daze as I recount every detail of this afternoon's events with Brad, starting with the memory of his soft lips against mine. Intermittently, we would pause our kissing to discuss each other's interests and plans for after high school. He wants to pursue professional rugby while I am still uncertain whether I want to become a literary teacher or follow a career in creative writing. I was disappointed to hear he preferred movies over books, but his kissing made up for it. Oh, the kissing. I could relive those moments over and over again…

"Something on your mind?" Will asks, snapping me out of my trance.

"No, why do you ask?"

"I've asked you twice if you want to read my journal, and you haven't looked away from the window."

"Oh, right, sure."

He hands over the leather-bound journal. The spine is so worn, the binding is giving away. I'm surprised the fragile pages are still intact.

"Are you sure?" he asks.

"Yeah, I'd love to read it."

"No, I meant if everything is all right. You seem disconnected. Maybe this is all too much?"

"It's not that. I just had a rough day at school, that's all."

"How so?"

"Are you sure you want to know? You might be here for a while."

"I've got all the time in the world," he says, unfolding his hands like he's about to show me a magic trick.

I let out a big sigh and roll back on the bed. "I was the topic of conversation today."

"I thought girls liked to be the center of attention?"

"It wasn't the kind of attention anyone would want. I was the focal point of cruel gossip that spread around our school faster than a wildfire."

"So, what happened that was so terrible everyone was talking about you?" he asks.

"That's the long part."

I share with Will about Saturday night with Brad, the kiss, the ride home, and him telling me he liked me. I described the endless rumors spread about me by the whole school, Brad's relationship with Allison, and his predicament because of his father's career. Lastly, I tell him about my deal with Brad to meet secretly. I do, however, leave out the part where we kissed in the abandoned locker room until the last bell rang for the day.

"I just feel so confused. I've never had so many emotions running through me at once!" I hit my hand on my forehead.

"It sounds like Brad doesn't have your best interest at heart."

I am taken aback by Will's response. Even with my clear explanation, I am shocked about how he arrived at that understanding.

"He's not like that."

"Oh, really?" Will plucks away at his nail. "Is that why he sat back and watched the rumors spread about you? It seems to me he had several opportunities to defend the truth."

I grip the bed cover tight with my fingers. "He's just confused. Everything is a mess right now."

"He had every opportunity to make a move. He's playing it safe, if you ask me."

"He *wants* to be with me. It's more complicated than that!" I realize that I'm almost shouting. As though the louder I get, the more I convince Will—or myself.

"If you say so," he says. His nonchalant tone—I find it more irritating than his laissez-faire reply.

"Let's just not talk about this right now. Can we just focus on this necklace, since that's why you're here?"

Will's eyes narrow. He twirls the tip of his pen in his mouth with his tongue like he wants to make a cheeky remark but refrains from doing so. "Sure, no problem."

Why does he have to say it like that? *"Sure, no problem,"* so indifferently. I feel my anger rising. I take a deep breath and let it out slowly to calm myself down.

"So, this journal is from when?" I ask, using the leftover adrenaline to flip to the first page with force.

"It's from 1884. I believe it could be from one of my last trips before I was killed."

The first page has a collection of handwritten notes in ink. On the side of the page is an illustration of a great-tailed grackle drawn in ink pen. The illustration looks like it could be in an Encyclopedia.

"Did you draw this?"

"Judging by the similarity between my current and previous sketches, I believe I did. It seems certain passions persist even when you become a ghost." He emits a gentle snort from his nose.

"Wow. You're really good," I say, careful not to boost his ego too much as I'm still bitter about his comment concerning Brad.

"Thank you," he answers proudly.

Above the bird illustration is a note in cursive handwriting. I read aloud:

"April 16th, 1884 - MEXICO CITY: A bird landed next to me, and I fed it part of my lunch of rye bread and an apple. Dr. Wallace and our crew are waiting for our guide, Fransisco Díaz, who is a local here. He is to take us to Teotihuacán. Because of the heat, we will need to stop often for the horses to rest. We are predicting we will be at the Avenue of the Dead by day four, where we'll find The Pyramid of the Moon and the Pyramid of the Sun."

"The name Dr. Wallace sounds familiar," he says. "I know I've come across something with his name on it before. For the life of me, I can't recall where."

"I've heard the name, too," I say, then it occurs to me. "I read a letter in the pink room the night I found the necklace. It was from your mother. She mentioned you were under the observation of Dr. Wallace and something about an archeology hobby. That must be why you were in Mexico City with him."

He puts his hand to his chin as though he's trying to recall what I'm talking about.

"I hardly ever go into that room," he says solemnly. A moment passes and I can tell he's deep in thought.

"I'm sorry about your parents, Will," I say, trying to show my sympathy.

He lifts his shoulders, but I can see the pain in his eyes.

"Oh well," he says casually.

I frown at his closed-off demeanor, but I can understand his pain. I might not remember my parents, but that doesn't mean I don't miss them.

"Maybe we should go over tonight and collect some items in the house that could be clues. We can bring anything we find back with us, since it's getting too dark to see anything in the manor," I suggest. "We can even make a conspiracy board with anything we think could lead us back to the necklace."

He wrinkles his brows and puts his fingers over his mouth like he's trying to stifle a laugh.

"What the hell is a conspiracy board?" he asks.

"You know, like what detectives have in movies. Where they place maps on walls and connect images and notes with red string," I explain, half-excitedly.

He's unable to hold back the laugh. I'm glad to see him smile, even if it's at the price of mocking my idea.

"A crime analysis chart, you mean?"

"That's exactly what I mean," I say, sitting straight up with my head held high.

He shakes his head in amusement. His eyes glimmer with admiration as he looks at me. "Your mind amazes me," he says, and my cheeks flush. "That's a brilliant idea. I don't know why I never thought to do something like that before."

"See? That's exactly why I get to be Sherlock," I declare with a grin.

"Well, Sherlock would be absolutely lost without Watson."

"I couldn't agree more," I reply, nodding and matching his infectious smile.

As our eyes meet, a moment of playful tension remains, causing my breathing to quicken. Sensing the need to break the spell, I clear my throat, and he rises to his feet.

"All right, Sherlock. Gather your things and meet me outside."

I instantly regret my choice of attire—a beige trench coat gifted by Aunt Ruth from our trip to New York City—instead of my reliable and less fashionable corduroy coat that would have kept me warm. The weather is chillier now that the sun is beginning to set. I cling onto the straps of my now-empty bookbag and brace myself as a gust of wind nearly knocks me off my feet. I meet Will outside by the gate. He doesn't seem to be bothered by the cold weather; I guess that's one perk of being a ghost.

"Do you have a lantern we could use?" he asks.

"You mean a flashlight? No. My aunt's flashlight died the night I found the necklace. I'll have to buy more batteries."

"Batteries." He shakes his head and sighs. "I never understood why lanterns became so unpopular. Unlike flashlights, they give out 360 degrees of light."

"You sound like my grandfather." I giggle. "He was always grumbling about new technology. I'm pretty sure he thought a floppy disk was slang for melted vinyl."

"What's a floppy disk?"

I let out a laugh. "It's a square disk you use to store computer data and programs," I explain, looking up at Will's face. He appears even more confused than before. "Nevermind."

"Well, as much as I would love for you to explain to me the technologies of the twentieth-century, we should pick up our pace. I don't think we will have much light left judging by those heavy clouds," he says.

I look up and spot the cluster of clouds moving in. I hope they aren't full of rain.

"Let's grab what we can and come back," he suggests.

As we approach Montgomery Manor, which looks just as chilling as always, an idea pops into my head that I think is worth exploring.

"I have an idea, Will. It's about the locket," I say, keeping up with his fast pace.

"What's that?" he asks.

"My friend told me about this man downtown who owns the bookshop. His name is Mr. Willoughby. He's a retired history professor from Harvard. Maybe he can tell us the history behind the locket?"

I look up at Will to gauge his reaction to my idea. He lowers his head and looks at the locket.

"I don't know," he says.

"Don't you think a history professor from Harvard might know something we can't find in an abandoned house?"

Will puts both of his hands on top of the brick wall. He uses his long legs to climb over to the front yard of Montgomery Manor.

"How do we know we can trust him?" he calls from the other side.

"My friends say he's a great man. He comes highly recommended," I yell back at him.

I wait for a car to go by before I step through the shrubs in the wall's opening. I brush off a few loose leaves from my red trousers.

"Can you give me some time to think about it?" Will asks as I meet him.

I can understand if he's overprotective of something he's been searching for over the last century. After all, it's only been a couple of days since we've met and he's been reunited with the locket. Though, I was hoping he'd be more accepting of my idea.

"Of course. Give it some thought," I say, trying not to push him.

I follow Will behind the back of the house and through the broken ballroom window. The manor feels less sad now that I know Will has been inhabiting its rooms for the last hundred years.

With all the heavy-leaved beech trees shading the house and the rain moving in, it's almost impossible to see anything in the manor. No doubt, in fifteen minutes, darkness will cover every room. We start in the study the same room I found the portrait of the man with the two bullet holes underneath. We grab anything we see off the floor—newspaper clippings, books, letters. It doesn't take long for my backpack to fill up.

"We might have a little light left to go into your mother's room. I can grab the letters off her desk," I say.

He nods. "Sure. That sounds like a good idea."

I follow Will up the steps, watching as he walks gracefully in his Victorian clothes. It feels like I'm viewing a historical reenactment of the Gilded Age. Sometimes I have to remind myself this is all real.

"Do you want to come in with me?" I ask him as I stand outside his mother's room.

"No, thank you. I'll wait out here," he says.

"Sure."

I walk over to the desk in the pink-colored room. I take the stack of letters and carefully place them in the front pocket of my backpack. It feels wrong taking someone else's notes, but I'm sure Will's mother wouldn't mind if anything in the letters could help her son. Before leaving the bedroom, I stand in front of the oil painting of Will's mother on the floor. Her delicate features make her seem softer and more approachable, even with her serious expression, similar to Will's.

"Don't worry. I'm going to help your son," I whisper to her.

I return to the hallway and find Will propped up against the wall. His head is down, and he is looking at his shoes. I sense a touch of strain behind his smile.

"I'm going to grab something from my room to bring back with us," he says.

"Will, I don't think I have any room left in my backpack."

"Don't worry. I won't be needing your bag."

When we get to his bedroom, he pulls back a dirty, frayed curtain to give us more light, but it's hopeless.

"Stay by the doorway. It's impossible to see in here. I don't want you getting hurt," he says. "I am aware of its location. I won't be long."

Following his instructions, I wait by the door. I watch him pull something out from under his bed.

"What's that?" I ask.

"It's a leather boot trunk," Will says. "I think it contains belongings from a previous time when I traveled. They could be valuable clues."

"Wow, that's fantastic!" I exclaim, feeling excited.

"Do you think you'll be able to carry it back? I would transport it, but we wouldn't want any passersby to witness a floating trunk beside you."

I grasp the handle of the medium-sized trunk, surprised by its lightness. "I'll be all right to carry it."

"Great," Will replies. He extends his hand in a gesturing manner, signaling for me to lead the way into the hallway. Overhead, we hear the start of rain drops on the roof. "We should move quickly."

We venture outside just as the rain pours from the dark clouds. I wish I was wearing my thick jacket to shield my body from the freezing wind. Water droplets pierce my skin like a shower of icy glass. I drape my trench coat over my backpack, guarding it against the downpour of rain. Will urges me to quicken my pace as the rain intensifies.

Once we reach Aunt Ruth's house, our paths split, and Will meets me upstairs. Nigel has already lit a fire in my room, and it casts a flickering glow throughout the space. I position myself in front of the fireplace, desperate for the warmth from the flames. A frigid chill has taken over my entire body. Numbness has claimed my fingers, causing them to be unsteady and nearly unresponsive as I struggle to unbutton my drenched jacket. Each tiny fastening becomes a daunting obstacle as my body rattles with shivers.

"Let me help you," Will offers.

I wasn't expecting my heart to thump like a tribal drum, echoing in my ears, when he steps closer, only inches from me. It's bizarre to witness his hands gliding through mine, unbuttoning the top button first, while the absence of his touch remains an unexplainable enigma. I'm having a hard time fully grasping what my eyes are seeing.

"I can s-s-see your hands, but I c-c-can't feel them. How does this w-w-ork?" I ask.

A soft, cynical laugh flees from his curved lips. "I'm not certain why I'm unable to feel you beyond your jacket or why you are unable to feel my hand. As long as I've been dead, I have been stripped of the capability to touch any living thing. It seems to be a curse that haunts me as long as I live—well exist—in this hollow body of mine. To be unable to touch someone," he begins, his eyes meeting mine, causing a flittering feeling in my stomach, "you don't realize how valuable the presence and weight of another human is until you have been deprived of it for so long."

"How l-l-lonely that m-m-must feel, Will?"

He frowns, betraying a look of shame, or maybe its vulnerability, and he averts his gaze from mine.

"Your teeth are chattering so loud, everyone a mile away can probably hear it," he says, deftly unbuttoning the last button on my jacket.

"I-I-I am fr-ree-zing. A-a-aren't you-u-u?"

"No, I don't feel anything," he says, looking at me pitifully, like you would at a stray dog begging for food. "Why don't you take a hot bath? It will be the fastest way to bring your body temperature back up. I'll start organizing all the material we've collected."

"O-o-okay."

I close the bathroom door behind me and hear Will humming to himself in the bedroom. I hesitate to turn on the faucet, feeling uneasy about taking a bath while a man I barely know is in my room. But he's right; it's the quickest way for me to warm up. I take a deep breath and turn on the faucet, letting the hot steam from the water wash over my face. I strip out of my wet clothes and climb into the bathtub. I lean my head against the tub's edge and let the warm water gradually bring my body temperature back to normal.

Will knocks on the door. "I found something interesting."

"Oh? Yeah?" I shrill. I quickly cover my lady-parts with my hands and water splashes out the sides.

"Relax." He laughs. "I have no plans of coming in."

I exhale a sigh of relief that he's not going to walk in on me.

"There's a letter addressed to my father from me."

"What does it say?"

He clears his throat and begins to read:

"The 12th of April, 1885

Dear Father,

I am glad to hear you both are well and your new neighbors in the Hollow have finished with the build. Mother must be thrilled the construction noise is over and it will not interfere with her busy summer season. I will arrive in Brooklyn on the third of May and will take the train in from there. I would not miss Letty's masquerade debutante ball for anything. You know I care for her deeply.

Oxford is cold and rainy, a lot like the spring and fall seasons in New York. You will be pleased to know my grades are above average in all my studies at the University. I am still waiting to hear if I am enrolled in the business courses, upon your request. In regards to how long I am staying in New York, my plans are tentative. Dr. Wallace is currently working on the itinerary for the next trip in the fall. Once the dates are set, I will have more solidified plans. I promise, when I return, we shall meet and discuss the railroad business.

Please make sure mother does not fill out my dance card for the ball before I step back on American soil.

Best,

Willy"

"You said the letter was written in 1885?" I ask. "That's the year you died. Do you think you went on the trip with Dr. Wallace in the fall?"

"I'm not sure. We know Dr. Wallace was a professor at Oxford University. There's a chance I went on a trip he was planning, that's if I even returned to England. I wonder where the trip was?"

"Who is Letty?" I ask curiously through the door.

"I cannot recall. Probably a daughter of a friend of my mother's."

"Oh." I strive to maintain an air of nonchalance, even as a strange wave of jealousy floods my thoughts. I'm curious if this Letty person could be a past lover. "Maybe we should try to find out more about her?"

"I'm not sure how that would be useful."

"Well, it's clear that she was someone important to you. Since you're having a hard time remembering people and your relationships with them, maybe we should try to find out more about your neighbors," I say, trying to be sensitive to his struggles with memory, all while not sounding too intrusive. "Your family's murder could have a connection with other families living in these mansions."

He's silent for a moment. I'm wondering what he's thinking behind the bathroom door.

"I suppose that couldn't hurt," he finally agrees. "I'll continue looking through the bag. There are still a few more items I need to go through."

The water in the bathtub is starting to get cold, and my fingers look like wrinkled prunes. I climb out of the tub, careful not to slip on the wet floor. I let my hair air-dry into its natural waves and step into a clean pair of underwear. I look around for my clothes but realize I must not have brought any dry ones into the bathroom. Aunt Ruth's silk, feathered evening robe from Saturday night hangs on a hook behind the bathroom door. I let out a sigh and wrap myself in it, feeling ridiculous in the frilly frock. I open the door and walk into my room.

Will is reclined on the bed, reading more letters from the bag. He seems deep in thought, so I make my way over to sit beside him. When he looks up and sees me in the robe, he sits up quickly, looking shocked and a bit uneasy.

"Did you find anything else in the letters that could be helpful?" I ask.

"Um"—he shuffles through some pages—"I think so."

I pick up one of the letters and start to read it, trying to ignore the embarrassed look on Will's face. As I scan the paper, I see he's still wearing the same awkward expression.

"What's the matter?" I ask, lowering the letter.

"You're… you're wearing a… a dressing gown," he stammers.

I forget that Will is from a different era. I find his flustered reaction hilarious.

"Why are you laughing?"

"It's just a robe, Will. In 1985 it isn't a big deal to wear them in front of people. But if it makes you uncomfortable, I'll put on some sweats."

"No. No, it's fine," he says, still looking bashful. "It's just that, in my day, women who wore those in front of men were usually... anyway, see what you think of this."

He drops the open journal and leaves the bed to search for more materials to read. On the open page, there's an ink drawing of a coin, with a carving of a jaguar in the center. Underneath the picture he has written:

I found a chipped, gold medallion while digging near a teocalli by The Pyramid of the Moon, using my trowel and brush. Fransisco explains that the jaguar, or ocelotl, was believed to be a beast of the stars and the earth to the Teotihuacan's. They believed the jaguar is able to move between worlds and see at night. Dr. Wallace is pleased with my discovery and we will take the medallion back to Oxford for more research. I feel like we are making progress.

Interesting… an artifact with references to magical symbols. I examine the locket around my neck.

"Could a green beetle have any symbolism in the Teotihuacan culture?" I ask Will, who is rummaging through some newspaper clippings.

"I'm not sure, but it's definitely possible I found the necklace on that trip."

I pick up the letter that Will was reading, addressed to his mother from the Duchess of Kent. The Duchess is concerned about Will's lack of interest in courting her daughter, Lady Georgiana. She writes that Will's attitude toward Georgiana at a recent dinner party was cold and indifferent. A giggle escapes me. It seems the dinner party designed for matchmaking purposes was more of a misery for Will than a triumph, given that he managed to come across as aloof and uninterested to Lady Georgianna.

Will sits on the floor, bent over the materials we found. The light from the fireplace flickers across his face, accentuating the shadows that playfully tease his strong features. Mesmerized, I watch his fingers gently comb through his raven hair while his eyes study a faded piece of paper. He's a very attractive guy—if you're drawn to someone who exudes an aura of confidence and mystery, of course. I find myself wondering if he ever had a lover in his mortal life and if he would even remember her now.

I head back to the bathroom and change into sweatpants and a T-shirt. When I return, I find Will lying on the bed with his head propped on a pillow.

"Much better," he says, approving my more modest outfit.

I let out a chuckle that's filled with amusement as I settle beside him. Casually, I gather my hair and sweep it to one side, idly toying with the tips. As I glance at him, I catch him giving me a curious look—

the kind one gives when attempting to remember where they've seen someone before. Uncertain of how to decipher his intent, I am at a loss, questioning the meaning behind his lingering stare.

"What's the matter now? Is my T-shirt too revealing?" I joke.

"No," he says somewhat seriously. "You remind me of someone sometimes."

"Maybe we met in my past life," I say playfully.

His eyes squint. "Maybe."

With a quick glance, I spy a handful of items resting inside the open boot trunk. Intentionally, I steer our conversation toward the intriguing objects.

"Were these your items?" I ask. I arrange the contents of the small trunk. I find an empty water canteen, a lone woman's glove, a pair of dirty men's Victorian trousers, an aged ticket of some sort, and a weathered book among the items.

He points to the side of the trunk where a faded name tag is stitched into the leather. "I think so. My name is written here, so it must be mine." He turns his attention to the collection, looking over the lone woman's glove. "Feel free to examine the items."

I look at the piece of paper in my hand. It's a first-class ticket for the SS Aurora Majesty passenger ship. The ink has faded significantly due to water damage.

"I can't make out the date, part of it has been washed away," I say.

He examines the ticket. "I can't seem to make out a date either."

"It looks like the ship was leaving the Port of Southampton in England and was sailing to New York," I say, peering over him. "Do you remember why you were in Southampton, England?"

"My guess is it's an old ticket from one of the times I came back from school," he answers. "But maybe we can figure out more by examining what we've found."

I pick up the first-edition book from the trunk called *Journal of the Discovery of the Source of the Nile,* by John Hanning Speke, published in 1863. I remove the necklace from around my neck and look at the green beetle locket.

"What if you found the locket in Egypt?" I ask, holding up the book. "What if that was your next trip?"

He purses his lips in thought as he thinks about the possibility. "Maybe, but I would expect to have more evidence of my travels to Egypt than just a single old book."

I frown. "I still think we should consider talking to Mr. Willoughby."

Will shakes his head. "I think we need to look through more of the contents we gathered from the house."

"Just think about it some more." I yawn. "I'll ask my aunt if she has an old corkboard we can use to organize everything."

He lets out a chuckle. "Sure, but you should really consider getting some rest. How about we reconvene tomorrow?" He rises from the bed.

As he turns to leave, a sense of guilt washes over me, knowing that he'll be returning to his dark, empty house all alone.

"Will?" I call out to him just as he reaches the balcony doors. "Why don't you stay a while longer? You can look through the items some more, or read while I catch up on my homework."

"Really?" he asks, withdrawing his hand from the door handle.

"Of course," I reply warmly, sensing that he might also welcome the company.

"All right," he says, settling himself back onto the bed.

I shift to lie flat on my stomach, cracking open my copy of *Les Fables de la Fontaine.* On the other side of the bed, he stretches out on his back, resting his head on the pillow as he resumes his perusal of the journal. The quietness feels natural and peaceful, with only the sound of turning pages breaking the silence as we enjoy each other's company.

CHAPTER XVI
SEALING THE DEAL

Throughout my morning classes, my mind wanders to the question of when Will had left last night. When I woke up, I discovered he had completed my unfinished French homework and arranged it neatly on my bed while I was asleep under a cozy blanket he placed over me. I find the gesture really sweet.

By lunchtime, I'm no longer the pinnacle of gossip, and I couldn't be happier. According to Julian, who heard the news during chorus practice, two sophomores got caught together in a wardrobe cabinet by the drama teacher this morning. My escapades with Brad seem to be old news.

"Mrs. Patterson saw the wardrobe rocking back and forth and when she opened it—well, let's just say they had some shirts and pants unbuttoned." Julian puts his hands over his mouth like he spilled a secret.

Davy wipes the milkstache from his upper lip. "So, did they bone or what?"

Julian waves his hands dismissively. "They didn't get too far. Mrs. Patterson got to them before it could go past PG-13."

"Aw, man," Wes and Davy whine in unison.

"I guess they never heard about the old shower room on the fourth floor," I let slip. The four of them look at me wide-eyed.

"How do you know about the fourth floor?" Aubrey asks with a smirk.

"I—uh, I heard about it in my American History class." It's impossible to keep my cheeks from flushing, and I hide them with my hands.

"We should go up there sometime," Wes says, winking to Aubrey.

"Ew! Don't make me ralph!" Davy says, looking like he's going to hurl into his carton of milk.

"Sorry, man. Sometimes I forget she's your cousin." Wes slaps Davy on the back, and he almost chokes on his Hostess Pudding Pie.

My mind trails off to my time on the fourth floor with Brad yesterday. I put my finger over my lips to relive the memory of kissing him, wondering if he has also been thinking about it. I glance over at his usual spot in the lunchroom. I watch as he talks to his friends beside him. I love how his animated hands move as he speaks with the same mouth that kissed me yesterday. I find him irresistible to look away from, with his chiseled features and muscular build that make him look like a mythical God, like Apollo himself. My eyes drift down to see his hands locking with Allison's. It feels like I'm being stabbed in the chest with a hot knife. I try to convince myself that his interaction with her is just for show and that he truly wants to be with me, all while feeling like I'm drowning in uncertainty. He turns his head, and our eyes lock from across the room. He sends me a gentle, reassuring smile before returning to his conversation. That one subtle hint is all I need to keep my confidence afloat.

After lunch, Aubrey and I walk to the library for study hall. Aubrey sits at our usual table to catch up on her reading homework while I take the opportunity to look for books on Mesoamerican and Egyptian jewelry. I set my bag down in my chair and approach the library desk. I'm greeted by a kind middle-aged woman.

"What can I do for you?" she asks sweetly.

"Hi, I was wondering if this library has any books on Mesoamerican or Egyptian jewelry?"

She taps her fingers on the desk while trying to think.

"Let me go in the back and check our Dewey Decimal System—

hang tight."

She leaves the desk and goes through a door to a back room. While I wait, I look at a returned book on the desk. It's *The Picture of Dorian Gray,* by Oscar Wilde. It's one of the few classic novels I have never read before. I read the summary on the back of the book:

"The Picture of Dorian Gray" is a story about a youthful individual who is gifted a portrait that embodies his true essence. As his soul is contained in the painting, it bears the aging process instead of him, allowing him to remain young and beautiful. However, as the story unfolds, Dorian becomes corrupted, indulging in a life of pleasure-seeking and extravagance, eventually resulting in his own destruction.

I'm immediately reminded of Will. If Dorian Gray's soul could be placed in a portrait, what if Will's soul is trapped in this necklace? Is something like that even possible? I feel for the necklace under my blouse. I let out a sigh of relief when I find the beetle locket resting just below my neck. I remind myself that *The Picture of Dorian Gray* is a fiction novel written by a famous, imaginative author—but after my recent adventures with a real-life ghost, anything seems possible.

The woman returns holding an index card in her hand. "I'm afraid we don't have much on Mesoamerican jewelry. Also, it looks like one of the books called *Treasures of Ancient Egypt* was checked out three years ago and never returned, but here is my book suggestion." She hands me the index card with the book title and the Dewey Decimal number in the 930's, which is under the category History of the Ancient World. "The books in this section are mostly about the history and archaeology of ancient civilizations, including Egypt. I hope it will be useful. I've been after them for years to update this library with better material. Goodness, our Encyclopedia Britannica collection is from 1960. Maybe if they put more funding into their books instead of their sports—" She catches herself complaining. "Anyway, I hope my suggestion helps."

"Thanks," I say, remaining hopeful I might find some useful information in her book suggestion.

The history section of the library is in the back of the room. It's six bookshelves deep and in the dark due to a couple lightbulbs that haven't been replaced. I scan the shelves for the 930's, and after a few moments of searching, I spot the book tucked between two others on North African history. It's called *The Kings and Queens of Egypt.* I stand on my toes and stretch my arm to reach for the book, but my fingers barely touch the bottom of the shelf. I put my feet on the ledge of the bottom bracket to give myself a lift. Before I can grab it, someone's hand reaches over mine and pulls the book out. Startled, I fall backward, and the person behind me grabs my waist. I turn to face my savior and thank them for catching me.

"Are you okay?" Brad asks, his bright smile shining down on me.

"Never better," I reply, surprised to see him. I straighten myself between his arms, still wrapped around me. The scent of rosemary from his cologne fills my nose, causing my knees to feel weak. "You shouldn't sneak up on people like that," I say playfully.

"You're easily spooked," he teases back. "Egyptian kings and queens, huh? Is that what you're interested in, my little nerd?"

"It's for a project." I reach under my blouse to retrieve the locket and toy with it.

"I haven't stopped thinking about you since yesterday," he says in a quiet, sweet hum.

I bite the edge of my lip. "Me neither."

He looks over his shoulder before placing his hands on the bookshelf on either side of my head, trapping me in. He leans in close, with his lips inches away from my ear. I can feel his heart beating against my chest, strong and steady.

"I wish I could kiss you again, right now." He speaks softly, his warm breath caressing my cheek.

As he stands close, I feel a mix of emotions welling up inside of me. My heart is pounding with excitement, my palms sweaty from my nervousness. The conflicting sensations create a thrill, and it feels like my heart might burst at any moment. Every girl at one point in her life has probably fantasized about being kissed between the stacks of a gothic-style library, and this is my perfect opportunity. I close my eyes, part my lips with anticipation, and draw myself closer. I wait for him to meet me, but my dreams of being kissed in a library are shattered as he shifts away. When my eyes open, I find him anxiously focused on the girl walking down a row of shelves close by.

"We need to be careful," he mutters.

He offers me the book and steps further away.

"This is going to be hard." I pout.

His mouth turns down slightly. "It won't be like this forever," he says. He takes more steps backward as the girl wandering through the shelves makes her way toward us. He blows me a kiss. "See you in class."

I watch as he disappears from the bookshelves. I am finding the secrecy of our relationship both stimulating and frustrating.

I check out the book at the front desk and peer around the room for Brad. It appears he left the library with the rest of his study hall mates. I head back to the table where Aubrey is asleep on an open page of *Lord of the Flies*. I drop *The Kings and Queens of Egypt* book on top of the table. The loud thud wakes her up.

"Am I late for school, mom?" she mumbles, coming out of her slumbered state of mind.

I laugh. "Aubrey, we are in study hall."

She wipes the drool off her chin. "Oh, great. What book did you get?"

I show her the book of *The Kings and Queens of Egypt* with a golden head statue of an Egyptian Queen on the cover. She seems unimpressed. As much as I'd love to browse through the book, I need to finish my math homework. I take the worksheet out of my bag and open my pre-calculus textbook.

"Did you not get much sleep last night?" I ask, pulling out my Casio FX-81 calculator from my bookbag.

She stretches her arms out. "Nah, we had band practice at my house. Wes didn't leave until 2:00 a.m."

It makes me reminisce about my time with Will last night. I think about his comforting presence lying beside me on my bed while we were both immersed in reading. A tender smile spreads across my face.

"Are you ready for your show next week?" I ask her as she fixes her eye makeup.

"Totally." She yawns. "I hope we have a pretty good turnout."

"I think you will."

"Don't feel pressured to come. I know it's your birthday and all."

I shake my head. "I'd love to. Besides, I haven't been too excited about this birthday since my grandfather's passing. It's going to feel different."

"I have an idea!" she exclaims, startling the students studying next to us. "After the show, meet us in the back. We'll get you a cake and do the whole present thing!"

"Oh, I have plans to make a cake with my—uh, with my aunt," I quickly catch myself, not wanting to tell her about Will just yet.

"No problem. I'll sneak in some champagne instead."

"Even better! Do you think you could get strawberry-flavored champagne?" I ask, hoping for my favorite.

"Anything for the birthday girl," Aubrey says cheerfully.

The day feels like it's dragging on, but finally, it's time for the class I have been looking forward to all day: American History. Mr. Ryan greets me as I enter the room, and I can see the TV cart set up again. Brad is already sitting in his seat at the back of the room next to mine. He is talking to Jake in front of him. I feel excited at the thought of spending the next hour with him. Mr. Ryan hands out the worksheets for the day as we are to finish watching the remaining part of the documentary. I am relieved he doesn't mention Brad's and my absence from class yesterday. I sit at my desk and review the fill-in-the-blank questions on the worksheet. My attention shifts when I hear Jake bringing up Allison's name.

"I saw you two holding hands at lunch. Danielle told me you two got together last night after practice. I'm assuming you worked out the fight?"

My eyes glance over at Jake. He nudges Brad and raises his eyebrows suggestively, implying that something more might have happened between them. Brad shushes him, and I see him tilt his head in my direction. I'm sure he doesn't want me to overhear their conversation, so I pretend to be engrossed in the worksheet questions.

"Um," Brad starts, "it's only a Band-Aid. I am thinking about ending it with her."

"Ending it with Allison Ashmore? Dude, are you insane? She's the hottest girl in the school and maybe in all of the east coast. Not to mention her family is ridiculously rich, your dad works for her dad, and—"

"I *know*, Jake!" Brad snaps at him. "You heard about the guy from

Venice, right?"

"Bro, you need to get over that. She slipped up. I'm sure you've had a weakness or two." Jake nods his head toward me.

Swiftly, I avert my gaze as I catch sight of Brad placing his fingers on his lips, emitting a low, cautionary grunting sound from his throat.

"If you blow it off now with Allison, it will destroy your reputation and your dad's career will go down the drain," adds Jake. "You and I both know that. Just keep banging her until you both go to college. I'm sure she'll find someone else by then, then you and your parents will be off the hook!"

Brad sighs. "It's not that simple, Jake."

Mr. Ryan interrupts Jake and Brad's conversation with roll call. I find Jake's advice shallow and disgusting, but I'm also curious how Brad and Allison made up last night. The thought of the two of them intimately together makes me feel a sense of betrayal, even though he warned me he needed time to figure everything out. It never occurred to me that their relationship would carry on physically while I waited. My thoughts spiral down a dark rabbit hole of unwanted imagery of the two of them. I don't know if I can continue seeing him secretly, knowing he will be intimate with her. But if I do, I will have to accept it. It will be a hard pill to swallow.

"Jade," Brad says to me, and I look over.

"Yeah?"

He points at Mr. Ryan.

"Jade Whitney?" Mr. Ryan calls again.

"Here!" I raise my hand.

I turn to look at Brad, who is looking at me across the aisle. He gives me a longing smile and I return with a grin. I know that our relationship is complicated, but I also know I don't want to let him go.

Mr. Ryan presses play on the VHS player and the room fills with quiet chattering. Partway through the documentary, Brad tosses a piece of paper folded up like a rugby ball onto my desk. I unfold the paper and scan the words. He's asking if he can come over to my house after practice. I scribble a response, telling him that I would love that and pass the note back to him. Our hands brush against each other, intentionally this time, as he takes the paper from me. I see the smile stretch from ear to ear on his face as he reads the note. He seems just as eager to see me as I am to see him.

The bell signals the end of the school day. Mr. Ryan wishes us farewell as half the students race to exit the classroom. I remain in my seat, taking extra time to pack up my belongings as I notice Brad is doing the same. Jake sticks around to wait for him.

"You go ahead," he tells Jake. "I'll meet you in the locker room."

Jake suspiciously looks at me and then at Brad. "Okay dude, but don't be too long," he says.

Mr. Ryan waves to both Brad and I as we step outside the classroom. The third floor hallway is empty. Brad holds my hand, brushing his finger against the top of my wrist. There's so much I want to ask him about last night, but I don't want to spoil this moment.

"I'll come by around 5:30 tonight if that works for you?"

"I can't wait." I beam.

He gives me a quick, gentle kiss on the lips and squeezes my hands tightly.

"See you tonight," he whispers in my ear, and we part ways in the empty hallway.

I head down to my locker and find Aubrey, Wes, Julian, and Davy waiting for me.

"Are you all walking with us?" I ask them.

"We're going to grab some burgers and go see *Back to the Future* with Greg and Sarah," Aubrey says, running up to me. "Come with us!"

"We promise Eddie won't be there this time," Davy says. Everyone gives him a warning look.

"I would love to, but—uh, my aunt and I already have plans after school," I say, trying to come up with an excuse. I don't want to tell them the actual plans that I am meeting with Brad. They probably won't be too happy about the idea that I'm spending time with the "king of douchebags" instead of them.

"Oh? What kind of plans?" I wasn't expecting Wes to ask for more details.

"I'm not sure, something about birthday preparations, I think," I say quickly.

Wes raises his eyebrows. I wonder if he can see right through my lie.

Luckily, the other three seem to believe me.

"No worries," Aubrey says, joining the dudes. "We'll be at the Beacon Theater at 6:00 tonight in Poughkeepsie if you change your mind."

"Thanks! You all have fun," I say.

I'm grateful it's not raining for once as I race home to Blythe House. I look downstairs for Nigel or Aunt Ruth and find neither of them. I hear rustling in the kitchen, and I open the door to find Chef Martin and the cooks preparing dinner. All six of them pause what they're doing to greet me with a bow.

"Afternoon, Miss Whitney," Chef Martin says.

"Hello everyone." I'm uncomfortable with their attentive treatment. It makes me feel like royalty. "I was wondering if you knew where Nigel and my aunt are?"

"Mr. Winslow drove madam to Albany for a play rehearsal."

"That's right. I forgot she was involved in the theater there," I say. "Did they say when they'll return?"

The head chef shakes his head. "No, miss. I imagine they will be gone until after dinner as they've instructed me and the staff to only cook for you tonight."

"Thank you," I say to them. As I'm about to leave the kitchen I turn my feet to face them again. "Would it be too much trouble to add a second plate? I will be having a guest tonight."

The chef hides his curiosity with a polite head nod. "No trouble at all."

"Great!" I cheer, skipping out the door.

I run upstairs to clean my room and change out of my school clothes. I find Will's belongings on the floor. I completely forgot he will be coming over sometime this afternoon. Since there's no working phone at Montgomery Manor, I can't phone him to reschedule our meeting. I'll have to tell him when he gets here, I guess.

It takes me close to ninety minutes to straighten my room, put away the items from Montgomery Manor, and work on my hair and makeup. I model three outfits to Toby, who is laying flat on my bed, before deciding on a mauve Giorgio Armani silk blouse and my high-waisted pleated brown trousers. I tuck the beetle locket under the ruby-detailed collar to keep it safe. I look at the clock and it's almost 4:45 p.m.

"5:30 feels like an eternity away, Toby," I whimper. He answers with a loud, deep snore.

Without getting in anyone's way in the kitchen, I collect a snack and return to my room and settle on my bed. Occasionally, I glance out the window anticipating Will's arrival. I tell myself he should be here any minute now, considering that a ghost doesn't have much to do in a day. As fifteen minutes pass without any sign of him, I occupy my time by flipping through the pages of my library book, *The Kings and Queens of Egypt.* I read the book's first chapter. It introduces the first King of Egypt, Narmer, also known as Menes or so historians believe. Menes was thought to be the one who united upper and lower Egypt around 3150 B.C.

"That was a long time ago!" I say to Toby, who is still fast asleep.

I flip more pages to browse a different chapter and stop at Hatshepsut. A photo to the left of the page shows a statue of a sphinx with a beard. At first glance, I assume Hatshepsut a male king, but to my surprise, she was the second female to declare herself Pharaoh. Her husband and half-brother, Thutmose II, inherited his father's title as king after his death, making Hatshepsut his consort. When Thutmose II died, Hatshepsut became the regent of her stepson, Thutmose III, and eventually, they co-ruled. Hatshepsut was the longest-reigning woman of nearly twenty years. She is considered one of the greatest Pharaohs in Ancient Egyptian history. Some of her more notable contributions were her success in establishing a thriving economy through trade, becoming trading allies with the Land of Punt, and creating a flourishing economy for her land. This proved she made a great ruler, regardless of her gender.

"What a badass," I say to myself.

Toby's ears perk up as he wakes from his nap. I quickly set my book aside and get up from the bed to see what has caught his attention. I unlock the balcony door and peer over the railing, looking for any sign of Will making his way up the lattice. To my surprise, there's no one there. I check the time and realize it's almost 5:30 p.m. Maybe Toby heard Brad's car pulling up instead.

I race down the stairs, with Toby trotting behind me. He veers off down the hallway toward the kitchen, no doubt in search of dinner. My giddiness builds as I catch sight of Brad's silhouette behind the stained-glass door. I feel a sudden surge of excitement, and the elated feeling lifts me off the ground. He greets me with his electrifying smile. It's the first time I've ever seen him in denim and a casual knitted-sweater. He looks so suave, like he crawled out of an advertisement for Ralph Lauren.

"Hey, pretty lady."

"Come on in," I say cheerfully.

He leans in and gives me a peck on my cheek, and the feeling is pure bliss. I open the door for him to step inside the foyer. He looks around, his eyes widening as he takes in Aunt Ruth's crowded and eclectic decor.

"Don't mind my aunt's decorations," I say, my cheeks flushing. "She has an unusual sense of style." It's the first time I've felt self-conscious about my aunt's decor choices. I imagine neither his house nor Allison's are decorated with this much chaotic flare.

"It's fine," he says, knocking into the taxidermied ostrich behind him.

"Why don't we go up to my room?"

"That sounds good," he says, a little too quickly.

He follows behind me, occasionally stopping to look at the naked 1930's mannequins in the upstairs hallway.

"Is your aunt all right?" he asks, sounding uneasy.

I laugh out loud. "I know her decorations look like we're on the set of a Twilight Zone episode, but she's pretty cool once you get to know her."

I open the door to my room and to my surprise, I find Will sitting on my bed reading the library book. He looks shocked as well when Brad enters the room behind me. I freeze in place, giving him a concerned *you-should-leave* look. He counters with a cunning smirk and clasps his hands behind his head, assuming the stance of a spectator about to witness a theatrical performance.

"Maybe we should go somewhere else to talk?" I propose in a panic.

"Your room is fine," Brad says, looking around.

My eyes dart toward Will, who doesn't seem eager to move.

"It's just a bit"—I scratch my head—"cluttered."

"Nah, it's great. I like it. It's pretty, like you."

Will rolls his eyes. I blush, feeling the awkward air in the room as Brad unknowingly compliments me with Will present. I anxiously wait for an opportunity when Brad's back is turned and gesture toward the balcony, signaling for Will to make his exit.

"I'm quite content here and thoroughly enjoying myself," Will responds, sounding smug.

"Leave or I'll force you to!" I mouth to him.

Will laughs to himself. "How do you plan on doing that?"

Brad turns to see me talking to the bed. He lifts an eyebrow.

"Ugh. I hate when my dog puts the throw pillows at the end of the bed," I say, in an attempt to thwart my unusual behavior. I take a round throw pillow by the footboard and chuck it at Will's face. Will puts his hands up in surrender.

"All right, all right, I'll go," Will says with a crooked smile.

"Do you want to go out on the balcony?" I ask Brad, opening the door for Will. As Will exits, I whisper to him, "I'll see you tomorrow."

He looks at me and then back at Brad.

"Sure," Will says with a shadow of disappointment in his tone.

Will steps over the balcony edge, gripping the lattice for support. He observes from that vantage point as Brad emerges and firmly grasps my hips, repositioning my body to face him. An unexplainable sense of guilt passes over me, knowing that Will is about to witness the unfolding scene.

"I like being right here," Brad says leaning into me.

I peek my eyes open mid-kiss to make sure Will has left. Not spotting him anymore, I let go of my worries and thoroughly enjoy what I've been longing for since I left school earlier today.

Guiding his hand, I lead him into the warmth of my room. I close the balcony door and draw the curtains. It feels surreal that Bradley Phillips, the captain of the rugby team and the most attractive guy in the entire school, is standing in my bedroom. He intertwines his fingers with mine, delicately tracing the inside of my palm. The sensation tickles, causing me to giggle.

"I haven't stopped thinking about you all day," he says. "I left as soon as I could after practice."

"Really?" I say, rotating the locket between my fingers. "I wish we didn't have to meet in secret."

He stops running his fingers along my hand and lets out a sigh. "I know. I'm still trying to figure that out."

"Is that why you made up with Allison last night?" I ask, even though a part of me regrets it. By asking, I realize I'm admitting that I overheard his conversation with Jake earlier today, but it's important to bring it up. "I heard you and Jake talking about it in class," I confess.

He looks at me with a startled expression, like a deer caught in the headlights. He exhales as if he has done something wrong and is feeling ashamed.

"You weren't supposed to hear that," he says.

"I know, but I did." I pause for a moment. "I'm worried you might keep things from me as you continue your relationship with her."

He sits in silence. I can feel the worry radiating off him. He grabs my hand tightly. "I want to be with *you*. I have to keep up the show for a while so she isn't… suspicious. Which means I'll have to sleep with her."

The jealous pain in my chest rises to my throat, making it difficult for me to speak. "I don't know if I can bear knowing that and wanting to carry this on, Brad."

"Are you giving me an ultimatum? You know my situation isn't an easy decision."

"I understand the consequences if you break up with Allison, but can you imagine how it would feel for me? It was hard enough seeing the two of you holding hands at lunch today."

He lays back on the bed. With a loud groan, he slaps both hands over his face in frustration. I play with the ends of my hair. I wish our relationship didn't have to be so complicated.

"I'm tempted to just do it," he finally says.

"Do what?"

"Break up with her. I don't think I can put on a convincing show even if I tried. Not to mention, there's already talk about you and me."

As much as I'm excited to hear him roll around the idea of bringing our relationship into the open, I worry about his father's career.

"What about your dad's position in her father's company?"

He removes his hands from his face and he stares up at the bed canopy. "Maybe it won't be that big of a problem."

I lay beside him, hoping to give him some comfort. He rolls over on his elbows to face me, moving my hair away from my face.

"What am I going to do with you, Jade Whitney?" He sighs. "You certainly know how to turn someone's world upside down."

I giggle softly and lower my head. "I feel horrible. Maybe it would have been better if I never moved to Grove Hollow."

I feel the strength of his gaze, and I look up at him.

"Screw it," he says, sounding tired and defeated. I don't say anything, waiting for him to continue. "Forget about everyone else. I like you, Jade. That's all that matters, right?" he says, as though he's trying to convince himself as much as me. I hide my smile behind my hand, shaking my head instead. He shifts closer to me and grins, but I can tell how uneasy he feels about the situation. I can see it in his fretful eyes as he looks at me.

"Are you sure you want to do this?" I ask, feeling anxious that he might change his mind.

"Yes, I'm sure," he whispers. He leans forward and his lips rest on mine, like he's sealing his decision with a kiss.

As Brad's hands move around my neck to bring me close, I hear the clink of the beetle necklace shifting under my collar. For some reason, I think of Will's bright-blue eyes. Why, of all times, am I thinking of him now?

CHAPTER XVII

CLUES AND SCANDALS

Brad and I spend the rest of the school week secretly smiling at each other and passing notes in American History class. We decide to wait until Monday to make our relationship exclusive. It will give him the weekend to end things with Allison and tell his parents about us. I'm anxious about how his family, our classmates, and most importantly, how my friends will react when our relationship becomes public. I'm hoping no matter what obstacles come our way, everything will work itself out.

While I've been away at school, Will has been engrossed in *The Kings and Queens of Egypt* book I borrowed from the library. Every evening, we pore over the collection of artifacts we retrieved from the mansion, but we've yet to uncover any new leads on the beetle locket. The items we recovered from the estate—old newspaper clippings about railroad strikes, his mother's party planning notes, and engineering manuals—have all been dead ends.

On the other hand, I finally convinced Will to meet with Mr. Willoughby. We agree to go on Sunday, since I already made plans to spend Saturday with Aunt Ruth.

As Sunday arrives, my nerves tingle with anticipation for the day I'll spend with Will. As the moment to leave and meet him approaches, I catch myself absentmindedly twirling the beetle locket, feeling it's cool metal against my skin. Having learned from my previous mistake of not wearing a thicker coat, I venture out to meet Will in my corduroy jacket, bravely confronting the biting wind that paints my cheeks with a rosy hue.

I see him leaning against the brick wall outside Montgomery Manor's gate, impervious to the frigid air. He greets me with a tilt of his head, and his raven hair cascades away from his eyes. My heart flutters—a feeling that has become all too common since Brad's kiss the other night. Unsure of these newfound sensations, I feel guilty for not thinking more about Brad when they happen. The butterflies are even worse when Will wears a smile, like right now, as he sees me approaching him.

"Ready?" he asks.

"Let's do this," I say, joining him.

We walk down Fairview side by side. I notice Will slows his pace, so my short legs don't have to struggle to keep up with his long strides.

"I discovered something interesting in your library book last night," he says excitedly. "I believe you were right in suggesting that I might have traveled to Egypt."

"Really?" I look up at him, excited to hear more. "What did you find?"

"I came across an image on one of the pages of the entrance to the Khepri Tomb of Nefertari," he begins. "It was a wall painting of a God by the name of Khepri, who had a human body but the face of a black beetle. The beetle was quite similar to the locket on the necklace."

"That means there's a good chance you made it on your trip in the fall with Dr. Wallace after all."

"A very good chance."

"Wow, Egypt," I say, unable to imagine traveling to such an exotic place. "Let's hope Mr. Willoughby has more information on the origin of this beetle."

As we walk through Main Street of Grove Hollow, I find myself falling in love with the town's quaint atmosphere and rich architectural history each day. It's beginning to feel like a place I could call home. I can understand why someone would want to establish roots in this old town.

Will and I stand by the side of the road, waiting for the passing cars to clear before we make our way to Mr. Willoughby's bookshop. I love the smell of bookshops, with their scent of new and old books. If I could, I would bottle it up and make it into a candle so I could enjoy the scent whenever I wanted. Mr. Willoughby's small shop is cluttered and cramped, with books spilling out from every nook and cranny. Despite the disorganization, I find the little bookshop charming all on its own. Will and I look around the store for Mr. Willoughby, but there's no sign of him anywhere.

"We should take a look around and see what we can find." Will suggests. "Perhaps we can find a book on the beetle or something similar."

We divide and conquer, with Will heading toward the history section and me walking down an aisle of books on ancient theology. The shelves range from Scottish folklore to Greek mythology. I stop when I reach a small section on Egyptian gods and goddesses. A black book with gold markings catches my eye. *The Egyptian Book of the Dead.* I feel intrigued and pull it off the shelf to take a closer look.

As I flip through the book's pages, I overhear an intense discussion on the other side of the bookshelf. I peer through the stacks and see a group of middle-school boys having a debate, drinking sodas, and eating candy while sitting on worn-out armchairs.

"Do you think parallel universes really exist? Like how Jack could travel to the Territories in *The Talisman?*" The freckled boy with curly hair asks the group.

"I think so. I mean, there's no way to know for sure, but there has to be a way," the boy with dark black hair and a red puffer vest replies. "Imagine there are kids just like us, living nearly identical lives in some other universe, and we'll never know."

"But what if we *actually* found the talisman and flipped to a parallel universe? And then we meet our parallel twin, our 'twinner', and find out they are psychotic murderers?" The worried kid with thick glasses swallows. "I don't think I could handle that kind of information."

I can't help but laugh to myself. The intense worry on the boys' faces over something so unrealistic is amusing.

"Ah, Teddy, Nicholas, and Benjamin—I see you boys have been reading Stephen King's, *The Talisman,"* an old man with a cheerful voice says to the group of boys.

"Mr. Willoughby, do you think it's possible to travel to parallel universes?" the boy with the thick glasses asks anxiously.

Mr. Willoughby lets out a hearty laugh and rests his hands on one of the armchairs. "Now, Nicholas, I don't see why not. If scientists believe in the theory of time travel through wormholes or 'bridges' of space and time, I don't see why the idea of jumping universes would be so far-fetched. Anything is possible, wouldn't you agree?"

"You mean like the Einstein-Rosen bridge or the Grandfather Paradox theory, but for parallel universes?" Teddy asks.

"Yes, that could be the case." Mr. Willoughby chuckles.

The boys' hopeful eyes grow in size, and they look at each other with excitement. They grab their bookbags and hastily get up from their chairs.

"You boys off already?" Mr. Willoughby asks.

"Yes, Mr. Willoughby! We are going to figure out how to jump parallel universes!" they say in unison.

Mr. Willoughby laughs and shakes his head. "Let me know how it goes!" he calls out to the boys as they exit the shop and ride away on their bikes. I close *The Egyptian Book of the Dead* and place it back on the shelf.

"Mr. Willoughby?"

He turns to face me as I walk out of the theology section.

"May I help you with something, miss?"

"Hi, my name is Jade, sir, and my friend—"

"Ah, Jade, like the beautiful green mineral, believed to have healing and protective properties," he says, brushing his white whiskers. "What can I help you with?"

"Well, sir, my friend Aubrey told me you are a retired professor from Harvard. I was wondering if you might be able to help me? You see, I have this necklace." I unclasp the locket from my neck and show him the beetle. "I was wondering if maybe you could tell me more about it?"

He adjusts his round framed glasses and examines the locket in my hand.

"Follow me into my office."

I follow Mr. Willoughby into a small room at the back of the bookshop. His office is messy with disorganized piles of books strewn across every surface. He moves a stack of books aside, allowing me to sit on the chaise lounge. He pulls out his desk chair, rotates it to face me, and takes a seat. An old Scottish terrier climbs out of a basket from under the desk and sniffs my leg.

"Don't mind my little old man, Comrie," he says. "He's a good boy, but I'm afraid he's not as spritely as he used to be."

"He probably smells my English Sheepdog."

"Ah, I dare say he does." We watch as Comrie finishes sniffing my pants and walks back to the basket. "Do you mind if I take a closer look at your piece of jewelry?"

I hesitate for a moment, unsure if I want to entrust Will's precious necklace to this old man, but if I want to ask him questions, I need to show some trust. I carefully place the locket in his weathered palm. Mr. Willoughby picks up a magnifying loupe from the desk and brings the beetle locket closer to his face.

"Where did you get this remarkable piece of jewelry?" he asks, turning the beetle around in his fingers.

"I—It's a family heirloom." I hate lying, but if I were to tell him the truth about where I found it, I might not be able to get it back.

"Fascinating, simply fascinating," he remarks and continues to inspect the necklace.

"I think it's a locket. If you look closely, you can see that it looks like it could open up between the beetle's wings."

"Yes, I dare say you are right about that." He uses his thumbs to try and pry open the wings, but they don't budge. "You said this is a family heirloom?"

I am nervous that he has caught on to my lie. "Yes, sir. My great aunt gave it to me," I say, trying to keep my voice steady.

"Well, this might be one expensive heirloom. What you have there is a scarabaeid beetle. Ancient jewelry isn't my department, but if I trust my gut, I would say that is a very old scarab." He gently places the necklace back in my palm.

"A scarab?" I ask, my curiosity piqued.

"Believe it or not," he says, picking up his wooden pipe and lighting the tobacco inside. He takes a few puffs. "It's a dung beetle!" He laughs to himself. "Scarabs are a very well-known symbol in Ancient Egypt. They were often used in amulets, jewelry, and other items. In fact, a very good friend of mine who works for Stuard's Auction House in London helped the Metropolitan Museum of Art retrieve more information about some Egyptian jewelry pieces a couple of decades ago. I remember him telling me about a blue scarab ring with the names of the joint rulers Thutmose III and Hatshepsut inscribed on the underside of it."

"I just learned about Hatshepsut. She was the oldest reigning female Pharaoh."

He nods. "The museum bought the ring in the 1920's from Lady Carnarvon." He shakes his head and laughs. "My friend wanted it so badly for his personal collection, he would have *killed* for it! He obsessed over the ring for weeks. The piece could swivel, so one side was a beetle, and when flipped over, the underside could be used as a seal on documents."

"Like a signet ring?" I say, thinking of Will's signet family ring.

"Exactly." He smiles behind his pipe. "You would make an excellent historian, Miss Jade."

I grin. "So, why a dung beetle? Why not something more like a butterfly or dragonfly?"

He puffs on his pipe and exhales a plume of smoke. "The dung beetle was a big deal in ancient Egypt," he says. "It was linked to the sun god Khephri, who symbolized rebirth and all that jazz. The beetle was seen as a symbol of the circle of life, like the sun. And let's not forget how strong it was—it could roll a ball of dung that was way bigger than itself. The Egyptians thought that was pretty fascinating. They even saw the dung ball as a metaphor for the world. Very poetic, don't you think?"

"I guess so," I say, even though I don't find anything related to dung romantic. I feel lost and confused about why this beetle locket is essential to Will's life. What if it's just a piece of jewelry and nothing more? I'm starting to doubt this mission, but Will said his life depended on it. I am trying to understand why.

"Is something else on your mind, Jade?"

"I'm having a hard time understanding why a beetle locket would be so important," I answer.

Mr. Willoughby raises an eyebrow. "The importance would depend on whether the person the locket belonged to was alive or deceased," he says and I feel a cold chill trail down my body. "In Ancient Egyptian culture, the scarab was believed to have powerful regenerative abilities. You see, they believed the sun died and was reborn every day. The scarab was seen as a symbol of rebirth and resurrection in the afterlife. Therefore, the locket would serve a greater purpose once they've died."

"So, what you're saying is, it's kind of like a talisman, used to transport you to a parallel universe—only this one in particular is the afterlife?"

He laughs, causing a cloud of smoke to billow out from his nostrils. "Exactly!"

"Thank you, Mr. Willoughby, I appreciate any information I can get on this locket."

"I hope my knowledge can be of some use," Mr. Willoughby says. "I would be happy to reach out to my friend, the one who works for Stuard's in London. If you'd like, I can send him a couple photos of the scarab and see if he can find out more information for you."

I grin. "That would be wonderful!"

"Wait here, I'll go grab my Polaroid."

He opens the door and exits the office. I see Will wandering around the shop looking for me. I let out a whistle, which wakes up Comrie, and I wave to Will.

"Why are you in here?" he asks.

"I'll fill you in later," I whisper.

We both hear Comrie growl from under the desk.

"Oh Comrie, calm down," Mr. Willoughby says, coming back into the office with his camera. I give him the locket.

"Jade, are you mad? I agreed we would come here to ask this man questions and questions *only,"* Will cries out in alarm. "Do not give the locket to this man. We don't know if we can trust him!"

I ignore Will's comment, as there's no way I could answer him in front of Mr. Willoughby. Mr. Willoughby sets the locket on his desktop and snaps a few photos. Will breathes impatiently. I'm sure he's anxious for me to explain what is going on.

"There, that should do the trick. I will send these through the post tomorrow. Come back in a couple of weeks, and I should have more information regarding your heirloom."

"You told him it was an heirloom?" Will asks.

"Thank you, Mr. Willoughby. For all of your help." I shake his hand.

"It was my pleasure."

Will moves out of the doorway to give space for me to leave the office.

"One more question, if you don't mind?" I pause before leaving. "Your conversation earlier with the boys, do you believe it's possible one could time travel?"

He takes his pipe out of his mouth and grins. "Like I said, anything is possible."

Will asks me an endless stream of questions as we leave the bookstore. I steer us down Artist's Alley to get some privacy from the busy sidewalk. I do my best to retell the information I received from Mr. Willoughby. He's quiet and listens closely as I talk.

"So, you think this necklace is some sort of cursed relic with magical powers?" his eyebrows pull inward.

"I know it sounds ridiculous, but Mr. Willoughby said the Ancient Egyptians believed it had regenerative powers and that the dead needed the scarab to be reborn in the afterlife," I explain again, all in one breath.

"Then why am I a ghost that never passed over?"

"I don't know," I admit.

"Hypothetically, if what you're saying is true, then how would I use it to pass over to the other side?"

"I don't know that either." I slump against the painted wall. "Maybe his friend in London might have some information for us."

Will's face droops in concern as he sees how overwhelmed I am.

"Let's take a break for today," he recommends.

I let out a sigh. "But we're so close."

"We can keep searching again this week."

"Maybe we should lay out all of our findings and take a step back to process it all," I suggest, trying to keep a straight face while looking up at him. "I still need to ask my aunt about the corkboard for my conspiracy board idea."

I was expecting him to laugh again at my idea, but instead his head tilts and nods slightly. He maintains eye contact with me as he gives me a faint smile. "Sure, we can do that if that's what you want to do."

"Definitely," I say, swallowing hard to suppress the fluttering butterflies in my stomach.

When we return to Blythe House, Will sticks close behind me, careful not to bump into anything. We find Aunt Ruth sitting at the table in the conservatory, throwing her crows leftover muffins from brunch. As usual, she holds a cocktail in her hand and a cigarette in the other.

"Come to join the crows and me for happy hour?" She hiccups and takes a sip of her cocktail.

"I think she has been drinking for longer than an hour," Will remarks.

"No, thank you, Aunt Ruth," I say, trying not to laugh at Will's comment. "I was wondering if you had a corkboard I could use?"

"Hm." She taps the filter-end of her cigarette, scattering ash over the ashtray. "If I did, it would probably be in the attic."

"We have an attic?" I ask, surprised.

"Of course, dear. Where else would we store party decor?"

"Great! How would I get there?"

Aunt Ruth rings the bell next to her cocktail. Not more than a minute later, Nigel walks into the room.

"Yes, madam?" he pants, wiping the sweat from his forehead.

"Nigel, please show Jade how to get to the attic."

He bows to her. "Certainly, madam. Follow me."

Will and I follow Nigel through a door between the U-shaped staircase that I had never gone down before. The long, ornate hallway leads to a pair of gold double doors. Instead of going through them, we stop at a small door camouflaged by wainscoting panels. He fiddles for the appropriate key, and it opens.

"Where do those gold doors lead to?" I ask Nigel.

"To the ballroom, miss."

"We have a ballroom?"

"Of course, miss. Every old house on Fairview Avenue has a ballroom," he says, as if offended by the question. "If you go through this door, and up the staircase, it will lead you to the attic," he explains, handing me a brass key.

"Thank you, Nigel."

After Nigel leaves, we make our way up the stairs to the attic. By the time we reach the top, I am out of breath and need to take a break. Will offers to unlock the door, but it's stuck. He braces his foot on the wall, pulls the handle hard, and it finally opens.

"Wow." I cough as a cloud of dust hits my face. "This place is like an antique shop."

I was expecting the attic at Blythe House to be one of those creepy, haunted-looking attics you see in horror movies. Instead, I get a sense of excitement and mystery at the musty space. It is full of elaborate furniture and intricate antiques with old boxes scattered about. As I look around, I experience a feeling of curiosity toward every object. How many treasures in this room connect to my ancestral history?

"Well, this should be an adventure," Will says, with a hint of sarcasm in his voice. "I'll start at the back if you want to look around the entrance?"

"That's a good idea." I nod to him.

We begin exploring the room in search of a corkboard. I'm careful not to knock anything over as I twist and turn around the fragile items. A brown trunk catches my eye. Written in white paint is the name Clyde Alton Whitney on the lid. My grandfather's name. I lift the top of the trunk and inside are old keepsakes and mementos. Under an antique Steiff teddy bear and a first edition of *The Wind in the Willows* is a folded piece of paper. I open it to discover a child's illustration of a little boy holding a sword at a red-faced monster called "The Beast" with a little girl shivering behind the boy. A smile stretches across my face as I imagine my grandfather doing this illustration. He had quite an imagination.

I hear a rustling behind me, and I turn to see Will undraping a large painting partially covered by a linen cloth. I walk over to him, curious to see what he has found. As the fabric pulls away, it reveals a stunning portrait of a girl seated on a tufted chair. She has long black hair pulled back in a ribbon, wearing an emerald green Victorian dress to match her eyes. Will and I both stare at the painting closely.

"She looks a lot like me."

"The resemblance is very close," he agrees, almost in a whisper.

"I wonder who she is?"

When I look up at Will, who is silent and focused on the painting, I see beside him a chalkboard on an old wooden easel.

"What about that?" I point to the chalkboard.

Will finally breaks his gaze from the painting. "That should suffice."

Before we conceal the girl in the painting with the linen cloth, Will casts a final look at the portrait. We carefully cover it and proceed to transport the chalkboard down a single flight of stairs. Once placed inside my room, we start by gathering the materials. Anything we think could be connected to the beetle locket and Will's possible travel to Egypt, we attach it to the board. I grab a couple of vibrant red ribbons from my grandmother's impressive ribbon collection and try to trace any leads that could connect to the beetle... but there aren't many clues to work with. At the very least, this will help us visually organize and keep track of what we do have.

I ask Will for his opinion, taking a step back to look at the few clues. When he doesn't respond, I turn to him and see that he's leaning against the bedpost with his arms crossed.

"What's wrong?" I ask.

He sighs deeply and scratches the top of his head. "I can't seem to shake that painting out of my mind."

"Really? Do you think she could be an important connection to your past?"

"I'm unsure, but I have a strange feeling that I once knew her."

"I'll tell you what. I'll ask my aunt about the painting and see if I can get some answers for you."

He tips his head and grins. "I don't think I've ever properly thanked you for everything you're doing for me."

"You're welcome." I smile up at him.

I notice his eyes linger on me longer than usual. I can't help but wonder if he's looking at me because he sees a resemblance to the girl in the painting or for some other reason I can't quite pinpoint. Whatever the cause, his gaze makes it challenging to keep my breathing even.

A knock at the door disrupts the connection of our eye contact. It's Nigel.

"Dinner is ready, miss. Your aunt was wondering if you would be joining her?" he asks.

"Sorry, I didn't realize the time! Yes, I'll be right down."

"I suppose I should leave you to eat something." Will says as I close the door behind Nigel.

Will starts for the balcony. I invite him to stay in my room while I meet Aunt Ruth downstairs for dinner. He politely declines, indicating he wants some time alone to think. I understand his desire for solitude. I, too, should take some time to organize my thoughts and prepare for tomorrow, as Brad and I plan to reveal our relationship. Who knows what challenges could come of it? I say goodnight to Will and hurry to change into something less dirty for dinner.

Aunt Ruth doesn't seem too bothered by my delay in arriving for dinner. She continues to smile as she mixes more olives into her martini.

"There she is, the girl of the hour," she says, raising her glass to me.

"Sorry I'm late for dinner." I pull out my chair. "Dinner smells amazing."

"I hope you don't mind, I ordered you the sole meunière."

"Thank you, I'm sure it will be delicious."

Nigel sets a cup of clam chowder in front of me. I don't hesitate to eat a spoonful of the buttery broth.

"Were you able to find what you were looking for in the attic?" Aunt Ruth asks, barely touching her soup.

"Yes, thank you. We—I mean, I found a chalkboard that should work."

"Good." She cheers with a sip.

"In fact, while I was in the attic, I found a portrait of a girl with black hair in a green dress. It was covered by a linen cloth. Do you know who she is? Is she related to us in some way?"

Aunt Ruth adjusts her position in her seat, clearly discomforted by the mention of this person.

"They called her Poppet," she replies with a downcast expression. "She was the daughter of your great-great-great-grandfather's twin brother. We don't like to talk about her in this family."

I am caught off guard by her response, causing me to accidentally drop my spoonful of chowder on the tablecloth. Nigel quickly replaces it.

"Why not?" I press, hoping she will open up and share the whole story.

She retrieves a fresh cigarette from her pack and lights it. She takes a deep drag before saying, "She nearly destroyed the reputation of the Whitney name in every way. After she disappeared, they did their best on damage control and erased her from the family."

I'm shocked by this revelation. "What did she do that was so terrible?"

Aunt Ruth takes another puff of her cigarette and blows the smoke upwards before replying, "She murdered the entire Montgomery family."

CHAPTER XVIII

THE BIG REVEAL

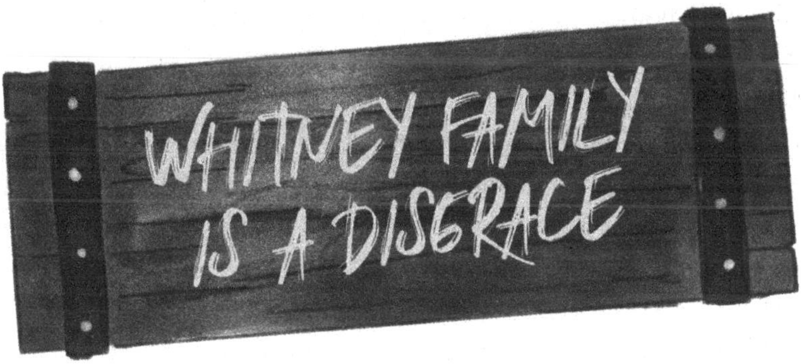

Okay, it's no big deal. It's not like I was the one who killed Will and his family, right? But it was a relative of mine. I could just not tell him, but it would be very wrong to keep something like this a secret. I mean, if someone knew who murdered me and my whole family, I'd want to know. But what if he gets angry and never wants to see me again? I've been biting my nails so hard that I didn't realize they were bleeding.

"I'll worry about this later," I say out loud to myself, dabbing the blood with toilet paper.

I hurry, tying my hair back in a ribbon. Brad will arrive to pick me up in just a few minutes. I grab my backpack from the bed and give Toby a quick pat on the head before heading downstairs. Nigel, who notices I missed breakfast, is waiting for me at the front door with a pain au chocolat. I quickly stuff it into my mouth. As I walk outside, I see Aubrey arrive on her bike with a sour expression. She recognizes Brad's red Ferrari in front of my gate.

"Hey, what's pretty-boy doing in front of your house?" she asks as I close the gate.

"He offered to drive me to school," I reply, feeling uncomfortable with her disapproving look. Brad ducks his head to peer out the passenger's window, and I wave to him. "Want a ride? I'm sure he won't mind."

"No thanks," she says, bitterly. "I'd rather get attacked by a pack of wild hogs."

I respond with a forced laugh, aware that she wasn't trying to be funny.

"I'll walk home with you, okay?" I reassure her.

She lets out a sigh. "Sure. See you at your locker."

I feel disappointed as I watch her pedal away. I wish my friendship with her and my relationship with Brad didn't have to feel so separated. I open the car door and slide into the seat next to him. His smile instantly lifts my spirits, like a delicious ice cream sundae, and his kiss is the cherry on top.

"Hey, pretty," he says, pulling his lips away from mine.

"Hi." I gleam and my cheeks flush. "How did your weekend go?"

He glances down at the stick shift and puts the car into drive. "It went okay, I guess," he says with notes of unease. I can only imagine how stressful his weekend was, considering he ended his relationship with Allison and had to tell his parents the news.

"How did your parents handle the breakup?"

He clears his throat. "They were okay with it."

"Really?" I reply, surprised and pleased. "That's great!"

He gives me a wide, closed-mouth smile. He takes my hand in his, squeezing it gently. Well, that is one less thing we have to worry about.

The ride to school with Brad isn't as nerve-wracking as I thought it would be. I tease him for liking Bryan Adams, whose music I consider very banal and bland. We also joke about our mutual dislike of Mr. O'Connor, who is returning to class today. I mention how intimidated I am by his military-like attitude, and Brad shares that Mr. O'Connor served in Vietnam. Hearing this makes me feel a little more sympathetic toward him.

From Main Street, I can see the school perched on top of the hill. Brad turns onto a winding drive that leads up to the school's parking lot, situated on the side of the building. Huddled around their sports cars are rugby players and cheerleaders, all waiting for Brad. As we pull into his parking spot, my anxiety grows knowing the entire school will soon see me arrive with him. Brad notices I'm holding onto the hem of my school skirt, trying to control my shaking legs.

"Don't worry, everything will be fine." Brad squeezes my hand. "These are my friends, and you're my girlfriend now, so they'll have your back."

"Right. Yeah, of course. Don't worry—got it."

Brad parks his Ferrari and comes to my side to open the door. The athletic crowd is surprised to see me in the passenger's seat.

"Where's Allison?" A girl with red hair asks as I exit the car.

Brad disregards the girl's question and offers a fist bump to the guy beside her. Meanwhile, I feel uneasy and unsure of how to integrate into the group of rugby players and cheerleaders, uncertain of whether they will accept me or not. Two girls whisper to the red-haired cheerleader, prompting her to scurry off toward the building. As Brad chats with his friends, I avoid acknowledging the cheerleaders keeping their distance while they privately watch Brad's new girlfriend. My stomach is churning with nerves as I struggle to blend in with an unfamiliar crowd.

"Are you ready to go inside?" Brad finally asks. I nod nervously, thinking I am as prepared as I'll ever be.

As Brad and I walk through the school, heads turn, and eyes follow us like a royal procession through a village. Although I feel a mix of unease and self-assurance, an underlying discomfort settles within me. It's as if I've grabbed the attention of someone with whom any girl at Grove Hollow Academy would love to be with—except for Aubrey. Her expression turns pale and troubled when she witnesses Brad and me intertwined, holding hands.

"I'll see you at lunch," Brad says as he kisses me on the cheek and glowers at Aubrey, who responds with disdain by narrowing her eyes.

"Lower the heat," I whisper to her.

"Sorry, old habits die hard."

I shake my head as I open my locker. "Look, I can't ask you to like him, but can you at least try to be cordial? It would mean a lot to me."

"I will if he does." She sighs.

"Good."

"Hi, Jade," a girl I've never seen before says while waving to me across the hallway. As I look around, I notice other students are looking at me.

"He's a great guy if you get to know him," I add.

"Do *you* even know him, Jade? I'm sorry, it's just that I told you about what happened with Julian. Something about this doesn't feel right."

"I love your hair today, Jade," another girl says as she walks past us, causing Aubrey to roll her eyes.

"There's nothing to worry about, Aubrey. You said so yourself, Brad didn't beat him up," I say, grabbing a couple of textbooks.

"I also remember saying he's guilty by association," Aubrey replies.

"That's not fair," I say, slamming my locker shut and hugging my books. "He's not like that."

"I just don't want to see you get hurt, that's all," Aubrey says, shifting her weight to the side and bringing her hands to her hips. I know she means well, but I hate feeling pulled in different directions.

"I'll be all right," I say, smiling to let her know I appreciate her concern. "You're a really good friend, Aubrey. I don't want our friendship ruined over this."

"Hah, it's going to take a lot more than Bradley Phillips to get in the way of that," she says, and we laugh. "Does Allison know?"

"I'm not sure. I am a little worried about that," I admit.

Aubrey swings her arm around my shoulder. "As long as you're my friend, and we have Wes and Davy on our side, you don't have to worry about that."

The bell rings, and Aubrey and I say our goodbyes as we part ways. I can't keep my eyes off the clock during homeroom. I'm feeling anxious about seeing Allison's face next period.

I am relieved when I see Allison isn't in French class today. Perhaps she called out sick, or even better, is on a week-long vacation.

Julian passes me a note that reads:

heard about your new beau – congrats.

I glance up at him, but he focuses on the worksheet Madame Gaël handed us on passé composé with the French verb "avoir." I can't tell from his note if he is genuinely happy for me.

My body tenses as the door swings open and Allison enters. She slams the door shut with a loud, jarring sound that makes the whole class jump. I'm afraid to make eye contact with her, fearing the heat of her anger could burn me with just one look. I hear her throw her bookbag on the ground and mutter something to a few people in the back row. One of them says my name, so I strain to listen to their hushed conversation.

"Céline, is there something you would like to share with the class that is more important than your worksheet?" Madame Gaël interrupts Allison's chatter. Everyone except me turns to look toward the back row.

"Sure, I'd love to," Allison responds.

Madame Gaël gestures for her to continue. "Continuez, s'il vous plaît."

"I was just telling Meghan and Anthony that Jade Whitney is a whore who can't keep other people's boyfriends out from between her legs," Allison says, causing everyone's mouth to drop and loud gasp sounds throughout the room. They all turn to look at Madame Gaël, whose face is red as a tomato. The rush of adrenaline makes me feel faint. Although I had suspected something might happen today involving Allison, I try to convince myself this isn't really happening.

"Actually," Julian says, standing up from his chair. The entire room turns to him. "Maybe Brad dumped your ass because you're a massive, vacuous bitch, and no one, not even someone as shallow and of such little intelligence as Brad, can stand to be around you." He starts packing up the stuff on his desk. "Don't worry, I'll see myself to the office, Madame Gaël," he says, slamming the door behind him.

"Céline, you can join him in the Headmaster's office, too. You'll both be getting detention and don't think for a second your dad's going to get you out of this one. I will not tolerate this type of behavior in my classroom," Madame Gaël says, pointing her index finger toward the door.

Allison stops before exiting the classroom. "You made a big mistake, Jade."

"That's enough, Céline! Get moving," Madame Gaël says sharply.

I feel ill. I bow my head, burying it in my hands. I contemplate the consequences of Julian receiving detention for standing up on my behalf. I wonder how Aubrey and the guys will take the news.

By fourth period, I am overwhelmed by the number of people greeting me and showering me with compliments in the hallways. It's baffling how my social standing can change so drastically in such a short period of time, going from the subject of torturous rumors to being treated like a celebrity simply because I am dating Brad.

As the lunch bell rings, I see Aubrey fidgeting with her braided-pigtails at my locker.

"Did you hear the news?" I ask her as we head toward the cafeteria.

"I did, and that asshole didn't even get detention!" she replies.

"What? How is that possible? Madame Gaël said her dad couldn't buy her way out of this one."

"It's totally bogus! They just continue to give Allison warnings, like these little slaps on the wrist, so she can continue to cheer," Aubrey says with a scoff. "And that's not even the worst of it. Julian will probably get grounded by his strict father and be unable to go to the show."

"It's all my fault," I say, shaking my head.

"No, it's not. Julian was defending one of his friends. That's what friends do. I'm sure you would have done the same."

I bow my head and bite my lip.

"You would do the same for one of us, right?" she repeats.

"Of course I would," I say, looking up at her as she wears a proud smile.

"Good. At least Julian will be remembered as a legend for calling Allison out in front of a teacher. It gives us Misfits some street credit."

I try to laugh, but I still feel guilty about the situation.

"It's okay. We'll find a way to sneak him out Thursday. It's not the first time he's been grounded," Aubrey reassures me as we enter the cafeteria.

I grab my food tray and head in the direction of our table. Brad calls my name from across the room and waves for me to come sit with him. I feel torn. On the one hand, I want to sit with Aubrey and the guys, especially after Julian's sacrifice in defending me. On the other hand, as Brad's girlfriend, I'm likely expected to sit next to him.

"Go on," she says genuinely but with a touch of disappointment. "Go sit with your guy."

"I feel bad."

"Don't." She shakes her head. "Maybe you can alternate days and sit with us tomorrow."

I nod. "Good idea. Tell the guys I said hello."

"Will do."

I walk over to Brad's section of the lunchroom in front of the fireplace. I glance over at Allison, who is sitting on the side of the cafeteria with Samantha, Danielle, and the entire cheerleading squad. I'm just glad I won't have to be in close proximity to them. Brad pats his hand on the free spot next to him on the velvet couch. When I sit down, he places his hand on my thigh, like he used to do with Allison.

Aside from Jake, I don't recognize any of the guys. Brad proceeds to introduce me. It seems like a majority of them are rugby teammates. I feel awkward and unsure of what to say to Brad and his friends, so I do the first thing that comes to mind and comment on the decor.

"It's so nice back here," I say.

"It is, isn't it?" Brad agrees with a polite grin.

"You must be thrilled not to have to sit with those freaks anymore," Jake says, grabbing a fry from my tray.

"I'm not sure I understand what you mean," I reply uncomfortably, knowing exactly what Jake means.

"It means you get to sit with the cool kids now," Jake says pompously.

"He's just messing, Jade," Brad whispers and squeezes my leg. "Ready for American History?" he adds quickly, switching topics.

Jake groans. "Shit. I forgot O'Connor was back today. We'll probably have a quiz on the documentary."

"I'll probably fail if we do. I barely paid attention." Brad winks at me and squeezes my thigh again, making my heart flutter.

"Better not fail. We need you, bro. We can't lose to Syracuse on Friday like we did last year," Jake says, chewing on a massive bite of his steak sandwich.

Contemplating how to join Brad and Jake's conversation about last night's practice and the upcoming games, I merely listen in. Occasionally, my mind drifts away with thoughts about what Will might be doing at this very moment. I giggle, picturing him skipping rocks. I wish I could be reading a book with him instead of being stuck at school. I hear boisterous laughter coming from my old lunch table.

Undoubtedly, Davy has shared one of his timeless jokes. I sigh and feel horrible remembering Jake's comment. I didn't defend my friends when they've always had my back. Sitting with Brad elevates me to cloud nine, yet it feels unnatural. His group of friends is so different from mine. Maybe with time, that will change.

"I noticed you didn't eat much," Brad says as we walk out of the lunchroom holding hands. "Are you feeling okay?"

"Oh, I hadn't really noticed," I lie. I fiddle with the beetle locket through the opening of my blouse. "I think it's just from all the nerves about today."

He brings my hand around to the back of him. "Would it make you feel better if I took you out on a date Saturday night?"

I look up at him in surprise, my eyes sparkling. "Really?"

"Sure," he laughs. "That's what boyfriends do, right?"

"What should we do?" I ask excitedly.

"Leave that part up to me." He winks.

I find myself grappling with the idea of confessing to Brad that I have never been asked out on a date. There is a nagging fear that he might see me differently, as if something is fundamentally wrong with me. None of the guys back in Coos Bay found me desirable due to my fisherman-tomboyish look and quiet demeanor. These doubts make me hesitant to open up to him. Still, I'm excited to see where Brad will take me. I bet he knows all the most romantic spots around here.

Two cheerleaders witness Brad kissing me by my locker. They glare at me as if I am some sort of sorceress. They spin around and whisper to one another. Brad puts his hand on my locker, so his arm blocks my view.

"Don't worry about them."

"It's not them I'm worried about," I say, biting my lip.

"Allison? She won't mess with you. Not if you're dating me," he says. The girls walk away, glancing back at us every so often. "They'll come around—the cheerleaders, I mean. They just need to get to know you a little more."

"Maybe..." My voice trails off, wondering what will happen if they don't accept me.

"I'll see you in American History." He leans in and gives me a peck on the cheek. "Don't worry," he adds, walking backward and pointing at me. I force a smile and shake my head at him, grasping the beetle locket tighter with my fingers before concealing it back under my shirt.

Even with Brad sitting next to me in American History, it still feels unbearable with Mr. O'Connor's return to class. As everyone predicted, he gave us a pop quiz on the material from the documentary. I am pretty sure I bombed it.

"Last week you were to watch a documentary about the industrial revolution," Mr. O'Connor says after the quiz. "Miss Whitney."

He walks up to my desk and everyone's eyes follow him. I glance over at Brad, who looks worried for me. My legs bob up and down and my desk rattles with them.

"Yes?" I gulp back air in my throat.

"Your family was one of the founders of oil, is that correct?" he asks, peering down with his dark, beady eyes.

I swallow more air. "That's correct, sir."

He places a new textbook in front of me and turns to walk back to the front of the room. "Oil was a huge part of the industrial revolution. Did you know that the Whitneys were once closely connected to the Beaumont family, a rising railroad company of the nineteenth century?"

"No, sir. I only just learned about my family's history when I arrived in Grove Hollow."

A cruel smile shifts up on Mr. O'Connor's face. "Well, let me help you learn a bit more about your family history." He starts writing on the chalkboard the name of James Hill, Jay Gould, Cornelius Vanderbilt, Collis P. Huntington, Charles Beaumont, and lastly, Arthur Montgomery. "What we have here are America's six major railroad tycoons. Turns out, there's a conspiracy scandal surrounding the Whitney family and the Montgomery family," says Mr. O'Connor as he underlines Arthur Montgomery's name.

"Oh?" I say, holding my breath, hoping he doesn't reveal to the classroom that one of my ancestors killed Will and his parents.

He folds one hand behind his back and uses the other to massage his mustache. "The Montgomery railroad enterprise was in fierce competition with Charles Beaumont, a close associate of the Whitney brothers. Beaumont, ambitious to establish monopolies in various industrial sectors like steel and manufacturing, posed a significant threat to the Montgomery railroad enterprise. Now, this is not an Economics class, but it's safe to say, it is not ethically and legally encouraged for one company to harm another to gain an advantage in any market intentionally."

I feel the sweat beads pour off my head, and I wipe them with the back of my blazer. Mr. O'Connor begins slowly pacing back and forth in front of the classroom.

"However, it was rumored that the Whitney & Whitney oil company was colluding with the Beaumonts. Some think the Whitney brothers were the culprits of bringing down the Montgomery railroad company through sabotage and spreading false information. The news spread like wildfire around the country. Attempting to take down a railroad company through nefarious means resulted in legal consequences for your family's oil company. Did you have knowledge of this as well, miss Whitney?"

"N—no, sir. I did not." I barely get the words out.

"As a result, no one wanted to do business with the brothers of Whitney & Whitney anymore. Railroads and other transport companies, merchants, politicians, even the most notable bank owners... like the Ashmores."

Loud gasps echo through the silent room. I believe Mr. O'Connor enjoys airing my family's dirty laundry, even if it is public knowledge, in front of the whole classroom. He seems to relish that everyone's eyes turned to me and Brad, who looks physically uncomfortable.

"Perhaps if you and Mr. Phillips didn't skip last Monday's video lesson, you would have learned about this." Mr. O'Connor smirks. "I expect you both to write a five-hundred word essay on the importance of the steam engine, the spinning jenny, cotton gin, and the telegraph. If I don't have those essays on my desk Thursday, you both will receive detention."

"But, Mr. O'Connor—" Brad calls out.

"One more word and it's an immediate detention, Mr. Phillips. Now, open your textbooks to page 453."

For the rest of the class, my body remains in a state of fight-or-flight, with my heart racing and my palms sweating. Every so often people glance back at me. It is as if Mr. O'Connor has placed a large sign around my neck, branding me with the message 'THE WHITNEY FAMILY IS A DISGRACE' as a form of public humiliation, similar to the punishment methods used in medieval times.

None of this is even my fault but rather the result of the actions of my ancestors. To make matters worse, I had no idea that my family and Allison's family had such a tumultuous and unfavorable history. A heavy weight settles in my stomach as I remember Brad's dad works for Allison's father. Do his parents know about the Whitney family's connection to Allison's family's business? As I look over at Brad during the class reading assignment, I see that he has both hands on the side of his head, tugging at his hair. I wish I could read his mind and know what he is thinking. Then again, maybe it's best I can't, as I'm sure it's about what just transpired.

As he and I walk out of the classroom, neither of us say anything to one another. I suppose this confirms he was thinking about the assignment or what Mr. O'Connor had exposed about my family. Or both. I stop him before we reach the stairwell.

"Did you know about my family's history with Allison's?" I ask him.

"No, I didn't," he replies, looking down at the floor.

The sight of him avoiding my eye contact makes me nervous. "Is this going to affect us?" I ask as the tears well up in my eyes.

"Mr. O'Connor likes to make people miserable," Brad says, trying to sound hopeful. "No one needs to know about this. Besides, it happened like a hundred years ago." He gives me a half-smile and brings his hand up to my cheek. "The essay will be worth it."

I smile, remembering our time in the fourth-floor bathroom.

"Call you after practice?"

"Okay," I sniffle.

"Don't worry." He gives me a peck. If I had a quarter for every time he told me not to worry, I would be richer than my ancestors.

Aubrey mentions several times as we walk home from school that the boys are not mad about my relationship with Brad. She has some errands to run for her mom, so we part ways on Main Street. As I pass Montgomery Manor on my left, I am reminded of all the information

I learned about the Whitney and Montgomery families. My anxiety creeps in. I'm not sure how I'll tell Will.

"I have been wondering where you've been," I hear someone say above me.

I look up and see Will perched atop the roof of Montgomery Manor, appearing calm and unfazed by the height.

"What the hell are you doing up there?" I call up to him. He gets up and starts walking across the peak of the roof like a balance beam. "Will, get down from there! You're going to hurt yourself!"

"Impossible," he says, steadying his balance with his hands. "Come join me."

"No, thanks. I'd rather not fall off a roof today."

"Come on, join me. You won't fall."

I grumble under my breath and give in. He meets me on the second floor. I follow him up a narrow set of stairs to a dead-end with only a ladder leading up to a round door.

"Ladies first," he says, ushering me forward with his hand.

I hesitate for a moment. I'm not particularly comfortable with the idea of climbing up a ladder onto the roof of an abandoned mansion. Will seems confident and unconcerned, so I decide to trust him and start climbing. When I reach the top, I find myself standing on a flat surface with a low wall around the edge. The view is stunning. On one side, I can see the entire town laid out before us, and on the opposite is the river with the rolling mountains and forests behind it. As the day moves toward sunset, the once-white clouds have taken on a yellow hue. The sun's rays now cast long shadows across the buildings' rooftops, creating a sense of peace.

"This is amazing," I say, taking in the scenery. "I've never been up on a roof like this before."

"I've spent enough time up here lost in thought to fill a century," Will muses, with some honesty in his pun. His gaze falls to the ring on his finger. "This place is perfect for clearing your mind. It's kept me from going insane all these years I've spent in solitude."

"I can't imagine what it must have been like to be alone for so long, Will. It must have been torture for you."

"It wasn't easy," Will continues. "Being alone for as long as I have can make you feel like you're losing touch with reality. There were times when I thought I *was* losing my mind." He laughs wryly and shakes his head. He looks out at the vast expanse of the town before us. "But I suppose even the most idyllic of places can't keep the loneliness away forever."

As he continues speaking, an overwhelming wave of distress and guilt consumes me. Thoughts of my family's involvement in Will's death penetrate my consciousness, leaving me feeling shaky and unstable. I quickly find a seat. I curl up and hug my knees tightly against my chest, desperately seeking comfort. I concentrate on taking deep, slow breaths, attempting to regain control and find relief amid this internal storm.

"What's the matter?" Will asks with worry in his voice, sitting down next to me. "Jade, are you all right?"

"I found out who that girl was in the painting," I pant.

"You did?"

I lock eyes with him. I'm struck by their radiance as they shine with pure innocence. The heavy burden of knowledge that the woman depicted in the painting, an uncanny reflection of myself, held responsible for his tragic end, pushes down on me with immense force.

I open my mouth to reveal my connection with his murderer. "She was"—the suffocating sensation tightens its grip around my throat and chokes the truth—"just a friend of the family's."

There it is. The lie of Poppet forever imprisoned inside me, causing the shame in my chest to intensify.

"A friend of the family's?" Will repeats. He raises an eyebrow.

"Yep," I say, shifting my eyes elsewhere and tucking my hair behind my ear. "My aunt didn't have any more information than that."

I peer through the opening of my hair at Will to gauge his reaction. I find myself questioning if the expression on his face reflects more skepticism than surprise.

"What a shame," he utters with a somber undertone. "Well, it appears the mystery has been solved."

He lies down on the roof with his hands behind his head as a pillow. I lay beside him, fiddling with the beetle nervously.

"Any other concern plaguing you?"

I stop playing with the locket. "No, why do you ask?"

"Are you certain?"

As his look shifts toward me, I redirect my gaze to the sky.

"Yep, all good." I let out a forced chuckle. If I don't relax soon, I fear Will will suspect something, as I'm not entirely convinced he bought into my lie.

I make a deliberate effort to shift my thoughts, directing my attention to the fluffy cumulonimbus cloud drifting by. I am grateful for his decision to stop probing for additional details, granting me temporary peace.

Unconsciously, I begin rotating the beetle necklace in my hand. I can't bring myself to confess the truth. Not just yet. We stand on the ridge of uncovering more about the necklace, and I want to ensure everything runs smoothly...

...Or, if I'm honest with myself, I don't want to lose him.

CHAPTER XIX

MAKE A WISH

Halloween has always held a special place in my heart, not just because it coincides with my birthday—or my love for the spooky stories and the traditional orange and black decorations—but because of the magic surrounding the holiday.

The crispness of the cool air and the overcast, gloomy sky create an ideal atmosphere for this enchanting day. Grove Hollow looks ready for Halloween with their festive shop window displays, jack-o-lanterns, and hay bales aligning the street. I lower the car window, allowing the smell of autumn leaves blended with the comforting scent of pumpkin spice from the nearby cafe to waft inside. I notice a cheerful parade of costumed children trailing down the sidewalk, making me smile. There's something truly special about witnessing the excited energy of kids preparing for a night of trick-or-treating.

I see a little boy dressed in a white sheet and two circles cut for eyes. He skips across the street while holding his mother's hand. My heart sinks. I'm reminded of my last conversation with my real life ghost. I feel awful hiding the truth about Poppet. It's been three days since I saw him last. I told him I'd be busy, using the American History essay as a buffer to avoid the pressure of my family's history and secrets, and that I would meet him tonight at Aubrey's show. The irony is, I didn't want to tell him anything to avoid losing him, but now that I haven't told him, I can't seem to face him.

Aubrey had invited me to get ready with her and the guys for the show at The Underground during study hall today. Since Aunt Ruth, Mable, Lolly, and Eileen are away in the city preparing for their annual Halloween party, it's an excellent opportunity to join my friends. I look forward to spending time with 'The Misfits' as I have not seen them much this week.

"Go figure, the one night Coach's wife makes him cancel practice to take their kids trick-or-treating, you have something planned," Brad grumbles in the car as he drives me to Aubrey's house after school.

"You can always come with me to the show."

"Nah, I hate The Underground. It gives me the creeps." He shudders.

I shoot him a cheeky grin. "Afraid you'll leave liking alternative music?"

"There's no way that's going to happen," Brad says, shaking his head as he turns up the volume to 'Thriller' by Michael Jackson on the radio.

The more time I get to know him, the more I realize how little we have in common. He's into sports, bands like White Snake and Europe, and thinks reading is boring, while I spend my free time reading classic literature, listening to new wave music, and watching Bette Davis films. I hope that the saying "opposites attract" holds true for us.

Brad turns onto Blackhill Road. The road's entrance is marked by a grand iron gate with tall stone walls stretching for miles. Surrounding us on both sides is an old cemetery with rows upon rows of weathered headstones that dot the gloomy fall landscape. Some of the tombstones are so old the engravings are barely legible. There is a sense of tranquility in the old melancholy cemetery that makes it feel like a place of rest and reflection. As Aunt Ruth mentioned, the Blackhill Cemetery is known for being the final resting place of the wealthy founders of Grove Hollow, as well as our ancestors. I feel the goosebumps rise on the back of my neck as I consider the possibility that Will's body might be buried here somewhere. I grab hold of the locket.

"I notice you're always wearing that bug necklace," Brad observes. "No offense, but it's pretty creepy."

I glance down at the beetle, feeling uncertain on how to respond. "I like it," I say, clutching the beetle tighter in my hand. "It's important to me."

"Okay," he responds, stretching out the word and shaking his head. "If you prefer that over diamonds, then it's fine with me."

I give him a joking side-eye. A smile breaks as he winks at me.

As we continue down the road, we come to an old one-room church at the cemetery's edge. There's a small stone house next to it, with a tarp covering the roof and a collapsed porch. I recognize Wes's car in the driveway. This must be Aubrey's house.

"Geez, what a dump," Brad lets slip.

"Be nice." I frown. "Aubrey's my friend."

"Sorry. Well, I think it's best if I don't walk you to the door," he says as we both see Aubrey looking out at us through the upstairs window. "But before you go—" He reaches into his coat pocket and pulls out a rectangular present.

"What is this?" I ask.

"What kind of boyfriend would I be if I forgot your birthday?"

I'm giddy as I unwrap the rose-patterned paper. It's a coral-colored box from Faberge perfume with the word 'Babe' written in a gold circle. I lift the gold bottle to my nose to smell the musky scent.

"I got it for you because you're my babe now," he says.

I chuckle at his cheesiness and spray some on my wrist. "Thank you, I love it."

He leans in to kiss me goodbye. I feel his lips press against mine and it's clear neither of us want the kiss to end. His hand moves up my thigh. I jump when it slips under my school skirt and reaches the hem of my underwear. I quickly pull away.

"I better get going!" I exclaim, grabbing his gift and putting it in my bookbag.

"Sure," he replies, looking awkward. "Everything okay?"

"Yeah, of course," I say, trying to sound casual. "Thanks again for the birthday present. I'll see you tomorrow!" I give him a peck on the cheek and exit the car.

As he reverses out of the driveway, I wave goodbye to him, conscious of my flustered state. I'm certain he must have been surprised by my behavior. However, the prospect of being intimate with Brad hasn't crossed my mind in great detail until now. The idea makes me nervous, given that I've only just experienced my first kiss not that long ago.

I walk onto the porch and knock on the door. A petite woman with a massive perm, dressed in an oversized sweatshirt and Lycra leggings, greets me. I assume she must be Aubrey's mom, and she invites me inside. I find the scent of laundry detergent and smoke from the woodstove comforting—it transports me back to the Coos Bay shack with my grandfather. I hadn't realized how much I miss this smell. I feel a burn in my throat as it travels to my nostrils and the tears pool under my eyelids. I've thought of my grandfather off and on all day and I miss him terribly. I wipe my eyes, hoping her mom won't notice their shininess.

"Don't mind the mess," she says, gesturing to the half-folded laundry on the couch.

"No, it's great." I sniffle.

"Aubrey and the boys are upstairs," she says with a smile.

When I get to the top floor, I follow the sound of music and the beeping of a Nintendo to a room down the hall.

"Jade!"

Aubrey leaps over Davy and Julian's Nintendo controller cords and gives me a big hug. Her heavy makeup, daring tight shorts, and ripped T-shirt revealing a black bra, all contribute to her rebellious punk rock image.

"Come in! I'm finishing Wes's makeup. I'll do yours after Davy's," she says.

Wes is wearing bold, androgynous makeup and a black stripe down the center of his face. It looks perfect as it accentuates his Victorian-military jacket, complete with epaulets on the shoulders and army boots worn over his leather pants. He looks like a true new wave musician.

"Julian, you made it." I give him a hug. "Your dad won't find out you left?"

"He thinks I'm in bed with a headache." He puts his finger up to his lips. "Plus, he and my mom are attending the Halloween party tonight at Town Hall. They'll never know I left."

"Ah." I laugh. "Great idea."

"Jade, did you bring a change of clothes?" Aubrey asks as she starts teasing Davy's mullet.

"I thought you said I could wear street clothes?"

"I said dress street—like punk and grunge. Our school uniform is hardly streetwear!" She chucks back a laugh. "Look in my closet and find something to wear."

I open Aubrey's closet door, covered in concert posters, and sift through her collection of black, studded, and torn clothes. In the far back, I find a black strapless dress with a bustier top and a black mesh layered flouncy skirt. It's the only thing she owns that I'd feel comfortable wearing.

"How about this?" I ask Aubrey.

"I'm getting Madonna vibes," Julian says with a theatrical nod.

She looks up from applying eyeliner under Davy's eyes. "Totally bitchin. There's a bathroom across the hall—go put it on!" she says with excitement.

It takes me a few minutes to adjust myself in Aubrey's dress. The beetle necklace hangs front and center above my chest, drawing the eye to my pushed-up bust. I stare at myself in the bathroom mirror and giggle. I've never worn something so provocative.

When I return to the room, I receive whistles from the four of them, and I blush. Davy has finished his makeup and is now dressed in a tight tailored suit with a Baroque bow tie.

"Sit down, birthday girl," Aubrey says, motioning to her vanity chair. "Julian's going to help me with your hair."

"Not too edgy," I caution them both. They exchange sneaky smiles, and it makes me nervous.

Julian transforms my hair with a few tugs of a comb, a spritz of hairspray, and a plethora of hairpins, while Aubrey works on my face. When they spin me around to reveal the final product, I'm surprised by how much I enjoy my smoky, sultry look and fanned-out waves. Davy and Wes stand alongside Aubrey and Julian. As I look at all five of us in the mirror, we could almost fool anyone into believing we are a legitimate new wave band.

At around 9:30 p.m., Wes parks the car on the side of the street, and we make our way to Mr. Willoughby's bookshop. Aubrey, Davy, and Wes go around the back to help load their equipment into the building. Julian explains we need to buy tickets to get in, so we stand in the long queue in Artist's Alley with the rest of the concertgoers.

Julian talks with the edgy guy in front of us, and I scan the crowd for Will. In a sea of punk rockers, a man in Victorian-style clothing should stand out like a sore thumb, but I don't see him anywhere. He's probably just running late.

Julian and I find things to talk about while the line crawls, mostly about the challenges of adjusting to Grove Hollow Academy. Having a friend who understands the struggle of trying to fit in at such a prestigious school feels like I'm less alone.

"There's one other thing I wanted to talk to you about," Julian says as we get closer to the bookshop's entrance.

"What's that?" I ask.

"Well, Aubrey mentioned you've been stressing about my feelings toward you dating Brad. Is that true?"

"Oh," I say, not prepared for his question. I sigh. "Yes, that's true."

"I really don't mind that you're dating him."

"Really?"

"Of course. I'll support whoever you choose to date. Same with the others."

"Julian, I feel terrible about what happened to you Monday with detention. I also feel guilty dating Brad, especially after what happened to you."

"I'm not a fan of the guy, but I know what it's like to want to date someone no one agrees with," Julian says, looking at the edgy guy in front of us. "Sometimes, we can't help who we like—even if people disagree."

I am overwhelmed with happiness, and a little relieved, as I realize the depth of my feelings for my new friends and their unconditional acceptance of me. I throw my arms around Julian and hold him tightly. Both of us take a moment to wipe away the tears of joy from our cheeks.

After thirty minutes of waiting, we make our way to the back of the bookshop. I'm so focused on looking around for any sign of Will that I don't realize it's our turn to buy tickets. A bouncer in front of a tall bookshelf takes our money and checks our IDs. Once we're cleared to go, he pulls down Arthur Conan Doyle's, *Hound of the Baskervilles,* and the bookshelf slides away to reveal a hidden set of stairs leading down into a cellar. Will was right—this must have been a speak-easy back in the day.

The music gets louder as we make our way down the stairway. Alternating red and blue lights flash around us. The music hall is much bigger than I had expected, about the size of an Olympic-sized swimming pool. The 1920s Art Deco interior has been well-preserved. The mahogany bar looks unchanged, displaying rows of liquor bottles. On either side of the room are nooks with booths embedded into the wall, separated by black curtains for privacy. Portions of the gold and black wallpaper, authentic to the decade, are worn away and reveal the red brick behind it. I pass a few people retiring from dancing and sitting on tufted couches.

"Hey, sweetie, want a seat next to me?" a girl asks, shifting her body to the side.

I shake my head, as we press our way through the tight crowd toward the dance floor. I don't see Aubrey and the guys performing on stage—a different band is playing.

"Where's Moxie Youth?" I yell over the noise to Julian.

"They are playing after this! This is just an opening band!" he yells back.

I follow Julian to the bar—he seems to know the bartender well enough to sneak us an alcoholic drink. Meanwhile, I'm standing on my tiptoes in Aubrey's ankle boots, searching the room for Will. As I scan the crowd, I begin to accept that Will must have forgotten about my birthday. Disappointment fills me. It's all my fault. Maybe he would have remembered if I hadn't avoided him in the first place.

"Who are you looking for?" Julian notices as he hands me a gin and tonic. I take a sip. It tastes sort of like a Christmas tree.

"Me? Nobody. I'm trying to get a better view of the band!"

"Let's move closer to the middle." He nudges me away from the bar.

We spot the edgy guy Julian was talking to earlier. He turns to give Julian a look that seems to say he wants to dance. I can tell by Julian's body language he wants to accept the invitation.

"Go for it," I say.

"No way, I'm here with you tonight." He throws his arm around my shoulder but peers over at the guy again.

"Julian, he keeps looking at you," I tell him.

"But it's your birthday."

"I'll be fine." I cheers his cup with mine. "Go have fun."

He kisses me on the cheek, like a giddy schoolboy, and goes over to join the guy.

I finish my drink, welcoming the gentle buzz of the gin just as the opening band finishes their last song. The staff quickly sets up Moxie Youth's equipment, and the lights dim lower. A blue light shines on the stage as Wes, Davy, and Aubrey walk out to perform. The crowd claps and cheers in excitement.

Instead of picking up the bass guitar, Aubrey stands behind a synthesizer keyboard and plays a low, slow, moody tune. The dance hall is silent as we all take in the chilling melody. As she continues to play, Davy starts on the drums. I recognize the alluring sound of a train horn on Wes's guitar as the introduction to "How Soon is Now" by The Smiths. No one moves or makes a sound while the three of them play their dramatic rendition.

My heart pounds with a confusing and unnatural fervor as I see Will standing in the shadows. He leans against the wall, his arms crossed as he watches the keyboard. The flicker of stage lights create playful shadows that dance on the sharpness of his cheekbones and the contours of his strong face. I find my eyes tracing the path from his long, dark eyelashes that flutter like wings with each blink down the straight bridge of his nose to his full lips, which hold a thoughtful expression. Seeing him casts a spell over my body, leaving me unable to move as I admire him.

Our eyes meet across the bustling dance floor, and I gasp. The flame I've long sensed smoldering within me is suddenly set ablaze. While the surroundings fade into nothingness, it's like we transform into the only stars shining in the boundless void of the night sky. I give in to the powerful pull that forces me to move closer to him.

I rise up on my tiptoes, leaning toward Will's ear so he can hear me clearly. "You're here."

"I am." He releases a slow breath. I swear I can feel it brush my cheek, as a cold chill climbs up my arms.

I lower myself back onto my feet. I'm spellbound by his widening smile that spreads across his face, so close to mine.

"You look absolutely incredible tonight," he says, and for a moment, the ground beneath me falls away.

"Thank you." My cheeks flush, and I tuck a strand of hair behind my ear.

There's a suspended energy in the air between us, and I teeter on the edge of losing myself under his charming gaze. I manage to regain control and pull myself back before getting completely lost in his irresistible eyes.

"So, um, what do you think so far?" I point to the stage.

"This band is very good. I find the young lady playing the peculiar-sounding piano quite fascinating."

"The synthesizer you mean? That's my friend, Aubrey. Isn't she amazing?"

"Very talented. It's incredible to see how concerts have changed over the years," he adds.

"I guess in your day everyone was wearing tuxedos and fancy dresses," I say as we both scan the sea of guests adorned in piercings, tattoos, and mohawks.

"We're a far cry from the prim and proper of the nineteenth century," he says and we mirror each other's laugh. "But I'm enjoying it."

"I'm glad you came."

Will leans in so his mouth is close to my ear. "I wouldn't miss your birthday for the world."

Goosebumps rise on my skin as I break into a wide grin.

The couple leaning against the wall next to us looks on in confusion. Will notices this, too, and I remember no one can see him. I must look ridiculous, talking to a wall.

"We should seek a more secluded area," he suggests.

"Good idea."

I follow him to a dark corner of the dance hall to avoid being seen talking to an invisible apparition.

"I suggest we stand here!" he yells from the more private area.

"It's perfect!" I yell back.

As the band finishes their song, Will and I clap along with the rest of the crowd. Aubrey stands up and takes a bow. She receives whistles from around the room and blows kisses to everyone. Wes greets the audience and announces their next song is an original, inspired by the band New Order.

"It's an upbeat song, so get dancing!" Wes shouts through the microphone and the cheers grow louder.

Will offers his hand, asking permission if I'd like to dance.

"Why, of course, sir," I say, impersonating his British-Victorian-dialect, and I bow my head.

Will laughs. "In my day, you would curtsey."

"In 1985, we do as we please," I say, proudly.

I accept his invitation and place my hand on top of his, even though it passes through his ghostly palm. I move close to him, holding one hand steady above his, while the other I pretend to put on his shoulder. I follow his lead as we dance, swaying side to side.

"You make an excellent dance partner," he says with a funny smirk. I know he is joking because I am struggling to follow his steps. He's lucky I can't step on his feet. I have never danced with a boy before, let alone waltzed with a ghost.

"I don't know these steps," I say.

"You're overthinking it," he replies. "Feel the music and follow my lead."

I do as he says and listen to the music. Before I know it, I'm following the dance effortlessly under his gentle guidance. He sweeps me into circular motions, and all my worries melt away. I don't pay any attention to the confused people watching as it must look like I'm waltzing alone. I want to pretend Will is present and just as much alive, because I can't imagine the dancing ever coming to an end.

He pretends to dip me, and I fall to the floor without his support. We both laugh loudly. He offers his hand to help me, but then remembers I can't grab it and withdraws it.

"What wouldn't I give to have a real chance to dance with you," he says, his words tumbling out. I stand up from the floor, surprised by his comment. "I mean, it would be wonderful to have a dance partner once again," he clarifies, rubbing the back of his head.

As I look down at the beetle locket, I hope it will give Will a chance to live beyond the age of twenty-one and continue dancing into old age. The alternative is too heartbreaking to consider.

"Maybe someday we will have that chance," I say to him.

"I'll hold on to that thought," he replies, his face lighting up with a grin.

In the secluded corner of the concert hall, we continue swaying and twirling, spinning around in circles. My eyes stay fixed on his as we dance. It feels like we've done this countless times before, like moving in and out of a labyrinth of memories and fantasies. With each turn, I feel a sense of comfort and familiarity, and he creates a safe haven where I can truly be myself. If time were endless, I would happily continue dancing with Will forever.

After the show, Will remains close to me as we go backstage with Julian and Elliot, the edgy boy, to congratulate our friends.

"Great job, guys!" Julian cheers.

"You guys were amazing!" I say from the open doorway. Aubrey rushes over and gives me a big hug.

"You really think so?" she asks.

"Absolutely," Julian, Will and I say in unison.

"This is…" I'm about to introduce Will to Aubrey, Wes, and the others, when I remember he can't be seen by anyone but me. "Oh, right," I whisper to him, thankful no one else seems to have heard my mistake. "No one can see you."

Will shrugs. "I suppose I'll have to be content with existing as your invisible dance partner."

Aubrey holds out a small bag with black tissue paper and a bottle of strawberry champagne.

"Happy Birthday from all of us," she says.

"You all are so thoughtful," I reply, taking the bag from her. Inside, I find a mixtape labeled 'Happy Birthday Mix - Love the Misfits,' written in marker.

"It's not much, but we all picked our favorite songs for you to jam out to," Aubrey explains.

"Especially when you want to escape Brad's terrible taste in music," Davy adds. Aubrey nudges him and I hear Will laughing.

"Thank you. Really," I say.

"Jade, we're all going to our friend's Halloween party. Want to come?" Wes asks.

"I'd love to, but it's getting late. I just wanted to say hi before I left."

I say farewell to the crew, giving hugs to Julian and Aubrey. I wait for everyone's back to turn before motioning Will to follow me.

"What's next?" Will asks as we leave backstage.

"What's a birthday without cake?" I smile.

Will and I walk to Blythe House. The autumn moon is hidden behind clouds, casting a dark and foggy veil over Fairview Avenue. We are coming up to Montgomery Manor on our left. I feel chilled by its uncanny appearance, hidden in the shadows.

"Your house looks spooky tonight—like something out of a horror movie. Aren't you scared to live there alone?" I ask.

"Isn't it a prerequisite for a ghost to live in an eerie, abandoned mansion?"

"You're welcome to stay in one of the many guest rooms Aunt Ruth has. That's if you can stand her decorating."

"Thank you, but Montgomery Manor is my home. It's the only connection I have with my family and who I am."

I understand what he means. Even though Blythe House isn't where I grew up, and I've only met Aunt Ruth recently, it feels like home because it's a part of my family's history.

"You seldom talk of your parents or your grandfather," Will says.

I run my fingers along the brick privacy wall. I feel guilty that I don't think of my parents more often than I should, but I'd rather not talk about my family's history right now.

Will sighs. "I apologize if I upset you. I thought since I can understand the pain of losing both parents, it may bring you some comfort to speak of them."

"It's not that. If I don't talk about my parents and grandfather, I don't have to revisit losing them. If I push it aside, I don't have to feel the pain… if that makes sense."

"It does," Will says somberly, putting his hands in his jacket pocket. "But the pain persists and festers within, doesn't it? Suppressing the pain will only lead to emotional and physical problems in the long run."

"Is that why you don't go into your mom's room?" I grit my teeth.

"Wouldn't it be easier to heal if you spent time in there?"

He stops to gaze at Montgomery Manor. I was expecting him to tense up, but instead he looks mournful. "You're right, it probably would."

"Sorry. That was thoughtless of me." I realize some of my own suppressed emotions might be causing me to feel defensive. "Do you miss your parents?"

"I may not recall much of my old life, but I do miss them. How could you not? It's like we are a puzzle, each made up of pieces of the souls of those we love." His eyes are now fixed on me. I sense he is not only referring to his parents.

"I—I think I know what you mean," I stammer, breaking our connection and starting to walk again.

If I could go back in time, I would write down my grandfather's delicious yellow cake recipe, as it was only stored in his memory. I flick the kitchen lights on. I search the pantry bookshelf for a baking cookbook with a recipe for a simple cake that we can follow.

"You've never made a cake before?" I ask Will as I flip through the pages of a cookbook.

"Not that I can remember," he says, examining the toaster oven. "I don't believe I spent much time in the kitchen, as we had our own kitchen staff at the manor."

"Makes sense," I say. I stop at a basic vanilla cake recipe that looks easy to follow. "I think I found one we can try."

Will helps me gather ingredients and we set everything on the long wooden prep table in the center of the kitchen. The recipe says to preheat the oven to 350-degrees, but the kitchen still operates with wood-burning stoves as they did in the early days. I don't know why Aunt Ruth never paid to update the appliances. I'm not confident I can cook this cake in these archaic ovens. I start to panic.

"You look worried," Will examines.

"I don't know how to work these old ovens."

"Not a problem." He takes a couple of logs stacked on the side of the kitchen. He opens the lid of one of the burners, tosses a log in, and lights the kindling. "Done. What's next?"

"Whisk together the flour, sugar, baking powder, baking soda, and salt in a medium-sized bowl."

Will rolls up the sleeves of his linen, high-collar shirt and measures the ingredients into the bowl while I plug in the 1960s hand mixer. When I turn it on, the dry ingredients fly up, and a cloud of white flour mixture blinds us.

"Turn it off! Turn it off!" Will yells.

"I'm trying!"

He places his hand through mine to shut it off. The situation's absurdity overtakes us, and we burst into roaring laughter.

"Let's try a slower setting," he suggests.

With my hands wrapped tightly around the mixer's handle, Will's ghostly hands merge seamlessly through mine to help steady the device. Though I cannot feel his touch in the physical sense, a flood of sensations rushes through my body as he stands close behind me. I hear the gentle rise in his deep breaths as he leans in, his head bending to rest near my cheek. I wonder if he's feeling the same swirling chest vibrations that mimic the rhythmic whirring of the mixer. I add in the wet ingredients, and our hands continue to move in perfect synchrony until the cake batter is smooth.

"Looks like we've got it," Will whispers, his lips close to my ear.

"I think so, too," I reply, my voice unsteady from the thrill of the intense feelings.

We pour the batter into the baking dish, and Will slides it into the oven. Over the next hour, we work together to clean up the mess. While the cake bakes and cools, we prepare the icing. Will remains silent throughout. Meanwhile, I wrestle with a whirlwind of thoughts and emotions, trying to make sense of the intimate moment that transpired between us.

Will insists that I wait in the dining room while he prepares to decorate the cake. I take the opportunity to calm my racing heart. With the bottle of the strawberry champagne in hand, thanks to my friends, I perch myself atop the dining room table. Disregarding the need for a cup, I drink the fizzy liquid straight from the bottle.

"Close your eyes," Will says from behind the kitchen door. I obey him and close them. The door swings open, and the smoke of a candle hits my nose. "Okay, you may open them now."

When I open my eyes, I see that Will has placed a beautifully decorated cake with a single, long, mint-colored candle in front of me on the table. Sitting beside me is a round present wrapped in old newspaper with twine tied around as a ribbon. He hops up on the table to sit across from me.

"First, you must open my present."

"All right," I say, filled with anticipation. I tear off the paper to reveal a full hunter pocket watch. I trace the curve of the case with my finger, mesmerized by the two green moths carved out of jade.

"It belonged to me. I'm afraid it doesn't work anymore."

"It's beautiful," I reply, admiring the case. "I remember seeing one of these moths the night I came to Grove Hollow."

"They are luna moths. You're lucky. They're very rare, especially for this time of year. They are sad, unfortunate creatures, though. They have no mouths to feed and only live for about a week. Their sole purpose in life is to find a mate before they die."

"How tragically romantic," I comment.

Will tilts his head with a soft laugh. "I suppose so."

I open the lid and see that the French words "pour toujours" are written on the face of the clock.

"Pour toujours means—"

"For all time," I say. I look at him with admiration so he knows how much his thoughtful present means to me. "Thank you, Will. It's a beautiful gift."

"Happy Birthday, Jade," he whispers. "Make a wish."

The candle flickers brightly between us. While I know it's unrealistic to believe that a simple birthday wish could bring someone back to life, the flame in Will's blue eyes seems to glimmer with possibility. I close my eyes and silently make the wish.

As my eyes flutter open, an unmistakable transformation happens within me. I watch the warm glow of candlelight paint Will's handsome face. His shoulders move up and down as his breathing picks up. I can't restrain the irresistible power tugging at my core, forcing me toward him. I sense he feels it as he places his hands on the table for stability and leans closer. My heart flaps like a spirited winged creature inside the cage of my chest, trying to break free. The unseen link between us tightens as we draw nearer, intensifying the gravitational pull. Just as our lips are about to meet, I lower my head and blow out the candle.

CHAPTER XX
CONFESSIONS

I cannot believe I let my emotions take over last night. Will and I were on the brink of a kiss, even though it's impossible to kiss a ghost—I think? But my feelings for Will feel real. I haven't decided if I should tell Brad because Will isn't even alive—which makes this all the more complicated.

I am starting to feel like all the lies and secrets I'm keeping are overwhelming me. My life before Grove Hollow was never so filled with drama. I never had to keep details from people, but now I find myself telling small white lies or withholding information on a daily basis. I don't even know who I've become. The burden of it all is becoming too much to bear. I have decided to confide in Aubrey during study hall on Friday about everything—I mean *everything.*

"Hold on, let me understand this. You've befriended the ghost that's haunting you, who lives in the creepy house next door, who was murdered by some girl named Poppet you're related to. You stumbled on a cursed necklace that might help him pass over into the afterlife. And you're the only one who can see him and you two almost *kissed* last night?" Aubrey asks, her eyes wide with excitement as if this is some romantic movie plot.

"Shh!" I glance over at Brad, who is absorbed in his studies at his library table. I unhook my necklace and retrieve the photograph of Will from my bag and hand it to her. "This is the necklace and this is him."

She examines the picture. "Wow, this guy is sexy!"

"You can't tell anyone about this," I implore her.

"I won't," Aubrey promises, but I'm not fully convinced.

"I mean it, Aubrey. Not even Wes."

"I promise, my lips are sealed," she assures me by pretending to zip her mouth shut. "So, what do you plan to do about Will? Do you think he has feelings for you, too?"

I nervously twist a strand of hair around my finger, peering over at Brad again. "I don't know. It doesn't really matter either way. He's a ghost."

Her expression turns serious. "It may be best for you to keep your emotions in check when it comes to your mission with Will. I mean, considering the unpredictability of the necklace and the fact that he's… well, dead."

I let out a staggered sigh, pushing back the tears.

"You're right," I admit, disheartened by the truth of her words.

"I just don't want to see you get hurt," she says, patting my hand on the table.

She's right. The truth is that Will is dead. Regardless of my feelings, there is no future for us, unlike Brad, who is living and real. Despite everything, why am I still shrouded in a web of confusion?

After school, I walk out with Brad, who is dressed in his rugby uniform, to the charter bus in the parking lot. The rugby and cheerleader coaches stand in front of the buses doing roll call.

"Are you sure you don't want me to come to your away game? I can have Nigel drive me to Syracuse," I suggest.

"Nah, don't trouble yourself. It's two hours away and it will be freezing up there," he says. "I have everything set for our date tomorrow. You will love where I'm taking you."

"I can't wait. I've been thinking about it all day."

"Me, too." He takes my hands and brings them to his lips for a kiss.

"Bradley Phillips!" his coach calls out, interrupting the moment.

"I better go. I'll pick you up tomorrow evening at seven," he says.

"I can hardly wait!"

He begins to walk away and then, unexpectedly, turns back to give me a swift peck on the lips.

"Brad, let's go!" his coach calls out again. I blush with embarrassment.

I watch as he boards the bus and disappears from view. The cheer coach calls out Allison's name, and as she's about to climb aboard, she turns to give me a cunning look. I should probably feel uneasy thinking about a two-hour ride with Brad and Allison sitting so close to one another, but I'm surprised by my sense of assurance in our relationship. I feel like there is nothing to worry about.

I plan to take my time walking home from school and reflect on how I should approach the almost-kiss with Will. The memories of last night swirl in my mind, a chaotic blur of strawberry champagne and misguided intentions. I decide it's best to play it cool like nothing happened. If he should broach the topic first, I'll simply pretend it meant nothing. As Aubrey suggested, I must remind myself to keep things platonic with Will…

…Even though the flame of attraction in my heart still burns, no matter how hard I try to extinguish it.

I change out of my school uniform into a cozy turtleneck, a thick maroon skirt, and the emerald earrings Aunt Ruth bought for my birthday. As I'm about to leave to find Will, I discover Aunt Ruth in the study, where she's painting a portrait of Toby dressed as a pirate.

"Would you like me to paint your portrait next?" she asks, beaming with pleasure at my appearance.

"No, thank you, Aunt Ruth. I was wondering, how did you maintain your composure during your romantic affairs?"

She peers over her reading glasses, her eyes questioning. "Caught between multiple lovers?"

I nod sheepishly.

She places her paintbrush in the water glass with a soft clink. "When it came to juggling multiple partners, I treated each one as its own unique experience," she says with dramatic undertones. "Each one deserved to be appreciated and valued for what it was, even if they overlapped in time. But above all, I never lost sight of my own wants and needs and stayed true to myself. It was a delicate tango, but I reveled in it."

"But what if I don't want multiple lovers? What if I just want to be in love with one but can't stop thinking about the other?" I ask.

"Well, my dear, the mind is a powerful thing. It's easy to get confused in the whirlwind of thoughts and emotions. It's important to listen to your heart, too, but to not get lost in it. Take a step back, try to understand what you really want, and let it guide you. But most importantly, enjoy the ride." She lets out a cackle, and I can't help but smile.

"Thanks, Aunt Ruth."

"Need any more love advice?"

I shake my head. "I think I got what I needed."

When I get to the ballroom of Montgomery Manor, I see an envelope with my name on it sitting on the grand piano. I open it to find a note from Will.

Meet me in the garden

-Will

The hidden garden door is slightly ajar. I find Will sitting by the pond with a book open in his lap. His dark hair is tousled and falls across his forehead, partially obscuring his eyes. He is deep in concentration, his strong jawline propped up by one hand as he flips to the next page with the other.

I inhale a deep breath.

"Here we go," I whisper to myself.

He looks up from the pages of his book when he sees me coming and smiles. "I was wondering when you'd be joining me," he says as he closes the book.

I sit beside him, and he turns toward me.

"I hope you weren't waiting long. I stopped to talk to my aunt before coming over," I say.

"Oh? What of?"

"We just talked about my birthday," I say, regretting my lack of a better excuse.

A smile forms on his face. I don't have to be a mind reader to know he's thinking about the almost-kiss. I attempt to conceal my emotions behind a facade of nonchalance, pretending the undeniable attraction does not exist. This only amplifies the charged silence. His smile falls away when he meets my gaze. With a solemn expression, he turns away and looks toward the pond.

"I see," he says, his voice linked with disappointment.

"Will," I begin, "about last night—"

"I would like to apologize for my behavior," he interjects, his tone empty of emotion. "I was out of line. It meant nothing and it will not happen again."

I should be relieved that he is the first to acknowledge that our almost-kiss was a mistake. Instead, I feel a chill settle within me as he pours water on the flame inside my chest, and it flickers and dies.

"Same here," I agree.

We sit in silence. The weight of the uncomfortable atmosphere pressing down on us like a leaden blanket. Each of us lost in our own thoughts. We occupy ourselves with our own pursuits; he fiddles with his signet ring, while I play with the pocket watch he had given me as a birthday present. I turn the crown clockwise to move the hands. Will releases a heavy sigh, as though to blow away some of the tension between us. I look up at him and see his eyes are relaxed, with his lips curled up symmetrically.

"Are you enjoying your present?"

I stop the hands once they get to 3:00.

"It's really beautiful. When did it stop working?"

Will shrugs. "I'm not sure it ever worked."

"Do you think you got it on one of your expeditions?" I ask, studying the French script on the clock's dial.

Will thinks for a moment. "It's possible. Speaking of which, have you heard from your friend Willoughby?"

I shake my head. "Nothing yet."

Will's expression falls. "Oh."

His deflated tone makes me sad. As each day passes, it's becoming difficult to imagine life without Will in it.

"If the beetle locket can truly shift you into the afterlife, are you sure that's what you want?"

As he looks into my eyes, his face contorts with anguish. "I've wandered alone in this world for far too long," he whispers. My heart breaks hearing his voice heavy with remorse. "Each day, I am reminded of my lack of history and future, left only with an endless present, Jade." I see the frustration in his eyes as they rest on my lips before dropping to the watch in my hands. "Time is just an illusion anyway. In the end, all of us will be summoned to the next realm, even you."

As Will's presence reminds me of my own mortality, I am reminded to cherish and appreciate the fragility of life. To make the most of every moment and not take the gift of existence for granted. It's crazy to think, through a twist of fate, I've crossed paths with Will. An encounter that seems so improbable, yet it was destined to happen.

"Will?"

"Yeah?" he asks, as he lays down in the grass.

"I'm glad that out of all the infinite possible people you could have met in the last one hundred years, it was me."

He glances at me, his face alight with a smile as radiant as the sun. "Me, too."

CHAPTER XXI
CROSSROADS

After talking with Will, I feel relieved. I'm glad my birthday didn't harm our special friendship. On Saturday afternoon, we search for a book about a fictional island nation described by Plato's dialogues "Timaeus" and "Critias" in Will's family library. Will remembered that the ancient Greek philosopher made references to pyramids and obelisks. As it approaches five o'clock, I keep glancing at my watch. I have a date with Brad later in the evening, but I have yet to tell Will about it.

"Have somewhere to be?" he says, pulling a book off one of the shelves. I keep my head down as I flip through the pages of *Atlantis The Antediluvian World,* by Ignatius L. Donnelly.

"I have a date tonight."

"Is that so?" he says nonchalantly, but I detect some envy in his tone. "Will your Aunt be accompanying?"

"Aunt Ruth?" I burst into laughter at the thought. "No. Thankfully, we don't need chaperones anymore."

"You should still have one," he says, sounding almost defensive. "A chaperone should be present to ensure your *date* doesn't engage in any inappropriate behavior."

"Things aren't like that anymore. People make out and mess around on dates all the time."

"You wouldn't let him take advantage of you willingly, would you?"

"I'm not letting anyone take advantage of me," I reply firmly. "I'm eighteen now and capable of making my own decisions. I don't need anyone trying to protect me."

He slams the book shut. "Jade, you can't be that foolish."

"I'm not being *foolish,"* I snap. "Will, it's really not any of your business what I do and don't do in private."

His teeth are clenched, and his jaw muscles are visibly bulging. He starts to speak, but I interrupt him by throwing the book at him, which he catches.

"Here's your book. I have a date I need to get ready for."

"So much for our special friendship," I grumble to Toby, as I tug at my hair with the hairbrush. "I'm perfectly capable of figuring things out for myself. After all, I like Brad a lot. I trust him."

Toby wimpers, peering up at me.

"Sorry, big guy. I'm just so frustrated. Who is he to tell me what I can and cannot do? If I wish to go that far with Brad"—I look down while playing with the bristles of the hairbrush and my tone drops—"then that's for me to decide."

I look at myself in the mirror while considering the idea of taking my relationship to the next level with Brad. My nerves are getting the best of me, and I question my own readiness. How does one know when it's the right time and how to prepare for it?

My thoughts are put on hold as Aunt Ruth enters the room. She offers to assist with my makeup and fasten the back of my midnight-blue sweetheart dress.

"Don't you think the pearls would look better with this outfit instead of that beetle necklace?" she suggests.

I grip the scarab tightly in my hand, thinking about my promise to Will. "No, I want to wear this one."

Aunt Ruth doesn't press the matter further. Instead, she focuses on fluffing the ribbon in my hair.

"How do I look?" I ask her.

"Stunning. You have nothing to be afraid of when he sees you." She smiles.

I spot Brad pulling up outside the gate. Walking to the car, I focus on not stumbling in my high heels. I close the gate behind me and spot Will walking up the sidewalk. I glance at him quickly before opening the car door.

"What kind of gentleman doesn't bother to open the door for his date?" Will asks.

I shake my head at his mocking comment and slam the car door shut.

"Is everything all right?" Brad asks.

"Yes," I reply. I avoid looking at Will, who now has his arms crossed.

Brad puts his free hand on my knee. "Shall we get going?"

"Absolutely," I say, impatient to get out of Will's view.

Brad navigates down a secluded road off Fairview Avenue that takes us to a bridge to the otherside of the river. I find myself forgetting about my previous conversation with Will and enjoy sitting beside my date. The air in his car is infused with a different cologne. This time it's a heady blend of leather and wood. The scent heightens his already irresistibly handsome appearance, if that's even humanly possible. Tonight, his hair is slicked back. He is dressed in a dark blue blazer with a black sweater underneath, making him look polished and sophisticated. He catches me admiring him, and we share a smile.

"So, where are you taking me tonight?" I finally ask.

"You'll have to wait and see," he says, squeezing my hand. "Do you like surprises?"

"Not particularly."

"You'll like this one," says Brad proudly.

We pull up to an old stone castle lit up with spotlights. Brad tosses his keys to the valet and meets me on the passenger side before we enter. This is the first time I have been on a date, especially to a fancy and upscale restaurant like Restaurant Bonaparte. If it weren't for the language spoken by the staff, I could have thought Brad had taken me to an old chateau in the south of France. The hostess sits us at a table with a view of the Hudson River. The water sparkles under the starry, moonlit sky. As I take in my surroundings, I am struck by the ornate architectural details—the high ceilings, intricate moldings, and the stone walls decorated with grand paintings. A string quartet plays behind us, making it the perfect backdrop for a romantic date. I feel like the luckiest girl in the world right now.

"Now I know why you wanted to keep this a surprise. This place is breathtaking," I say.

"And so are you," Brad replies, causing me to blush and hide my face behind the menu.

The waiter returns with a club soda for Brad and regular water for me.

"Have either of you been here before?" the waiter asks.

"I have, but it's her first time," Brad responds.

"Welcome," the waiter greets, with his arm tucked behind his back. "Allow me to give you a brief history of Restaurant Bonaparte. The vineyard was established in the mid-1800s by Jaque Moreau, a renowned winemaker from Bordeaux, France. His French wine was a favorite amongst the Grove Hollow families and caught the eye of the wealthy banker, Nicholas Ashmore," he says, placing a wine menu at the center of the table. "Nicholas partnered with Moreau to bring his wine to America, providing this estate as a wine cellar. After Moreau's passing in the early 1900s, the Ashmore family continued running the winery in this small chateau, eventually converting part of it into Restaurant Bonaparte."

Brad's expression tightens upon hearing the name Ashmore. My swooning mood deflates. Suddenly, the restaurant no longer feels as special as it did just a few moments ago.

"Would either of you be interested in a bottle for the table?" asks the waiter.

"We're underage still," Brad says.

"Not to worry. I'll give you some time to look over the menu." The waiter bows and steps away.

"Sorry, I forgot her family owned this place."

"It's all right," I reply, trying to downplay the situation.

Brad drums his fingers on the tablecloth as an awkward silence creeps in.

"Who won the game last night?" I ask.

"We won. It was so cold and windy, you would have hated it."

"You're probably right." I nod my head. "How was the two-hour bus ride? It's great you got to ride in charter buses instead of regular school buses."

He clears his throat and drinks his club soda before responding, "It was fine. What did you do last night?"

"Not much. I just read my book," I say, taking a sip of water. I omit the part where Will and I stayed up until midnight reading together in my room until I fell asleep on the pages.

During the lull in our conversation, we take the opportunity to browse the menu. Most of the dishes are listed in French. I decide to order ratatouille, and Brad opts for the bouillabaisse. I glance around the room, noticing that all the tables are now occupied by deeply engaged couples. I think of something to say to Brad as we wait for our food to arrive. I consider some topics that come naturally between Will and me, such as our favorite Charles Dickens novel, our preference between an opera or a play, or what the 1920s were like. Still, none of those would be relevant nor interesting to Brad.

I settle on a simple topic. "What's your favorite movie?"

"Probably Rambo," he says. I shudder at all the blood and gore. He notices my reaction and laughs. "Not a gore fan, I see?"

"Definitely not. Although, I love watching Alfred Hitchcock films. That's about as gory as I get," I reply.

"Alfred-Who?"

If it wasn't for the fancy restaurant setting, I would have thrown a bread roll at him for not knowing one of the most legendary directors.

"The Birds? Psycho? Rear Window? You've never heard of Hitchcock?"

"Wait, are those, like, the boring black-and-white movies?" he teases.

"Are you talking about the classics?" I respond with a teasing smirk. "Why don't we watch a black-and-white movie after this and see if you like it?"

He hesitates, and his mouth sinks to the side.

"Well, I thought we could go to my friend's party after this," he says. My eyebrows gently arch in surprise, and my mouth instinctively forms a perfect "o" shape, not realizing that a party was part of his plan for our date. Seeing my reaction, he quickly adds, "But it's totally okay if you want to watch a movie instead."

"No. No, that's fine," I say. "Let's go to your friend's party."

So much for alone time…

Brad pays for our dinner. We walk out of the restaurant hand-in-hand and wait for his car from the valet. I can't shake off the anxiety that overcomes me as we head to the party, especially since I hardly know Brad's friends. Even though I would rather be doing something else, I know I will have a good time with Brad no matter what we do.

We pull into the driveway of The Willows—the same house I had gone to for the costume party and where I had met Will for the first time.

The party is just as crowded as it was the last time I was here. I stay close to Brad, as I don't recognize anyone, though he seems to know everyone. We go to the massive kitchen, which has been updated with modern appliances unlike the one at Blythe House, where there is a keg and a place to make your own drink. Brad makes a rum and coke for me, which has a bit too much rum for my liking. A tall guy I have never seen before—who looks much older than a high school student—approaches Brad. They give each other a high-five.

"Phillips!" The guy exclaims.

"Eric! Hey, man. How's it going?" Brad asks.

"Good, bro. I didn't think you were going to come tonight. Allison said you were busy volunteering your time to the less fortunate," Eric says and laughs. "I said it didn't sound like what my buddy Phillips would do on a Saturday night." Eric notices that I am clinging tightly to Brad's arm. "And who is this?"

"Jade, this is my buddy, Eric Goldman. His family owns this house," Brad says.

"Hi." I nod to him politely. "Nice to meet you."

As Eric lifts his cup in a toast, his face contorts into an uneasy expression, hinting at his disapproval of me being Brad's date for the evening.

"You kids carry on and have fun," Eric says. "I'm gonna go make sure no one's jumping off the roof. Excuse me."

I look around the room nervously, looking for Allison.

"Don't worry, I don't think she's coming tonight." Brad assures me.

That's a relief.

He leads me to the billiard room where teams on either side of a ping-pong table are throwing ping-pong balls into cups across from them.

"What is this game?" I ask him.

"It's beer pong, wanna play?"

"Sure, but I don't know how."

"The rules are simple. Whoever sinks their ping-pong balls into a cup makes their opponent drink a beer. The first team to clear all their cups from the table wins. Let's play a round."

Brad and I get ready to play a game against two opponents wearing matching red bandanas around their foreheads. Brad seems eager for a competition, removing his blazer and rolling up his sleeves, exposing his muscular arms. We set up six cups of beer in a triangle formation for the other team.

"Remember, if they land their ball in a cup we have to drink it," he says.

"But it's so much beer!"

"Then we better make sure they don't make it in." He winks.

Brad prepares to make the first throw. Spectators gather around us in anticipation. He releases the ball and it misses the cup, hitting the floor instead.

"Your turn, babe," he says excitedly, making me feel elated at the pet name.

As someone not particularly interested in sports and barely passing gym class, I focus on the rows of cups in front of me. I try to pick the best target. I take aim and throw the ball, which lands perfectly in the center cup.

"You did it! You got one in!" He cheers and picks me up by the waist for a celebratory kiss.

Unfortunately, the one shot I made was all my luck, as Brad is the one carrying the weight of our team. The beers we had to drink give me a pleasant buzz, loosening my inhibitions and kindling a flirtatiousness with Brad. Whenever he's not throwing the ball, he seizes the chance to pull me closer by resting his hands on my waist. This leads me to believe that he's enjoying our date just as much as I am.

We are neck and neck with the other team. Our opponents whisper to one another. They bargain that the losers of the game have to jump into the pool.

"Deal," Brad decides for us.

I tug at his shirt.

"The pool water's going to be freezing!" I exclaim through boozy hiccups.

"We better not lose then," Brad says with a smile as he prepares for his final throw. "A kiss for good luck?"

I give him a quick peck on the cheek. He focuses on the cup across from us with narrowed eyes fixed on the target. I bite my lip, praying he makes it in. As Brad throws the ball, the crowd watches in silence.

The ball misses the cup and hits the table's edge

"No!" we both cry out with laughter.

"POOL TIME!" someone next to us shouts.

Brad grabs me by the waist to throw me over his shoulder. His goofy laugh echoes in my ear as he carries me outside. A crowd surrounds us, cheering for him and me to jump into the pool.

"No! No!" I shout as he holds me in his arms.

"One! Two! THREE!" The crowd counts down.

With a mighty leap, Brad plunges into the pool with me cradled securely in his arms. We sink beneath the water, and my hair flows wildly around us like an ethereal halo. As we come together in a passionate embrace, his lips press against mine. The heated water engulfs us as we sink deeper into the pool, locked in our intimate moment. An upward force is caused by the surrounding individuals jumping into the water. Bubbles escape from our mouths as we break the surface for air and cling to each other. Brad pulls me close as we tread water. I can feel the strength of his muscles through his wet shirt pressed up against me. I wonder if he can feel the wild beats of my heart.

"You drive me crazy," he whispers before claiming my lips in a long, passionate kiss. "Let's get out and dry off."

He extends a helping hand, offering to assist me out of the pool. I hesitate to take it. In that fleeting second, I remind myself of the stark contrast between the ability to grasp Brad's hand and the inability to hold Will's. I place my palm onto his and he lifts me up effortlessly.

We giggle the whole way inside, shivering from the cold, as we hurry for warmth. An unwelcome sight fills me with dread as I see Allison talking to Eric from across the foyer. We make our way up the steps, hand-in-hand, and Allison watches us with her fierce eyes. Nerves stir within me, regardless of being with Brad at the party. Brad notices her as well and pulls me up the steps.

"Don't worry about her," he says as we make it to the second floor. "Let's go into one of these rooms and hang out for a bit."

Brad opens the last door in the hall. I recognize it as the same room where I first met Will. He hands me his blazer to wear while I change out of my wet dress in the adjacent bathroom. The jacket is revealing and barely reaches the top of my thighs. The lace of my bra appears through the deep opening of the blazer.

I open the bathroom door and find Brad's muscular back illuminated by the soft, radiant light. Maybe it's the effect of the alcohol or his sculpted physique with each muscle sharply defined that stimulates a curious desire inside of me. He turns around and sees that I am looking at him, and his face flushes. I make my way to him from across the room. I stand on my tiptoes to reach his lips, and his mouth is eager to meet mine. His strong arms reach around my back, pulling me close to his half-naked body. My longing to touch his muscular chest is irresistible, so I give in to temptation and rest my hands on him.

I remind myself to breathe as our kissing intensifies. His fingers move to the front of his blazer and undoes the first button, the second, and the third. I hear the blazer fall to the floor. The intense pounding of my heart makes it feel like it might explode from my chest as I stand before him, more exposed than I have ever been in front of any man. I look at his dark eyes as they depart from mine and slowly travel to my navel. I'm wondering how he sees me, as he takes it all in.

Gently, his hands caress my shoulders. Goosebumps rise as his warm fingers and my bra straps glide down my arms.

"Wait," I say nervously and pull back.

His eyebrows furrow. "We don't have to do anything, Jade."

"I know," I say, biting my lip.

I turn my head to look out the window at the balcony. I grasp the beetle locket in my hand, twisting and turning it around in my fingers. I'm at a crossroad where one path leads to a continuation of our date as it is, with no significant change. On the other hand, the second choice would take me down an unexplored path, one that fills me with both nerves and a curious longing. With Brad by my side, the one I'm sure I want to be with, I think I know which path to take...

I think I'm ready.

"I want to," I say.

I unclasp my bra and let it fall to the floor. A small smile appears on his lips as he takes in every inch of my body. My cheeks flush with a mix of fear and arousal. He pulls me close, kissing me deeply as he guides me onto the bed. I fold my arms around his broad shoulders, using my hands to press him closer. He responds to my touch, and his hands roam my body. My pulse quickens as he kisses me with increasing passion.

His hands tuck away my hair. His kisses move down my neck, stopping at the scarab locket. He reaches behind to unclasp the necklace. I watch as he places it on the nightstand beside the bed before continuing where he left off.

His kisses return with his hot breath tickling my neckline. My breathing picks up as his hands move further down my body and stop at the hem of my underwear. With one swift motion, he removes them. As he unfastens his pants and puts on a condom, I stare at the ceiling, unsure what to do besides inhaling and exhaling anxiously through my mouth. With his weight pressing against my hips, he positions himself over me. I cling my shaking hands to his shoulders, allowing him to take control. As I prepare for what's to come, I take a deep breath and think, *"This is it."*

CHAPTER XXII

GO YOUR OWN WAY

It's impossible to fall asleep after Brad drives me home. I toss and turn the whole night, feeling like something within me has changed. The next morning, I hold on to my body while sitting on the floor of the bathtub. I embrace my knees and tenderly stroke my arm as the lukewarm water flows over me like a soothing waterfall. Through my bathroom window, I stare at the bleak gray hue that covers the mid-morning sky—a shade lacking vibrancy and clarity, much like my current mood and state of confusion.

I always dreamt my first time would be nothing short of a fairy tale. I assumed it would have the same passion and heat of a bodice-ripper romance novel—where the cover depicts a half-naked couple in front of a castle, and the woman is swept away in ecstasy by a Duke. But, the reality is far from what I imagined. It was painful, anticlimactic, and not as enjoyable as I thought it would be. Luckily, the whole experience was short. If it had lasted any longer, I fear my tears would have flowed like a river. It seems the only enjoyable part was the cuddling in bed afterward, but it was short-lived as Brad wanted to carry on with the festivities downstairs.

I feel like I should be over the moon. Last night, I gave myself to Brad. All of me. As there is no manual on how falling in love should feel, the experience is so new to me. I mean, I might be falling for Brad… I think. While I hug myself tighter, I question why I'm not feeling as happy as I should.

I drag myself out of the tub and make a conscious effort to get dressed. I look at my naked reflection in the mirror, trying to comprehend the person staring back at me. My appearance is unchanged—same body, hairstyle, face—yet everything feels different. Like the flick of a switch. I no longer feel like a young girl, but a woman embarking on a journey of self-discovery. Though, I'm not yet sure if it's a positive or negative one.

Dressing in comfortable attire, I settle onto my bed, hoping to immerse myself in a book to distract my fragmented thoughts. The raindrops begin to hit hard onto the balcony, adding to my dismal mood.

A knock on my window startles me. There stands Will, his body drenched from head to toe on the balcony. I unlock the door for him. As he enters, he shakes his wet hair, and water droplets scatter in every direction. I can't bring myself to look directly at him. I'm afraid he'll sense every conflicting emotion I'm battling internally, and he will be able to link them to my semi-regretful choice of giving myself to Brad. It's the burden of my guilt for not being true to myself last night. Perched on the bed's edge, I embrace myself by wrapping my arms tightly around my body again while absentmindedly scratching my arm.

"Are you okay?" he asks as he sits next to me.

"I'm fine," I manage to choke out, wringing my hands to distract myself.

I make the mistake of meeting his eyes, and they narrow in disbelief. If only the tension between us weren't so thick, if only he wasn't so right about everything, and if... if only I could touch him without barriers, I would find sanctuary in his arms and let my tears flow freely.

As tears well up in my eyes, I shift my focus to the floor. I see his hands clenching tightly on his knees, his knuckles turning white. I nervously bite my nails.

"Jade, are you sure?"

I release an audible sigh, pretending to be annoyed by his concern to avoid revealing my vulnerability.

"Did you come here to lecture me or something? Because I'm really not in the mood."

"Lecture you? I came here to apologize for my behavior yesterday. I realize your personal life is none of my business, and you won't have to worry about me interfering."

"Good," I snap.

He clears his throat. "I won't take up too much of your time." His tone becomes monotone and carries a sense of sadness, jealousy, or perhaps both.

He takes a book on gemstones out of his jacket, reminding me of the passage about the Koh-i-Noor Diamond I had read the night I had found the necklace.

"I was reading through my gemstone book and was curious if the beetle's body is made of malachite. Apparently, Ancient Egyptians believed malachite had protective powers. It was used in amulets, talismans, and decorating tombs to protect the deceased in the afterlife. If that's the case, there could be some truth to your talisman theory."

"Wait here. I'll grab it."

I search for the locket, starting at my vanity, but it's not there. I move to my bedside and rummage through my jacket, but it's not there either. My stress rises as I empty my purse onto the bed, frantically searching through every pocket. I'm finding nothing but old receipts, chapstick, and my wallet.

"What's the matter?"

"I can't find the necklace," I say, my voice shaking.

Will loses all color in his face and his eyes widen.

"I'm sure it's around here somewhere." He begins searching around the bed. I do the same on the other side. "When was the last time you saw it?"

"I had it on last night and—" My stomach drops like a rollercoaster.

"What? What is it?" he asks.

"Brad took the necklace off of me last night," I begin slowly. "He placed it on the nightstand."

Will's chest puffs up and down. His eyes are an icy-cold blue as they stare at me from the other side of the bed. I can see the hurt and anger reflected in them.

"I'm so sorry, Will," I say, approaching him from across the room, but he shifts away from me.

"Where did you go last night?" he asks, his voice demanding.

"We went to The Willows."

"Which room did you leave it in?"

I hesitate, feeling guilty about the words I'm about to say. "The one where we met."

He swiftly turns around and storms out of the room. I chase him, leaning over the railing to watch him climb down the lattice.

"Will, where are you going?"

He looks up once his feet hit the ground.

"To The Willows."

"I'll come with you."

"No. You've done enough."

You've Done Enough. The words still echo in my ears four hours later. I don't understand what's taking Will so long. Nigel brings me a cup of tea and shortbread cookies. I nibble on them only to pass the time. I force myself to read the book from earlier, but it's useless. No amount of words can distract me from the thought of leaving the necklace behind and the hurt in Will's eyes.

I hear commotion on the balcony. I look up from my book, filled with hope that he has found the locket. I see the tormented expression on his face and my hope vanishes.

"The locket wasn't there," he says, sitting down on the couch with his head in his hands.

"That's impossible. We were the last ones in that room. Did you check under the bed and behind the nightstand?"

"Yes, of course I did," he snaps with narrowed eyes. "I can't believe you would be so careless. You know how valuable that necklace was to me—to my life."

"I'm sorry, Will. I just—"

"Did it really mean nothing to you?" he interrupts, his voice tinted with pain. "That you let *him* remove it from your neck, after you promised me—"

"That's not fair," I respond, my anger rising. "Brad has nothing to do with this."

"Do you know what he says about you? When you're not around?" he says. I look down at his hands and notice they are clenched into tight fists. "He was at The Willows this afternoon, talking to his friends about you. All of them taking bets on how long he'll last with you."

"You're lying," I say, my voice trembling.

"Do you know he's been keeping information from you as well? How he hasn't told his parents about you. How he kissed someone on a bus ride just two nights prior—"

"You're just saying this because you're jealous that he's real and you're not."

I didn't mean to say those things, but I wanted to hurt him. I wanted to lash out at him for admitting the things he heard. To put blame on someone else other than myself for being too trusting… too willing.

"What if I am?" He stands up and towers over me. "Would it change anything?"

His face is inches from mine. The fierce passion in his eyes makes my heart feel like it will burst any moment.

"You-you can't just throw blame at Brad and me without proof," I breathe.

"You want proof? I heard it from his own mouth, Jade. I saw him with my own eyes. But you've made it clear you don't believe me. You'd rather stand by that liar than believe my truth."

"This isn't about the locket anymore, is it?" I say, my voice firm, despite feeling on fire. "You're biased against Brad because of your own feelings."

"*My* feelings? You think this is about my feelings?" He laughs maniacally and shakes his head in frustration. "This is about *you,* Jade. This is about the kind of person you're dating and the kind of person you deserve. But clearly, you're too shallow to see it."

I feel a burst of heated pressure explode inside of me.

"The only thing I see is that my ancestor cursed me the day she killed you, and now I'm forever haunted by someone who tries to control me and my choices!"

A look of shock washes over him. "What did you just say?"

I put my hand over my mouth as I realize the deep secret I just shared. "I wanted… the woman in the painting… I didn't—"

"Here, you call *me* a liar when *you're* keeping information from *me*. Perhaps you shouldn't throw stones at glass houses, Jade."

I scramble for an excuse to avoid confessing that the thought of losing him terrifies me.

"I didn't think it mattered. I thought it wouldn't make a difference," I counter.

"You didn't think telling me that your ancestor—the girl in the painting—who killed me and my family was important?" he asks. His matter-of-fact, rhetorical comment makes me feel worse.

"I'm sorry, Will."

"Sorry doesn't change the fact that you kept it from me," he responds. "I can't believe I put trust in you, Jade. I knew you were withholding something from me on the roof that afternoon."

I look into Will's uncompromising eyes. There are no words to express how deeply I wish I could go back in time and start over, just so I never have to see him look at me the way he is right now. The shame and guilt is unbearable. He turns to open the balcony door without a glance back.

"Will, don't go!" I call to him, tears streaming down my face.

"It's clear that I was wrong about all of this."

"No, that's not true! Please, we can keep looking! We will find the locket!"

I grab his hand to pull him back inside, but it moves right through him. He looks down at my hand and then back up at me.

"Goodbye, Jade. Enjoy the rest of your life."

CHAPTER XXIII

TAKING IT PERSONAL

I lay staring at the glowing red numbers on my digital clock. The alarm will go off in a matter of minutes. I had tried to drift off last night, but it was in vain. I feel trapped in an endless nightmare. In less than a day, I lost the necklace, I lost my trust in Brad, and I lost Will. The pain is unbearable, and it's swallowing me whole.

It takes me an eternity to get dressed. My feet feel like they're dragging through heavy mud. I pull at the bags under my puffy eyes in front of the bathroom mirror. There's no amount of makeup that can conceal them. I guess it doesn't matter anyway. I'm sure at some point today, I'll find myself crying again.

Nigel intercepts me on my way out the door. He hands me a thermos of tea and a lemon muffin on Aunt Ruth's insistence that I try to eat something. I'm sure my loud cries traveled through the halls of the massive mansion in the night.

I hold my breath when I spot Brad's car parked outside the gate. I know this car ride to school is going to be intense. Brad notices something is wrong as soon as I get in the passenger seat.

"Everything ok?"

I fiddle with my hands. "Not really."

"Okay," he says, slowly and puts the car in drive. "Are you going to tell me what's on your mind?"

I shrug, deep in thought about how to bring up what Will overheard yesterday. Should I start with how he never told his parents about me or the possibility that he kissed someone on Friday night? As we drive past Montgomery Manor, the pain in my chest intensifies, a reminder of the tears I've been holding back.

"Jade? Are you not going to talk to me?" he asks with concern.

My emotions are too raw to be placated.

"Why didn't you tell your parents about us?" I question him, my voice cracking.

A look of surprise and embarrassment appears on his face. "I'm going to tell them, Jade. I swear. It's just that—"

"You lied to me."

"Look, it's not that easy. Before making a big deal, I thought I'd wait and see how things go. I'm sure Allison's dad knows we broke up. So far, it hasn't been a problem."

I shake my head in confusion. "So, what *is* the problem then?"

"I don't know. After what Mr. O'Connor said about your family's history, I'm afraid my parents won't approve of you."

"Do *you* disapprove of me?" I ask, my voice barely audible.

He bends his brows and focuses on the red light on Main Street.

"Why are you acting so crazy, Jade?"

His gaslighting only fuels my next question.

"Who did you kiss on the bus ride Friday night?"

A fake grin spreads across his face as he shakes his head. "What are you talking about?"

"Don't lie to me, Brad. Tell me the truth. Did you kiss someone?"

His hesitant response is enough confirmation for me.

"Who was it?"

"It wasn't like that," he says in a whisper. "I didn't want to do it."

"Tell me who it was."

"Fine." He pauses. "It was Allison."

I feel like my heart is being crushed inside my chest. A part of me had hoped Will was wrong about this. All I see now is that he was trying to protect me.

"I swear on my life I didn't want to kiss her, Jade. We were playing a game and she—"

"Pull over. I want to get out."

"What? No. Can we just talk about this?"

"Pull over, or I'll jump out." I grip the door handle to emphasize my point.

"Okay! Okay!"

Brad pulls over just outside Mr. Willoughby's shop. I exit the car without a word, and he speeds away. I turn down Artist's Alley and collapse to the ground. Tears stream down my face. It feels like a year's worth of pain is being released in these tiny droplets. I cling to my knees, ignoring the people walking by the alley staring.

"Jade!" I hear Aubrey's voice and look up. "What happened? Why are you crying?"

I can't find the words to explain. I can only shake my head in response. Aubrey kneels beside me, wrapping her arms around me in a comforting embrace. She doesn't say a word. She holds me as I cry into her shoulder.

"You were right, Aubrey. You all were right," I sob.

"Right about what?"

"About… Brad."

"What about him?"

I spill everything to her: the part where I lost the locket, my argument with Will, how I gave myself to Brad, and how he kissed Allison Friday. I watch Aubrey's face turn from a cold white to fuming red.

"I'm going to kill that son of a bitch. No one messes with my friends!" she snarls.

"Please, I can't handle any more drama right now," I say, laying my head in my hands.

"Sorry." She rubs my back. "What about Will? Maybe he just needs some space to calm down. I'm sure he'll understand once you give him some time."

"Maybe," I sniffle. I wipe the trail of tears off my chin. "Ugh. There's no way I can go to school today."

"Who says you have to? Come on, you are in dire need of a personal day."

"I've never skipped school before," I say, drying my eyes. "Won't we get in trouble?"

"Only if we get caught," she says with a smile. "Hang tight, I'll be right back."

I force myself to eat part of the lemon muffin and sip on the hot tea while I wait for Aubrey to return. I look up at the almost-finished David Bowie mural Wes and Julian have worked hard on. The lyrics from the song "Heroes" comes into my head.

Maybe there is hope Will won't be mad at me forever.

"Who's ready to get the hell out of here?" I hear Davy shout.

My spirits lift when I see Aubrey and Julian walking behind him. The sound of a car honking catches my attention. Wes is waiting in his car on the street.

"Come on, let's get you cheered up!" chimes Julian.

We cram ourselves into Wes's car. I have no clue where we are headed or what we are going to do, but I'm just happy to be with my friends while I struggle at rock bottom.

I roll down the window and stick my head out, feeling invigorated by the chilly breeze. Davy asks Aubrey to turn up the volume as the song "Take on Me" by the Norwegian band A-ha starts playing. I giggle as the four of them belt out the chorus. Davy strains his voice to hit the high notes.

"Come on, Jade, sing! It will make you feel better!" Julian encourages.

I join in as Julian uses his hand as a microphone. It feels great to sing with my friends. The song's catchy melody and upbeat tempo helps boost my morale.

We arrive at a grocery store just outside of town. Wes and Davy grab shopping carts while Aubrey and Julian sit in them. They race each other through the parking lot. I run to catch up with them, laughing. Once inside, we split up to fill our carts with as many snacks and caffeinated drinks as possible. I walk with Wes through the candy aisle while Aubrey, Julian, and Davy tackle the frozen food section.

"How are you feeling?" he asks, taking a bite of an unpaid for Twizzler.

"I'm not sure," I say, grabbing a bag of Reese's Pieces and placing it in the cart. "You were right about Brad. He was a liar after all."

"I'm sorry he hurt you."

"Well"—I sigh—"it's not like you didn't warn me."

"You know, it sucks that people think Davy and I are unworthy just by looking at us. I'm artistic and self-expressive and that scares people. Davy's fearless outspokenness and jokester personality often add to the perception of him as a troublemaker. They think suave and refined guys like Brad make worthy partners for their daughters. But I can assure you, Davy and I would never treat a woman like most of those jocks do. People see what they want to see, I guess."

"I suppose I fit into that category," I admit. "I was so quick to think that Brad was different. That if someone as popular and attractive as him could like a girl like me, I would feel seen and valued." I frown, realizing Will and my friends made me feel that way all along.

Wes sighs. "Guys like Brad are the perfect example of aposematism."

"What's that?"

"It's like the poison dart frog. They're beautiful, and their bright colors are attractive, but it's a warning to stay away from them because they're venomous."

"So what you're saying is that I should stay away from pretty people?" I chuckle.

Wes scratches the back of his head. "All except Aubrey. She's not venomous—well, just sometimes," he teases, seeing her come down the aisle with Julian and Davy.

"We're ready to go. Let's motor!" Aubrey says.

We spend the afternoon indulging in snacks, watching an early movie at the cinema, grabbing burgers at a diner, and browsing records at the record store. I'm able to forget about Brad and Will for a time. It makes skipping school worth it. By 3:00 p.m., the five of us retreat to Artist's Alley. Aubrey puts in the new cassette she bought, Simple Minds, "Once Upon a Time," into the boombox.

With a final stroke, Wes and Julian unveil their masterpiece. The wall comes alive with David Bowie's visage, surrounded by a cosmic array of stars and planets. As we stand in awe, admiring the mural, a trio of Brad's rugby buddies and their cheerleader companions saunter by.

They snicker and scoff at our celebration of art. But their disdain cannot diminish the brilliance of the artwork or our appreciation of it.

Mr. Willoughby comes outside and sees us looking at the mural.

"It's perfect," he says, holding up his Polaroid camera. "Mind if I take a photo of you all in front of the mural?"

"Not at all, Mr. W.," Davy replies excitedly.

The four stand in front of the brick wall. Wes stands in the center and his arm around Aubrey. Julian stands on the other side of Wes, holding his paintbrush in his mouth. Davy positions himself next to him, with his arms crossed and his foot resting against the brick wall.

"Come on, Jade, get in the picture!" Wes calls. I join the group, standing next to Aubrey as she puts her arm around my shoulders.

"Everyone say 'Ziggy Stardust'," Julian says. We all say it together as Mr. Willoughby takes the photo.

"Ah, Jade, while I've got you here, I received a letter from my friend Saturday. It seems he was very excited to respond," says Mr. Willoughby. "Stay here, I'll go grab it."

Aubrey overhears my conversation with Mr. Willoughby and comes over.

"What letter is he talking about?"

"It's about Will's necklace." I lower my voice to her. "I pretended it was a family heirloom to get more information about it."

Mr. Willoughby walks back outside with a white envelope in his hand.

"Thank you, Mr. Willoughby. I really appreciate it."

"Anytime," he says with a half-moon smile and returns to the bookshop.

The guys begin packing up their paint and discuss grabbing fries at the arcade.

"Hey, Aubrey," I call and pull her aside. "Do you mind if I head home?"

"Want me to come with you?" she asks.

"It's okay. I think it's best if I find Will and show him the letter." Not that he'll be happy to read it since I've lost the locket, but there's always a chance.

"Sure thing. I'll see you tomorrow," she says.

I say goodbye to Aubrey and the guys, giving them all big hugs, and start walking to Fairview Avenue.

I bolt toward Montgomery Manor, clutching the letter from Mr. Willoughby's friend in my hand. My pulse quickens as I hope Will will be pleased to see me. I make my way to the back of the house and through the grand ballroom entrance.

"Will!" I shout, my voice ringing out in the empty room. "Will! I have the letter!" But there is no response. My feet carry me up the stairs and through each room. I search from the rooftop to the servants' quarters in the basement. Will is nowhere to be found. I have a feeling he must be in the garden, so I make my way there.

"Will?" I call as I open the garden door. But the only inhabitant is a lone rabbit. I sit on the bench under the marble gazebo, pondering Will's whereabouts. I head back to the manor to wait for him in the ballroom.

The hours pass. The darkness surrounds me. Still, there is no sign of Will. I contemplate the various places where he could have gone. Has he left for good? No, I can't bring myself to believe it. Besides, he mentioned before that he doesn't like to leave Grove Hollow. With no sign of him, I grab my belongings and make my way back to Blythe House with a heavy heart.

I get to my room and sit on the bed. I open the letter and read it, careful not to splash any tear droplets on the ink.

Albert,

Your letter and accompanying images have truly piqued my interest. I delved into our archives and uncovered information about a similar scarab necklace we sold in the 1930s, though it was less ancient than the one in your photos. As the Ancient Egyptians believed, scarab amulets were used to guide the soul into the afterlife.

What makes this particular scarab amulet so unique is its locket-like chamber, a metaphor for the chambers of the heart. Typically, lockets were popularly used as jewelry in the 16th century, but this piece appears to be far older. Without the opportunity to examine it in person, it's difficult to determine its exact age, but it's safe to say it belongs in a museum display, not around someone's neck!

Such a necklace would have been expensive to craft and was commonly worn by Ancient Egyptian Pharaohs. A lover likely commissioned it as a symbol for their souls to be reunited in the afterlife. The Ancient Egyptians had a complex understanding of the soul, believing it to be made up of multiple parts and able to travel between worlds. It's possible that the original owner of this amulet may need it to guide their soul's journey.

The scarab appears to be made of malachite, a gemstone believed to possess resurrection powers. In ancient Egypt, the color green was associated with the god of the underworld, Osiris, making this a powerful and potentially dangerous piece if it were to fall into the wrong hands. But, it is also believed that this gemstone can attune spiritual guidance and open the heart to unconditional love. It is thought that the wearer of this gem is encouraged to take risks to mature the soul, something like Punarjanma or reincarnation.

I trust that this information is helpful to your friend. Regardless, the locket is invaluable. If your friend is considering selling, I would be very interested for my own personal collection!

Take care dear friend,
Frederick Kraus

Stuard's International Auction House
London Office
Senior Director
Head of International Jewelry

This letter confirms that the scarab locket serves as the amulet for transporting Will's soul into the afterlife. Except there are no instructions in the letter to tell us how, and the locket is still missing…

CHAPTER XXIV

DOG EAT DOG

I rush to get ready for school. With a sliver of hope that Will returned in the night, I race over to Montgomery Manor. I call out his name so loud, the echo scares the mourning doves off the roof. But still no Will. I wait for Aubrey outside Will's house, rereading the letter I received from Frederick Kraus.

"It is thought that the wearer of this gem is encouraged to take risks to mature the soul, something like Punarjanma or reincarnation." I wonder if that's why Will never crossed over. But he isn't the one wearing the necklace. I am. And how does the gemstone's abilities to attune spiritual guidance and help open the heart to unconditional love apply to his situation? I scratch my head, trying to piece the information together.

"I thought you got a ride with Asshole when I didn't see you outside your gate," Aubrey says as she interrupts my detective work.

"No way," I reply, my thoughts still on Will.

As we make our way to school, I fill Aubrey in on the new information about the necklace I received from Mr. Willoughby's friend.

"I am kicking myself for taking off that necklace," I confess.

"Maybe we can make flyers and put them around town? Wes is great at drawing," Aubrey suggests.

"I doubt whoever took it from The Willows will turn it in," I say, my spirits sinking.

"Yeah, you're probably right."

As much as I don't want to come to terms with it, I fear the necklace is long gone.

We turn down Artist's Alley. Our mouths drop at the sight of the word 'FREAKS' scrawled in large black letters over Julian and Wes's David Bowie mural.

"Who would do this?" Aubrey shouts, her eyes glistening with tears.

"I know who would do this," I say, my anger boiling. "The people who get away with everything around here."

We hurry to school, where Wes, Davy, and Julian huddle by Davy's locker near the cafeteria entrance. They look confused when they see the distressed looks on our faces.

"The jocks… cheerleaders… they—" Aubrey pants, trying to catch her breath.

"They vandalized the Bowie mural," I finish for her.

"Stop messing," Julian says, his eyes wide.

"They wrote in black paint the word 'FREAKS' over it," I say. "I saw some of them walk by yesterday."

Wes rolls up his sleeves. Davy is cracking his knuckles. Even Julian's hands are clenched.

"I've had enough of this bullshit," Wes says, gritting his teeth.

We trek to the familiar spot where the rugby team congregates outside the boy's locker room. My anxiety peaks as I spot Allison, Samantha, and Danielle mingling with them.

"Jake," Wes bellows, "We know what you did."

Jake slowly pivots to face us with a sharp gaze. The other guys around him stand at attention, their eyes narrowing in response.

"What the hell are you talking about, freaks?" Jake sneers.

"You guys defaced our mural," Julian says, standing firm.

Jake folds his arms across his chest. "Why don't you girls go back to playing with your makeup?"

Davy growls beside me.

"We know you did it. We want you to apologize," Aubrey speaks up.

Allison cackles like an evil witch. "Apologize? You live in some fantasy world if you think we'll lower ourselves to that level."

I spot Brad emerging from the locker room, drying his hands with a paper towel. With a startled look, he catches sight of our group ready for a fight with his friends.

"What's going on here?" he asks, putting himself between Wes and Jake.

I step forward to defend my friends. He looks surprised to see me.

"We want you guys to apologize. Your friends vandalized my friends' mural."

"Everyone take a chill pill. I'm sure this is just a big misunderstanding, right guys? They probably didn't know it was your mural," Brad says, looking back at his friends.

"Why are you defending them?" I say, my voice steady. He really is one of them.

Brad is silent. Allison puts her arm on his shoulder. He glances away.

"What we wrote was nothing but the truth. You should be grateful this school takes you in as a charity case. You are the town's outcasts, the lowly filth that doesn't deserve to exist alongside decent human beings. You're nothing but vermin, crawling out from The Underground where you belong."

Before I have a chance to speak up, Aubrey has Allison pinned to the ground, gripping a handful of her blonde locks. Brad struggles to separate Jake from Wes, who are wildly throwing punches. Davy lunges at two other guys standing behind him. Three jocks slam Julian against the wall and viciously kick him in the side. Surrounding us are the screams from Samantha and Danielle on the sidelines.

A whistle pierces the air. Mr. Miller, the boy's gym teacher, emerges from the locker room. No one seems to hear it, and the fight rages on. I stand motionless processing the chaos. Mr. Miller takes a deep breath and blows the whistle with all his might. That's when everything comes to a halt.

"THAT'S ENOUGH!" Mr. Miller yells. "What the devil is going on here?"

Wes shoves Jake off of him and helps Aubrey up off the ground. Davy struggles to get Julian back on his feet, and I assist him.

"Sir," Wes says through a split lip, "they vandalized our mural."

Mr. Miller shakes his head in disbelief. "All of this over some artwork?"

"But sir—" I begin, but Mr. Miller cuts me off.

"You five, to the Headmaster's office—*now!*" he shouts, pointing to my friends and me. "Brad, gather up your teammates. You're running laps until you all throw up."

All of us walk with our tails between our legs to the Headmaster's office.

"Did you see how Allison and her posse went unrecognized?" Aubrey muses as she tends to Wes's cut lip.

"It's hard to miss," Davy grumbles in frustration. "Not to mention, we're the only ones ordered to go to the Headmaster's office."

Wes steps forward to help Julian, who's still reeling from the altercation, with Davy's and my support.

"Maybe we'll get off easy? They were the ones who called us freaks," I offer, trying to stay hopeful.

Aubrey sighs. "You've still got a lot to learn about this school."

The five of us huddle in the wooden seats outside the Headmaster's office. My nerves are high. I've never been summoned to a principal's office before. I can only assume that the punishment dealt out by a prestigious institution like this would be severe. My mind races with the possibilities of suspension or expulsion. Oh gosh, how would Aunt Ruth react to such news?

The door swings open. We all tense up, holding our breath as the Headmaster emerges with his usual stoic expression. He gestures for us to enter his office. The five of us stand before his desk. I hope he recognizes the severity of the injuries inflicted upon my cut, bruised, and beaten friends by the school's athletes.

"Let me make one thing clear," the Headmaster begins sternly, "violence is not tolerated at Grove Hollow Academy. It seems this school is becoming more of a reformatory than a preparatory institution."

"Sir, if I may, I'd like to explain the situation," Wes says.

"I hope you have a good explanation, Mr. English. I'll be calling each of your parents and guardians to inform them of this incident," the Headmaster warns.

Wes takes a deep breath. "You see, sir, Julian and I finished a mural in the Artist's Alley yesterday. The rugby players and cheerleaders defaced it with a derogatory word written in black paint."

"What happens outside the school's grounds is not of my concern," the Headmaster states.

"But sir, you always stress the importance of setting a good example for the community," Aubrey counters. The Headmaster's expression darkens. His annoyance at being called out for his hypocrisy is clear.

"Miss Jackson, let me remind you that you were in this office just a couple weeks ago for attacking Miss Ashmore in the bathroom. It seems you have a tendency to initiate violence."

"Sir, I was there that day in the bathroom. Aubrey didn't lay a finger on Allison," I say. He waves his hand dismissively.

"I also recall it was only a year ago that Mr. English, Mr. Jackson, and Mr. Jones were in here for a fight in the locker room as well," notes the Headmaster. As Davy is about to defend the locker room incident with Julian's bullying, the Headmaster scribbles something on a piece of paper. "Not to mention the five of you skipped school yesterday. While I should be suspending you all for this conduct, I've decided to teach you a lesson. The five of you will serve in-school suspension with Mr. Grayson every day until the holiday break to prevent any more incidents. Let this be a warning to you all. Next time I won't be as forgiving."

"Will the rugby and cheerleading team be served the same sentence?" Julian speaks up.

"No, Mr. Jones. To my knowledge, Miss Jackson was the one that started the fight. Therefore, I don't see it as necessary."

"That's bullshit!" The five of us cry out.

"Don't make me change my mind!" the Headmaster bellows. He stands up and slams his hands on his desk. "Now get moving to the detention hall and drop Mr. Jones off at the nurse's office on your way there."

Defeated, we turn to exit the Headmaster's office.

"Miss Whitney, I'd like to have a word with you, please," the Headmaster asks.

Aubrey, Davy, Julian, and Wes all turn to look at me. I'm sure my fear is reflected in my eyes.

"Close the door behind you," the Headmaster commands. I stand before him, my gaze fixed on the hourglass sitting atop his desk.

"Miss Whitney, I am concerned for you."

"Sir?" I ask, confused.

"I suggest you reevaluate the company you keep. I understand that you're new here and may be misguided. You might want to make amends with Miss Ashmore and seek her friendship. Both of you come from prominent founding families of Grove Hollow and this academy. She could be a great influence for you."

I take a deep breath before speaking. "Sir, with all due respect, true friendship is not about the size of one's bank account but the depth of one's character."

I notice a muscle in his forehead twitch as if I hit a nerve.

"Very well," he replies, and his face stiffens. "You're dismissed."

As I make my way to the detention hall on the third floor, I hear Aubrey's voice in the hallway and find my destination. The room is small, with no decorations on the walls. There is a wooden desk with a man sitting behind it reading a newspaper. A plaque with the name "Mr. Grayson" rests on his desk.

"Find a seat," he says, never glancing up as he sips his coffee.

Apart from two unfamiliar freshman boys, the five of us are the only ones in detention. I sit behind Aubrey. Wes and Davy sit across from us. We sit quietly as the four of us feel the heaviness of the Headmaster's unfairness.

The bell for a new period rings out. Mr. Grayson rises from his desk, announcing that he is going to refill his coffee cup. As soon as Mr. Grayson is out of earshot, we whisper to one another, trying to make sense of what had just happened.

"It's totally unfair nothing ever happens to them," Aubrey whines.

Davy sighs. "He was unfazed by how hard Julian got hit, too."

"What did the Headmaster want when he called you to stay, Jade?" Wes asks curiously.

"He wanted me to make amends with Allison and consider her friendship."

Aubrey looks disgusted. "Why?"

"Because our families are two of the school's founders and he thinks you all are a bad influence," I say reluctantly, knowing it will likely make my friends feel worse about themselves.

"Asshole," comments Davy.

"What did you tell him?" Wes asks.

"I told him the truth," I reply.

"Which is?" the three of them ask at the same time.

"That you guys are the best of friends I've ever had," I say.

Their faces light up with happiness. I realize that being different doesn't equate to being bad. My friends are simply misunderstood. I feel a sense of pride standing up for them.

I spend the entire day in detention re-reading the letter from Mr. Kraus. Every time I read it, I feel like a part of me is still connected to Will—that maybe, if I keep re-reading it, he will be able to forgive me. It probably sounds silly, but I guess when someone is in a state of desperation, they find themselves more open to accepting beliefs that are not based on what is real.

"How many times did you read that letter?" Aubrey asks as we walk to my locker as school lets out.

"I lost count after twenty-seven."

"Holy cow!" She laughs, then stops when she notices I wasn't intending to be funny. I'm more or less depressed at the thought that Will might never forgive me. "He'll forgive you, Jade," she says to me.

"But what if he doesn't?"

"If you mean that much to him, he'll forgive you. Trust me. Wes and I fight like cats and dogs and always find a way to mend things."

"I hope you're right." I open my locker and grab the books I need for tonight. A folded up piece of paper falls onto my shoe when I open the door.

"What's that?" Aubrey asks.

"Probably an old note from Brad or something." I tuck the note in my backpack pocket and close the door. I'm not in any mood for reminders of Brad.

We head to Artist's Alley. The mood is somber. The guys pull out paint buckets from Wes's trunk, ready to cover up the hateful message. Julian sits against the wall. Tears fall down his cheeks as he takes in the word "FREAKS" scrawled in front of him. Aubrey grabs the boombox from the arcade's backroom and sets it beside Julian.

"You choose the music," she insists.

He plays a cassette from his backpack. The first track starts to play. It's "Changes" by David Bowie.

As we listen to the lyrics, I think about how Bowie embraces the weird and the different. Maybe being a freak isn't such a bad thing after all. Maybe it's cooler to be unique than to conform. With that thought in mind, I open a can of black paint and dip a brush into it. I start to write beneath the vandalized word on the wall.

"What is she doing?" Davy whispers to the others.

I step back, and we all read the full phrase on the wall: "FREAKS UNITE. EMBRACE THE STRANGE." I sign it as, "The Misfits."

A smile spreads across Julian's face. "It's perfect."

With Aubrey leaning her arm on my shoulder, Davy, Julian, and Wes behind us, we all admire the inclusive words. Together, we are The Misfits—embracing our differences and standing proud.

On the way home, I bask in the warmth of having them as my friends. It feels great to be counted among their ranks. My lips bend into a smile for the first time today, but the joy is short-lived. Montgomery Manor looms before me, shrouded in darkness. I inhale and forge ahead through the cold grounds, passing through the ballroom and into the empty manor.

Still no sign of Will.

I twirl my fettuccine on my fork, lost in a spiral of thoughts as I sit at the dinner table. My heart aches with the knowledge that Will's likely gone for good. The guilt of driving him away rests heavily on me, but the pain of losing him is even greater. Aunt Ruth's voice pierces through the heavy silence.

"I got a call from the school today," she begins. My shoulders slouch as I anticipate her scolding me for my recent fight and in-school suspension. "They told me you started a fight."

"Yes," I reply. "Allison Ashmore and some rugby guys wrote the word 'FREAKS' over my friends' mural."

"Ashmore? No one mentioned an Ashmore," she says, her voice hardening. "Bunch of pretentious snobs. Either way, I'm glad you stood up for your friends. Worth every bit of punishment, if you ask me."

"Really?" I'm surprised by her comment.

"It takes loyalty, bravery, and integrity to stand up for your friends. Lord knows I've had to do the same for mine." She giggles to herself. "I'm proud of you."

"Thanks Aunt Ruth."

I find myself lost in thought again about Will. Aunt Ruth notices my silence and raises an eyebrow.

"How are things going with your lovers?"

I sigh. "Not good."

"It seems Eileen's prediction came true after all about having two lovers," she says. She had warned me to be careful about which lover I chose. I realize now that I made the wrong choice in choosing Brad. But Will isn't technically alive, so how *could* I choose him?

"I picked the wrong guy and now I've lost them both," I say, feeling the pain of my regret.

"I'm sorry, dear. The loss of a lover can be harsh on the heart," she says, almost in tears. I realize that she's talking about Reggie, her own lost love.

"How did you know Reggie was the one for you, out of all your lovers?"

"He felt like home," she says, with a glint of nostalgia in her eyes. "He was the only man I ever felt as though our souls were cut from the same cloth. He was my best friend. Not to mention, he could make me laugh on a dime," she chuckles, wiping away a tear.

"Will feels like that," I admit, choking on the lump in my throat.

"Well, perhaps there's still hope for you two after all."

If only she knew the truth. The truth that even if Will does come back, there's no chance for us, ever. Especially if he crosses over.

After dinner I retire to my room to tackle the work I missed in class. A thick pile of papers in a manila folder awaits me. The stack feels so daunting. As I look in my front pocket for a pencil, I see the note that fell on the floor from my locker. I open it, wondering which one of Brad's notes it was. I discover it's one I've never read before.

JADE,

WORDS CAN'T DESCRIBE HOW SORRY I AM. THE KISS WITH ALLISON WAS A MISTAKE. WE WERE ALL PLAYING A GAME OF TRUTH OR DARE ON THE BUS. JAKE DARED HER TO KISS TONY, WHO WAS SITTING NEXT TO ME. INSTEAD, SHE LEANED OVER AND KISSED ME. I SWEAR I PULLED HER OFF AS SOON AS I COULD.

IF YOU NEVER WANT TO TALK TO ME AGAIN, THAT'S FINE. BUT I WANTED TO EXPLAIN MY SIDE OF THE STORY.

I MISS YOU - BRAD

I crumple the note in my hand, anger and disappointment coursing through me. Accident or not, he lied to me about the kiss. He defended his friends. He—and I then realize that I did the exact same thing he had done. I fall back on the bed feeling more confused than I ever have in my life.

CHAPTER XXV

DANCES AND DREAMS

As the days drift by, I find myself counting them on a calendar I've hung on the chalkboard in my room. It hangs between the clues Will and I found, the letter from Frederick Kraus, and the black and white photo of Will. Four weeks have passed since Will left. Each day ticking by slower than the day before. I've been plagued with thoughts of where he could have gone.

The first flakes of December snow fall gently in Grove Hollow. The somber weather here has become a familiar friend. I embrace the snow more than Aubrey and the guys. They are crossing their fingers for an early dismissal. Mr. Grayson, who is more laid-back than I thought would be, reminds us that our recent week-long Thanksgiving break makes it unlikely.

I've oddly found that I enjoy in-school suspension. I'm with my friends all day, it's quiet, and drama-free. Most importantly, I don't have to see Brad or confront the jumbled mess of emotions he's left me with.

Julian trudges into detention. His head hangs low, and his shoulders slump. He has just come from a mandatory meeting with the dance committee, where he was tasked with organizing the upcoming Winter

Formal.

"What's the matter, Jules?" Aubrey asks him as he takes a seat.

"The gymnasium roof caved in from the snow last night," he replies, his voice fueled with frustration.

"We hate gym. So what?" Davy comments.

"We no longer have a venue for The Winter Formal, that's what," Julian says, agitated.

"What about The Hollow Hotel?" Wes offers the idea. "My dad designed the owner's house, I'm sure he can hook us up—"

Aubrey chimes in. "Or the country club?"

"The hotel has a wedding that night, and someone's retirement party is already booked with catering at the country club. We are screwed. Unless we find a venue by the end of the week, we'll have to cancel the dance."

I have a stroke of brilliance. "We have a ballroom at Blythe House. Why don't we host it there?"

Julian's face lights up. "For real? Do you think your aunt will be okay with it?"

"I'm sure she won't mind. She lives for parties," I say. "I'll ask her after school. When's the dance?"

"It's on Friday the twentieth," Julian says, the sparkle returning to his eyes.

He provides me with a detailed list of everything required for the dance. The school will provide the music—which Aubrey, Wes, and Davy offered to provide with their band—food and refreshments, and decorations. I couldn't imagine any of this being an issue. Our house was basically designed to host events like this back in the mid-1800s, with its grand ballroom and spacious lounge areas.

Now Julian's worries about finding a venue have ended, he is brimming with enthusiasm, and the group proceeds to discuss the songs for the formal. Julian strongly advocates for the inclusion of some contemporary pop music in their setlist. On the other hand, Wes appears unhappy with the idea initially but ultimately agrees, provided he doesn't have to perform any songs by REO Speedwagon.

Finally, the lunch bell rings. My grumbling stomach welcomes the thought of food. Normalcy has been restored again in the cafeteria as

Allison and her flock of cheerleaders gather around the rugby team. The only difference is the once vivacious and charming Brad now seems to be a pale imitation of his former self. Just thinking about speaking with him sets off a tornado of unresolved feelings in my gut.

As I stand in line for my Waldorf salad, I feel a tap on my shoulder and turn to see Brad. I am at a loss for words as I stare at him.

"Have a nice break?" he asks.

I can tell by his quivering eyebrow that he's nervous. A few people around us, Aubrey and the guys included, are watching our interaction.

"I—I did. Did you?"

"I did," he says, putting his hands in his pockets.

"Mr. Phillips, no talking to students in detention. Please return to your seat," a teacher tells him.

"Just a minute," he says. "I wanted to know if you got my note."

"I did." I grab my tray.

The teacher interrupts again. "Mr. Phillips—"

"Wait!" He holds a finger up at the teacher. "I just want to say, I'm really sorry, Jade—for everything."

I struggle to sort out my emotions as I feel conflicted and heartbroken, torn between the love I once had for him and the betrayal that shattered it all. I'm a hypocrite for not accepting his apology, yet I stare at him, unable to take his words. As the teacher walks toward us, Brad retreats back to his seat.

Throughout the remainder of my day at school, my thoughts are consumed by Brad's apology. Even as I make my way home, my mind remains preoccupied with him. I pause at the gate of Montgomery Manor—the dilapidated estate has been transformed into a quiet sanctuary by the snow. After my hopeless attempts to call Will for the past four weeks, I've come to terms with the fact that he's long gone, and the mansion now stands empty. I fumble with his pocket watch that I've been clutching tightly in my coat. I'm beginning to realize that the past is irreversible and cannot be changed.

I continue to Blythe House with my head held low. I'm greeted by Toby as I walk into the living room. Aunt Ruth sits on the couch, watching a video-recorded copy of the prime time television soap opera,

Dynasty, sipping a glass of wine.

"Why so gloomy?" She pats the empty spot next to her on the couch. "Come sit. Daniel is about to kiss Krystal. The Ball episode was one of my favorites from last season."

I sit down next to her. "Speaking of balls, our school's gymnasium roof caved in last night from the snow. My friend is organizing our Winter Formal and is frazzled because we no longer have a venue. I mentioned I'd ask you if we could host it here."

Aunt Ruth's eyes light up with excitement. "A ball? At Blythe House? What a splendid idea!"

"So, you're okay with it?"

"My dear, party planning is where I thrive!" she exclaims. "When is the ball taking place?" I tell her it's on the twentieth. "Three weeks? We must get planning!" she declares, pausing her show and running to the doorway.

"Wait, don't you want to hear the details?" I shout after her.

She turns around. "My dear, I'm a professional. I already know all that we will need. Call your friend and have him come for a planning meeting tomorrow. Pip-pip!"

After informing Julian over the phone of my aunt's eagerness to host the Winter Formal, I ascend the stairs to my room with homework before dinner. Nigel, ever the firestarter, has once again kindled the fireplace. I lie on my bed, watching the snow fall outside the window. The gentle crackling of the embers and the falling of the snowflakes lulls me into a dreamy state. As I drift off into an unexpected slumber, my mind wanders to the luxurious balls once held at Blythe House in its younger years. I wonder what it would have been like to attend such an event, surrounded by Victorian elegance...

With the grandeur of golden doors before me, I find myself in a dream where two dapper gentlemen bow and open the way to a magnificent ballroom. The ballroom is none other than the dilapidated Montgomery Manor. The mansion is now revived to its former glory, complete with ornate details and a polished sheen. As I take in the scene, I am surprised by the Victorian-era attire of the dancing guests. The men are clad in elegant black tailcoats, white wing-collared shirts, and bow ties. The women are adorned in vibrant hour-glass shaped dresses with bell-shaped skirts that swirl around the dance floor like a kaleidoscope of colors. But what catches my attention is the dramatic, embellished masks worn by the guests. I've entered into a masquerade ball. My bell-shaped skirt, embroidered in butterflies, swishes beneath me. I tie the feathered mask, in the shape of a winged luna moth, around my face. My free hand holds the beetle locket glowing green around my neck. I'm ready to join in the revelry.

I navigate the crowded ballroom. I find myself looking for someone in the crowd, but unsure who it is I'm looking for. Moving around the edges of the room, I weave in and out of conversations as the soft strains of the stringed orchestra drift through the air. The coordinated dance comes to a close. The guests erupt in applause and cheers as the dancers take their bows.

A man with blond hair tugs at my hand and leads me onto the dance floor. His dark eyes peer through the narrow slits of a ghostly Pantalone mask. His twisted smile under his thin mustache sends shivers down my spine, evoking an unexplainable fear. I attempt to break free, but his unyielding grasp constricts my fingers, denying my escape. He presses me closer with a firm hand on my back, jailing me within his hold.

The ballroom pulses with vibrant melodies, harmonizing with the sharp swaying of the dancers. Amidst the swirling sea of couples, my gaze locks on him—the man I've been looking for. He leans against a pillar at the ballroom's edge, observing me. Our eyes remain locked as I twirl across the floor, neither of us severing our connection.

As the final notes resound, I dip in a curtsey, eager to cut ties with my dreadful partner. I pivot, fixated on the mysterious figure emerging from the side of the ballroom. Every beat of my heart quickens, struggling against the confines of my corset, hindering my breath. He draws near, as the serenade of stringed instruments begin to play.

With a bow, he claims my hand.

As our palms meet, it feels as if fate itself orchestrated this serendipitous union of two souls. In an instant, the world synchronizes in flawless harmonies, like the beautiful melody of the orchestra surrounding us. Each note seamlessly melds with another, resonating in a deep unity, granting the world a newfound sense of purpose and meaning.

We are entangled in an endless cadence, balanced between the realms of reality and dreams, unaffected by the constraints of time. He moves with grace and confidence that is both mesmerizing and charming. Concealed behind his mysterious dark mask, his blue eyes, so hauntingly familiar, call to me from within the shadows. I find myself entranced, dancing within their cerulean depths, like a waltz beneath the boundless sky.

As he draws me closer, our chests collide like the union of two powerful flames. The desire within me blazes with newfound intensity. I know now that my attempts to suppress the fire was a blanket woven by fear and denial. But no matter how hard I tried to smother it, the flame in my heart for him never faded. It burns with an unquenchable passion. Love like this cannot be extinguished; it glows brightly, silently but persistently lighting the way toward him.

I've been in love with him all along. Somehow, I've always known.

"Will."

I awake with a start, my body jolting upright in bed. My covers are damp with tears and sweat, and my heart is pounding in my chest. I climb out of bed and step onto the balcony, seeking comfort from the cool night air.

The snow clouds are gone. The sky is clear and sparkles with an abundance of dazzling stars, with the crescent moon shining bright and cold above the river. As I stand there, taking in the beauty of the night, I wonder if Will is somewhere out there, staring at the same moon. Lost in his thoughts just as I am. The idea of him sends a pang of longing through my heart. But I feel a sense of peace, knowing that even if Will is miles away, we are still connected by the same star-studded sky above us. Maybe, just maybe, we are connected by something more than coincidence.

CHAPTER XXVI

THE WINTER FORMAL

Since Julian's initial sit-down with Aunt Ruth regarding the Winter Formal preparations, he and the dance committee have devoted each afternoon to priming the 63,000 sq ft mansion for the grand event. I welcomed the distraction from missing Will, as he still hasn't returned. After three grueling weeks of dedicated effort, I can hardly believe that the Blythe House decorations are complete. Julian and Aunt Ruth have led the charge, transforming the mansion into a winter wonderland. Aunt Ruth even poured some of her own money into the decor. She was determined to create an immersive experience for the guests. She left no detail unturned in her pursuit of this vision. I think she was also partly driven by a desire to restore the Whitney family's reputation to the town.

On the day of the Winter Formal, Julian and I arrive at Blythe House. We find Aunt Ruth chain-smoking in the study due to the predicted snowstorm.

"Of course, there would be a blizzard this evening—of all evenings!" Her cigarette bobs up and down in her mouth as we step outside to inspect the exterior decor. "I just hope it holds off long enough for the party."

"It will be all right, Aunt Ruth," I reassure her as I look at the snow falling. All of us cross our fingers that it doesn't get any heavier.

We begin the tour outside, where the entrance is graced by two massive holiday wreaths on the iron gates, making the gothic entrance more festive. Ten eight-foot tall ice sculptures of woodland animals, commissioned by Aunt Ruth's famous ice sculptor friend in NYC, line the driveway.

"Nigel, can we turn on the lights?" Julian calls out.

Nigel plugs in the extension cord. Thousands of lights illuminate the sculptures, setting off a breathtaking display of icicle lights on the sycamore trees. All of us are in awe of the magical atmosphere.

We make our way inside to check the rest of the house for any last-minute adjustments. The twelve-foot Christmas tree in the foyer is fully decorated with blue and gold ornaments to match the garland on the staircase. Aunt Ruth insisted we used her taxidermied birds as tree decorations, adding a life-like look.

We head to the study, which doubles as the refreshments room. Julian has transformed it into a winter wonderland, with bookshelves hidden behind panels of winter scenes. The room features buffet tables for the caterers, which will serve various food, drinks, and hors d'oeuvres for guests.

Aunt Ruth had a special surprise in store for the dining room. We were banned from entering for three weeks, so I had taken to eating my meals in the living room. As we close our eyes, Aunt Ruth finally opens the double doors to the dining room to reveal her creation. Julian and I can hardly believe our eyes as we admire the woodland ambience. On top of the table, now draped in sparkling white fabric, is a winter display of towering trees covered in faux-snow. Surrounding it are life-size deer, rabbits, raccoons, squirrels, and even a black bear. All are illuminated by spotlights. The scene is enchanting, like something out of a Harrods' window display. All of the dining room chairs have been replaced with tufted chairs and sofas to provide lounge seating for guests.

Last, but not least, we make our way to the ballroom. Several winter trees line the side of the room. They are frosted to look snow-covered and lit up by blue lights, casting a romantic shine on the room. Everything looks perfect.

"Thank you so much for everything," I say to Aunt Ruth. "You went above and beyond."

"I never had the chance to throw a party for a child," she says, putting her arm around myself and Julian. "I felt like a kid again watching your reactions to the decorations."

"It's by far the best looking formal the school has ever put on," Julian adds.

"Well, there's one more thing left to do now," Aunt Ruth says, curling the corner of her mouth.

"What's that?" we ask in unison.

"Time to get ready for the ball!"

Our attention is focused on getting ready for the Winter Formal, ignoring the increasing snow outside my balcony windows. Julian changes into his tuxedo in my bathroom while Aunt Ruth helps me do my hair and makeup. She finishes pinning back my curled hair. She sprays it with Aqua Net to keep it secure for the night. I stand before my mirror as Aunt Ruth helps me into an elegant all-black ballgown she had custom designed for me. The garment sparkles under the light of my bedroom chandelier, with its billowing puff sleeves revealing my bare shoulders, and fluffed layered skirt.

"You look like a princess," Julian says coming out of the bathroom, looking handsome in his tuxedo.

"What time is Elliot coming?" I ask him. I see the frown form on his face. "Oh, Julian. I'm sorry."

Julian shrugs and puts his arm through mine. "We can be each other's date."

"Splendid!" Aunt Ruth claps her hands together. "Now off you go. The guests will be arriving soon, and I must get ready!"

As Julian and I make our way to the foyer, Nigel informs us the band has arrived.

"I'll take care of Aubrey and the guys while you greet the guests," Julian directs.

The doorbell chimes. I see the caterers come into view, peering through the glass. An army of twenty black and white suited men enter, wheeling in countless carts of tiered food. Nigel guides them to the study.

I open the door to welcome the first guests. It's a small group of sophomores. Their mouths drop as they peer up at the mixture of the gold interior decorated in winter decor.

"Isn't this where the witch lives?" I overhear one of the kid's whisper.

"Come in," I welcome them nervously.

As more guests arrive, my anxiety grows. With this many people in my home, it feels overwhelmingly intimate. Aunt Ruth, dressed like a true Snow Queen in her white peacock feather ball gown and matching hat, confidently greets each new arrival with me. She basks in the compliments from a couple faculty members about the house's grandness.

"Please, come in. Make yourselves at home with refreshments in the study, lounge seating in the dining room, and music in the ballroom," she offers as she invites a group of awestruck rugby players and their dates inside.

I see a black Jeep pull up through the falling snow, and Brad and his rugby friends hop out of it. I turn to Aunt Ruth, asking if I can be dismissed from greeting our guests. I want to avoid the responsibility of welcoming Brad into my home.

"Go, have fun." She gleams.

I make my way to the ballroom and stand by Julian in front of the stage, listening to Aubrey and the guys play a cover of "Tenderness" by General Public. I see Brad enter, his arm linked with a girl I've never seen before. I grab Julian's fruit punch from his hand. Before he can warn me that it's full of smuggled vodka, I chug the entire thing.

"I needed that," I say, wiping my mouth.

"Come on, let's forget about guys and dance," Julian says, twirling me around.

About an hour into the formal, the whole ballroom is at full capacity. The sound of Aubrey and the guys' music filling the room. As the night goes on, the energy in the room only increases. I can see people laughing, chatting, and having a great time. The dance floor is packed, with couples swaying to the beat and single people showing off their dance moves. The night is turning out to be a huge success.

"Ladies and gentlemen, brace yourselves for an epic tune," Davy's voice echoes through the mic. "It's a slow one, so grab your partner."

Aubrey walks over to the keyboard, launching into the opening notes of Yazoo's, "Only You." The sound of the poignant lyrics surround us. I stand on the sidelines watching the dancers sway with their partners. I feel a pinch in my chest as I think back to the time I danced with Will on my birthday. I wish he was here.

As I watch the couples dance, I spot Brad slow-dancing with his date. We lock eyes from across the room, and I quickly look away.

"Fancy a dance?" Julian asks, snapping me out of my reverie.

"Absolutely," I reply, ambitious to lose myself in the music.

We rotate ourselves in a slow circle while dancing like everyone around us. I enjoy listening to Wes sing. Laura from the dance committee approaches Julian. She whispers something in his ear, and he nods in agreement.

"Excuse me, Jade. I have to go and help announce the king and queen winners."

I use this time to step away from the view of Brad dancing with his date. I move to the study instead for refreshments. I join the line behind two freshman girls. I smile at their innocence, as they chat about Aunt Ruth, remarking "how cool of a witch" she is. I reach the punch bowl, but the bartender is currently refilling it.

"Hey," I hear Brad say from behind.

"Hi," I answer, not turning to face him.

He comes up next to me. "The place looks great."

"Thanks," I say as I turn to him. "Is your date having a good time?" I ask, letting him know I saw him arrive with someone new.

"Dana? She's my cousin. Not exactly the best date material."

For some reason I am pleased to know it's his cousin.

"I came over here to ask you—" But before he can finish his sentence, Julian's voice booms over the ballroom speakers.

"Bradley Phillips!"

"I think you've just been crowned king," I say.

"BRADLEY PHILLIPS?"

"Oh, shit!" Brad turns to hurry toward the ballroom. "Save the next dance for me!" he yells.

I make it back to the ballroom just as Julian opens an envelope to announce the Winter Formal queen.

"Now for this year's queen, give it up for"—he picks up the card inside—"Allison Ashmore."

The crowd continues to clap. Allison and Brad are in the spotlight as Julian places the crowns on their heads. We form a large circle on the ballroom floor, giving them space to shine. Brad places his hands on her back, but she repositions them to her waist.

My pulse races, drumming louder in my ears with each beat.

As I watch the two together, my eyes zero in on the pendant that dangles from Allison's neck. It's Will's locket. I rub my eyes, to make sure I'm not hallucinating. I struggle, wondering how she could have claimed it on the night of the party. And then it clicks. She saw Brad lead me upstairs that night. Nervousness grips me as I frantically pull my hair, unable to remain still. I *need* to get that locket back. Finally, The King and Queen's dance ends with people clapping around me. I see it as the perfect chance to approach Allison. I scan the crowd and see her heading toward the foyer.

I quickly call out, "Allison!" I follow her, shouting her name once more.

She turns around with a glare. "What the hell do you want?"

I keep my voice even. The last thing I want to do is upset her. "I would like my locket back."

She rolls her eyes and keeps walking. I jump in front of her before she can enter the dining room.

"The necklace you're wearing, I need it back."

"You just want everything of mine, don't you?" she barks.

My hands clench into fists. "I left it at The Willows. I really need it back."

"What's going on here?" Danielle and Samantha approach her from behind.

"Jade thinks she can take yet *another* thing that doesn't belong to her," Allison says.

My body starts to shake, fearing I may not get the locket back.

"I'll do anything. Please just give it back."

Allison considers my offer and whispers to her friends. They give me a look that frightens me.

"You'll do anything?" she asks.

"Anything."

She smirks. "Meet us outside behind the house in five minutes or forget about the locket."

I am caught off guard by the proposal, confused why she wants to go outside in a blizzard.

"What?"

"Meet us there in five minutes or no locket," Allison says.

I force down a large breath and nod in agreement. I know Allison and whatever she has planned will not be easy. I go to my room to grab my jacket. I change out of my heels and put boots on under my dress. The flashlight in the utility closet is still dead from the night of manhunt so I take a lantern instead. As Will once said, it will provide more light. I race downstairs. Julian, who is at the bottom of the steps, notices I'm bundled up.

"Where are you going?" he asks.

"I'll be right back. I have to go outside for something."

"Okay," he says, looking confused. "But hurry back, we still have more dancing to do."

Nodding, I only partly hear what he says as my mind is consumed with retrieving the necklace. I will get it back, no matter what Allison has in store for me.

I step outside. There must be at least a foot of snow on the ground. It sticks to my dress, making it heavier and harder to move. I use the lantern to find my way behind the house. I see light from a flashlight at the edge of the dock over the river. Following Allison and her friends' footprints and voices from afar, I make my way to the pier.

"Allison, it's freezing. Can't we just go back inside?"

"Shut up, Samantha. If you can't handle it, go back to the party," I hear Allison snap.

"Shh! Someone's coming."

The dock rocks as the river's strong waters hit it. I walk carefully, not wanting to lose my balance.

"So, you finally decided to show up," Allison growls.

"I'm here. Can I have the locket now?" I shout over the wind.

"First, promise me you'll stay away from Brad."

"Is that what this is about?"

A strong gust of wind causes the dock to wobble.

"Allison, we need to go inside," Danielle pleads.

"No! Not until she promises," Allison orders.

"Fine. I promise. Now can I have the locket?"

Allison unhooks the locket from her neck. I go to take it and she snatches it back to her chest.

"I change my mind," she declares.

"Why?" I yell in frustration.

"Because I don't make deals with people like you."

I match the audible gasps coming from Danielle and Samantha as she throws the locket into the river. I let go of the lantern and it plummets with a metallic clang. A voice calls out my name as I take a deep breath and plunge into the icy water. I'm consumed by a million shards of glass, slicing through my flesh as the bitter chill seizes me. The water around me is a murky void. My dress soaks through and it grows heavy, dragging me deeper. I tear off my jacket as it feels like an anchor pulling me down. Desperate to find the locket, I flail in the darkness. The river's depth is unknown, but I pray I'm close. Panic creeps in as I'm pulled further under by the weight of my dress. My lungs are begging for air. I know I'm running out of time.

With a fierce kick, I fight to reach the top. The more I struggle, the more exhausted I become. I switch to frog kicks and sweep my arms in circles. I break through the surface with all my might, gasping for air. Ahead, on a dock, a figure stands shouting my name. With my last bit of strength, I cry out for help.

"Jade, reach for this branch!" the voice on the dock calls out.

I clench the branch with my frozen fingers as the person yanks me toward them. The branch splinters, and I am pulled away from the safety of the dock.

"Hold on, Jade! Help! Somebody, help us!" Will's voice pierces the air. His face, aglow with the lantern's light, brings a glimmer of hope. But I'm too weak. The water's icy grip claims me, and I sink into the darkness yet again.

The once icy water now feels serene, empty of any sensation except for tranquility. My dress flows effortlessly, a beautiful canvas for the gentle swirl of the fabric. A brilliant, almost otherworldly green orb drifts by, inviting me to touch it. I reach out and it spirals around my fingers. As I drift into a quiet slumber, I wonder if this is all just a dream.

CHAPTER XXVII

OSIRIS, GOD OF THE UNDERWORLD

As I surrender to a deep sleep, I'm transported to a celestial chamber reminiscent of the angelic fresco painted on Will's ballroom ceiling. But this is no painting. I float amidst billowing clouds. I am the only soul in this ethereal sunset universe. Though I'm alone, I feel at peace.

I soar through the boundless sky. A distant glimmer draws me closer. Approaching, I realize it's the reflection of a glowing green orb in a shimmering golden mirror. It is coming from the scarab locket around my neck. My reflection fades, replaced by the image of a person consumed by fear and worry. Tears fall down his face as he watches me sleep on a bed. He is still as a statue, never looking away from me, even as the room fills with escalating commotion and the tearful cries grow louder. The sight saddens me. I'm seized by a burning urge to reach out to him. I place my hand on the glass, causing it to ripple like a calm lake. I push forward, plunging into an empty darkness, like the space of consciousness just before waking from a dream.

Muffled voices surround me. I long for the quiet stillness of before. All of them leave, except one voice stays as they talk to themselves. A faint beeping noise pierces my ears, growing louder with each passing moment. I struggle to lift my heavy arms to my ears, my strength failing me. The beeping grows louder still, leading me to wonder if I've stumbled into the depths of Hell.

An antiseptic odor assaults my senses, and my gut churns, threatening to send bile spilling up my throat. My eyes, still closed, are pummeled by a fierce brightness. I flutter my lids, desperately trying to soothe the burning of my retinas. The room around me swirls in a disorienting haze. I shut my eyes tight, hoping to stop the dizzying spin.

I open my eyes. The room transforms from a bright, sterile environment to a warm and cozy haven. The beeping fades into a distant hum. The unpleasant odor is replaced by the sweet fragrance of blooming flowers. I lay still, too weak to move. My gaze falls upon a figure in the corner. Perched on a chair, their foot moves nervously, and their head rests in their hands.

"Will," I whisper, my voice raspy and strained. He doesn't respond. I gather all my strength and try again louder this time. "Will."

Will's head snaps in my direction. His eyes widen with shock. In an instant, he's at my bedside. His ghostly hand slips through mine, offering comfort despite its intangible form. I know, in his own way, he is holding it. Through his smile, I can see the worry carved on his face.

"I thought I lost you, Jade," he says, his words trembling.

"I thought I lost you, too," I say, my voice hoarse and barely audible. A cough wracks my body, causing pain to ripple through my chest.

"Just rest," Will says, his tender eyes fixed on mine.

A commotion at the door draws our attention as a nurse enters the room. She runs out in the hallway, calling for the doctor that I'm awake.

"Miss Whitney, you're awake," the doctor says. "Amelia, can you help Miss Whitney sit up?" He turns to me and asks, "How are you feeling?"

The inside of my chest burns, and my body feels weak. I feebly wave my hands, indicating not so well. The nurse gently lifts me into a semi-upright position, adjusting my gown for modesty. Will steps away, giving me privacy behind the curtain. The doctor places his stethoscope on my back.

"Good. Just breathe normally for me," the doctor instructs, moving the stethoscope to my chest. He checks his watch and counts. "I'm sure you have many questions right now. This must all be very confusing for you," the doctor says, putting away his stethoscope and making notes on the clipboard at the end of my bed. "I'm Dr. Marshall. You were brought in five days ago. We've been treating you for severe hypothermia and we performed CPR after your near-drowning incident. The fact that you were underwater for so long in those temperatures is simply astonishing. It's a miracle you're even conscious now. Do you remember anything about what happened, Miss Whitney?"

I try to speak, but my throat hurts too much. Instead, I shake my head to indicate that I don't.

"I figured as much," Dr. Marshall continues. "You went into a coma. I was not confident you would make it." He takes a moment to continue. "Your body has been through a lot of stress. It will take time for it to recover."

"How long?" I manage to force a whisper before coughing.

"Let's see how things progress for a week or so before I can give you a definitive answer," Dr. Marshall says. "For now, get some rest. Amelia, please ring Mrs. Mayfield and alert her that her niece has woken up."

Will walks back from behind the curtain after the doctor finishes examining me. I have a hard time wrapping my head around everything Dr. Marshall explained. Will sits by my bedside, a frown on his face. I attempt to moisten my parched throat with a gulp of saliva and ask, "What's wrong?"

"Jade, you were so close to death. The physician had serious concerns about your well-being just hours ago. He expressed his worries to your aunt, suggesting she prepare herself for the possibility you might not pull through." He shifts himself even closer. "I've been in a constant state of worry, unsure if each day would bring us good news or bad. I couldn't bear the thought of losing you forever. It's all my fault."

I shake my head and place my finger on my chest to indicate that I disagree. He attempts to take my hand in his and it glides through it.

"Absolutely not," he says seriously. His face reveals a raw emotional state that might just bring him to tears. "I let my foolish pride, selfishness, and jealousy get the better of me. Driven by my stubbornness, I journeyed to my mother's ancestral home in North Carolina. I wanted to…" His voice trails off for a moment. "I wanted to finally confront my grief."

"Oh, Will," I whisper, with a mix of remorse and care for him.

He lets out a deep sigh. "However, the moment I left Blythe House, I knew I was wrong. I wasn't in North Carolina longer than a few days when I realized the mistake I made by leaving you."

A smile crosses my face. I don't have the energy to reveal I've been waiting for a knock on my window each night. I had hoped and prayed for it, fearing I would never see him again. But now, here he is by my side.

"I'm sorry, too—" I manage to say before a cough violently erupts from my chest.

"Save your voice," Will says as he rummages through the drawers of my bedside table, pulling out a small notepad and pen. "Here, this might help," he says, handing me the tools.

I begin to write:

what happened?

"You really don't remember anything?" Will asks, and I move my head side to side. "I was on my way to your house when I heard loud music. Through the reflection of the ballroom window, I spotted a light by the dock. I heard your voice and ran over, confused as to why you were by the river in the middle of a blizzard." He takes a brief pause before inhaling deeply. "I shouted your name as I reached the dock, but you already dove into the water. I kept a close eye on you. When I realized you were struggling, I managed to find a long tree branch. You were close enough to grab it, but it broke. The water carried you away. That's when Brad jumped in and saved you." I stare at him in shock. "If it weren't for him asking Julian where you had gone, you would have drowned. He was in the hospital for a few days, but not as long as you," he says, hesitating to continue. "I might find myself liking the lad now for saving your life." A soft laugh accompanies his words, as though he still holds some uncertainty about his newfound admiration.

My fingers play with the blanket's hem. The staggering revelation that Brad risked his own life to save mine has unleashed a wave of feelings from within. I'm caught in a conflicting barrage of feeling both grateful and guilty. In some ways, it's altered my view of him.

I let go of the blanket and look at Will. Our eyes communicate with one another as if the unspoken words between us are louder than any spoken language. I have missed their vivid blue hue. I don't want to imagine another day without looking at them.

"Why did you jump into the river, Jade?" Will whispers.

I lower my head. I remember the last thought before jumping into the river was fighting to retrieve the necklace. I write on the pad of paper, explaining what happened. How I wasn't able to retrieve the locket.

Will gives me a weak, empathetic smile. "It doesn't matter now."

A hacking cough escapes me, shaking my weary body to its core.

"How are you feeling?" Will asks with genuine worry in his voice.

I scrawl a simple response:

tired

"You need some rest."

I shake my head, afraid that when I wake up, he'll be gone. I quickly write:

don't leave!

He reassures me with a smile. "I'll be right here the entire time."

I croak out a quiet plea, "Promise?"

Will extends his hand, tenderly caressing my cheek with a touch as soft as a breeze.

"I promise."

"So let me understand this—Barnabus can time-travel?" Will asks, leaning back in his chair.

"Correct. His name is Barnabus Collins, and he's a vampire," I reply, turning up the volume on the hospital TV to hear the conversation between Barnabus and Victoria Winters from the show "Dark Shadows".

"Do people know he's a vampire?"

"Eventually they find out," I answer.

"I see. If Barnabus and Victoria met in 1795, and he covered for her when she was accused of witchcraft, why don't they recognize each other in the present era?" Will queries.

"Do you ever stop asking questions?" I ask, trying to keep a straight face.

"The show's weak plot is confusing. How do you keep up with it?"

"If you paid attention, you'd understand. Dark Shadows was a top-rated soap opera of its time," I retort, defending my favorite show.

"A show so incredible they canceled it before the series ended?" Will teases. I shoot him a glare. I throw my empty paper cup at him, which he dodges. "Okay, I'll stop talking," he says with a laugh. It has been six days since I emerged from my coma. Will has remained by my side throughout. His constant presence has played a significant role in my recovery. It's like I found strength having him near.

Our time alone is interrupted as Aunt Ruth enters the room with more flowers and opens the blinds to let more light in.

"If your aunt or your friends bring any more bouquets, your room will start to look like a funeral parlor," Will says, and I nearly choke on my soup.

Will stands up from the chair next to me as Aunt Ruth unknowingly takes his seat. He climbs onto the radiator, his usual spot during Aunt Ruth's visits, causing it to bang loudly as his foot hits it.

"That radiator needs fixing. It sounds like a gunshot every time I come in. I can't wait until you're back home where you can rest better," Aunt Ruth says, placing the back of her hand on my forehead. "Nigel has already freshened up the bed with clean sheets and added more pillows for you."

"Do you know when I'll be out of here?" I ask.

"I just spoke with the nurse. Since you're feeling better, the doctor decided to discharge you this afternoon," she says, and I clap at the news. Will looks excited to be leaving early, too. "One other thing to celebrate is that I just heard from the school. The Headmaster and Superintendent agreed to punish those wretched girls. They'll have to do community service after school for a month." Aunt Ruth looks satisfied with the decision.

On the one hand, I'm happy the girls got what they deserved. But on the other hand, I am concerned about what will happen once I go back to school. I know they won't take the punishment lightly. For now, I am just grateful to be getting out of the hospital.

The doctor arrives to release me, prescribing rest until the end of the holiday break. The days are all a blur, and I realize tomorrow is New

Year's Eve already. Aunt Ruth hands me a set of comfy clothes, and I change in the bathroom. The nurse brings me a bag containing the black ball gown I had arrived in.

Before leaving, I thank Dr. Marshall and his team for saving my life. The nurse escorts me out of the building in a wheelchair, with Will following closely. Nigel is waiting in the car for us. Before we leave, Will tells me he will come by later to check on me. I watch him recede into the distance as we drive away.

When we get home, Toby greets me with excitement, nearly knocking me to the ground with his enthusiastic licking. Aunt Ruth scolds him for his lack of house manners, and Toby obediently takes a saluted stance beside her. No matter how much I object to spending more time in bed, Aunt Ruth insists that I retreat to my bedroom and rest.

While I wait for Will's knock at the window, I take a moment to touch up my appearance. I add blush to my cheeks to look less sickly and tie my hair back with a white ribbon. I tidy the room and empty my belongings from the hospital bag. As I hang the now-wrinkled ball gown on the outside of my armoire, I hear a thud and look down. A whirling motion travels through my body from head to toe, as I stare at the scarab locket by my feet.

My shaking hands reach down to retrieve it from the floor. Its wings slide away from one another to reveal the mysterious contents within. It's a message in hieroglyphic symbols. Inscribed and painted inside are interesting markings around a man and a woman facing one another. Above them rests some sort of cross surmounted by a loop. The woman's arms, made of falcon wings, are stretched out in the direction of the green-colored man. Behind her, is a marking in red. It is similar to the looped-cross above the man and woman, except it is tied with a sash that hangs down below the loop on two sides. I find it interesting that the man's torso faces the woman, while his feet face the opposite direction. Behind him shows a long tree with four horizontal branches at the top, resembling something of a pillar. Between the two figures is a red heart-like symbol, and surrounding them is a serpent swallowing its tail. The whole image is very alarming.

A loud tap at the window startles me. I quickly usher Will inside. I can hardly contain my excitement as I reveal not only did I somehow retrieve the locket from the river, but, even more incredible, its miraculous opening.

"Will, the locket—it's open!" I say.

Will's eyes grow in disbelief. My hands shake from the rush of adrenaline as I try to show him the images inside the beetle, but I drop it in the process. In a fluid instinctive motion, Will catches it mid-air. Our eyes lock as we realize the impossible—Will can hold the locket.

"How is this even possible?" Will whispers. His eyes widen at the extraordinary occurrence. We stand frozen, staring at the enigmatic locket in his hands. "What do these markings mean?"

"I'm not sure, but perhaps..." I dart to the chalkboard where I retrieve the letter from Frederick Krauss. "Perhaps there's something in this letter that can shed some light on this."

"Is that—"

"Yes," I interrupt, my excitement spilling out of me. "The letter from Frederick Krauss, Mr. Willoughby's friend. I received it while you were..." I trail off, not wanting to dwell on the painful memory of his absence and cause him any further guilt.

Will and I sit on the bed. He reads the letter aloud. With every passing word, his pace slows until he reaches the end. "'*The scarab appears to be made of malachite, a gemstone said to hold resurrection powers. In ancient Egypt, the color green was associated with the god of the underworld, Osiris, making this a powerful and potentially dangerous piece if it were to fall into the wrong hands.*' Wait a minute... Jade, the man in the locket, is green," he exclaims.

"Could he be Osiris?" I ask.

"It has to be," Will says with conviction.

I gaze at the mysterious woman with falcon wings. "Who do you think the woman is?"

"Maybe we should visit Mr. Willoughby. You can ask him to send another letter to Frederick Kraus. Maybe he will have more information about the message inside," Will suggests.

"We can go tomorrow!"

Will gives me a stern look. "You're not going anywhere. You need to rest, remember?"

"But Frederick might have the answers we need. It could take weeks to get a reply," I argue.

Will speaks with a calm and measured pace. "There's no rush. We have all the time in the world."

I let out a labored sigh; the faster we decipher the locket's secrets, the quicker Will can transition to the afterlife. A reality I'm selfishly not prepared to face. Suddenly, the day's excitement begins to fade and a flood of exhaustion consumes me. I lay down on the bed. Will nestles beside me, his head finding its spot on the pillow beside mine. A sense of deep contentment fills me, knowing he's inches away. The hypnotic motion of his fingers playing with the scarab locket soothes me into a peaceful sleep.

CHAPTER XXVIII

NEW YORK BOUND

Light flickers across my eyelids. I hear the soft rustle of movement. The sound of a door clicking shut snaps me awake. Will has left. I leap out of bed and race to the balcony, peering over the railing in search of him.

"Will?" I call out, but he's already disappeared around the side of the house. I quickly dress in my warmest winter gear—a white button down under a cozy wool sweater and my trusty denim. As I brush through my hair and search for a ribbon in my grandmother's box of ribbons, I spot a note from Will on my vanity next to the locket.

I didn't want to wake you. You looked so peaceful. I've gone to the bookstore to look for literature on Egyptian hieroglyphics. I'll return later.
-Will

Despite the physician's advice to stay put to recuperate, the thought of spending another day in bed is unbearable. I've got to find a way to sneak out and join Will. I'm sure some fresh air would benefit my recovery, anyway. I go out to the balcony to observe the lattice next to the railing, the same one Will always effortlessly descends. I could use it to slip out of the house without being noticed. A knock at my door interrupts my scheming. I find Nigel standing outside with a tray of mini-sandwiches and tea.

"Lunch, miss," he says, placing the tray on my bedside table.

"Thank you, Nigel," I reply. As he's about to leave, I recall Julian's ruse to sneak out to the show and borrow it for my own plan. "Will you please tell Aunt Ruth that I have a headache and will be spending the day resting?"

Nigel nods. "Certainly, miss."

With that, I put on my boots, grab the locket on the vanity, fasten it around my neck, and swing my bag over my shoulder. I am free to join Will on his quest, undetected and unfettered—or so I hope.

By the time I reach the bookstore, I am panting. My lungs are protesting the exertion. The store is stirring with activity. I scan the busy aisles until I catch sight of Will. He is perusing the shelves in the theology section. Steeling myself for his inevitable disapproval, I approach him, trying to hide my labored breathing.

"Excuse me, sir," I whisper, drawing up beside him. "Do you have any books on communicating with the paranormal? I seem to have a ghost haunting me, and they left without saying goodbye."

Will turns at the sound of my voice, his eyes widening in surprise. "You're supposed to be in bed," he scolds, his face pulled into a stern expression, except the smile that breaks through like sunshine on a cloudy day belies his words.

"I've rested enough," I reply, matching his grin with my own.

"All right," he agrees, his warm eyes conveying his approval. "I spotted a book I've been wanting to grab. I've been waiting for the place to quiet down so I can take it without anyone noticing."

"Which one?" I ask.

"It's the black volume titled, *The Egyptian Book of the Dead.*"

I recognize the book immediately. I flipped through it when we first visited the bookstore.

"I'll grab it and pay for it. Then we can bring it back to my place and take our time reading it."

Will nods in agreement.

I pay for the book, breaking the last twenty-dollar bill in my wallet. As we're about to leave the store, Mr. Willoughby's jovial voice reaches us from his office.

"Will, it's Mr. Willoughby," I whisper to him.

I wait outside Mr. Willoughby's door as he finishes his phone call. Once I hear the phone hang up, I knock. Comrie, sensing Will's presence, growls from under the desk.

"Mr. Willoughby?" I peek into his office.

His face lights up in delight. "Jade, come in! Come in," he beckons. "As a matter of fact, I was just thinking of you."

"Really?" I ask, turning to Will, who looks equally surprised by Mr. Willoughby's statement.

"Yes! I just hung up the phone with my friend from London, Freddy. You remember the one I wrote to about your locket?"

"That's why we—why I am here. The locket opened." I hold out my hand to show him. "I was wondering if you could write to your friend again and send him some photos to decipher the message."

Mr. Willoughby pushes his glasses up his nose and gives me an odd smile. "Of course, but it would be *quicker* to show him in person."

"Show him in person?" Will and I say in unison.

"He's in New York tonight for a private New Year's Day auction tomorrow. He invited me to dinner, but I'm too old for these spontaneous trips."

"Ask him when he's leaving town," Will suggests.

"When is Mr. Kraus returning to London?"

Mr. Willoughby rubs his chin. "It's his last show before he takes a three week winter holiday to the Bahamas, or was it Bermuda? Blast! My memory's shot!"

"Three weeks? We won't hear back from him for over a month," Will laments.

Noticing my disappointment in the news, Mr. Willoughby scribbles something on an old receipt. "*If* you decide to go, here is the address for Stuard's Auction House in Manhattan."

"Thank you, Mr. Willoughby," I say, grabbing the paper from him.

"Just tell them I sent you! I'm sure he'll love to see the necklace in person!" he calls out, chuckling, as I exit his office. "Oh! And have a Happy New Year!"

When we get outside, I cross the street to the payphone.

"Jade, where are you going?" Will asks, confused.

"I'm calling Aubrey to see if her boyfriend can give us a ride to New York City."

Will shakes his head. "This is madness. You need to rest."

"Will, it could take weeks for us to receive an answer."

I search for change for the payphone at the bottom of my bag. There's a lone quarter resting next to the pocket watch. My heart sinks at the reminder of how fickle time can be.

"We don't know how long the locket will be open for or why it's even open now."

Will frowns. "I hadn't considered that. I think you're right about going to New York."

I look up at his worried eyes. We share a moment of unease as the significance of the locket's sudden opening sinks in. The when and why of it all had only now just occurred to us. I can tell by the concerned look on his face we are both wondering what could have prompted the locket to open and what it might mean.

The phone rings, and Aubrey finally answers on the other end. "Hello?"

"Aubrey, it's Jade! I need your help," I say, urgency in my voice.

"Jade! How are you feeling?" Aubrey asks.

"I'm doing much better," I say. "Listen, is Wes there? Will and I need a ride to Manhattan. I know it's a lot to ask, but—"

"Will? As in your hot-ghost friend, Will?"

"Yes, that one," I reply, lowering my voice.

"Awesome! Will I get to meet him?"

"Yeah, yeah, sure. Listen, can you ask Wes for me?"

"Let me go ask him. He's in the other room, playing Nintendo," Aubrey says.

As I wait for Aubrey to return, the payphone's automated voice informs me I have only one minute left. My legs start to shake and worry settles in. We might get disconnected before she gets back and I don't have any more change.

Aubrey returns. "He has a New Year's Eve party to go to with his dad."

"Shit," I say under my breath. Will's eyes narrow as he waits for me to explain.

"But, he said he can drop you off at the Hudson Train Station nearby. It's about a two hour Amtrak ride into the city."

"Perfect! Meet us by Artist's Alley. We'll be waiting there." I sigh with relief.

"Artist's Alley?" Aubrey begins to ask before the automated voice interrupts, ending the call.

While we wait for Wes, I fill Will in on the plan. When I mention the commuter train, I see a hint of discomfort in his expression.

"Is there a problem with trains?" I ask.

Will remains silent for a moment before responding. "Since my parents' deaths, I haven't been able to bring myself to ride a train. The railroad was my father's passion, as you know, so I prefer to travel by foot." It occurs to me that Will had walked all the way to North Carolina. My heart breaks as I imagine Will, a lonely ghost, wandering the empty roads alone. "I guess it's one way to finally close that chapter," he adds.

"I'll be there with you," I say, wishing I could offer him physical comfort. He tilts his head and gives me a comforting smile that tells me he wishes I could, too.

We hear a honk and see Wes's black car parked by the alley. Aubrey's head hangs out the passenger's window. I open the door, let Will get in the car first, and then sit next to him. Aubrey starts mouthing as soon as I sit, asking if Will is sitting next to me. I nod in affirmation. Her eyes grow in size, and her mouth drops open in shock.

"Everything okay?" Wes asks, noticing our strange behavior.

"Yep, all good! Let's go!" Aubrey says enthusiastically.

The thirty-minute journey seems to fly by in no time. Aubrey keeps glancing in my direction, which seems to add to Wes's confusion. Will also notices. I'm sure he has it figured out Aubrey knows. When we reach the train station, there is a queue of people waiting to board a train on the south side.

"Call me if you need a ride back," Aubrey says, rolling down the window as Will and I step out of the car.

"Will do," I reply, anxious to get a ticket before the train arrives.

"Tell her I said thank you," chimes Will.

I convey the message. "Will says thank you."

"No problem! Take care of my friend, ghosty," she says and Wes looks lost. Will nods, but she can't see it. I say goodbye and thank them.

I hurry to the ticketbooth of the small red station to buy a ticket before the next train arrives.

"A ticket to New York City on the three o'clock train, please," I request of the bubblegum-chomping man behind the ticket window. It feels like an eternity before he hands me the ticket, only adding to my anxiety. "What's the latest train back tonight?"

He takes his time to consult the schedule, his chewing growing louder.

"The last train tonight departs from Penn Station at 10:30 p.m.," he says.

"Perfect. Maybe I can make it back at a decent hour and slip back into my room before Aunt Ruth knows I've been missing," I tell Will, eliciting no reaction from the ticket guy.

Will and I find a spot to stand and wait for the train. Will's hands fidget as we wait.

"You don't have to come if it's too much, Will," I say, trying to hide my concern.

"Are you mad? We're in this together. I'm coming with you," he replies as his posture relaxes.

The distant sound of a train horn signals our ride's approach. A uniformed man blows his whistle, yelling for everyone to stand back as the Amtrak train rolls to a stop. We wait for the passengers to disembark before boarding. Will leads the way to the back of the car, where we find two empty seats facing each other. The train sets off, gliding alongside the snowy trees. I notice Will looking out the window deep in thought.

"What are you thinking about?" I ask, breaking the silence.

"It's really not a thought," he says, turning to me.

"Tell me anyway."

"It's just that my father was one of the pioneers in the railroad industry when he came to America from England. Here I am, a hundred years later, riding an electric train to New York City. If only he could see this," he says with a trace of sadness before looking back out the window.

"I bet he would be ecstatic to know his son had the chance to ride an electric train," I say, hoping to bring a smile to his face.

He rests his head on the window. "I think you're right."

As the conductor makes his rounds, I hand him my ticket and watch as he punches a neat hole through it. I ask him how much longer until we reach Penn Station. He informs me it will be another hour. My eyes shift to Will, who continues staring out the window with a contemplative look. I spot a hint of a smile playing at the corners of his lips, and he catches me looking at him.

"So, what are you thinking about now?"

"Sorry, this one is for my own thoughts," he says, crossing his arms.

"Oh, come on, why the secret?"

"Because some things are better kept a secret," he replies with a charming grin that makes me blush.

"Fine, be that way." I pout, playfully sticking my tongue out at him. I'm glad to see it makes him laugh. "I'm excited to spend time in New York with you. I hope I'll get back before Aunt Ruth finds out I've been missing. She'll ground me for all eternity if she finds out I left."

"Don't worry. Your Aunt is pretty laid-back. I'm sure she won't be too hard on you," Will reassures me.

"Fingers crossed, she's five drinks in and passed out by the time we get home," I joke.

"Wow, that's the most un-Jade-like thing you've ever said." He claps his hands in amusement.

A bashful smile spreads across my face as I bow my head and join in his boisterous laughter. When our eyes meet again, I'm breathlessly stunned by the way he looks at me. There's something about the way his eyes changed, as if they've undergone a metamorphosis. They're so warm and inviting, calling me with open arms, and I can't resist. My heart races faster than the train's speed. I feel myself losing control, falling hopelessly and completely in love with him.

"We've arrived," Will says, as we pull into Penn Station. The bustling hub is teeming with travelers from all corners of the globe, coming and going from the city. However, when exiting the station, Will and I are at a loss as to where to go.

"Have you been here before?" I shout over the honking of cars and taxis. I cup my hands over my ears to block out the sirens from an ambulance.

"Not since the early 1900s, and it wasn't this chaotic!" he yells back.

Two women push past me and I almost stumble into the street.

"Maybe we should hail a taxi!" I suggest.

"Good idea!"

When I came to New York City with Aunt Ruth, people whistled and waved their hands above their heads to flag down a cab. I stand as close to the edge of the sidewalk as possible without stepping into the road. I put my hand above my head, attempting to whistle. Although, my poor whistling skills are of no use, as every yellow taxi cab is occupied.

Finally, after ten minutes, a yellow taxi pulls up. Will and I jump in the back. I retrieve the receipt Mr. Willoughby gave me from my bag, and provide the address to the impatient driver.

"Stuard's Auction House, between 71st and 72nd street on York Ave, please."

The taxi driver starts the meter. I check to ensure the locket is safely around my neck. I start wringing my hands. Will notices my nervousness and floats a comforting hand over mine.

"I don't know why I'm so nervous," I whisper to him.

"It will be all right," he says.

I lay my palm face up on my lap, and his hand continues to hover over it.

After lots of weaving through traffic, the taxi finally pulls up in front of a grand glass and granite building. Seven international flags fly proudly above the entrance. I pay the driver, and we step out of the cab. I watch as he merges back into the busy traffic. Outside the auction house, banners featuring the late Grace Kelly, the Princess of Monaco, are displayed. A sign in front of us reads, "New Year's Day Private Event at 8:00 p.m."

"Here goes nothing," I say to Will as I open the front door of Stuard's Auction House.

The contemporary lobby boasts black and white marble, with minimalistic decorations of abstract paintings in contrasting colors hanging from floor to ceiling. Every step I take echoes throughout the gigantic hall. A scowling security guard stands between us and the elevators. I'm intimidated by his weathered face. He raises his rough hands for me to stop.

"Excuse me, sir," I say, "I'd like to see Mr. Frederick Kraus."

The security guard gives me a skeptical look. "Do you have an appointment?" he asks in his distinct New York accent.

"Not exactly," I reply, "but I'm sure Mr. Kraus will know who I am."

"Sorry, without an appointment, you won't be able to get in," he states firmly.

I try again. "Can you please just check with Mr. Kraus? I'm sure he'll want to see me."

The security guard rolls his eyes. He picks up the phone beside him and dials a number.

"Yeah, there's a young lady here claiming to know Mr. Kraus," he says and pauses to listen to the person on the other line. "What's your name?" he asks.

"Jade Whitney."

"Tell him you know Mr. Willoughby, too," Will interjects.

"I'm a friend of Mr. Willoughby," I add.

"Jade Whitney. She knows some Willoughby-man? Yeah, I'll wait," he says through the phone.

A few minutes later, the person on the other line comes back.

"Uh-huh. Thank you. Uh-huh, sure thing," he says and hangs up the phone. The huffy look on his face makes me take a step back. "Follow me."

We take the elevator to the eleventh floor, where we are greeted by an attractive woman behind a gold-tiled desk.

"Thank you, Lloyd," the lady says, dismissing the security guard. She makes a call, and in no time at all, she leads us to a waiting room. "Mr. Kraus will be with you shortly. Can I offer you anything to drink while you wait?"

I decline her offer, feeling nervous as I sit in one of the plush Catalonia chairs. Will sits down next to me. The waiting area is more luxurious than the lobby. Everything in the room is white and gleaming. The walls are intricately carved into curves and sharp geometric shapes. Display cases line the room, each showcasing a piece of shiny jewelry. I nervously tap my fingers on my bag, taking in the surroundings. Will calmly reclines in his chair with his arm resting on the cushion.

"Jade?" A deep, unfamiliar voice with a British accent calls out.

I quickly turn around to see a man in a pristine suit with neatly combed white hair standing in a doorway. I stand up and approach him.

"Frederick Kraus," the man greets me with a grin. "Come into my office."

I look back at Will, who nods, and I follow Mr. Kraus into his spacious office. The modern room consists mostly of bookshelves, a case of Middle Eastern jewelry, and one large safe on the wall. His desk is neat and tidy, with only a lamp and a small stack of papers.

"What brings you to see me?" Mr. Kraus asks, closing the door behind us.

"Mr. Willoughby mentioned you were in town for an auction. I apologize as it's last minute without a call-ahead, but I had to see you before you left for your vacation."

He sinks into his leather office chair. I sit in one of the mid-century chairs in front of the desk while Will stands behind me. Mr. Kraus lights a pipe, filling the air with the fragrant aroma of tobacco. He extinguishes the flame and places the match on a crystal ashtray.

"I'm flattered," he says with a sly smile. "I take it you received my letter regarding the locket? It's quite a piece, I must say. I would love the opportunity to lay eyes on it in person."

"Actually, that's why I'm here," I say, unclasping the locket around my neck. Will steps forward, his hand resting on the back of my chair. I place the necklace on Mr. Kraus's desk. I open its wings with delicate care to reveal the mysterious symbols etched within.

"Fascinating, truly fascinating," Mr. Kraus says, his voice filled with wonder. He strokes his fingertips over the green stone of the locket's surface, his gaze focusing on its cryptic symbols inside. "Where did you say you acquired this object, my dear?" he asks, lifting his eyes to meet mine.

"It is a family heirloom," I say, watching Mr. Kraus examine the locket with great interest.

"I have a horrible feeling about this guy," Will says. I trust Mr. Willoughby's judgment and believe in Mr. Kraus's authenticity. It's hard for me to imagine he would send us all the way here if he didn't trust his friend.

Mr. Kraus rises to his feet, cradling the locket in his palms. "May I take this in the back to call a colleague?"

I nod in agreement. Will starts to move as if he wants to follow. I put a hand out to stop him.

"I'll be back in a jiffy," Mr. Kraus smiles, flashing his pearly whites. He heads toward the door behind his desk, closing it behind him. The sound of his muffled voice can be heard through the walls.

"Let's grab the locket and get out of here," Will suggests, but I resist.

"What's so shady about him? He took the time to meet with us and is trying to help by consulting his friend. He might be our only hope."

Will shrugs. "I didn't appreciate how he looked at the locket with covetousness. It was definitely an intense fixation."

"Will, he was just admiring the locket. Anyone with a passion for jewelry would do the same," I counter. I don't want to admit to Will that I may have felt uneasy about giving him the locket. But our hesitation is likely due to our attachment to it now that it's no longer lost.

Nearly fifteen minutes have passed. Mr. Kraus is still on the phone in the back room. Will approaches Mr. Kraus's bookshelf to peruse the literature.

"He has the same book we purchased today. Look, *The Egyptian Book of the Dead,* but with a more tattered binding," he says.

Just then, the door swings open. Mr. Kraus exits with his finger raised, grabbing the black book from the bookshelf.

"I'll only be a moment longer," he says.

As Mr. Kraus reenters, Will slips into the back office while the door shuts before I can motion for him to stay out. Nervous, I remain waiting, my leg shaking. I worry about Will trusting Mr. Kraus; there's a possibility he might do something impulsive, such as grabbing the locket from him. A reckless act like that could complicate the entire situation, especially concerning my story that the locket is a family heirloom.

As the minutes tick by, I become more anxious, knowing Will is in there with Mr. Kraus. Finally, the door opens, and Mr. Kraus emerges from the back room. This time, he looks concerned. I notice that he clutches the locket and a compact mirror in his hand. Will stands to the side, casting a wary look in my direction. I feel uneasy and stand up as well.

"Did your friend have any information on the locket?" I ask.

Mr. Kraus lets out a forced laugh. His eyes fall to the table.

"I don't know how else to say this," Mr. Kraus begins. I observe as he sets the mirror on his desk. His other hand grasps the locket tightly, and then it disappears into his pocket. "But unfortunately, I can't let you leave with this. You must understand, it's for the good of the relic."

Will's reaction is noticeable—his nostrils are flaring, and his body is taut.

"Sir, that is an heirloom," I protest. "It belonged to my great grandmother—"

He raises his hand to stop me. "I believe that your *heirloom,* which is a clever lie, I must say, is indeed a stolen item. Unless you're a descendant of an ancient Egyptian goddess, which I highly doubt, this doesn't belong in the hands of a little schoolgirl. It will stay here at Stuard's, in my possession."

At that moment, there's a knock on the door. Lloyd, the security guard from downstairs, enters the room.

"You called, sir?" he asks.

"Yes. Please escort Miss Whitney outside. Make sure she is no longer allowed in this building," Mr. Kraus says. The guard looks more than happy to comply.

"I'm not leaving without the locket," I declare. The guard's grip on my arms is so tight that I let out a cry. He starts pulling me away from the room.

"Let go of her!" Will exclaims, but it's no use. No one can hear him.

"Please, give me back the locket," I plea with Mr. Kraus, struggling to free myself from Lloyd's grasp.

"I'm sorry, we had to have this rift between us," Mr. Kraus says in a condescending way. He walks over to the safe on the wall. He lifts a finger toward the door and Lloyd shoves me away. "Get her out of here."

"Wait!" I yell and Lloyd stops. Mr. Kraus turns around. "My aunt, she has a lot of money. She can pay you for it."

"Hah! You can't put a price on something as old as this, you silly child!" Mr. Kraus exclaims. He opens the safe and places the locket inside. Will swiftly grabs the necklace before the door can close.

"W-w-what the devil?" Mr. Kraus shrieks.

Lloyd's jaw drops, as I'm sure all he can see is the locket hovering in front of Mr. Kraus. Will backs away, and the locket moves with him.

"Oh, I forgot to mention, it's cursed," I chime in.

"There's no such thing as a curse!" Mr. Kraus lunges to grab the floating locket.

Will snatches a pile of books from the shelf and hurls them onto the ground—he's a convincing poltergeist. Mr. Kraus cries out in terror as the lamp lifts from his desk and smashes on the floor.

"You should be careful, Mr. Kraus," I warn, playing along with Will's act, "as you mentioned in your letter, the stone is not very forgiving."

With a final flourish, Will sends the stack of papers flying from the desk. Mr. Kraus screams and locks himself in the back room. Lloyd finally releases my arms and flees, shouting, *"Ghost!"* down the hallway.

"Come on, Jade!" Will shouts.

We race out of the building as fast as our feet can carry us.

CHAPTER XXIX

THE ACTIAS HOTEL

Will and I sprint as far away from Stuard's Auction House as possible. After ten blocks, we come to a halt, my recovering lungs working hard for me to catch my breath. We exchange expressions of shock and disbelief, only to suddenly burst into uncontrollable laughter.

"Holy shit. I never thought we'd see that locket again." I double over, clutching my knees.

"I had a sour feeling about him," Will says. "The way he was fixated on the locket, it was like he was under a spell or something."

"I didn't want to admit it, but he gave me major Gollum vibes," I admit.

"Who's Gollum?" Will asks.

"You'll just have to read the books," I say, finally catching my breath.

"Regardless, maybe that locket really does belong to an ancient Egyptian goddess," Will says, leaning against the wall of a building. "There was something in that black book that was important to him. He was obsessed with taking the locket to the mirror, believing it would trigger something. They continued referring to a lost tomb of Isis and something concerning Osiris's Amulet of Resurrection."

"Do you think it's in that book?" I ask him.

"Maybe we're closer than we think."

I quickly retrieve it from my bag. "Let's read through it on the train ride home," I say with determination. He drops the locket in my hand and I fasten it around my neck.

I hail a cab for us. It takes a little while before we arrive at Penn Station. I pay the driver, noticing my cash is running low. Panic sets in when we discover all the train terminals are closed except for the subway.

"Excuse me," I say to the only person behind the ticket booth. When the elderly lady doesn't look up from her book, I tap the bell on the counter to try and get her attention. "When's the next train to Albany departing?"

"What's that?" she yells, cupping a hand to her ear. "Speak up!"

"When is the next train to Albany?" I ask again, raising my voice this time.

The elderly lady gestures toward a sign on the window that I hadn't seen until now. The bold letters read: "NEW YEAR'S EVE AND NEW YEAR'S DAY - ALL AMTRAK TRAINS WILL RUN UNTIL 5:00 P.M." A quick glance at the clock behind her shows it is almost 6:30 p.m.

"But the man in the ticket booth back at Hudson Station said they run until 10:30 p.m."

"Well, I don't know what to tell you. He must not have been paying attention to the holiday hours," she says.

Desperate to get home, I ask, "Are there any buses going that way?"

The lady consults with the computer before her, typing painfully slow.

"No, they're all booked," she says. "Your best bet is to head to Port Authority. I'll warn you, they're probably booked out, too, with the Time's Square New Year's Eve show and people coming in and out for the holidays."

It's not worth the risk paying to get there without a guarantee I can get a bus ticket, I think to myself.

"My aunt is going to kill me," I say, feeling hopeless.

"The next morning's trains are available, sweetheart. Why don't you come back tomorrow?"

I nod. "Thank you, ma'am."

I slink away from the booth, feeling guilty and defeated. I never intended to stay the night in the city. Will steps in front of me and offers a comforting smile.

"We're here now, so let's find a place to stay and catch the first train in the morning."

"I suppose I should do the right thing and call Aunt Ruth to let her know where I am." I scratch my head. "How will I break the news to her that I fled to New York City?"

Will taps his foot as he thinks of a plausible excuse. "Why don't you tell her that you came to the city to get her a late Christmas gift? She might be less angry with those intentions in mind."

It's not a guarantee, but it's my best plan.

We wander around the bustling city, searching for a place to stay. Every hotel we come across is fully booked for New Year's Eve. Our worries grow until we spot a beacon of hope across the street, The Actias Hotel. Its vibrant neon lights draw us in as we exchange hopeful glances. We approach the revolving doors beneath the dazzling Art-Deco sign. Stepping into the mysterious and evocative atmosphere of the moody lobby, we're surrounded by a world of shiny emerald accents and infinite reflections. Mirrors line the walls on either side, multiplying our image a million times. Ahead of us, the gold front desk is a work of art in itself, with its horizontal lines and vertically lit pillars adding a bold, dramatic touch to the space. An intricately cut mosaic of a green silk moth looms behind it as the room's focal point. I hear the sound of glasses clinking from what I assume is the hotel's lounge nearby. I ring the bell on the counter. A man in a velour suit emerges from a nearby room.

"Can I help you?" the desk clerk asks.

"Yes, I'd like to reserve a room for tonight."

"Wonderful. Have you ever stayed at The Actias Hotel before?"

"No, it's my first time here."

"Welcome. We're glad to have you as our guest," he says looking through the computer. "We only have a king suite available at the moment. How many nights are you planning to stay?"

"Just for tonight," I reply.

He inputs the information into the computer and then looks back at me. "A room for one night will cost $395.00."

The amount catches me off-guard. I wasn't anticipating it to be that high. Knowing I have only a few dollars left, I reach for the credit card my Aunt Ruth gave me for emergencies. I think my situation qualifies.

"Would you like to try another hotel?" Will offers. I shake my head slightly.

The man swipes the card.

"Great, let me finalize the booking for you. Checkout is at eleven in the morning tomorrow," the receptionist says. He hands me a key with the mosaic green moth emblem on the tag. Room 714 is painted in gold underneath. "Your room is on the top floor, all the way to the right down the hall."

"Thank you," I say.

We ascend to the seventh floor in an old, creaky 1920s elevator. Our hotel room is at the far end of the ambient-lit hallway. When I try to unlock the door, it proves to be stubborn.

"Allow me," Will offers. With a strong push, he opens the door.

"You always come to my rescue when it comes to doors." I giggle.

He shakes his head with a grin and gestures for me to go in.

The king suite is a spacious wonder. The decor features cool hues that coordinate with the lobby's moody palette. The room harmoniously blends its architecture's geometric lines and flowing curves with elegant floral prints, seamlessly marrying the artistic styles of Art Nouveau and 1920s Art Deco. The kitchen, dining room, and round living room are separated by an emerald lucite wall with a half-moon opening. To my delight, I find a complimentary bottle of wine and a charcuterie board in the mini-fridge. I fix myself a small plate of cheese and pour a glass of chardonnay into a vintage martini glass. With each sip and bite, I feel my spirits lift.

I spot Will standing with his hands tucked in his pockets by the row of windows in the living room. His expression is serious and pensive as he looks at the sparkling cityscape.

"The moon is bright tonight," he says, admiring how the light reflects off the river below. "This must be the Hudson River."

"It's like a home away from home," I add.

"Speaking of home, maybe you should phone your aunt."

I groan, almost having forgotten about Aunt Ruth. I realize that

Will is right—for all I know, she might have called the police looking for me.

"I'll see if there's a phone in the bedroom," I say, hoping the long-distance call won't add too much more to the hotel bill.

The bedroom is just as spacious as the living room. It boasts a massive bed with a tufted, velvet headboard shaped like butterfly wings. On the other side of the room are carpeted steps leading up to a platform, which houses a full-length mirror surrounded by four gold panels. The mirror's design is another nod to the hotel's Art Deco style. Though I think large wall mirrors in hotel rooms look tacky, this handcrafted one is enchanting.

I sit on the bedside and grab the rotary phone from the nightstand. I take a large gulp of chardonnay, hoping the alcohol will soothe my nerves. I start dialing. The phone repeatedly rings before I hear Nigel's voice on the other end.

"Blythe House residence, Nigel speaking."

"Hi Nigel, it's Jade," I say.

"Jade? Why are you calling from the upstairs phone? If you're looking for your dinner, the chef left it in the refrigerator."

I pause. How has no one realized I am missing?

"I am in New York City for the night." I wince, anticipating a scolding.

"New York City?" he repeats. "For heaven's sake, what are you doing all the way over there? Thank goodness your aunt is asleep on the couch! She'll have my head when she finds out you've escaped to the city—"

"I-I-I am getting a surprise for her as a late Christmas present," I say. Before he can say anything, I quickly continue. "Don't worry, Nigel. I'm fine. I'm staying at a hotel in Manhattan for the night."

"What hotel? A present?" Nigel asks urgently, his questions pressing with alarm.

Realizing Aunt Ruth doesn't know I'm missing, I find an opportunity.

"Can you cover for me until tomorrow?" I ask. "I promise I will take the earliest train home in the morning."

Nigel lets out a massive sigh. "I suppose you've left me with no choice. Your surprise better be worth all this trouble—"

"Okay, well, I have to go! Goodnight, Nigel!" I say, hurrying off the phone.

"Miss!" I hear him say on the other end before hanging up.

I better think of a special surprise for Aunt Ruth while I'm here. I'm too tired to think about it now, so I'll worry about it tomorrow. I collapse back onto the soft comforter and rest my head on the pillow. The chardonnay takes effect, and I finally feel relaxed for the first time today.

Will enters the room. His tall, handsome figure and self-assured demeanor command my attention as he makes his way to the other side of the bed. Never in my wildest dreams did I imagine that a ghost could look like him. Typically, ghosts are portrayed as haunting figures, lacking limbs and shrouded in a ghostly white sheet with empty, black eye sockets. But not Will. His entire presence radiates an irresistible attractiveness—from his striking features to his intelligent mind. I've been drawn to him since the first moment I saw his portrait in the manor, but tonight, my feelings for him are stronger than ever. Without a doubt, he is the missing puzzle piece that completes my soul. I was a fool to think I could suppress these feelings, which have always been harbored deep within me.

"That chat was brief." He settles down on the bed next to me, leaning his head against the headboard.

"I guess nobody realized I was gone," I say. "Nigel agreed to cover for me as long as we catch the earliest train tomorrow."

"That should be doable." Will nods. "How are you feeling?"

I turn to face him. His hair falls in front of his eyes, unforgivingly concealing their brilliant blue that has the ability to ignite a fiery passion within me with just one glance. His curved lips are parted slightly. I imagine what it would be like to be kissed by Will. Would he be slow and sensual, drawing me in with each kiss? Or would he be passionate, with intense kisses that I'd forget to come up for air? As I study his mouth, I'm lost in thought, completely ignoring his question. An irresistible smile lights up his face, making me believe he's flattered by my distraction.

"What's on your mind?" he asks with a voice as sweet as honey.

"Some things are better kept a secret," I reply.

"Very well," he says, flashing a playful smirk.

I find the light teasing amusing, and from the soft laughter coming from Will's lips, it seems he does too.

"If I shared what I was thinking on the train earlier, would you be willing to reveal your current thoughts?" he proposes, his eyes glinting with mischief, causing a slight nervous gulp to fall down my throat.

"That depends on what you were thinking," I reply. My cheeks heat up at the thought of him discovering I was daydreaming about kissing him. I bring my hands to my face, feeling the warmth spread throughout my body.

"That takes the fun out of the game," he says, angling his head sideways.

I look up at him through half-lowered lashes. "Did it involve me?"

A sly smile forms on his lips as he nods. I inhale, as the butterflies in my stomach flap their wings in a frenzy. My mind is consumed by the curiosity of wanting to know more.

"Fine, you go first." My breathing quickens as he moves closer.

"I was thinking about how different things would be if we had met years ago," he says, his face mere inches from mine.

"Like, in the early 1950s or something?"

He shakes his head with a light laugh. "No, as in the years I was still alive."

A strand of hair falls in front of my face. I see him reflexively reaching out to push it away, only to hesitate and let his hand fall onto the bed.

"How would it have been different?" I ask in a hushed tone, almost in a whisper. I sense that he means the difference would be physical, but I want to hear him say it. I need to know if he feels the same intense pull between us as I do.

I see a blush spread across his usually pale cheeks. He responds with an uncharacteristically shy smile, a sight I haven't seen before. In reaction, I let out a gentle chuckle.

"What? Now you have to tell me," I say, teasing him to reveal more.

"I'll save the details for after you tell me what you were thinking."

I groan, feeling like I'm being set up for failure. The thought of Will being repulsed by my thoughts of kissing him is too much to bear.

"That's not fair." I pout.

"I think it is."

I roll my eyes playfully. Taking a deep breath to prepare myself to spill the truth and let it out slowly.

"I was thinking," I begin, and my hands grow sweaty as I fidget with them, delaying the inevitable. "I was thinking what it would be like to... to kiss you."

My eyes fall to his hand resting on the bed. I gather the courage to meet his gaze, fearful of being turned away. The beating of my heart echoes like a pounding hammer in my ears. My head swirls like a carousel of thoughts, wondering what he is thinking. I force myself to look up at him, trembling with the overwhelming heat of embarrassment. The intensity of his stare catches me by surprise. My chest is rising and falling fast, as I wonder what might be going through his mind. Suddenly, his lips part as if he's about to say something, or perhaps he's considering the thought of kissing me, too.

"Jade," he says, his voice low, "I've wanted to kiss you since the moment we met."

The room around us spins as my breathing becomes labored. I struggle to catch it.

"You have?" I whisper.

"Yes," he continues, his voice barely audible. "My heart was captured from the moment I first laid eyes on you, fast asleep and so breathtakingly angelic. Your innocence called to me, stirring a primal need to protect you." He stares warmly, recalling that fateful night at The Willows. "I became spellbound when I watched you dancing with such vulnerability. It was as though you were revealing your true self to the world as if nothing else mattered. I found it impossible to look away." His eyes lower with a soft laugh. "You, with your mesmerizing spirit and beauty—were the most extraordinary soul I had ever seen." My heart embraces his gentle and affectionate words as a soft tear finds its way down my cheek. No one has ever expressed such genuine feelings to me before. He pauses, his voice now a tender murmur. "It's been pure torture. Sometimes I feel like you were brought into my life as some sort of cruel punishment."

"I'm so sorry," I reply.

He shakes his head, a look of frustration crossing his face. "Don't you see, Jade? You're the best thing that's happened to me in a hundred years. You make me feel *alive.*"

With his confession, he reaches out and brushes his fingers down my arm. Each hair on my body stands up straight, accompanied by a prickling sensation with every rise of a goosebump. This electric feeling isn't from his phantom caress but from the deep-rooted desire of longing to feel his touch.

"I've wondered," he begins, his voice soft and sweet, "what it would feel like to touch my lips to yours. I've imagined it over and over, playing it like a film in my head."

His hand moves from my arm to my neck, settling just below my chin. The tip of his finger grazes my mouth. I close my eyes, imagining the feel of his lips pressed to mine.

"It's like you're a million miles away, yet you're right next to me," I whisper.

"It feels like that, doesn't it?"

"It's not fair," I breathe.

I open my eyes. His head shifts—ever so slightly—as though he is going to kiss me. Instead, he releases a deep, pained sigh. He shifts away, stretching his arms behind his head. His focus moves to the mirror on the opposite side of the room.

"I know," he says, his jaw clenched tight.

An all-encompassing silence lingers between us but carries no awkwardness or discomfort. Instead, it's infused with a longing for something that seems impossible. I draw closer to him, and rest my head on the other side of his pillow. It's a surreal aching pain that torments your heart—to want to be with someone so close to you, yet they're untouchable. It's like a beautiful dream that refuses to materialize.

Despite our wishes to eliminate the physical barrier that separates us, it feels as though only our proximity and imagination are within reach. Together, we lift our hands into the air. He weaves his fingers in and out of mine, but the lack of physical contact persists, haunting us both. I watch his chest rise and fall with every breath. I would rest my head on it and be cocooned in his loving arms, if I could. Instead, I am left to satisfy myself with these thoughts, which do little to calm my aching heart.

"I wish I could hold you," he mutters softly. My body flutters as though he has read my mind. "I would never let you go."

I contemplate the depths to which a person can fall in love with someone. Given the opportunity, it would be an eternal, beautiful abyss, delving unfathomably deep, with Will. Fate seems unkind, for it has brought us together, fully aware that the chance to uncover the answer will never occur—and yet, I am truly grateful for its gift of leading me to him.

"Will?" I ask softly.

"Hm?" he whispers.

"Do you think there's a reason we met?"

"Yes," he says, his voice filled with certainty. "I do."

"Me, too," I agree, knowing we'll never know why.

He presses a tender kiss to my forehead, but it is as light as a whisper of wind on my skin. He heaves a heavy sigh, battled with want and frustration. Nestling my head near his, he continues gliding his hand up and down my arm.

Time eludes us as we lie still, oblivious to its passing. Amid the somberness, a subtle beam of sunshine graces my heart being so close to him. But the longer we relax, I become aware of the toll I've inflicted on my recovering body throughout the day. I gently rub my eyes and release a tired yawn, succumbing to the overwhelming exhaustion that consumes me.

"You should try to get some rest," he says.

"I don't want to," I protest with another yawn.

"You are still recovering. You had a big journey today."

"So did you."

"Yes, but I don't need sleep. You do. Who knows what tomorrow will be like for you."

"True," I sigh, "but what about you? What will you do?"

"I'll find a way to preoccupy myself," he reassures me. "Would you mind if I looked at the locket again?"

"Of course," I say, unfastening it and dropping the beetle into his palm.

I watch as his gentle hands meticulously toy with the delicate beetle, unfolding and folding its wings. My eyelids grow heavier with each passing moment.

"You never told me your secret of how things would be different," I ask.

A soft laugh escapes his lips, a sound like a lullaby. "I'll tell you all about it when you're fully rejuvenated," he says.

With one final yawn I ask, "Promise me you won't leave?"

"I promise," he vows.

I wake up, unsure of the time. It takes my eyes a moment to adjust to the room's darkness. Glancing over, I see Will on the bed with the locket open, engrossed in *The Egyptian Book of the Dead* book resting against his bent legs.

"You're awake," he says.

Stretching my arms, I ask, "What time is it?"

"It just turned midnight," he replies. "You've been asleep for a few hours."

"Happy New Year," I murmur, as I crawl up beside him, wishing I could rest my sleepy head on his shoulder while he reads.

"Happy New Year, Jade." He gives me an airy kiss on the forehead, filling my body with the warmest feeling, before returning to the book. As he flips through the pages, he stops at an illustration of a green man and a woman with wings.

"It's the image of the people in the locket. It seems like I've come across what Mr. Kraus and his companion were discussing—it appears to be some kind of story."

"What does it say?"

He clears his throat and begins reading, *"The god of the sky, Geb, and the goddess of the earth, Nut, had four children: Osiris, Isis, Set, and Nepthys. In the depths of their mother's womb, a profound love blossomed between Osiris and Isis, surpassing all comprehension. Their love was pure and mighty, transcending boundaries. Osiris embodied the quintessential Divine Masculine, symbolizing life cycles, fertility, and the realms beyond death. On the other hand, Isis embodied the essence of the Divine Feminine, emanating feminine energy that exuded healing, enchantment, and the transformative strength of motherhood.*

Their love was legendary, a powerful union symbolizing the balance of nature's forces. Through their bonded love was a beacon of hope and inspiration, a shining example of the heights that love could reach.

Osiris, the eldest son, became the king of Egypt and was widely respected on earth and in the underworld. However, Set, Osiris's brother, was envious of his older brother's rise to Pharaoh and plotted to kill him. He tricked Osiris into getting into a decorated chest, which he then sealed and threw into the Nile river. Believing he had succeeded in his murder, Set became King of Egypt, ruling alongside his wife and sister, Nepthys—"

"That's horrible," I interrupt.

Will nods and continues to read. *"The news of Osiris's death caused great grief and sorrow for Isis. She wept tears that filled the Nile, but she did not give up hope. Instead, she used her magic to bring her beloved back to life. With the help of her sister, Nepthys, she set out to search for Osiris's body. They found the chest containing his remains in Byblos. Isis brought it back to Egypt.*

Fuming with rage, Set discovered the chest and chopped Osiris's body into pieces. He scattered them across the land. But Isis was undeterred. With her magical powers, she transformed into a bird and, together with Nepthys, collected all the pieces of her husband's body.

Piece by piece, she put him back together and breathed life into him once again. Although their reunion was short-lived, Isis spent time with her love, Osiris, and became pregnant with their son, Horus.

Before Osiris was sent to the underworld, he gave Isis a gift to remember him by. He chose a scarab, which symbolized renewal and was colored green like his skin. The locket contained a djed-pillar to represent his strength, a tyet knot for her protection, an ankh mirror to symbolize her soul was a reflection of his, a shared heart between them for their love, and a circle to show it is infinite. Scholars refer to it as Osiris's Amulet of Resurrection."

Stunned, I look down at the engraved locket nestled in Will's palm and exclaim, "It's the locket!"

"Yes, I believe it is."

"An ankh mirror to symbolize her soul was a reflection of his," I say slowly out loud. The words echo through my head. In a sudden epiphany, I realize the locket was trying to convey a message to us all along. "Will, I remember catching glimpses of you in the reflection of my room's mirror and through the window of Montgomery Manor, even before discovering the locket," I say. Will's eyes watch me intently as I piece the clues together. "It must have opened underwater because water has the ability to reflect."

"Then that's the reason behind Mr. Kraus's obsession with the mirror!"

"Exactly!" I say, adding to his excitement. "But how does any of this help you?"

"Hm." He bites his lip. "Let's see." He looks down at the book and continues: *"The Sema amulet, traditionally represented by a stone and symbolizing the union of two entities, was frequently depicted as a set of lungs connected to a windpipe and commonly positioned on the chest of a mummy to bestow vitality upon it in the realm of the afterlife. Instead of a stone, this Sema amulet takes the shape of a pendant locket, a scarab, with an accompanying chain. Isis breathed magic from her lungs into the locket to activate the amulet's powers and reunite her with her one true love—a mirror of her own soul, Osiris. The incantation she uttered can be translated as:*

Through the amulet's power, twin flames unite.
In a union of breath and life, its brilliance shines.
A passionate love burning beyond life's final bend.
May this sacred magic foster an eternal unity."

As Will begins to turn another page, a shimmering green orb captures my attention. The room is bathed in an eerie glow as it dances and shimmers across the surface of the polished mirror. The light intensifies with each passing moment. Like a call from another realm, the glowing green light in the mirror summons our attention.

"Will?" my voice trembles. "Do you see that green light?"

He raises an eyebrow. "A green light?"

With my shaking hand, I gesture toward the mirror on the podium across from us. A green glow brightens and fades, like the light of a firefly, in the center of the mirror.

"Stay here."

"What are you doing?" I ask him.

"I'm going to find out what it is."

Ignoring his request for me to stay put, I follow him closely. As we near the mirror, I see two dark figures in the reflection. The only feature I can make out is their piercing white eyes as they stand motionless, watching us.

"Will, I'm scared," I whisper.

"It's all right," he says, but I can hear the fear in his voice.

I stand beside him in front of the mirror, but neither of our reflections can be seen. The figures' features become more apparent. It's a man with green skin and a woman with a cape made of falcon wings.

It's them.

"What do you want?" Will demands.

The woman in the mirror glances up at the man, who keeps his eyes fixed on Will. With his palm facing up, he extends his hand toward us.

"What do they want?" I ask him.

Will grips the necklace. "They want the locket," he replies. I am confused by the heartbreaking tone in his words.

"What? Why?"

His gaze falls to the necklace in his hand before meeting my eyes. I can see a mixture of sorrow and knowledge in his expression. The situation is clear to me without the need for words. They have come to claim him, a fact we both recognize.

"No," I gasp, my voice shaking.

His lips form a grim line. His tormented eyes are starting to glisten. A heavyweight smashes to the pit of my stomach and forcefully spreads up my body. This can't be the end. I'm not ready to face it.

"Maybe just give them the locket, and then you can stay," I suggest, but I can sense that it's not as simple as that.

Will looks at the man, whose hand remains extended. Suddenly, it feels hard to breathe and I begin to panic. My heart thumps in my chest, as the growing lump in my throat begins to form. I wasn't prepared for this moment. I had foolishly hoped it would never come.

Will turns toward me. He takes a deep breath, as he struggles to look at me through my tears.

"You have made these last few months worth waiting a hundred years for—"

"No, Will," I protest.

"Jade—"

"Please, Will, don't go," I beg, praying my plea can sway his decision. He averts his gaze momentarily, clearing his throat, his entire body trembling. With a relentless effort, his face regains composure and directs his eyes back to me.

"You have made me feel so alive in these last few months—"

"No. No. No," I cry, shaking my head fiercely.

"My time here was gone a long time ago—"

"This can't be happening." The intensity of my trembling body grows stronger. "No, Will. You *can't* leave me—"

"Jade, you have your whole life ahead of you," he says, with a thoughtfulness in his unsteady voice that's supposed to convince me that everything will be okay, when the thought of never seeing him again feels unbearable. I see him fighting bravely, trying to be strong for both of us in the face of the inevitable. I wish I could hold him tightly, to make sure he never leaves my side.

"And I want you in it, Will. I can't live without you." I sob. "We can find a way to make this work," I cry out, but I know that my words are just empty solutions that offer no real resolution.

"I couldn't take away all the incredible possibilities life has to offer you—the opportunities I missed and will forever remain beyond my grasp. Live for me."

"Will, please," I choke, making one last desperate plea. But my words are met with a deluge of tears.

He leans in with a tender, weightless kiss on my cheek.

"It won't be forever," he whispers in my ear as he pulls away. "It's just goodbye for now."

A searing pain rips through my chest, as a flood of treasured memories swallows me, shattering my heart into a million pieces. My soul grieves over the undeniable truth that this is where the story, about a girl who fell in love with a ghost, will end.

Our attention is drawn to the glowing mirror, a silent witness to our predicament. With each passing moment slipping through our fingers, we desperately cling to the dwindling time we have left. Will turns to look at me and our eyes connect. Those stunning blue spheres, usually filled with warmth, now reveal a vulnerability that tugs at my heartstrings. He clenches his jaw, valiantly fighting off the unshed tears. The deep, trembling inhale and subtle quiver of his lips reveal this decision is just as hard for him. The glowing green orb casts a shimmer on his ring as he brings his hand up to my cheek.

"Goodbye, Jade."

I hold my breath as he turns toward the mirror. My knees buckle beneath me as I crumple to the floor. The emptiness within feels like a physical wound, one I try to shield with my arms. I clutch my chest, unable to control the pain tearing me apart. Will enters the mirror, the locket in his grasp. The icy sting of irreversibility strikes me, a haunting reminder of mortality, as I understand that this will be the last time I will ever see him. I watch with a heavy heart as the man I love fades away and is gradually replaced by my own lonely reflection.

"Goodbye, Will."

EPILOGUE

In the still of the night, a hush that fills the air can bring solace to a weary soul. The calm of quietude can soothe the mind, erasing the day's anxieties and preparing yourself for sleep. However, not all silences are equal. Some silences are harrowing and excruciating, like the quietness that follows after the loss of someone. It's a sudden, agonizing realization that strikes without warning. No amount of preparation or diversions can prevent the loneliness that creeps in its wake. The yearning to fill the emptiness with the comforting sounds from those you miss will drive you mad. Now, I lay in this desolate, dark hotel room alone. Waiting for the tormenting heartache to ease just a little.

Hugging my knees close to my chest, I curl up into a tight ball and glance at the bedside alarm clock, which shows three in the morning. It's been three hours since I said goodbye to Will. The duration of time confuses me as it seems much longer, and yet, at the same time, not so long ago. My head rests on the soaked pillow where he once laid beside me. The muffled song of the Four Tops, "Reach Out I'll Be There," comes from the TV as the news station replays their performance from Dick Clark's New Year's Rockin' Eve celebration. I let out a sardonic laugh as I listen to the lyrics of this song—they seem to mock my painful situation. My tear ducts have dried up, leaving my eyes swollen and weary. I close them in a vain attempt to escape into sleep, but it's an unattainable dream. I reach for another handful of tissues to wipe my runny nose, joining the other discarded, crumpled ones on the bedspread. This wasn't meant to be like this... or was it? Everything happened in an instant, with no warning.

The sadness inside me transforms into a storm of anger. I rise to my feet and attempt again. I push against the mirror with all my strength, hoping I'll be able to go through. Yet, my hands are met with the unyielding surface of the glass, a cruel reminder that Will is never coming back. When he left me before, there was a glimmer of hope that he might return someday. However, now that hope is lost forever. As I face the idea of confronting each day without him, I attempt to persuade myself with a sense of denial, but the burning in my chest sharpens when I acknowledge that this is how it will be from now on. Ultimately, this was always going to be the outcome. I bear the responsibility for not preparing for it… and I'm terrified I won't be able to suppress this amount of pain this time.

I'm startled by a sudden ticking sound from my bag at the foot of the bed. My heart pounds as I dart to grab the pocket watch that Will had given me. In disbelief, I find that the watch has sprung back to life. Its second-hand crawls leisurely, taking its sweet time. I examine the back, the clock's face, and the metal case where the etched luna moths are. Everything seems normal and unchanged, except for the resurrection of this seemingly broken timepiece.

An unsettling sound pierces the silent room, like nails scratching at glass. I pivot to see the ghostly green orb materializing from the mirror. My hand trembles and I drop the watch onto the bed. Perhaps they've come to take me too. With bated breath, I move toward the light. The two figures become visible again, emerging from the shadows.

"What do you want?" I demand, trying to hide the worry in my voice. The man and woman remain silent. I yell again, "What do you want?"

The man extends his hand, revealing the scarab locket. It's the source of the green light. I hesitate, unsure of how I want to proceed. The woman's eyes comfort me in a way that makes me feel like I can trust them.

With quivering hands, I reach out, placing my palm on the glass. My hand passes through it, similar to the feel of flowing water grazing my skin like falling feathers. I let out a sharp gasp as the man's hand clasps mine from the other side. The grip is strong yet gentle. He's not pulling but instead pushing his way toward me. As I bring the hand into view, my heart races like a herd of galloping mustangs. I immediately recognize the gold ring with a rose in the center.

Will.

ACKNOWLEDGEMENTS

I want to thank my gifted friend, Terry Beale, whose magical, intuitive advice became the guiding light that sparked my journey into crafting this series. To the brilliant mind and discerning eye of Andrea Mast, my beta reader, your invaluable insights and feedback sculpted the very heart of book one. And lastly, I pay tribute to the remarkable Friel Black, a master of words and a beacon of support, whose editorial prowess breathed life into the pages, lifting the story and characters to new heights.

Thank you.

www.ingramcontent.com/pod-product-compliance
Ingram Content Group UK Ltd.
Pitfield, Milton Keynes, MK11 3LW, UK
UKHW041137181125
9024UKWH00016B/172/J

9 798988 874607